By George R.R. Martin

A Song of Ice and Fire
  Book One: A Game of Thrones
  Book Two: A Clash of Kings
  Book Three, part one: A Storm of
    Swords: Steel and Snow
  Book Three, part two: A Storm of
    Swords: Blood and Gold
  Book Four: A Feast for Crows
  Book Five, part one: A Dance with
    Dragons: Dreams and Dust
  Book Five, part two: A Dance with
    Dragons: After the Feast
  The World of Ice & Fire: The
    Untold History of Westeros
    and the Game of Thrones

  Dying of the Light
  Windhaven (with Lisa Tuttle)
  Fevre Dream
  The Armageddon Rag
  Dead Man's Hand
    (with John J. Miller)
  Hunter's Run
    (with Gardner Dozois and Daniel
    Abraham)
  The Ice Dragon

Short Story Collections
  Dreamsongs: Volume I
  Dreamsongs: Volume II
  A Song for Lya: And Other Stories
  Songs of Stars and Shadows
  Sandkings
  Songs the Dead Men Sing
  Nightflyers
  Tuf Voyaging
  Portraits of His Children
  Quartet

Edited by George R.R. Martin
  New Voices in Science Fiction,
    Volumes 1–4
  The Science Fiction Weight Loss
    Book (with Isaac Asimov and
    Martin Harry Greenberg)
  The John W. Campbell Awards,
    Volume 5
  Night Visions 3
  Wild Cards I–XXII

Co-edited with Gardner Dozois
  Warriors I–III
  Songs of the Dying Earth
  Songs of Love and Death
  Down These Strange Streets
  Old Mars
  Dangerous Women
  Rogues
  Old Venus

A KNIGHT OF THE SEVEN KINGDOMS

George R.R. Martin

* * *

Illustrations by Gary Gianni

HARPER
Voyager

HarperCollins*Publishers*
1 London Bridge Street
London, SE1 9GF

www.harpervoyagerbooks.co.uk

Legends I originally edited by Robert Silverberg and
published by Tor Books in 1998.
Legends II originally edited by Robert Silverberg and
published by Del Rey in 2004.
Warriors originally edited by George R.R. Martin and Gardner Dozois
and published by Tor Books in 2010.

Published by Harper*Voyager*
An imprint of HarperCollins*Publishers* 2017
7

Book design by Virginia Norey

A catalogue record for this book
is available from the British Library

ISBN: 978-0-00-823809-4

Printed and bound by CPI Group (UK) Ltd, Croydon, CR0 4YY

A KNIGHT OF THE SEVEN KINGDOMS

THE
HEDGE KNIGHT

The story offered here takes place about a hundred years prior
to the events described in A Game of Thrones.

The spring rains had softened the ground, so Dunk had no trouble digging the grave. He chose a spot on the western slope of a low hill, for the old man had always loved to watch the sunset. "Another day done"—he would sigh—"and who knows what the morrow will bring us, eh, Dunk?"

Well, one morrow had brought rains that soaked them to the bones, and the one after had brought wet, gusty winds, and the next a chill. By the fourth day the old man was too weak to ride. And now he was gone. Only a few days past, he had been singing as they rode, the old song about going to Gulltown to see a fair maid, but instead of Gulltown he'd sung of Ashford. *Off to Ashford to see the fair maid, heigh-ho, heigh-ho,* Dunk thought miserably as he dug.

When the hole was deep enough, he lifted the old man's body in his arms and carried him there. He had been a small man, and slim; stripped of hauberk, helm, and sword belt, he seemed to weigh no more than a bag of leaves. Dunk was hugely tall for his age, a shambling, shaggy, big-boned boy of sixteen or seventeen years (no one was quite certain which) who stood closer to seven feet than to six, and had only just begun to fill out his frame. The old man had often praised his strength. He had always been generous in his praise. It was all he had to give.

He laid him out in the bottom of the grave and stood over him for a time. The smell of rain was in the air again, and he knew he ought to fill the hole before it broke, but it was hard to throw dirt down on that tired old face. *There ought to be a septon here, to say some prayers over him, but he only has me.* The old man had taught Dunk all he knew of swords and shields and lances, but had never been much good at teaching him words.

"I'd leave your sword, but it would rust in the ground," he said at last, apologetic. "The gods will give you a new one, I guess. I wish you didn't die, ser." He paused, uncertain what else needed to be said. He didn't know any prayers, not all the way through; the old man had never been much for praying. "You were a true knight, and you never beat me when I didn't deserve it," he finally managed, "except that one time in Maidenpool. It was the inn boy who ate the widow woman's pie, not me, I told you. It don't matter now. The gods keep you, ser." He kicked dirt in the hole, then began to fill it methodically, never looking at the thing at the bottom. *He had a long life,* Dunk thought. *He must have been closer to sixty than to fifty, and how many men can say that?* At least he had lived to see another spring.

The sun was westering as he fed the horses. There were three; his swaybacked stot, the old man's palfrey, and Thunder, his warhorse, who was ridden only in tourney and battle. The big brown stallion was not as swift or strong as he had once been, but he still had his bright eye and fierce spirit, and he was more valuable than everything else Dunk owned. *If I sold Thunder and old Chestnut, and the saddles and bridles too, I'd come away with enough silver to . . .* Dunk frowned. The only life he knew was the life of a hedge knight, riding from keep to keep, taking service with this lord and that lord, fighting in their battles and eating in their halls until the war was done, then moving on. There were tourneys from time to time as well, though less often, and he knew that some hedge knights turned robber during lean winters, though the old man never had.

I could find another hedge knight in need of a squire to tend his animals and clean his mail, he thought, *or might be I could go to some city, to Lannisport or King's Landing, and join the City Watch. Or else . . .*

He had piled the old man's things under an oak. The cloth purse contained three silver stags, nineteen copper pennies, and a chipped garnet; like most hedge knights, the greatest part of his worldly wealth had been tied up in his horses and weapons. Dunk now owned a chain-mail hauberk that he had scoured the rust off a thousand times. An iron halfhelm with a broad nasal and a dent on the left temple. A sword belt of cracked brown leather, and a longsword in a wood-and-leather scabbard. A dagger, a razor, a whetstone. Greaves and gorget, an eight-foot war lance of turned ash topped by a cruel iron point, and an oaken shield with a scarred metal rim, bearing the sigil of Ser Arlan of Pennytree: a winged chalice, silver on brown.

Dunk looked at the shield, scooped up the sword belt, and looked at the shield again. The belt was made for the old man's skinny hips, it would never do for him, no more than the hauberk would. He tied the scabbard to a length of hempen rope, knotted it around his waist, and drew the longsword.

The blade was straight and heavy, good castle-forged steel, the grip soft leather wrapped over wood, the pommel a smooth, polished, black stone. Plain as it was, the sword felt good in his hand, and Dunk knew how sharp it was, having worked it with whetstone and oil-cloth many a night before they went to sleep. *It fits my grip as well as it ever fit his,* he thought to himself, *and there is a tourney at Ashford Meadow.*

Sweetfoot had an easier gait than old Chestnut, but Dunk was still sore and tired when he spied the inn ahead, a tall, daub-and-timber building beside a stream. The warm yellow light spilling from its windows looked so inviting that he could not pass it by. *I have three silvers,* he told himself, *enough for a good meal and as much ale as I care to drink.*

As he dismounted, a naked boy emerged dripping from the stream and began to dry himself on a roughspun brown cloak. "Are you the stableboy?" Dunk asked him. The lad looked to be no more than eight or nine, a pasty-faced, skinny thing, his bare feet caked in mud up to the ankle. His hair was the queerest thing about him. He had none. "I'll want my palfrey rubbed down. And oats for all three. Can you tend to them?"

The boy looked at him brazenly. "I could. If I wanted."

Dunk frowned. "I'll have none of that. I am a knight, I'll have you know."

"You don't look to be a knight."

"Do all knights look the same?"

"No, but they don't look like you, either. Your sword belt's made of rope."

"So long as it holds my scabbard, it serves. Now see to my horses. You'll get a copper if you do well, and a clout in the ear if you don't."

He did not wait to see how the stableboy took that but turned away and shouldered through the door.

At this hour, he would have expected the inn to be crowded, but the common room was almost empty. A young lordling in a fine damask mantle was passed out at one table, snoring softly into a pool of spilled wine. Otherwise there was no one. Dunk looked around uncertainly until a stout, short, whey-faced woman emerged from the kitchens and said, "Sit where you like. Is it ale you want, or food?"

"Both." Dunk took a chair by the window, well away from the sleeping man.

"There's good lamb, roasted with a crust of herbs, and some ducks my son shot down. Which will you have?"

He had not eaten at an inn in half a year or more. "Both."

The woman laughed. "Well, you're big enough for it." She drew a tankard of ale and brought it to his table. "Will you be wanting a room for the night as well?"

"No." Dunk would have liked nothing better than a soft straw mattress and a roof above his head, but he needed to be careful with his coin. The ground would serve. "Some food, some ale, and it's on to Ashford for me. How much farther is it?"

"A day's ride. Bear north when the road forks at the burned mill. Is my boy seeing to your horses, or has he run off again?"

"No, he's there," said Dunk. "You seem to have no custom."

"Half the town's gone to see the tourney. My own would as well, if I allowed it. They'll have this inn when I go, but the boy would sooner swagger about with soldiers, and the girl turns to sighs and giggles every time a knight rides by. I swear I couldn't tell you why. Knights are built the same as other men, and I never knew a joust to change the price of eggs." She eyed Dunk curiously; his sword and shield told her one thing, his rope belt and roughspun tunic quite another. "You're bound for the tourney yourself?"

He took a sip of the ale before he answered. A nut-brown color it was, and thick on the tongue, the way he liked it. "Aye," he said. "I mean to be a champion."

"Do you, now?" the innkeep answered, polite enough.

Across the room, the lordling raised his head from the wine puddle. His face had a sallow, unhealthy cast to it beneath a rat's nest of sandy brown hair, and blond stubble crusted his chin. He rubbed his mouth, blinked at Dunk, and said, "I dreamed of you." His hand trembled as he pointed a finger. "You stay away from me, do you hear? You stay *well* away."

Dunk stared at him uncertainly. "My lord?"

The innkeep leaned close. "Never you mind that one, ser. All he does is drink and talk about his dreams. I'll see about that food." She bustled off.

"Food?" The lordling made the word an obscenity. He staggered to his feet, one hand on the table to keep himself from falling. "I'm going to be sick," he announced. The front of his tunic was crusty red with old wine stains. "I wanted a whore, but there's none to be found here. All gone to Ashford Meadow. Gods be good, I need some wine." He lurched unsteadily from the common room, and Dunk heard him climbing steps, singing under his breath.

A sad creature, thought Dunk. *But why did he think he knew me?* He pondered that a moment over his ale.

The lamb was as good as any he had ever eaten, and the duck was even better, cooked with cherries and lemons and not near as greasy as most. The innkeep brought buttered pease as well, and oaten bread still hot from her oven. *This is what it means to be a knight,* he told himself as he sucked the last bit of meat off the bone. *Good food, and ale whenever I want it, and no one to clout me in the head.* He had a second tankard of ale with the meal, a third to wash it down, and a fourth because there was no one to tell him he couldn't, and when he was done he paid the woman with a silver stag and still got back a fistful of coppers.

It was full dark by the time Dunk emerged. His stomach was full and his purse was a little lighter, but he felt good as he walked to the stables. Ahead, he heard a horse whicker. "Easy, lad," a boy's voice said. Dunk quickened his step, frowning.

He found the stableboy mounted on Thunder and wearing the old man's armor. The hauberk was longer than he was, and he'd had to tilt the helm back on his bald head or else it would have covered his eyes. He looked utterly intent, and utterly absurd. Dunk stopped in the stable door and laughed.

The boy looked up, flushed, vaulted to the ground. "My lord, I did not mean—"

"Thief," Dunk said, trying to sound stern. "Take off that armor, and be glad that Thunder didn't kick you in that fool head. He's a warhorse, not a boy's pony."

The boy took off the helm and flung it to the straw. "I could ride him as well as you," he said, bold as you please.

"Close your mouth, I want none of your insolence. The hauberk too, take it off. What did you think you were doing?"

"How can I tell you, with my mouth closed?" The boy squirmed out of the chain mail and let it fall.

"You can open your mouth to answer," said Dunk. "Now pick up that mail, shake off the dirt, and put it back where you found it. And the halfhelm too. Did you feed the horses, as I told you? And rub down Sweetfoot?"

"Yes," the boy said, as he shook straw from the mail. "You're going to Ashford, aren't you? Take me with you, ser."

The innkeep had warned him of this. "And what might your mother say to that?"

"My mother?" The boy wrinkled up his face. "My mother's dead, she wouldn't say anything."

He was surprised. Wasn't the innkeep his mother? Perhaps he was only 'prenticed to her. Dunk's head was a little fuzzy from the ale. "Are you an orphan boy?" he asked uncertainly.

"Are you?" the boy threw back.

"I was once," Dunk admitted. *Till the old man took me in.*

"If you took me, I could squire for you."

"I have no need of a squire," he said.

"Every knight needs a squire," the boy said. "You look as though you need one more than most."

Dunk raised a hand threateningly. "And you look as though you need a clout in the ear, it seems to me. Fill me a sack of oats. I'm off for Ashford ... alone."

If the boy was frightened, he hid it well. For a moment he stood there defiant, his arms crossed, but just as Dunk was about to give up on him the lad turned and went for the oats.

Dunk was relieved. *A pity I couldn't ... but he has a good life here at the inn, a better one than he'd have squiring for a hedge knight. Taking him would be no kindness.*

He could still feel the lad's disappointment, though. As he mounted Sweetfoot and took up Thunder's lead, Dunk decided that a copper penny might cheer him. "Here, lad, for your help." He flipped the coin down at him with a smile, but the stableboy made no attempt to catch it. It fell in the dirt between his bare feet, and there he let it lie.

He'll scoop it up as soon as I am gone, Dunk told himself. He turned the palfrey and rode from the inn, leading the other two horses. The trees were bright with moonlight, and the sky was cloudless and speckled with stars. Yet as he headed down the road he could feel the stableboy watching his back, sullen and silent.

* * *

The shadows of the afternoon were growing long when Dunk reined up on the edge of broad Ashford Meadow. Threescore pavilions had already risen on the grassy field. Some were small, some large; some square, some round; some of sailcloth, some of linen, some of silk; but all were brightly colored, with long banners streaming from their center poles, brighter than a field of wildflowers with rich reds and sunny yellows, countless shades of green and blue, deep blacks and greys and purples.

The old man had ridden with some of these knights; others Dunk knew from tales told in common rooms and round campfires. Though he had never learned the magic of reading or writing, the old man had been relentless when it came to teaching him heraldry, often drilling him as they rode. The nightingales belonged to Lord Caron of the Marches, as skilled with the high harp as he was with a lance. The crowned stag was for Ser Lyonel Baratheon, the Laughing Storm. Dunk picked out the Tarly huntsman, House Dondarrion's purple lightning, the red apple of the Fossoways. There roared the lion of Lannister gold on crimson, and there the dark green sea turtle of the Estermonts swam across a pale green field. The brown tent beneath a red stallion could only belong to Ser Otho Bracken, who was called the Brute of Bracken since slaying Lord Quentyn Blackwood three years past during a tourney at King's Landing. Dunk heard that Ser Otho struck so hard with the blunted longaxe that he staved in the visor of Lord Blackwood's helm and the face beneath it. He saw some Blackwood banners as well, on the west edge of the meadow, as distant from Ser Otho as they could be. Marbrand, Mallister, Cargyll, Westerling, Swann, Mullendore, Hightower, Florent, Frey, Penrose, Stokeworth, Darry, Parren, Wylde; it seemed as though every lordly house of the west and south had sent a knight or three to Ashford to see the fair maid and brave the lists in her honor.

Yet however fine their pavilions were to look upon, he knew there was no place there for him. A threadbare wool cloak would be all the shelter he had tonight. While the lords and great knights dined on capons and suckling pigs, Dunk's supper would be a hard, stringy piece of salt beef. He knew full well that if he made his camp upon that gaudy field, he would need to suffer both silent scorn and open mockery. A few perhaps would treat him kindly, yet in a way that was almost worse.

A hedge knight must hold tight to his pride. Without it, he was no more than a sellsword. *I must earn my place in that company. If I fight well, some lord may take me into his household. I will ride in noble company then, and eat fresh meat every night in a castle hall, and raise my own pavilion at tourneys. But first I must do well.* Reluctantly, he turned his back on the tourney grounds and led his horses into the trees.

On the outskirts of the great meadow, a good half mile from town and castle, he found a place where a bend in a brook had formed a deep pool. Reeds grew thick along its edge, and a tall, leafy elm presided over all. The spring grass there was as green as any knight's banner and soft to the touch. It was a pretty spot, and no one had yet laid claim to it. *This will be my pavilion,* Dunk told himself, *a pavilion roofed with leaves, greener even than the banners of the Tyrells and the Estermonts.*

His horses came first. After they had been tended, he stripped and waded into the pool to wash away the dust of travel. "A true knight is cleanly as well as godly," the old man always said, insisting that they wash themselves head to heels every time the moon turned, whether they smelled sour or not. Now that he was a knight, Dunk vowed he would do the same.

He sat naked under the elm while he dried, enjoying the warmth of the spring air on his skin as he watched a dragonfly move lazily amongst the reeds. *Why would they name it a dragonfly?* he wondered. *It looks nothing like a dragon.* Not that Dunk had ever seen a dragon. The old man had, though. Dunk had heard the story half a hundred times, how Ser Arlan had been just a little boy when his grandfather had taken him to King's Landing, and how they'd seen the last dragon there the year before it died. She'd been a green female, small and stunted, her wings withered. None of her eggs had ever hatched. "Some say King Aegon poisoned her," the old man would tell. "The third Aegon that would be, not King Daeron's father, but the one they named Dragonbane, or Aegon the Unlucky. He was afraid of dragons, for he'd seen his uncle's beast devour his own mother. The summers have been shorter since the last dragon died, and the winters longer and crueler."

The air began to cool as the sun dipped below the tops of the trees. When Dunk felt gooseflesh prickling his arms, he beat his tunic and breeches against the trunk of the elm to knock off the worst of the dirt and donned them once again. On the morrow he could seek out the master of the games and enroll his name, but he had other matters he ought to look into tonight if he hoped to challenge.

He did not need to study his reflection in the water to know that he did not look much a knight, so he slung Ser Arlan's shield across his back to display the sigil. Hobbling the horses, Dunk left them to crop the thick green grass beneath the elm as he set out on foot for the tourney grounds.

In normal times the meadow served as a commons for the folk of Ashford town across the river, but now it was transformed. A second town had sprung up overnight, a town of silk instead of stone, larger and fairer than its elder sister. Dozens of merchants had erected their stalls along the edge of the field, selling felts and fruits, belts and boots, hides and hawks, earthenware, gemstones, pewterwork, spices, feathers, and all manner of other goods. Jugglers, puppeteers, and magicians wandered amongst the crowds plying their trades … as did the whores and cutpurses. Dunk kept a wary hand on his coin.

When he caught the smell of sausages sizzling over a smoky fire, his mouth began to water. He bought one with a copper from his pouch and a horn of ale to wash it down. As he ate he watched a painted wooden knight battle a painted wooden dragon. The puppeteer who worked the dragon was good to watch too; a tall drink of water, with the olive skin and black hair of Dorne. She was slim as a lance with no breasts to speak of, but Dunk liked her face and the way her fingers made the dragon snap and slither at the end of its strings. He would have tossed the girl a copper if he'd had one to spare, but just now he needed every coin.

There were armorers amongst the merchants, as he had hoped. A Tyroshi with a forked blue beard was selling ornate helms, gorgeous fantastical things wrought in the shapes of birds and beasts and chased with gold and silver. Elsewhere he found a swordmaker hawking cheap steel blades, and another whose work was much finer, but it was not a sword he lacked.

The man he needed was all the way down at the end of the row, a shirt of fine chain mail and a pair of lobstered steel gauntlets displayed on the table before him. Dunk inspected them closely. "You do good work," he said.

"None better." A stumpy man, the smith was no more than five feet tall, yet wide as Dunk about the chest and arms. He had a black beard, huge hands, and no trace of humility.

"I need armor for the tourney," Dunk told him. "A suit of good mail, with gorget, greaves, and greathelm." The old man's halfhelm would fit his head, but he wanted more protection for his face than a nasal bar alone could provide.

The armorer looked him up and down. "You're a big one, but I've armored bigger." He came out from behind the table. "Kneel, I want to measure those shoulders. Aye, and that thick neck o' yours." Dunk knelt. The armorer laid a length of knotted rawhide along his shoulders, grunted, slipped it about his throat, grunted again. "Lift your arm. No, the right." He grunted a third time. "Now you can stand." The inside of a leg, the thickness of his calf, and the size of his waist elicited further grunts. "I have some pieces in me wagon that might do for you," the man said when he was done. "Nothing prettied up with gold or silver, mind you, just good steel, strong and plain. I make helms that look like helms, not winged pigs and queer foreign fruits, but mine will serve you better if you take a lance in the face."

"That's all I want," said Dunk. "How much?"

"Eight hundred stags, for I'm feeling kindly."

"*Eight hundred?*" It was more than he had expected. "I ... I could trade you some old armor, made for a smaller man ... a halfhelm, a mail hauberk ..."

"Steely Pate sells only his own work," the man declared, "but it might be I could make use of the metal. If it's not too rusted, I'll take it and armor you for six hundred."

Dunk could beseech Pate to give him the armor on trust, but he knew what sort of answer that request would likely get. He had traveled with the old man long enough to learn that merchants were no-toriously mistrustful of hedge knights, some of whom were little better than robbers. "I'll give you two silvers now, and the armor and the rest of the coin on the morrow."

The armorer studied him a moment. "Two silvers buys you a day. After that, I sell me work to the next man."

Dunk scooped the stags out of his pouch and placed them in the armorer's callused hand. "You'll get it all. I mean to be a champion here."

"Do you?" Pate bit one of the coins. "And these others, I suppose they all came just to cheer you on?"

* * *

The moon was well up by the time he turned his steps back toward his elm. Behind him, Ashford Meadow was ablaze with torchlight. The sounds of song and laughter drifted across the grass, but his own mood was somber. He could think of only one way to raise the coin for his armor. And if he should be defeated ... "One victory is all I need," he muttered aloud. "That's not so much to hope for."

Even so, the old man would never have hoped for it. Ser Arlan had not ridden a tilt since the day he had been unhorsed by the Prince of Dragonstone in a tourney at Storm's End, many years before. "It is not every man who can boast that he broke seven lances against the finest knight in the Seven Kingdoms," he would say. "I could never hope to do better, so why should I try?"

Dunk had suspected that Ser Arlan's age had more to do with it than the Prince of Dragonstone did, but he never dared say as much. The old man had his pride, even at the last. *I am quick and strong, he always said so, what was true for him need not be true for me,* he told himself stubbornly.

He was moving through a patch of weed, chewing over his chances in his head, when he saw the flicker of firelight through the bushes. *What is this?* Dunk did not stop to think. Suddenly his sword was in his hand and he was crashing through the grass.

He burst out roaring and cursing, only to jerk to a sudden halt at the sight of the boy beside the campfire. "You!" He lowered the sword. "What are you doing here?"

"Cooking a fish," said the bald boy. "Do you want some?"

"I meant, how did you *get* here? Did you steal a horse?"

"I rode in the back of a cart, with a man who was bringing some lambs to the castle for my lord of Ashford's table."

"Well, you'd best see if he's gone yet, or find another cart. I won't have you here."

"You can't make me go," the boy said, impertinent. "I'd had enough of that inn."

"I'll have no more insolence from you," Dunk warned. "I should throw you over my horse right now and take you home."

"You'd need to ride all the way to King's Landing," said the boy. "You'd miss the tourney."

King's Landing. For a moment Dunk wondered if he was being mocked, but the boy had no way of knowing that he had been born in King's Landing as well. *Another wretch from Flea Bottom, like as not, and who can blame him for wanting out of that place?*

He felt foolish standing there with sword in hand over an eight-year-old orphan. He sheathed it, glowering so the boy would see that he would suffer no nonsense. *I ought to give him a good beating at the least,* he thought, but the child looked so pitiful he could not bring himself to hit him. He glanced around the camp. The fire was burning merrily within a neat circle of rocks. The horses had been brushed, and clothes were hanging from the elm, drying above the flames. "What are those doing there?"

"I washed them," the boy said. "And I groomed the horses, made the fire, and caught this fish. I would have raised your pavilion, but I couldn't find one."

"There's my pavilion." Dunk swept a hand above his head, at the branches of the tall elm that loomed above them.

"That's a tree," the boy said, unimpressed.

"It's all the pavilion a true knight needs. I would sooner sleep under the stars than in some smoky tent."

"What if it rains?"

"The tree will shelter me."

"Trees leak."

Dunk laughed. "So they do. Well, if truth be told, I lack the coin for a pavilion. And you'd best turn that fish, or it will be burned on the bottom and raw on the top. You'd never make a kitchen boy."

"I would if I wanted," the boy said, but he turned the fish.

"What happened to your hair?" Dunk asked of him.

"The maesters shaved it off." Suddenly self-conscious, the boy pulled up the hood of his dark brown cloak, covering his head.

Dunk had heard that they did that sometimes, to treat lice or rootworms or certain sicknesses. "Are you ill?"

"No," said the boy. "What's your name?"

"Dunk," he said.

The wretched boy laughed aloud, as if that was the funniest thing he'd ever heard. *"Dunk?"* he said. "Ser Dunk? That's no name for a knight. Is it short for Duncan?"

Was it? The old man had called him just *Dunk* for as long as he could recall, and he did not remember much of his life before. "Duncan, yes," he said. "Ser Duncan of ..." Dunk had no other name, nor any house; Ser Arlan had found him living wild in the stews and alleys of Flea Bottom. He had never known his father or mother. What was he to say? "Ser Duncan of Flea Bottom" did not sound very knightly. He could take Pennytree, but what if they asked him where it was? Dunk had never been to Pennytree, nor had the old man talked much about it. He frowned for a moment, then blurted out, "Ser Duncan the Tall." He *was* tall, no one could dispute that, and it sounded puissant.

Though the little sneak did not seem to think so. "I have never heard of any Ser Duncan the Tall."

"Do you know every knight in the Seven Kingdoms, then?"

The boy looked at him boldly. "The good ones."

"I'm as good as any. After the tourney, they'll all know that. Do *you* have a name, thief?"

The boy hesitated. "Egg," he said.

Dunk did not laugh. *His head does look like an egg. Small boys can be cruel, and grown men as well.* "Egg," he said, "I should beat you bloody and send you on your way, but the truth is, I have no pavilion and I have no squire either. If you'll swear to do as you're told, I'll let you serve me for the tourney. After that, well, we'll see. If I decide you're worth your keep, you'll have clothes on your back and food in your belly. The clothes might be roughspun and the food salt beef and salt fish, and maybe some venison from time to time where there are no foresters about, but you won't go hungry. And I promise not to beat you except when you deserve it."

Egg smiled. "Yes, my lord."

"Ser," Dunk corrected. "I am only a hedge knight." He wondered if the old man was looking down on him. *I will teach him the arts of battle, the same as you taught me, ser. He seems a likely lad, might be one day he'll make a knight.*

The fish was still a little raw on the inside when they ate it, and the boy had not removed all the bones, but it still tasted a world better than hard salt beef.

Egg soon fell asleep beside the dying fire. Dunk lay on his back nearby, his big hands behind his head, gazing up at the night sky. He could hear distant music from the tourney grounds half a mile away. The stars were everywhere, thousands and thousands of them. One fell as he was watching, a bright green streak that flashed across the black, then was gone.

A falling star brings luck to him who sees it, Dunk thought. *But the rest of them are all in their pavilions by now, staring up at silk instead of sky. So the luck is mine alone.*

In the morning, he woke to the sound of a cock crowing. Egg was still there, curled up beneath the old man's second-best cloak. *Well, the boy did not run off during the night, that's a start.* He prodded him awake with his foot. "Up. There's work to do." The boy rose quick enough, rubbing his eyes. "Help me saddle Sweetfoot," Dunk told him.

"What about breakfast?"

"There's salt beef. *After* we're done."

"I'd sooner eat the horse," Egg said. "Ser."

"You'll eat my fist if you don't do as you're told. Get the brushes. They're in the saddle sack. Yes, that one."

Together they brushed out the palfrey's sorrel coat, hefted Ser Arlan's best saddle over her back, and cinched it tight. Egg was a good worker once he put his mind to it, Dunk saw.

"I expect I'll be gone most of the day," he told the boy as he mounted. "You're to stay here and put the camp in order. Make sure no *other* thieves come nosing about."

"Can I have a sword to run them off with?" Egg asked. He had blue eyes, Dunk saw, very dark, almost purple. His bald head made them seem huge, somehow.

"No," said Dunk. "A knife's enough. And you had best be here when I come back, do you hear me? Rob me and run off, and I'll hunt you down, I swear I will. With dogs."

"You don't have any dogs," Egg pointed out.

"I'll get some," said Dunk. "Just for you." He turned Sweetfoot's head toward the meadow and moved off at a brisk trot, hoping the threat would be enough to keep the boy honest. Save for the clothes on his back, the armor in his sack, and the horse beneath him, everything Dunk

owned in the world was back at that camp. *I am a great fool to trust the boy so far, but it is no more than the old man did for me*, he reflected. *The Mother must have sent him to me so that I could pay my debt.*

As he crossed the field, he heard the ring of hammers from the riverside, where carpenters were nailing together jousting barriers and raising a lofty viewing stand. A few new pavilions were going up as well, while the knights who had come earlier slept off last night's revels or sat to break their fasts. Dunk could smell woodsmoke, and bacon as well.

To the north of the meadow flowed the river Cockleswent, a vassal stream to the mighty Mander. Beyond the shallow ford lay town and castle. Dunk had seen many a market town during his journeys with the old man. This was prettier than most; the whitewashed houses with their thatched roofs had an inviting aspect to them. When he was smaller, he used to wonder what it would be like to live in such a place; to sleep every night with a roof over your head and wake every morning with the same walls wrapped around you. *It may be that soon I'll know. Aye, and Egg too.* It could happen. Stranger things happened every day.

Ashford Castle was a stone structure built in the shape of a trian-gle, with round towers rising thirty feet tall at each point and thick, crenellated walls running between. Orange banners flew from its battlements, displaying the white sun-and-chevron sigil of its lord. Men-at-arms in orange-and-white livery stood outside the gates with halberds, watching people come and go, seemingly more intent on joking with a pretty milkmaid than in keeping anyone out. Dunk reined up in front of the short, bearded man he took for their captain and asked for the master of the games.

"It's Plummer you want, he's steward here. I'll show you."

Inside the yard, a stableboy took Sweetfoot for him. Dunk slung Ser Arlan's battered shield over a shoulder and followed the guards captain back of the stables to a turret built into an angle of the cur-tain wall. Steep stone steps led up to the wallwalk. "Come to enter your master's name for the lists?" the captain asked, as they climbed.

"It's my own name I'll be putting in."

"Is it now?" Was the man smirking? Dunk was not certain. "That door there. I'll leave you to it and get back to my post."

When Dunk pushed open the door, the steward was sitting at a trestle table, scratching on a piece of parchment with a quill. He had thinning grey hair and a narrow, pinched face. "Yes?" he said, looking up. "What do you want, man?"

Dunk pulled shut the door. "Are you Plummer the steward? I came for the tourney. To enter the lists."

Plummer pursed his lips. "My lord's tourney is a contest for knights. Are you a knight?"

He nodded, wondering if his ears were red.

"A knight with a name, mayhaps?"

"Dunk." Why had he said *that*? "Ser Duncan. The Tall."

"And where might you be from, Ser Duncan the Tall?"

"Everyplace. I was squire to Ser Arlan of Pennytree since I was five or six. This is his shield." He showed it to the steward. "He was coming to the tourney, but he caught a chill and died, so I came in his stead. He knighted me before he passed, with his own sword." Dunk drew the longsword and laid it on the scarred wooden table between them.

The master of the lists gave the blade no more than a glance. "A sword it is, for a certainty. I have never heard of this Arlan of Pennytree, however. You were his squire, you say?"

"He always said he meant for me to be a knight, as he was. When he was dying he called for his longsword and bade me kneel. He touched me once on my right shoulder and once on my left, and said some words, and when I got up he said I was a knight."

"Hmpf." The man Plummer rubbed his nose. "Any knight can make a knight, it is true, though it is more customary to stand a vigil and be anointed by a septon before taking your vows. Were there any witnesses to your dubbing?"

"Only a robin, up in a thorn tree. I heard it as the old man was saying the words. He charged me to be a good knight and true, to obey the seven gods, defend the weak and innocent, serve my lord faithfully, and defend the realm with all my might, and I swore that I would."

"No doubt." Plummer did not deign to call him *ser,* Dunk could not help but notice. "I shall need to consult with Lord Ashford. Will you or your late master be known to any of the good knights here assembled?"

Dunk thought a moment. "There was a pavilion flying the banner of House Dondarrion? The black, with purple lightning?"

"That would be Ser Manfred, of that house."

"Ser Arlan served his lord father in Dorne, three years past. Ser Manfred might remember me."

"I would advise you to speak to him. If he will vouch for you, bring him here with you on the morrow, at this same time."

"As you say, m'lord." He started for the door.

"Ser Duncan," the steward called after him.

Dunk turned back.

"You are aware," the man said, "that those vanquished in tourney forfeit their arms, armor, and horse to the victors, and must needs ransom them back?"

"I know."

"And do you have the coin to pay such ransom?"

Now he knew his ears were red. "I won't have need of coin," he said, praying it was true. *All I need is one victory. If I win my first tilt, I'll have the loser's armor and horse, or his gold, and I can stand a loss myself.*

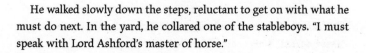

He walked slowly down the steps, reluctant to get on with what he must do next. In the yard, he collared one of the stableboys. "I must speak with Lord Ashford's master of horse."

"I'll find him for you."

It was cool and dim in the stables. An unruly grey stallion snapped at him as he passed, but Sweetfoot only whickered softly and nuzzled his hand when he raised it to her nose. "You're a good girl, aren't you?" he murmured. The old man always said that a knight should never love a horse, since more than a few were like to die under him, but he never heeded his own counsel either. Dunk had often seen him spend his last copper on an apple for old Chestnut or some oats for Sweetfoot and Thunder. The palfrey had been Ser Arlan's riding horse, and she had borne him tirelessly over thousands of miles, all up and down the Seven Kingdoms. Dunk felt as though he was betraying an old friend, but what choice did he have? Chestnut was too old to be worth much of anything, and Thunder must carry him in the lists.

Some time passed before the master of horse deigned to appear. As he waited, Dunk heard a blare of trumpets from the walls and voices in the yard. Curious, he led Sweetfoot to the stable door to see what was happening. A large party of knights and mounted archers poured through the gates, a hundred men at least, riding some of the most splendid horses that Dunk had ever seen. *Some great lord has come.* He grabbed the arm of a stableboy as he ran past. "Who are they?"

The boy looked at him queerly. "Can't you see the banners?" He wrenched free and hurried off.

The banners . . . As Dunk turned his head, a gust of wind lifted the black silk pennon atop the tall staff, and the fierce three-headed dragon of House Targaryen seemed to spread its wings, breathing scarlet fire. The banner-bearer was a tall knight in white scale armor chased with gold, a pure white cloak streaming from his shoulders. Two of the other riders were armored in white from head to heel as well. *Kingsguard knights with the royal banner.* Small wonder Lord Ashford and his sons came hurrying out the doors of the keep, and the fair maid too, a short girl with yellow hair and a round pink face.

She does not seem so fair to me, Dunk thought. The puppet girl was prettier.

"Boy, let go of that nag and see to my horse."

A rider had dismounted in front of the stables. *He is talking to me,* Dunk realized. "I am not a stableboy, m'lord."

"Not clever enough?" The speaker wore a black cloak bordered in scarlet satin, but underneath was raiment bright as flame, all reds and yellows and golds. Slim and straight as a dirk, though only of middling height, he was near Dunk's own age. Curls of silver-gold hair framed a face sculpted and imperious; high brow and sharp cheekbones, straight nose, pale smooth skin without blemish. His eyes were a deep violet color. "If you cannot manage a horse, fetch me some wine and a pretty wench."

"I ... m'lord, pardons, I'm no serving man either. I have the honor to be a knight."

"Knighthood has fallen on sad days," said the princeling, but then one of the stableboys came rushing up, and he turned away to hand him the reins of his palfrey, a splendid blood bay. Dunk was forgotten in an instant. Relieved, he slunk back inside the stables to wait for the master of horse. He felt ill at ease enough around the lords in their pavilions; he had no business speaking to princes.

That the beautiful stripling was a prince he had no doubt. The Targaryens were the blood of lost Valyria across the seas, and their silver-gold hair and violet eyes set them apart from common men. Dunk knew Prince Baelor was older, but the youth might well have been one of his sons: Valarr, who was often called the Young Prince to set him apart from his father, or Matarys, the Even Younger Prince, as old Lord Swann's fool had named him once. There were other princelings as well, cousins to Valarr and Matarys. King Daeron the Good had four grown sons, three with sons of their own. The line of the dragonkings had almost died out during his father's day, but it was commonly said that Daeron II and his sons had left it secure for all time.

"You. Man. You asked for me." Lord Ashford's master of horse had a red face made redder by his orange livery, and a brusque manner of speaking. "What is it? I have no time for—"

"I want to sell this palfrey," Dunk broke in quickly, before the man could dismiss him. "She's a good horse, sure of foot—"

"I have no time, I tell you." The man gave Sweetfoot no more than a glance. "My lord of Ashford has no need of such. Take her to the town, perhaps Henly will give you a silver or three." That quick, he was turning away.

"Thank you, m'lord," Dunk said before he could go. "M'lord, has the king come?"

The master of horse laughed at him. "No, thank the gods. This infestation of princes is trial enough. Where am I going to find the stalls for all these animals? And fodder?" He strode off shouting at his stableboys.

By the time Dunk left the stable, Lord Ashford had escorted his princely guests into the hall, but two of the Kingsguard knights in their white armor and snowy cloaks still lingered in the yard, talking with the captain of the guard. Dunk halted before them. "M'lords, I am Ser Duncan the Tall."

"Well met, Ser Duncan," answered the bigger of the white knights. "I am Ser Roland Crakehall, and this is my Sworn Brother, Ser Donnel of Duskendale."

The seven champions of the Kingsguard were the most puissant warriors in all the Seven Kingdoms, saving only perhaps the crown prince, Baelor Breakspear himself. "Have you come to enter the lists?" Dunk asked anxiously.

"It would not be fitting for us to ride against those we are sworn to protect," answered Ser Donnel, red of hair and beard.

"Prince Valarr has the honor to be one of Lady Ashford's champions," explained Ser Roland, "and two of his cousins mean to challenge. The rest of us have come only to watch."

Relieved, Dunk thanked the white knights for their kindness and rode out through the castle gates before another prince should think to accost him. *Three princelings,* he pondered as he turned the palfrey toward the streets of Ashford town. Valarr was the eldest son of Prince Baelor, second in line to the Iron Throne, but Dunk did not know how much of his father's fabled prowess with lance and sword he might have inherited. About the other Targaryen princes he knew even less. *What will I do if I have to ride against a prince? Will I even be allowed to challenge one so highborn?* He did not know the answer. The old man had often said he was thick as a castle wall, and just now he felt it.

Henly liked the look of Sweetfoot well enough until he heard Dunk wanted to sell her. Then all the stableman could see in her were faults. He offered three hundred silvers. Dunk said he must have three thousand. After much arguing and cursing, they settled at seven hundred fifty silver stags. That was a deal closer to Henly's starting price than to Dunk's, which made him feel the loser in the tilt, but the stableman would go no higher, so in the end he had no choice but to yield. A second argument began when Dunk declared that the price did not include the saddle, and Henly insisted that it had.

Finally it was all settled. As Henly left to fetch his coin, Dunk stroked Sweetfoot's mane and told her to be brave. "If I win, I'll come back and buy you again, I promise." He had no doubt that all the palfrey's flaws would vanish in the intervening days, and she would be worth twice what she was today.

The stableman gave him three gold pieces and the rest in silver.

Dunk bit one of the gold coins and smiled. He had never tasted gold before, nor handled it. "Dragons," men called the coins, since they were stamped with the three-headed dragon of House Targaryen on one side. The other bore the likeness of the king. Two of the coins Henly gave him had King Daeron's face; the third was older, well worn, and showed a different man. His name was there under his head, but Dunk could not read the letters. Gold had been shaved off its edges too, he saw. He pointed this out to Henly, and loudly. The stableman grumbled, but handed over another few silvers and a fist-ful of coppers to make up the weight. Dunk handed a few of the coppers right back, and nodded at Sweetfoot. "That's for her," he said. "See that she has some oats tonight. Aye, and an apple too."

With the shield on his arm and the sack of old armor slung over his shoulder, Dunk set out on foot through the sunny streets of Ash-ford town. The heft of all that coin in his pouch made him feel queer; almost giddy on one hand and anxious on the other. The old man had never trusted him with more than a coin or two at a time. He could live a year on this much money. *And what will I do when it's gone, sell Thunder?* That road ended in beggary or outlawry. *This chance will never come again, I must risk all.*

By the time he splashed back across the ford to the south bank of the Cockleswent, the morning was almost done and the tourney grounds had come to life once more. The winesellers and sausage makers were doing a brisk trade, a dancing bear was shuffling along to his master's playing as a singer sang "The Bear, the Bear, and the Maiden Fair," jugglers were juggling, and the puppeteers were just finishing another fight.

Dunk stopped to watch the wooden dragon slain. When the pup-pet knight cut its head off and the red sawdust spilled out onto the grass, he laughed aloud and threw the girl two coppers. "One for last night," he called. She caught the coins in the air and threw him back a smile as sweet as any he had ever seen.

Is it me she smiles at, or the coins? Dunk had never been with a girl, and they made him nervous. Once, three years past, when the old man's purse was full after half a year in the service of blind Lord Flor-ent, he'd told Dunk the time had come to take him to a brothel and make him a man. He'd been drunk, though, and when he was sober he did not remember. Dunk had been too embarrassed to remind him. He was not certain he wanted a whore anyway. If he could not have a highborn maiden like a proper knight, he wanted one who at least liked him more than his silver.

"Will you drink a horn of ale?" he asked the puppet girl as she was scooping the sawdust blood back into her dragon. "With me, I mean? Or a sausage? I had a sausage last night, it was good. They're made with pork, I think."

"I thank you, m'lord, but we have another show." The girl rose and ran off to the fierce fat Dornishwoman who worked the puppet knight while Dunk stood there feeling stupid. He liked the way she ran, though. *A pretty girl, and tall. I would not have to kneel to kiss that one.* He knew how to kiss. A tavern girl had showed him one night in Lannisport, a year ago, but she'd been so short she had to sit on the table to reach his lips. The memory made his ears burn. What a great fool he was. It was jousting he should be thinking about, not kissing.

Lord Ashford's carpenters were whitewashing the waist-high
wooden barriers that would separate the jousters. Dunk watched
them work a while. There were five lanes, arrayed north to south so
none of the competitors would ride with the sun in his eyes. A three-
tiered viewing stand had been raised on the eastern side of the lists,
with an orange canopy to shield the lords and ladies from rain and
sun. Most would sit on benches, but four high-backed chairs had

been erected in the center of the platform, for Lord Ashford, the fair maid, and the visiting princes.

On the eastern verge of the meadow, a quintain had been set up and a dozen knights were tilting at it, sending the pole arm spinning every time they struck the splintered shield suspended from one end. Dunk watched the Brute of Bracken take his turn, then Lord Caron of the Marches. *I do not have as good a seat as any of them,* he thought uneasily.

Elsewhere, men were training afoot, going at each other with wooden swords while their squires stood shouting ribald advice. Dunk watched a stocky youth try to hold off a muscular knight who seemed lithe and quick as a mountain cat. Both had the red apple of the Fossoways painted on their shields, but the younger man's was soon hacked and chipped to pieces. "Here's an apple that's not ripe yet," the older said as he slammed the other's helm. The younger Fossoway was bruised and bloody by the time he yielded, but his foe was hardly winded. He raised his visor, looked about, saw Dunk, and said, "You there. Yes, you, the big one. Knight of the winged chalice. Is that a longsword you wear?"

"It is mine by rights," Dunk said defensively. "I am Ser Duncan the Tall."

"And I Ser Steffon Fossoway. Would you care to try me, Ser Duncan the Tall? It would be good to have someone new to cross swords with. My cousin's not ripe yet, as you've seen."

"Do it, Ser Duncan," urged the beaten Fossoway as he removed his helm. "I may not be ripe, but my good cousin is rotten to the core. Knock the seeds out of him."

Dunk shook his head. Why were these lordlings involving him in their quarrel? He wanted no part of it. "I thank you, ser, but I have matters to attend." He was uncomfortable carrying so much coin. The sooner he paid Steely Pate and got his armor, the happier he would be.

Ser Steffon looked at him scornfully. "The hedge knight has matters." He glanced about and found another likely opponent loitering nearby. "Ser Grance, well met. Come try me. I know every feeble trick my cousin Raymun has mastered, and it seems that Ser Duncan needs to return to the hedges. Come, come."

Dunk stalked away red-faced. He did not have many tricks himself, feeble or otherwise, and he did not want anyone to see him fight until the tourney. The old man always said that the better you knew your foe, the easier it was to best him. Knights like Ser Steffon had sharp eyes to find a man's weakness at a glance. Dunk was strong and quick, and his weight and reach were in his favor, but he did not believe for a moment that his skills were the equal of these others. Ser Arlan had taught him as best he could, but the old man had never been the greatest of knights even when young. Great knights did not live their lives in the hedges nor die by the side of a muddy road. *That will not happen to me,* Dunk vowed. *I will show them that I can be more than a hedge knight.*

"Ser Duncan." The younger Fossoway hurried to catch him. "I should not have urged you to try my cousin. I was angry with his arrogance, and you are so large, I thought ... well, it was wrong of me. You wear no armor. He would have broken your hand if he could, or a knee. He likes to batter men in the training yard, so they will be bruised and vulnerable later, should he meet them in the lists."

"He did not break you."

"No, but I am his own blood, though his is the senior branch of the apple tree, as he never ceases to remind me. I am Raymun Fossoway."

"Well met. Will you and your cousin ride in the tourney?"

"He will, for a certainty. As to me, would that I could. I am only a squire as yet. My cousin has promised to knight me, but insists that I am not ripe yet." Raymun had a square face, a pug nose, and short woolly hair, but his smile was engaging. "You have the look of a challenger, it seems to me. Whose shield do you mean to strike?"

"It makes no difference," said Dunk. That was what you were supposed to say, though it made all the difference in the world. "I will not enter the lists until the third day."

"And by then some of the champions will have fallen, yes," Raymun said. "Well, may the Warrior smile on you, ser."

"And you." *If he is only a squire, what business do I have being a knight? One of us is a fool.* The silver in Dunk's pouch clinked with every step, but he could lose it all in a heartbeat, he knew. Even the rules of this tourney worked against him, making it very unlikely that he would face a green or feeble foe.

There were a dozen different forms a tourney might follow, according to the whim of the lord who hosted it. Some were mock battles between teams of knights, others wild melees where the glory went to the last fighter left standing. Where individual combats were the rule, pairings were sometimes determined by lot and sometimes by the master of the games.

Lord Ashford was staging this tourney to celebrate his daughter's thirteenth name day. The fair maid would sit by her father's side as the reigning Queen of Love and Beauty. Five champions wearing her favors would defend her. All others must perforce be challengers, but any man who could defeat one of the champions would take his place and stand as a champion himself, until such time as another challenger unseated him. At the end of three days of jousting, the five who remained would determine whether the fair maid retained the crown of Love and Beauty, or whether another would wear it in her place.

Dunk stared at the grassy lists and the empty chairs on the viewing stand and pondered his chances. One victory was all he needed; then he could name himself one of the champions of Ashford Meadow, if only for an hour. The old man had lived nigh on sixty years and had never been a champion. *It is not too much to hope for, if the gods are good.* He thought back on all the songs he had heard, songs of blind Symeon Star-Eyes and noble Serwyn of the Mirror Shield, of Prince Aemon the Dragonknight, Ser Ryam Redwyne, and Florian the Fool. They had all won victories against foes far more terrible than any he would face. *But they were great heroes, brave men of noble birth, except for Florian. And what am I? Dunk of Flea Bottom? Or Ser Duncan the Tall?*

He supposed he would learn the truth of that soon enough. He hefted the sack of armor and turned his feet toward the merchants' stalls, in search of Steely Pate.

Egg had worked manfully at the campsite. Dunk was pleased; he had been half-afraid his squire would run off again. "Did you get a good price for your palfrey?" the boy asked.

"How did you know I'd sold her?"

"You rode off and walked back, and if robbers had stolen her you'd be more angry than you are."

"I got enough for this." Dunk took out his new armor to show the boy. "If you're ever to be a knight, you'll need to know good steel from bad. Look here, this is fine work. This mail is double-chain, each link bound to two others, see? It gives more protection than single chain. And the helm, Pate's rounded the top, see how it curves? A sword or an axe will slide off, where they might bite through a flat-topped helm." Dunk lowered the greathelm over his head. "How does it look?"

"There's no visor," Egg pointed out.

"There are air holes. Visors are points of weakness." Steely Pate had said as much. "If you knew how many knights have taken an arrow in the eye as they lifted their visor for a suck o' cool air, you'd never want one," he'd told Dunk.

"There's no crest either," said Egg. "It's just plain."

Dunk lifted off the helm. "Plain is fine for the likes of me. See how bright the steel is? It will be your task to keep it that way. You know how to scour mail?"

"In a barrel of sand," said the boy, "but you don't have a barrel. Did you buy a pavilion too, ser?"

"I didn't get *that* good a price." *The boy is too bold for his own good, I ought to beat that out of him.* He knew he would not, though. He liked the boldness. He needed to be bolder himself. *My squire is braver than I am, and more clever.* "You did well here, Egg," Dunk told him. "On the morrow, you'll come with me. Have a look at the tourney grounds. We'll buy oats for the horses and fresh bread for ourselves. Maybe a bit of cheese as well, they were selling good cheese at one of the stalls."

"I won't need to go into the castle, will I?"

"Why not? One day, I mean to live in a castle. I hope to win a place above the salt before I'm done."

The boy said nothing. *Perhaps he fears to enter a lord's hall,* Dunk reflected. *That's no more than might be expected. He will grow out of it in time.* He went back to admiring his armor and wondering how long he would wear it.

Ser Manfred was a thin man with a sour look on his face. He wore a black surcoat slashed with the purple lightning of House Dondarrion, but Dunk would have remembered him anyway by his unruly mane of red-gold hair. "Ser Arlan served your lord father when he and Lord Caron burned the Vulture King out of the Red Mountains, ser," he said from one knee. "I was only a boy then, but I squired for him. Ser Arlan of Pennytree."

Ser Manfred scowled. "No. I know him not. Nor you, boy."

Dunk showed him the old man's shield. "This was his sigil, the winged chalice."

"My lord father took eight hundred knights and near four thousand foot into the mountains. I cannot be expected to remember every one of them, nor what shields they carried. It may be that you were with us, but ..." Ser Manfred shrugged.

Dunk was struck speechless for an instant. *The old man took a wound in your father's service, how can you have forgotten him?* "They will not allow me to challenge unless some knight or lord will vouch for me."

"And what is that to me?" said Ser Manfred. "I have given you enough of my time, ser."

If he went back to the castle without Ser Manfred, he was lost. Dunk eyed the purple lightning embroidered across the black wool of Ser Manfred's surcoat and said, "I remember your father telling the camp how your house got its sigil. One stormy night, as the first of your line bore a message across the Dornish Marches, an arrow killed his horse beneath him and spilled him on the ground. Two Dornishmen came out of the darkness in ringmail and crested helms. His sword had broken beneath him when he fell. When he saw that, he thought he was doomed. But as the Dornishmen closed to cut him down, lightning cracked from the sky. It was a bright, burning purple, and it split, striking the Dornishmen in their steel and killing them both where they stood. The message gave the Storm King victory over the Dornish, and in thanks he raised the messenger to lordship. He was the first Lord Dondarrion, so he took for his arms a forked purple lightning bolt, on a black field powdered with stars."

If Dunk thought the tale would impress Ser Manfred, he could not have been more wrong. "Every potboy and groom who has ever served my father hears that story soon or late. Knowing it does not make you a knight. Begone with you, ser."

It was with a leaden heart that Dunk returned to Ashford Castle, wondering what he might say so that Plummer would grant him the right of challenge. The steward was not in his turret chamber, however. A guard told him he might be found in the great hall. "Shall I wait here?" Dunk asked. "How long will he be?"

"How should I know? Do what you please."

The great hall was not so great, as halls went, but Ashford was a small castle. Dunk entered through a side door and spied the steward at once. He was standing with Lord Ashford and a dozen other men at the top of the hall. He walked toward them, beneath a wall hung with wool tapestries of fruits and flowers.

"—more concerned if they were *your* sons, I'll wager," an angry man was saying as Dunk approached. His straight hair and square-cut beard were so fair they seemed white in the dimness of the hall, but as he got closer he saw that they were in truth a pale silvery color touched with gold.

"Daeron has done this before," another replied. Plummer was standing so as to block Dunk's view of the speaker. "You should never have commanded him to enter the lists. He belongs on a tourney field no more than Aerys does, or Rhaegel."

"By which you mean he'd sooner ride a whore than a horse," the first man said. Thickly built and powerful, the prince—he was surely a prince—wore a leather brigantine covered with silver studs beneath a heavy black cloak trimmed with ermine. Pox scars marked his cheeks, only partly concealed by his silvery beard. "I do not need to be reminded of my son's failings, brother. He has only eighteen years. He can change. He *will* change, gods be damned, or I swear I'll see him dead."

"Don't be an utter fool. Daeron is what he is, but he is still your blood and mine. I have no doubt Ser Roland will turn him up, and Aegon with him."

"When the tourney is over, perhaps."

"Aerion is here. He is a better lance than Daeron in any case, if it is the tourney that concerns you." Dunk could see the speaker now. He was seated in the high seat, a sheaf of parchments in one hand, Lord Ashford hovering at his shoulder. Even seated, he looked to be a head taller than the other, to judge from the long, straight legs stretched out before him. His short-cropped hair was dark and peppered with grey, his strong jaw clean-shaven. His nose looked as though it had been broken more than once. Though he was dressed very plainly, in green doublet, brown mantle, and scuffed boots, there was a weight to him, a sense of power and certainty.

It came to Dunk that he had walked in on something that he ought never have heard. *I had best go and come back later, when they are done,* he decided. But it was already too late. The prince with the silvery beard suddenly took note of him. "Who are you, and what do you mean by bursting in on us?" he demanded harshly.

"He is the knight that our good steward was expecting," the seated man said, smiling at Dunk in a way that suggested he had been aware of him all the time. "You and I are the intruders here, brother. Come closer, ser."

Dunk edged forward, uncertain what was expected of him. He looked at Plummer but got no help there. The pinch-faced steward who had been so forceful yesterday now stood silent, studying the stones of the floor. "My lords," he said, "I asked Ser Manfred Dondarrion to vouch for me so I might enter the lists, but he refuses. He says he knows me not. Ser Arlan served him, though, I swear it. I have his sword and shield, I—"

"A shield and a sword do not make a knight," declared Lord Ashford, a big bald man with a round red face. "Plummer has spoken to me of you. Even if we accept that these arms belonged to this Ser Arlan of Pennytree, it may well be that you found him dead and stole them. Unless you have some better proof of what you say, some writing or—"

"I remember Ser Arlan of Pennytree," the man in the high seat said quietly. "He never won a tourney that I know, but he never shamed himself either. At King's Landing sixteen years ago, he overthrew Lord Stokeworth and the Bastard of Harrenhal in the melee, and many years before at Lannisport he unhorsed the Grey Lion himself. The lion was not so grey then, to be sure."

"He told me about that, many a time," said Dunk.

The tall man studied him. "Then you will remember the Grey Lion's true name, I have no doubt."

For a moment there was nothing in Dunk's head at all. *A thousand times the old man had told that tale, a thousand times, the lion, the lion, his name, his name, his name . . .* He was near despair when suddenly it came. "Ser Damon Lannister!" he shouted. "The Grey Lion! He's Lord of Casterly Rock now."

"So he is," said the tall man pleasantly, "and he enters the lists on the morrow." He rattled the sheaf of papers in his hand.

"How can you possibly remember some insignificant hedge knight who chanced to unhorse Damon Lannister sixteen years ago?" said the prince with the silver beard, frowning.

"I make it a practice to learn all I can of my foes."

"Why would you deign to joust with a hedge knight?"

"It was nine years past, at Storm's End. Lord Baratheon held a hastilude to celebrate the birth of a grandson. The lots made Ser Arlan my opponent in the first tilt. We broke four lances before I finally unhorsed him."

"*Seven,*" insisted Dunk, "and that was against the Prince of Dragonstone!" No sooner were the words out than he wanted them back. *Dunk the lunk, thick as a castle wall,* he could hear the old man chiding.

"So it was." The prince with the broken nose smiled gently. "Tales grow in the telling, I know. Do not think ill of your old master, but it was four lances only, I fear."

Dunk was grateful that the hall was dim; he knew his ears were red. "My lord." *No, that's wrong too.* "Your Grace." He fell to his knees and lowered his head. "As you say, four, I meant no ... I never ... the old man, Ser Arlan, he used to say I was thick as a castle wall and slow as an aurochs."

"And strong as an aurochs, by the look of you," said Baelor Breakspear. "No harm was done, ser. Rise."

Dunk got to his feet, wondering if he should keep his head down or if he was allowed to look a prince in the face. *I am speaking with Baelor Targaryen, Prince of Dragonstone, Hand of the King, and heir apparent to the Iron Throne of Aegon the Conqueror.* What could a hedge knight dare say to such a person? "Y-you gave him back his horse and armor and took no ransom, I remember," he stammered. "The old—Ser Arlan, he told me you were the soul of chivalry, and that one day the Seven Kingdoms would be safe in your hands."

"Not for many a year still, I pray," Prince Baelor said.

"No," said Dunk, horrified. He almost said, *I didn't mean that the king should die,* but stopped himself in time. "I am sorry, m'lord. Your Grace, I mean."

Belatedly he recalled that the stocky man with the silver beard had addressed Prince Baelor as brother. *He is blood of the dragon as well, damn me for a fool.* He could only be Prince Maekar, the youngest of King Daeron's four sons. Prince Aerys was bookish and Prince Rhaegel mad, meek, and sickly. Neither was like to cross half the realm to attend a tourney, but Maekar was said to be a redoubtable warrior in his own right though ever in the shadow of his eldest brother.

"You wish to enter the lists, is that it?" asked Prince Baelor. "That decision rests with the master of the games, but I see no reason to deny you."

The steward inclined his head. "As you say, my lord."

Dunk tried to stammer out thanks, but Prince Maekar cut him off. "Very well, ser, you are grateful. Now be off with you."

"You must forgive my noble brother, ser," said Prince Baelor. "Two of his sons have gone astray on their way here, and he fears for them."

"The spring rains have swollen many of the streams," said Dunk. "Perhaps the princes are only delayed."

"I did not come here to take counsel from a hedge knight," Prince Maekar declared to his brother.

"You may go, ser," Prince Baelor told Dunk, not unkindly.

"Yes, my lord." He bowed and turned.

But before he could get away, the prince called after him. "Ser. One thing more. You are not of Ser Arlan's blood?"

"Yes, m'lord. I mean, no. I'm not."

The prince nodded at the battered shield Dunk carried, and the winged chalice upon its face. "By law, only a trueborn son is entitled to inherit a knight's arms. You must needs find a new device, ser, a sigil of your own."

"I will," said Dunk. "Thank you again, Your Grace. I will fight bravely, you'll see." *As brave as Baelor Breakspear,* the old man would often say.

The winesellers and sausage makers were doing a brisk trade, and whores walked brazenly amongst the stalls and pavilions. Some were pretty enough, one red-haired girl in particular. He could not help staring at her breasts, the way they moved under her loose shift as she sauntered past. He thought of the silver in his pouch. *I could have her, if I liked. She'd like the clink of my coin well enough; I could take her back to my camp and have her, all night if I wanted.* He had never lain with a woman, and for all he knew he might die in his first tilt. Tourneys could be dangerous ... but whores could be dangerous too, the old man had warned him of that. *She might rob me while I slept, and what would I do then?* When the red-haired girl glanced back over her shoulder at him, Dunk shook his head and walked away.

He found Egg at the puppet show, sitting cross-legged on the ground with the hood of his cloak pulled all the way forward to hide his baldness. The boy had been afraid to enter the castle, which Dunk put down to equal parts shyness and shame. *He does not think himself worthy to mingle with lords and ladies, let alone great princes.* It had been the same with him when he was little. The world beyond Flea Bottom had seemed as frightening as it was exciting. *Egg needs time, that's all.* For the present, it seemed kinder to give the lad a few coppers and let him enjoy himself amongst the stalls than to drag him along unwilling into the castle.

This morning the puppeteers were doing the tale of Florian and Jonquil. The fat Dornishwoman was working Florian in his armor made of motley, while the tall girl held Jonquil's strings. "You are no knight," she was saying as the puppet's mouth moved up and down. "I know you. You are Florian the Fool."

"I am, my lady," the other puppet answered, kneeling. "As great a fool as ever lived, and as great a knight as well."

"A fool *and* a knight?" said Jonquil. "I have never heard of such a thing."

"Sweet lady," said Florian, "all men are fools, and all men are knights, where women are concerned."

It was a good show, sad and sweet both, with a sprightly sword fight at the end, and a nicely painted giant. When it was over, the fat woman went amongst the crowd to collect coins while the girl packed away the puppets.

Dunk collected Egg and went up to her.

"M'lord?" she said, with a sideways glance and a half smile. She was a head shorter than he was, but still taller than any other girl he had ever seen.

"That was good," Egg enthused. "I like how you make them move, Jonquil and the dragon and all. I saw a puppet show last year, but they moved all jerky. Yours are more smooth."

"Thank you," she said to the boy politely.

Dunk said, "Your figures are well carved too. The dragon, especially. A fearsome beast. You make them yourself?"

She nodded. "My uncle does the carving. I paint them."

"Could you paint something for me? I have the coin to pay." He slipped the shield off his shoulder and turned it to show her. "I need to paint something over the chalice."

The girl glanced at the shield, then at him. "What would you want painted?"

Dunk had not considered that. If not the old man's winged chalice, what? His head was empty. *Dunk the lunk, thick as a castle wall.* "I don't ... I'm not certain." His ears were turning red, he realized miserably. "You must think me an utter fool."

She smiled. "All men are fools, and all men are knights."

"What color paint do you have?" he asked, hoping that might give him an idea.

"I can mix paints to make any color you want."

The old man's brown had always seemed drab to Dunk. "The field should be the color of sunset," he said suddenly. "The old man liked sunsets. And the device . . ."

"An elm tree," said Egg. "A big elm tree, like the one by the pool, with a brown trunk and green branches."

"Yes," Dunk said. "That would serve. An elm tree . . . but with a shooting star above. Could you do that?"

The girl nodded. "Give me the shield. I'll paint it this very night and have it back to you on the morrow."

Dunk handed it over. "I am called Ser Duncan the Tall."

"I'm Tanselle," she laughed. "Tanselle Too-Tall, the boys used to call me."

"You're not too tall," Dunk blurted out. "You're just right for . . ." He realized what he had been about to say, and blushed furiously.

"For?" said Tanselle, cocking her head inquisitively.

"Puppets," he finished lamely.

The first day of the tourney dawned bright and clear. Dunk bought a sackful of foodstuffs, so they were able to break their fast on goose eggs, fried bread, and bacon, but when the food was cooked he found he had no appetite. His belly felt hard as a rock, even though he knew he would not ride today. The right of first challenge would go to knights of higher birth and greater renown, to lords and their sons and champions from other tourneys.

Egg chattered all through their breakfast, talking of this man and that man and how they might fare. *He was not japing me when he said he knew every good knight in the Seven Kingdoms,* Dunk thought ruefully. He found it humbling to listen so intently to the words of a scrawny orphan boy, but Egg's knowledge might serve him should he face one of these men in a tilt.

The meadow was a churning mass of people, all trying to elbow their way closer for a better view. Dunk was as good an elbower as any, and bigger than most. He squirmed forward to a rise six yards from the fence. When Egg complained that all he could see were arses, Dunk sat the boy on his shoulders.

Across the field, the viewing stand was filling up with highborn lords and ladies, a few rich townfolk, and a score of knights who had decided not to compete today. Of Prince Maekar he saw no sign, but he recognized Prince Baelor at Lord Ashford's side. Sunlight flashed golden off the shoulder clasp that held his cloak and the slim coronet about his temples, but otherwise he dressed far more simply than most of the other lords. *He does not look a Targaryen in truth, with that dark hair.* Dunk said as much to Egg.

"It's said he favors his mother," the boy reminded him. "She was a Dornish princess."

The five champions had raised their pavilions at the north end of the lists with the river behind them. The smallest two were orange, and the shields hung outside their doors displayed the white sun-and-chevron. Those would be Lord Ashford's sons Androw and Robert, brothers to the fair maid. Dunk had never heard other knights speak of their prowess, which meant they would likely be the first to fall.

Beside the orange pavilions stood one of deep-dyed green, much larger. The golden rose of Highgarden flapped above it, and the same device was emblazoned on the great green shield outside the door. "That's Leo Tyrell, Lord of Highgarden," said Egg.

"I knew that," said Dunk, irritated. "The old man and I served at Highgarden before you were ever born." He hardly remembered that year himself, but Ser Arlan had often spoken of Leo Longthorn, as he was sometimes called; a peerless jouster, for all the silver in his hair. "That must be Lord Leo beside the tent, the slender greybeard in green and gold."

"Yes," said Egg. "I saw him at King's Landing once. He's not one you'll want to challenge, ser."

"Boy, I do not require your counsel on who to challenge."

The fourth pavilion was sewn together from diamond-shaped pieces of cloth, alternating red and white. Dunk did not know the colors, but Egg said they belonged to a knight from the Vale of Arryn named Ser Humfrey Hardyng. "He won a great melee at Maidenpool last year, ser, and overthrew Ser Donnel of Duskendale and the Lords Arryn and Royce in the lists."

The last pavilion was Prince Valarr's. Of black silk it was, with a line of pointed scarlet pennons hanging from its roof like long red flames. The shield on its stand was glossy black, emblazoned with the three-headed dragon of House Targaryen. One of the Kingsguard knights stood beside it, his shining white armor stark against the black of the tent cloth. Seeing him there, Dunk wondered whether any of the challengers would dare to touch the dragon shield. Valarr was the king's grandson, after all, and son to Baelor Breakspear.

He need not have worried. When the horns blew to summon the challengers, all five of the maid's champions were called forth to defend her. Dunk could hear the murmur of excitement in the crowd as the challengers appeared one by one at the south end of the lists. Heralds boomed out the name of each knight in turn. They paused before the viewing stand to dip their lances in salute to Lord Ashford, Prince Baelor, and the fair maid, then circled to the north end of the field to select their opponents. The Grey Lion of Casterly Rock struck the shield of Lord Tyrell, while his golden-haired heir Ser Tybolt Lannister challenged Lord Ashford's eldest son. Lord Tully of Riverrun tapped the diamond-patterned shield of Ser Humfrey Hardyng, Ser Abelar Hightower knocked upon Valarr's, and the younger Ashford was called out by Ser Lyonel Baratheon, the knight they called the Laughing Storm.

The challengers trotted back to the south end of the lists to await their foes: Ser Abelar in silver and smoke colors, a stone watchtower on his shield, crowned with fire; the two Lannisters all crimson, bearing the golden lion of Casterly Rock; the Laughing Storm shining in cloth-of-gold, with a black stag on breast and shield and a rack of iron antlers on his helm; Lord Tully wearing a striped blue-and-red cloak clasped with a silver trout at each shoulder. They pointed their twelve-foot lances skyward, the gusty winds snapping and tugging at the pennons.

At the north end of the field, squires held brightly barded destriers for the champions to mount. They donned their helms and took up lance and shield, in splendor the equal of their foes: the Ashfords' billowing orange silks, Ser Humfrey's red-and-white diamonds, Lord Leo on his white charger with green satin trappings patterned with golden roses, and of course Valarr Targaryen. The Young Prince's horse was black as night, to match the color of his armor, lance, shield, and trappings. Atop his helm was a gleaming three-headed dragon, wings spread, enameled in a rich red; its twin was painted upon the glossy black surface of his shield. Each of the defenders had a wisp of orange silk knotted about an arm, favors bestowed by the fair maid.

As the champions trotted into position, Ashford Meadow grew almost still. Then a horn sounded, and stillness turned to tumult in half a heartbeat. Ten pairs of gilded spurs drove into the flanks of ten great warhorses, a thousand voices began to scream and shout, forty ironshod hooves pounded and tore the grass, ten lances dipped and steadied, the field seemed almost to shake, and champions and challengers came together in a rending crash of wood and steel. In an instant, the riders were beyond each other, wheeling about for another pass. Lord Tully reeled in his saddle but managed to keep his seat. When the commons realized that all ten of the lances had broken, a great roar of approval went up. It was a splendid omen for the success of the tourney, and a testament to the skill of the competitors.

Squires handed fresh lances to the jousters to replace the broken ones they cast aside, and once more the spurs dug deep. Dunk could feel the earth trembling beneath the soles of his feet. Atop his shoulders, Egg shouted happily and waved his pipestem arms. The Young Prince passed nearest to them. Dunk saw the point of his black lance kiss the watchtower on his foe's shield and slide off to slam into his chest, even as Ser Abelar's own lance burst into splinters against Valarr's breastplate. The grey stallion in the silver-and-smoke trappings reared with the force of the impact, and Ser Abelar Hightower was lifted from his stirrups and dashed violently to the ground.

Lord Tully was down as well, unhorsed by Ser Humfrey Hardyng, but he sprang up at once and drew his longsword, and Ser Humfrey cast aside his lance—unbroken—and dismounted to continue their fight afoot. Ser Abelar was not so spritely. His squire ran out, loosened his helm, and called for help, and two serving men lifted the dazed knight by the arms to help him back to his pavilion. Elsewhere on the field, the six knights who had remained ahorse were riding their third course. More lances shattered, and this time Lord Leo Tyrell aimed his point so expertly he ripped the Grey Lion's helm cleanly off his head. Barefaced, the Lord of Casterly Rock raised his hand in salute and dismounted, yielding the match. By then Ser Humfrey had beaten Lord Tully into surrender, showing himself as skilled with a sword as he was with a lance.

Tybolt Lannister and Andrew Ashford rode against each other thrice more before Ser Andrew finally lost shield, seat, and match all

at once. The younger Ashford lasted even longer, breaking no less than nine lances against Ser Lyonel Baratheon, the Laughing Storm. Champion and challenger both lost their saddles on their tenth course, only to rise together to fight on, sword against mace. Finally a battered Ser Robert Ashford admitted defeat, but on the viewing stand his father looked anything but dejected. Both Lord Ashford's sons had been ushered from the ranks of the champions, it was true, but they had acquitted themselves nobly against two of the finest knights in the Seven Kingdoms.

I must do even better, though, Dunk thought as he watched victor and vanquished embrace and walk together from the field. *It is not enough for me to fight well and lose. I must win at least the first challenge, or I lose all.*

Ser Tybolt Lannister and the Laughing Storm would now take their places amongst the champions, replacing the men they had defeated. Already the orange pavilions were coming down. A few feet away, the Young Prince sat at his ease in a raised camp chair before his great black tent. His helm was off. He had dark hair like his father, but a bright streak ran through it. A serving man brought him a silver goblet and he took a sip. *Water, if he is wise,* Dunk thought, *wine if not.* He found himself wondering if Valarr had indeed inherited a measure of his father's prowess, or whether it had only been that he had drawn the weakest opponent.

A fanfare of trumpets announced that three new challengers had entered the lists. The heralds shouted their names. *"Ser Pearse of House Caron, Lord of the Marches."* He had a silver harp emblazoned on his shield, though his surcoat was patterned with nightingales. *"Ser Joseth of House Mallister, from Seagard."* Ser Joseth sported a winged helm; on his shield, a silver eagle flew across an indigo sky. *"Ser Gawen of House Swann, Lord of Stonehelm on the Cape of Wrath."* A pair of swans, one black and one white, fought furiously on his arms. Lord Gawen's armor, cloak, and horse bardings were a riot of black and white as well, down to the stripes on his scabbard and lance.

Lord Caron, harper and singer and knight of renown, touched the point of his lance to Lord Tyrell's rose. Ser Joseth thumped on Ser Humfrey Hardyng's diamonds. And the black-and-white knight, Lord Gawen Swann, challenged the black prince with the white guardian. Dunk rubbed his chin. Lord Gawen was even older than the old man, and the old man was dead. "Egg, who is the least dangerous of these challengers?" he asked the boy on his shoulders, who seemed to know so much of these knights.

"Lord Gawen," the boy said at once. "Valarr's foe."

"*Prince* Valarr," he corrected. "A squire must keep a courteous tongue, boy."

The three challengers took their places as the three champions mounted up. Men were making wagers all around them and calling out encouragement to their choices, but Dunk had eyes only for the prince. On the first pass he struck Lord Gawen's shield a glancing blow, the blunted point of the lance sliding aside just as it had with Ser Abelar Hightower, only this time it was deflected the other way, into empty air. Lord Gawen's own lance broke clean against the prince's chest, and Valarr seemed about to fall for an instant before he recovered his seat.

The second time through the lists, Valarr swung his lance left, aiming for his foe's breast, but struck his shoulder instead. Even so, the blow was enough to make the older knight lose his lance. One arm flailed for balance and Lord Gawen fell. The Young Prince swung from the saddle and drew his sword, but the fallen man waved him off and raised his visor. "I yield, Your Grace," he called. "Well fought." The lords in the viewing stand echoed him, shouting, "*Well fought! Well fought!*" as Valarr knelt to help the grey-haired lord to his feet.

"It was not either," Egg complained.

"Be quiet, or you can go back to camp."

Farther away, Ser Joseth Mallister was being carried off the field unconscious, while the harp lord and the rose lord were going at each other lustily with blunted longaxes, to the delight of the roaring crowd. Dunk was so intent on Valarr Targaryen that he scarcely saw them. *He is a fair knight, but no more than that,* he found himself thinking. *I would have a chance against him. If the gods were good, I might even unhorse him, and once afoot my weight and strength would tell.*

"Get him!" Egg shouted merrily, shifting his seat on Dunk's shoulders in his excitement. "Get him! Hit him! Yes! He's right there, he's *right there!*" It seemed to be Lord Caron he was cheering on. The harper was playing a different sort of music now, driving Lord Leo back and back as steel sang on steel. The crowd seemed almost equally divided between them, so cheers and curses mingled freely in the morning air. Chips of wood and paint were flying from Lord Leo's shield as Lord Pearse's axe knocked the petals off his golden rose, one by one, until the shield finally shattered and split. But as it did, the axehead hung up for an instant in the wood . . . and Lord Leo's own axe crashed down on the haft of his foe's weapon, breaking it off not a foot from his hand. He cast aside his broken shield, and suddenly he was the one on the attack. Within moments, the harper knight was on one knee, singing his surrender.

For the rest of the morning and well into the afternoon, it was more of the same, as challengers took the field in twos and threes, and sometimes five together. Trumpets blew, the heralds called out names, warhorses charged, the crowd cheered, lances snapped like twigs, and swords rang against helms and mail. It was, smallfolk and high lord alike agreed, a splendid day of jousting. Ser Humfrey Hardyng and Ser Humfrey Beesbury, a bold young knight in yellow and black stripes with three beehives on his shield, splintered no less than a dozen lances apiece in an epic struggle the smallfolk soon began calling The Battle of Humfrey. Ser Tybolt Lannister was unhorsed by Ser Jon Penrose and broke his sword in his fall, but fought back with shield alone to win the bout and remain a champion. One-eyed Ser Robyn Rhysling, a grizzled old knight with a salt-and-pepper beard, lost his helm to Lord Leo's lance in their first course, yet refused to yield. Three times more they rode at each other, the wind whipping Ser Robyn's hair while the shards of broken lances flew round his

bare face like wooden knives, which Dunk thought all the more won-
drous when Egg told him that Ser Robyn had lost his eye to a splinter
from a broken lance not five years earlier. Leo Tyrell was too chivalrous to aim another lance at Ser Robyn's unprotected head, but even
so, Rhysling's stubborn courage (or was it folly?) left Dunk astounded.
Finally the Lord of Highgarden struck Ser Robyn's breastplate a solid
thump right over the heart and sent him cartwheeling to the earth.

Ser Lyonel Baratheon also fought several notable matches. Against
lesser foes, he would often break into booming laughter the moment
they touched his shield and laugh all the time he was mounting and
charging and knocking them from their stirrups. If his challengers
wore any sort of crest on their helm, Ser Lyonel would strike it off
and fling it into the crowd. The crests were ornate things, made of
carved wood or shaped leather, and sometimes gilded and enameled
or even wrought in pure silver, so the men he beat did not appreciate
this habit, though it made him a great favorite of the commons.

Before long, only crestless men were choosing him. As loud and often as Ser Lyonel laughed down a challenger, though, Dunk thought the day's honors should go to Ser Humfrey Hardyng, who humbled fourteen knights, each one of them formidable.

Meanwhile the Young Prince sat outside his black pavilion, drinking from his silver goblet and rising from time to time to mount his horse and vanquish yet another undistinguished foe. He had won nine victories, but it seemed to Dunk that every one was hollow. *He is beating old men and upjumped squires, and a few lords of high birth and low skill. The truly dangerous men are riding past his shield as if they do not see it.*

Late in the day, a brazen fanfare announced the entry of a new challenger to the lists. He rode in on a great red charger whose black bardings were slashed to reveal glimpses of yellow, crimson, and orange beneath. As he approached the viewing stand to make his salute, Dunk saw the face beneath the raised visor, and recognized the prince he'd met in Lord Ashford's stables.

Egg's legs tightened around his neck. "Stop that," Dunk snapped, yanking them apart. "Do you mean to choke me?"

"Prince Aerion Brightflame," a herald called. "Of the Red Keep of King's Landing, son of Maekar, Prince of Summerhall of House Targaryen, grandson to Daeron the Good, the Second of His Name, King of the Andals, the Rhoynar, and the First Men, and Lord of the Seven Kingdoms."

Aerion bore a three-headed dragon on his shield, but it was rendered in colors much more vivid than Valarr's; one head was orange, one yellow, one red, and the flames they breathed had the sheen of gold leaf. His surcoat was a swirl of smoke and fire woven together, and his blackened helm was surmounted by a crest of red enamel flames.

After a pause to dip his lance to Prince Baelor, a pause so brief that it was almost perfunctory, he galloped to the north end of the field, past Lord Leo's pavilion and the Laughing Storm's, slowing only when he approached Prince Valarr's tent. The Young Prince rose and stood stiffly beside his shield, and for a moment Dunk was certain that Aerion meant to strike it ... but then he laughed and trotted past, and banged his point hard against Ser Humfrey Hardyng's diamonds. "Come out, come out, little knight," he sang in a loud clear voice, "it's time you faced the dragon."

Ser Humfrey inclined his head stiffly to his foe as his destrier was brought out, and then ignored him while he mounted, fastened his helm, and took up lance and shield. The spectators grew quiet as the two knights took their places. Dunk heard the *clang* of Prince Aerion's dropping his visor. The horn blew.

Ser Humfrey broke slowly, building speed, but his foe raked the red charger with both spurs, coming hard. Egg's legs tightened again. *"Kill him!"* he shouted suddenly. *"Kill him, he's right there, kill him, kill him, kill him!"* Dunk was not certain which of the knights he was shouting to.

Prince Aerion's lance, gold-tipped and painted in stripes of red, orange, and yellow, swung down across the barrier. *Low, too low,* thought Dunk the moment he saw it. *He'll miss the rider and strike Ser Humfrey's horse, he needs to bring it up.* Then, with dawning horror, he began to suspect that Aerion intended no such thing. *He cannot mean to . . .*

At the last possible instant, Ser Humfrey's stallion reared away from the oncoming point, eyes rolling in terror, but too late. Aerion's lance took the animal just above the armor that protected his breastbone, and exploded out of the back of his neck in a gout of bright blood. Screaming, the horse crashed sideways, knocking the wooden barrier to pieces as he fell. Ser Humfrey tried to leap free, but a foot caught in a stirrup and they heard his shriek as his leg was crushed between the splintered fence and falling horse.

All of Ashford Meadow was shouting. Men ran onto the field to extricate Ser Humfrey, but the stallion, dying in agony, kicked at them as they approached. Aerion, having raced blithely around the carnage to the end of the lists, wheeled his horse and came galloping back. He was shouting too, though Dunk could not make out the words over the almost human screams of the dying horse. Vaulting from the saddle, Aerion drew his sword and advanced on his fallen foe. His own squires and one of Ser Humfrey's had to pull him back. Egg squirmed on Dunk's shoulders. "Let me down," the boy said. "The poor horse, *let me down.*"

Dunk felt sick himself. *What would I do if such a fate befell Thunder?* A man-at-arms with a poleaxe dispatched Ser Humfrey's stallion, ending the hideous screams. Dunk turned and forced his way through the press. When he came to open ground, he lifted Egg off his shoulders. The boy's hood had fallen back and his eyes were red. "A terrible sight, aye," he told the lad, "but a squire must needs be strong. You'll see worse mishaps at other tourneys, I fear."

"It was no mishap," Egg said, mouth trembling. "Aerion meant to do it. You saw."

Dunk frowned. It had looked that way to him as well, but it was hard to accept that any knight could be so unchivalrous, least of all one who was blood of the dragon. "I saw a knight green as summer grass lose control of his lance," he said stubbornly, "and I'll hear no more of it. The jousting is done for the day, I think. Come, lad."

He was right about the end of the day's contests. By the time the chaos had been set to rights, the sun was low in the west, and Lord Ashford had called a halt.

As the shadows of evening crept across the meadow, a hundred torches were lit along the merchants' row. Dunk bought a horn of ale for himself and half a horn for the boy, to cheer him. They wandered for a time, listening to a spritely air on pipes and drums and watching a puppet show about Nymeria, the warrior queen with the ten thousand ships. The puppeteers had only two ships, but managed a rousing sea battle all the same. Dunk wanted to ask the girl Tanselle if she had finished painting his shield, but he could see that she was busy. *I'll wait until she is done for the night,* he resolved. *Perhaps she'll have a thirst then.*

"Ser Duncan," a voice called behind him. And then again, "Ser Duncan." Suddenly Dunk remembered that was him. "I saw you among the smallfolk today, with this boy on your shoulders," said Raymun Fossoway as he came up, smiling. "Indeed, the two of you were hard to miss."

"The boy is my squire. Egg, this is Raymun Fossoway." Dunk had to pull the boy forward, and even then Egg lowered his head and stared at Raymun's boots as he mumbled a greeting.

"Well met, lad," Raymun said easily. "Ser Duncan, why not watch from the viewing gallery? All knights are welcome there."

Dunk was at ease among smallfolk and servants; the idea of claiming a place amongst the lords, ladies, and landed knights made him uncomfortable. "I would not have wanted any closer view of that last tilt."

Raymun grimaced. "Nor I. Lord Ashford declared Ser Humfrey the victor and awarded him Prince Aerion's courser, but even so, he will not be able to continue. His leg was broken in two places. Prince Baelor sent his own maester to tend him."

"Will there be another champion in Ser Humfrey's place?"

"Lord Ashford had a mind to grant the place to Lord Caron, or perhaps the other Ser Humfrey, the one who gave Hardyng such a splendid match, but Prince Baelor told him that it would not be seemly to remove Ser Humfrey's shield and pavilion under the circumstances. I believe they will continue with four champions in place of five."

Four champions, Dunk thought. *Leo Tyrell, Lyonel Baratheon, Tybolt Lannister, and Prince Valarr.* He had seen enough this first day to know how little chance he would stand against the first three. Which left only . . .

A hedge knight cannot challenge a prince. Valarr is second in line to the Iron Throne. He is Baelor Breakspear's son, and his blood is the blood of Aegon the Conqueror and the Young Dragon and Prince Aemon the Dragon-knight, and I am some boy the old man found behind a pot shop in Flea Bottom.

His head hurt just thinking about it. "Who does your cousin mean to challenge?" he asked Raymun.

"Ser Tybolt, all things being equal. They are well matched. My cousin keeps a sharp watch on every tilt, though. Should any man be wounded on the morrow, or show signs of exhaustion or weakness, Steffon will be quick to knock on his shield, you may count on it. No one has ever accused him of an excess of chivalry." He laughed, as if to take the sting from his words. "Ser Duncan, will you join me for a cup of wine?"

"I have a matter I must attend to," said Dunk, uncomfortable with the notion of accepting hospitality he could not return.

"I could wait here and bring your shield when the puppet show is over, ser," said Egg. "They're going to do Symeon Star-Eyes later, and make the dragon fight again as well."

"There, you see, your matter is attended to, and the wine awaits," said Raymun. "It's an Arbor vintage, too. How can you refuse me?"

Bereft of excuses, Dunk had no choice but to follow, leaving Egg at the puppet show. The apple of House Fossoway flew above the gold-colored pavilion where Raymun attended his cousin. Behind it, two servants were basting a goat with honey and herbs over a small cook-fire. "There's food as well, if you're hungry," Raymun said negligently as he held the flap for Dunk. A brazier of coals lit the interior and made the air pleasantly warm. Raymun filled two cups with wine. "They say Aerion is in a rage at Lord Ashford for awarding his charger to Ser Humfrey," he commented as he poured, "but I'll wager it was his uncle who counseled it." He handed Dunk a wine cup.

"Prince Baelor is an honorable man."

"As the Bright Prince is not?" Raymun laughed. "Don't look so anxious, Ser Duncan, there's none here but us. It is no secret that Aerion is a bad piece of work. Thank the gods that he is well down in the order of succession."

"You truly believe he meant to kill the horse?"

"Is there any doubt of it? If Prince Maekar had been here, it would have gone differently, I promise you. Aerion is all smiles and chivalry so long as his father is watching, if the tales be true, but when he's not ..."

"I saw that Prince Maekar's chair was empty."

"He's left Ashford to search for his sons, along with Roland Crakehall of the Kingsguard. There's a wild tale of robber knights going about, but I'll wager the prince is just off drunk again."

The wine was fine and fruity, as good a cup as he had ever tasted. He rolled it in his mouth, swallowed, and said, "Which prince is this now?"

"Maekar's heir. Daeron, he's named, after the king. They call him Daeron the Drunken, though not in his father's hearing. The youngest boy was with him as well. They left Summerhall

together but never reached Ashford." Raymun drained his cup and set it aside. "Poor Maekar."

"Poor?" said Dunk, startled. "The king's son?"

"The king's *fourth* son," said Raymun, "not quite as bold as Prince Baelor, nor as clever as Prince Aerys, nor as gentle as Prince Rhaegel. And now he must suffer seeing his own sons overshadowed by his brother's. Daeron is a sot, Aerion is vain and cruel, the third son was so unpromising they gave him to the Citadel to make a maester of him, and the youngest—"

"Ser! Ser Duncan!" Egg burst in panting. His hood had fallen back, and the light from the brazier shone in his big dark eyes. "You have to run, he's hurting her!"

Dunk lurched to his feet, confused.

"Hurting? Who?"

"*Aerion!*" the boy shouted. "He's *hurting* her. The puppet girl. *Hurry.*" Whirling, he darted back out into the night.

Dunk made to follow, but Raymun caught his arm. "Ser Duncan. Aerion, he said. A prince of the blood. Be careful."

It was good counsel, he knew. The old man would have said the same. But he could not listen. He wrenched free of Raymun's hand and shouldered his way out of the pavilion. He could hear shouting off in the direction of the merchants' row. Egg was almost out of sight. Dunk ran after him. His legs were long and the boy's short; he quickly closed the distance.

A wall of watchers had gathered around the puppeteers. Dunk shouldered through them, ignoring their curses. A man-at-arms in the royal livery stepped up to block him. Dunk put a big hand on his chest and shoved, sending the man flailing backwards to sprawl on his arse in the dirt.

The puppeteers' stall had been knocked on its side. The fat Dornishwoman was on the ground weeping. One man-at-arms was dangling the puppets of Florian and Jonquil from his hands as another set them afire with a torch. Three more men were opening chests, spilling more puppets on the ground and stamping on them. The dragon puppet was scattered all about them, a broken wing here, its head there, its tail in three pieces. And in the midst of it all stood Prince Aerion, resplendent in a red velvet doublet with long, dagged sleeves, twisting Tanselle's arm in both

hands. She was on her knees,
pleading with him.
Aerion ignored her.

He forced open her hand and seized one of her fingers. Dunk stood there stupidly, not quite believing what he saw. Then he heard a *crack*, and Tanselle screamed.

One of Aerion's men tried to grab him, and went flying. Three long strides, then Dunk grabbed the prince's shoulder and wrenched him around hard. His sword and dagger were forgotten, along with everything the old man had ever taught him. His fist knocked Aerion off his feet, and the toe of his boot slammed into the prince's belly. When Aerion went for his knife,

Dunk stepped on his wrist and kicked him again, right in the mouth. He might have kicked him to death right then and there, but the princeling's men swarmed over him. He had a man on each arm and another pounding him across the back. No sooner had he wrestled free of one than two more were on him.

Finally they shoved him down and pinned his arms and legs. Aerion was on his feet again. The prince's mouth was bloody. He pushed inside it with a finger. "You've loosened one of my teeth," he complained, "so we'll start by breaking all of yours." He pushed his hair from his eyes. "You look familiar."

"You took me for a stableboy."

Aerion smiled redly. "I recall. You refused to take my horse. Why did you throw your life away? For this whore?" Tanselle was curled up on the ground, cradling her maimed hand. He gave her a shove with the toe of his boot. "She's scarcely worth it. A traitor. The dragon ought never lose."

He is mad, thought Dunk, *but he is still a prince's son, and he means to kill me.* He might have prayed then, if he had known a prayer all the way through, but there was no time. There was hardly even time to be afraid.

"Nothing more to say?" said Aerion. "You bore me, ser." He poked at his bloody mouth again. "Get a hammer and break all his teeth out, Wate," he commanded, "and then let's cut him open and show him the color of his entrails."

"*No!*" a boy's voice said. "Don't hurt him!"

Gods be good, the boy, the brave foolish boy, Dunk thought. He fought against the arms restraining him, but it was no good. "Hold your tongue, you stupid boy. Run away. They'll hurt you!"

"No, they won't." Egg moved closer. "If they do, they'll answer to my father. And my uncle as well. Let go of him, I said. Wate, Yorkel, you know me. Do as I say."

The hands holding his left arm were gone, then the others. Dunk did not understand what was happening. The men-at-arms were backing away. One even knelt. Then the crowd parted for Raymun Fossoway. He had donned mail and helm, and his hand was on his sword. His cousin, Ser Steffon, just behind him, had already bared his blade, and with them were a half dozen men-at-arms with the red apple badge sewn on their breasts.

Prince Aerion paid them no mind. "Impudent little wretch," he said to Egg, spitting a mouthful of blood at the boy's feet. "What happened to your hair?"

"I cut it off, brother," said Egg. "I didn't want to look like you."

*　*　*

The second day of the tourney was overcast, with a gusty wind blowing from the west. *The crowds should be less on a day like this,* Dunk thought. It would have been easier for them to find a spot near the fence to see the jousting up close. *Egg might have sat on the rail, while I stood behind him.*

Instead Egg would have a seat in the viewing box, dressed in silks and furs, while Dunk's view would be limited to the four walls of the tower cell where Lord Ashford's men had confined him. The chamber had a window, but it faced in the wrong direction. Even so, Dunk crammed himself into the window seat as the sun came up, and stared gloomily off across town and field and forest. They had taken his hempen sword belt, and his sword and dagger with it, and they had taken his silver as well. He hoped Egg or Raymun would remember Chestnut and Thunder.

"Egg," he muttered low under his breath. His squire, a poor lad plucked from the streets of King's Landing. Had ever a knight been made such a fool? *Dunk the lunk, thick as a castle wall and slow as an aurochs.*

He had not been permitted to speak to Egg since Lord Ashford's soldiers had scooped them all up at the puppet show. Nor Raymun, nor Tanselle, nor anyone, not even Lord Ashford himself. He wondered if he would ever see any of them again. For all he knew, they meant to keep him in this small room until he died. *What did I think would happen?* he asked himself bitterly. *I knocked down a prince's son and kicked him in the face.*

Beneath these grey skies, the flowing finery of the highborn lords and great champions would not seem quite so splendid as it had the day before. The sun, walled behind the clouds, would not brush their steel helms with brilliance nor make their gold and silver chasings glitter and flash, but even so, Dunk wished he was in the crowd to watch the jousting. It would be a good day for hedge knights, for men in plain mail on unbarded horses.

He could *hear* them, at least. The horns of the heralds carried well, and from time to time a roar from the crowd told him that someone had fallen, or risen, or done something especially bold. He heard faint hoofbeats too, and once in a great while the clash of swords or the *snap* of a lance. Dunk winced whenever he heard that last; it reminded him of the noise Tanselle's finger had made when Aerion broke it. There were other sounds too, closer at hand: footfalls in the hall outside his door, the stamp of hooves in the yard below, shouts and voices from the castle walls. Sometimes they drowned out the tourney. Dunk supposed that was just as well.

"A hedge knight is the truest kind of knight, Dunk," the old man had told him, a long long time ago. "Other knights serve the lords who keep them, or from whom they hold their lands, but we serve where we will, for men whose causes we believe in. Every knight swears to protect the weak and innocent, but we keep the vow best, I think." Queer how strong that memory seemed. Dunk had quite forgotten those words. And perhaps the old man had as well, toward the end.

The morning turned to afternoon. The distant sounds of the tourney began to dwindle and die. Dusk began to seep into the cell, but Dunk still sat in the window seat, looking out on the gathering dark and trying to ignore his empty belly.

And then he heard footsteps and a jangling of iron keys. He un-coiled and rose to his feet as the door opened. Two guards pushed in, one bearing an oil lamp. A serving man followed with a tray of food. Behind came Egg. "Leave the lamp and the food and go," the boy told them.

They did as he commanded, though Dunk noticed that they left the heavy wooden door ajar. The smell of the food made him realize how ravenous he was. There was hot bread and honey, a bowl of pease porridge, a skewer of roast onions and well-charred meat. He sat by the tray, pulled apart the bread with his hands, and stuffed some into his mouth. "There's no knife," he observed. "Did they think I'd stab you, boy?"

"They didn't tell me what they thought." Egg wore a close-fitting black wool doublet with a tucked waist and long sleeves lined with red satin. Across his chest was sewn the three-headed dragon of House Targaryen. "My uncle says I must humbly beg your forgiveness for deceiving you."

"Your uncle," said Dunk. "That would be Prince Baelor."

The boy looked miserable. "I never meant to lie."

"But you did. About everything. Starting with your name. I never heard of a Prince Egg."

"It's short for Aegon. My brother Aemon named me Egg, he's off at the Citadel now, learning to be a maester. And Daeron sometimes calls me Egg as well, and so do my sisters."

Dunk lifted the skewer and bit into a chunk of meat. Goat, flavored with some lordly spice he'd never tasted before. Grease ran down his chin. "Aegon," he repeated. "Of course it would be Aegon. Like Aegon the Dragon. How many Aegons have been king?"

"Four," the boy said. "Four Aegons."

Dunk chewed, swallowed, and tore off some more bread. "Why did you do it? Was it some jape, to make a fool of the stupid hedge knight?"

"No." The boy's eyes filled with tears, but he stood there manfully. "I was supposed to squire for Daeron. He's my oldest brother. I learned everything I had to learn to be a good squire, but Daeron isn't a very good knight. He didn't want to ride in the tourney, so after we left Summerhall he stole away from our escort, only instead of doubling back he went straight on toward Ashford, thinking they'd never look for us that way. It was him shaved my head. He knew my father would send men hunting us. Daeron has common hair, sort of a pale brown, nothing special, but mine is like Aerion's and my father's."

"The blood of the dragon," Dunk said. "Silver-gold hair and purple eyes, everyone knows that." *Thick as a castle wall, Dunk.*

"Yes. So Daeron shaved it off. He meant for us to hide until the tourney was over. Only then you took me for a stableboy, and ..." He lowered his eyes. "I didn't care if Daeron fought or not, but I wanted to be *somebody's* squire. I'm sorry, ser. I truly am."

Dunk looked at him thoughtfully. He knew what it was like to want something so badly that you would tell a monstrous lie just to get near it. "I thought you were like me," he said. "Might be you are. Only not the way I thought."

"We're both from King's Landing still," the boy said hopefully.

Dunk had to laugh. "Yes, you from the top of Aegon's Hill and me from the bottom."

"That's not so far, ser."

Dunk took a bite from an onion. "Do I need to call you *m'lord* or *Your Grace* or something?"

"At court," the boy admitted, "but other times you can keep on calling me Egg if you like. Ser."

"What will they do with me, Egg?"

"My uncle wants to see you. After you're done eating, ser."

Dunk shoved the platter aside, and stood. "I'm done now, then. I've already kicked one prince in the mouth, I don't mean to keep another waiting."

Lord Ashford had turned his own chambers over to Prince Baelor for the duration of his stay, so it was to the lord's solar that Egg—no, *Aegon,* he would have to get used to that—conducted him. Baelor sat reading by the light of a beeswax candle. Dunk knelt before him. "Rise," the prince said. "Would you care for wine?"

"As it please you, Your Grace."

"Pour Ser Duncan a cup of the sweet Dornish red, Aegon," the prince commanded. "Try not to spill it on him, you've done him sufficient ill already."

"The boy won't spill, Your Grace," said Dunk. "He's a good boy. A good squire. And he meant no harm to me, I know."

"One need not intend harm to do it. Aegon should have come to me when he saw what his brother was doing to these puppeteers. Instead he ran to you. That was no kindness. What you did, ser ... well, I might have done the same in your place, but I am a prince of the realm, not a hedge knight. It is never wise to strike a king's grandson in anger, no matter the cause."

Dunk nodded grimly. Egg offered him a silver goblet, brimming with wine. He accepted it and took a long swallow.

"I *hate* Aerion," Egg said with vehemence. "And I had to run for Ser Duncan, uncle, the castle was too far."

"Aerion is your brother," the prince said firmly, "and the septons say we must love our brothers. Aegon, leave us now, I would speak with Ser Duncan privately."

The boy put down the flagon of wine and bowed stiffly. "As you will, Your Grace." He went to the door of the solar and closed it softly behind him.

Baelor Breakspear studied Dunk's eyes for a long moment. "Ser Duncan, let me ask you this—how good a knight are you, truly? How skilled at arms?"

Dunk did not know what to say. "Ser Arlan taught me sword and shield, and how to tilt at rings and quintains."

Prince Baelor seemed troubled by that answer. "My brother Maekar returned to the castle a few hours ago. He found his heir drunk in an inn a day's ride to the south. Maekar would never admit as much, but I believe it was his secret hope that his sons might outshine mine in this tourney. Instead they have both shamed him, but what is he to do? They are blood of his blood. Maekar is angry, and must needs have a target for his wrath. He has chosen you."

"Me?" Dunk said miserably.

"Aerion has already filled his father's ear. And Daeron has not helped you either. To excuse his own cowardice, he told my brother that a huge robber knight, chance met on the road, made off with Aegon. I fear you have been cast as this robber knight, ser. In Daeron's tale, he has spent all these days pursuing you hither and yon, to win back his brother."

"But Egg will tell him the truth. Aegon, I mean."

"Egg *will* tell him, I have no doubt," said Prince Baelor, "but the boy has been known to lie too, as you have good reason to recall. Which son will my brother believe? As for the matter of these puppeteers, by the time Aerion is done twisting the tale it will be high treason. The dragon is the sigil of the royal House. To portray one being slain, sawdust blood spilling from its neck ... well, it was doubtless innocent, but it was far from wise. Aerion calls it a veiled attack on House Targaryen, an incitement to revolt. Maekar will likely agree. My brother has a prickly nature, and he has placed all his best hopes on Aerion since Daeron has been such a grave disappointment to him." The prince took a sip of wine, then set the goblet aside. "Whatever my brother believes or fails to believe, one truth is beyond dispute. You laid hands upon the blood of the dragon. For that offense, you must be tried, and judged, and punished."

"Punished?" Dunk did not like the sound of that.

"Aerion would like your head, with or without teeth. He will not have it, I promise you, but I cannot deny him a trial. As my royal father is hundreds of leagues away, my brother and I must sit in judgment of you, along with Lord Ashford, whose domains these are, and Lord Tyrell of Highgarden, his liege lord. The last time a man was found guilty of striking one of royal blood, it was decreed that he should lose the offending hand."

"My *hand*?" said Dunk, aghast.

"And your foot. You kicked him too, did you not?"

Dunk could not speak.

"To be sure, I will urge my fellow judges to be merciful. I am the King's Hand and the heir to the throne, my word carries some weight. But so does my brother's. The risk is there."

"I," said Dunk, "I ... Your Grace, I ..." *They meant no treason, it was only a wooden dragon, it was never meant to be a royal prince,* he wanted to say, but his words had deserted him once and all. He had never been any good with words.

"You have another choice, though," Prince Baelor said quietly. "Whether it is a better choice or a worse one, I cannot say, but I remind you that any knight accused of a crime has the right to demand trial by combat. So I ask you once again, Ser Duncan the Tall—how good a knight are you? Truly?"

"A trial of seven," said Prince Aerion, smiling. "That is *my* right, I do believe."

Prince Baelor drummed his fingers on the table, frowning. To his left, Lord Ashford nodded slowly. "Why?" Prince Maekar demanded, leaning forward toward his son. "Are you afraid to face this hedge knight alone and let the gods decide the truth of your accusations?"

"Afraid?" said Aerion. "Of such as this? Don't be absurd, Father. My thought is for my beloved brother. Daeron has been wronged by this Ser Duncan as well, and has first claim to his blood. A trial of seven allows both of us to face him."

"Do me no favors, brother," muttered Daeron Targaryen. The eldest son of Prince Maekar looked even worse than he had when Dunk had encountered him in the inn. He seemed to be sober this time, his red-and-black doublet unstained by wine, but his eyes were bloodshot, and a fine sheen of sweat covered his brow. "I am content to cheer you on as you slay the rogue."

"You are too kind, sweet brother," said Prince Aerion, all smiles, "but it would be selfish of me to deny you the right to prove the truth of your words at the hazard of your body. I must insist upon a trial of seven."

Dunk was lost. "Your Grace, my lords," he said to the dais. "I do not understand. What is this *trial of seven*?"

Prince Baelor shifted uncomfortably in his seat. "It is another form of trial by combat. Ancient, seldom invoked. It came across the narrow sea with the Andals and their seven gods. In any trial by combat, the accuser and accused are asking the gods to decide the issue between them. The Andals believed that if seven champions fought on each side, the gods, being thus honored, would be more like to take a hand and see that a just result was achieved."

"Or mayhaps they simply had a taste for swordplay," said Lord Leo Tyrell, a cynical smile touching his lips. "Regardless, Ser Aerion is within his rights. A trial of seven it must be."

"I must fight *seven men*, then?" Dunk asked hopelessly.

"Not alone, ser," Prince Maekar said impatiently. "Don't play the fool, it will not serve. It must be seven against seven. You must needs find six other knights to fight beside you."

Six knights, Dunk thought. They might as well have told him to find six thousand. He had no brothers, no cousins, no old comrades who had stood beside him in battle. Why would six strangers risk their own lives to defend a hedge knight against two royal princelings? "Your Graces, my lords," he said, "what if no one will take my part?"

Maekar Targaryen looked down on him coldly. "If a cause is just, good men will fight for it. If you can find no champions, ser, it will be because you are guilty. Could anything be more plain?"

Dunk had never felt so alone as he did when he walked out the gates of Ashford Castle and heard the portcullis rattle down behind him. A soft rain was falling, light as dew on his skin, and yet he shivered at the touch of it. Across the river, colored rings haloed the scant few pavilions where fires still burned. The night was half-gone, he guessed. Dawn would be on him in a few hours. *And with dawn comes death.*

They had given him back his sword and silver, yet as he waded across the ford, his thoughts were bleak. He wondered if they expected him to saddle a horse and flee. He could, if he wished. That would be the end of his knighthood, to be sure; he would be no more than an outlaw henceforth, until the day some lord took him and struck off his head. *Better to die a knight than live like that,* he told himself stubbornly. Wet to the knee, he trudged past the empty lists.

Most of the pavilions were dark, their owners long asleep, but here and there a few candles still burned. Dunk heard soft moans and cries of pleasure coming from within one tent. It made him wonder whether he would die without ever having known a maid.

Then he heard the snort of a horse, a snort he somehow knew for Thunder's. He turned his steps and ran, and there he was, tied up with Chestnut outside a round pavilion lit from within by a vague golden glow. On its center pole the banner hung sodden, but Dunk could still make out the dark curve of the Fossoway apple. It looked like hope.

"A trial by combat," Raymun said heavily. "Gods be good, Dun-

can, that means lances of war, morningstars, battle-axes ... the swords won't be blunted, do you understand that?"

"Raymun the Reluctant," mocked his cousin Ser Steffon. An apple made of gold and garnets fastened his cloak of yellow wool.

"You need not fear, cousin, this is a knightly combat. As you are no knight, your skin is not at risk. Ser Duncan, you have one Fossoway at least. The ripe one. I saw what Aerion did to those puppeteers. I am for you."

"And I," snapped Raymun angrily. "I only meant—"

His cousin cut him off. "Who else fights with us, Ser Duncan?"

Dunk spread his hands hopelessly. "I know no one else. Well, except for Ser Manfred Dondarrion. He wouldn't even vouch that I was a knight, he'll never risk his life for me."

Ser Steffon seemed little perturbed. "Then we need five more good men. Fortunately, I have more than five friends. Leo Longthorn, the Laughing Storm, Lord Caron, the Lannisters, Ser Otho Bracken ...

aye, and the Blackwoods as well, though you will never get Blackwood and Bracken on the same side of a melee. I shall go and speak with some of them."

"They won't be happy at being woken," his cousin objected.

"Excellent," declared Ser Steffon. "If they are angry, they'll fight all the more fiercely. You may rely on me, Ser Duncan. Cousin, if I do not return before dawn, bring my armor and see that Wrath is saddled and barded for me. I shall meet you both in the challengers' paddock." He laughed. "This will be a day long remembered, I think." When he strode from the tent, he looked almost happy.

Not so Raymun. "Five knights," he said glumly after his cousin had gone. "Duncan, I am loath to dash your hopes, but ..."

"If your cousin can bring the men he speaks of ..."

"Leo Longthorn? The Brute of Bracken? The Laughing Storm?" Raymun stood. "He knows all of them, I have no doubt, but I would be less certain that any of them know *him.* Steffon sees this as a chance for glory, but it means your life. You should find your own men. I'll help. Better you have too many champions than too few." A noise outside made Raymun turn his head. "Who goes there?" he demanded, as a boy ducked through the flap, followed by a thin man in a rain-sodden black cloak.

"Egg?" Dunk got to his feet. "What are you doing here?"

"I'm your squire," the boy said. "You'll need someone to arm you, ser."

"Does your lord father know you've left the castle?"

"Gods be good, I hope not." Daeron Targaryen undid the clasp of his cloak and let it slide from his thin shoulders.

"*You?* Are you mad, coming here?" Dunk pulled his knife from his sheath. "I ought to shove this through your belly."

"Probably," Prince Daeron admitted. "Though I'd sooner you poured me a cup of wine. Look at my hands." He held one out and let them all see how it shook.

Dunk stepped toward him, glowering. "I don't care about your hands. You lied about me."

"I had to say *something* when my father demanded to know where my little brother had gotten to," the prince replied. He seated himself, ignoring Dunk and his knife. "If truth be told, I hadn't even realized Egg was gone. He wasn't at the bottom of my wine cup, and I hadn't looked anywhere else, so . . ." He sighed.

"Ser, my father is going to join the seven accusers," Egg broke in. "I begged him not to, but he won't listen. He says it is the only way to redeem Aerion's honor, and Daeron's."

"Not that I ever asked to have my honor redeemed," said Prince Daeron sourly. "Whoever has it can keep it, so far as I'm concerned. Still, here we are. For what it's worth, Ser Duncan, you have little to fear from me. The only thing I like less than horses are swords. Heavy things, and beastly sharp. I'll do my best to look gallant in the first charge, but after that . . . well, perhaps you could strike me a nice blow to the side of the helm. Make it ring, but not *too* loud, if you take my meaning. My brothers have my measure when it comes to fighting and dancing and thinking and reading books, but none of them is half my equal at lying insensible in the mud."

Dunk could only stare at him and wonder whether the princeling was trying to play him for a fool. "Why did you come?"

"To warn you of what you face," Daeron said. "My father has commanded the Kingsguard to fight with him."

"The Kingsguard?" said Dunk, appalled.

"Well, the three who are here. Thank the gods Uncle Baelor left the other four at King's Landing with our royal grandfather."

Egg supplied the names. "Ser Roland Crakehall, Ser Donnel of Duskendale, and Ser Willem Wylde."

"They have small choice in the matter," said Daeron. "They are sworn to protect the lives of the king and royal family, and my brothers and I are blood of the dragon, gods help us."

Dunk counted on his fingers. "That makes six. Who is the seventh man?"

Prince Daeron shrugged. "Aerion will find someone. If need be, he will buy a champion. He has no lack of gold."

"Who do you have?" Egg asked.

"Raymun's cousin Ser Steffon."

Daeron winced. "Only one?"

"Ser Steffon has gone to some of his friends."

"I can bring people," said Egg. "Knights. I can."

"Egg," said Dunk, "I will be fighting your own brothers."

"You won't hurt Daeron, though," the boy said. "He *told* you he'd fall down. And Aerion ... I remember, when I was little, he used to come into my bedchamber at night and put his knife between my legs. He had too many brothers, he'd say, maybe one night he'd make me his sister, then he could marry me. He threw my cat in the well too. He says he didn't, but he always lies."

Prince Daeron gave a weary shrug. "Egg has the truth of it. Aerion's quite the monster. He thinks he's a dragon in human form, you know. That's why he was so wroth at that puppet show. A pity he wasn't born a Fossoway, then he'd think himself an apple and we'd all be a deal safer, but there you are." Standing, he scooped up his fallen cloak and shook the rain from it. "I must steal back to the castle before my father wonders why I'm taking so long to sharpen my sword, but before I go, I would like a private word, Ser Duncan. Will you walk with me?"

Dunk looked at the princeling suspiciously a moment. "As you wish. Your Grace." He sheathed his dagger. "I need to get my shield too."

"Egg and I will look for knights," promised Raymun.

Prince Daeron knotted his cloak around his neck and pulled up the hood. Dunk followed him back out into the soft rain. They walked toward the merchants' wagons.

"I dreamed of you," said the prince.

"You said that at the inn."

"Did I? Well, it's so. My dreams are not like yours, Ser Duncan. Mine are true. They frighten me. *You* frighten me. I dreamed of you and a dead dragon, you see. A great beast, huge, with wings so large they could cover this meadow. It had fallen on top of you, but you were alive and the dragon was dead."

"Did I kill it?"

"That I could not say, but you were there, and so was the dragon. We were the masters of dragons once, we Targaryens. Now they are all gone, but we remain. I don't care to die today. The gods alone know why, but I don't. So do me a kindness if you would, and make certain it is my brother Aerion you slay."

"I don't care to die either," said Dunk.

"Well, I shan't kill you, ser. I'll withdraw my accusation as well, but it won't serve unless Aerion withdraws his." He sighed. "It may be that I've killed you with my lie. If so, I am sorry. I'm doomed to some hell, I know. Likely one without wine." He shuddered, and on that they parted, there in the cool soft rain.

The merchants had drawn up their wagons on the western verge of the meadow, beneath a stand of birch and ash. Dunk stood under the trees and looked helplessly at the empty place where the puppeteers' wagon had been. *Gone.* He had feared they might be. *I would flee as well, if I were not thick as a castle wall.* He wondered what he would do for a shield now. He had the silver to buy one, he supposed, *if* he could find one for sale ...

"Ser Duncan," a voice called out of the dark. Dunk turned to find Steely Pate standing behind him, holding an iron lantern. Under a short leather cloak, the armorer was bare from the waist up, his broad chest and thick arms covered with coarse black hair. "If you are come for your shield, she left it with me." He looked Dunk up and down. "Two hands and two feet, I count. So it's to be trial by combat, is it?"

"A trial of seven. How did you know?"

"Well, they might have kissed you and made you a lord, but it didn't seem likely, and if it went t'other way, you'd be short some parts. Now follow me."

His wagon was easy to distinguish by the sword and anvil painted on its side. Dunk followed Pate inside. The armorer hung the lantern on a hook, shrugged out of his wet cloak, and pulled a roughspun tunic down over his head. A hinged board dropped down from one wall to make a table. "Sit," he said, shoving a low stool toward him.

Dunk sat. "Where did she go?"

"They make for Dorne. The girl's uncle, there's a wise man. Well gone is well forgot. Stay and be seen, and belike the dragon remembers. Besides, he did not think she ought to see you die." Pate went to the far end of the wagon, rummaged about in the shadows a moment, and returned with the shield. "Your rim was old, cheap steel, brittle and rusted," he said. "I've made you a new one, twice as thick, and put some bands across the back. It will be heavier now, but stronger too. The girl did the paint."

She had made a better job of it than he could ever have hoped for. Even by lanternlight, the sunset colors were rich and bright, the tree tall and strong and noble. The falling star was a bright slash of paint across the oaken sky. Yet now that Dunk held it in his hands, it seemed all wrong. The star was *falling*, what sort of sigil was that? Would he fall just as fast? And sunset heralds night. "I should have stayed with the chalice," he said miserably. "It had wings, at least, to fly away, and Ser Arlan said the cup was full of faith and fellowship and good things to drink. This shield is all painted up like death."

"The elm's alive," Pate pointed out. "See how green the leaves are? Summer leaves, for certain. And I've seen shields blazoned with skulls and wolves and ravens, even hanged men and bloody heads. They served well enough, and so will this. You know the old shield rhyme? *Oak and iron, guard me well . . .* "

"*. . . or else I'm dead, and doomed to hell,*" Dunk finished. He had not thought of that rhyme in years. The old man had taught it to him, a long time ago. "How much do you want for the new rim and all?" he asked Pate.

"From you?" Pate scratched his beard. "A copper."

* * *

The rain had all but stopped as the first wan light suffused the eastern sky, but it had done its work. Lord Ashford's men had removed
the barriers, and the tourney field was one great morass of grey-
brown mud and torn grass. Tendrils of fog were writhing along the
ground like pale white snakes as Dunk made his way back toward the
lists. Steely Pate walked with him.

The viewing stand had already begun to fill, the lords and ladies
clutching their cloaks tight about them against the morning chill.
Smallfolk were drifting toward the field as well, and hundreds of
them already stood along the fence. *So many come to see me die,* thought
Dunk bitterly, but he wronged them. A few steps farther on, a woman
called out, "Good fortune to you." An old man stepped up to take his
hand and said, "May the gods give you strength, ser." Then a begging
brother in a tattered brown robe said a blessing on his sword, and a
maid kissed his cheek. *They are for me.* "Why?" he asked Pate. "What
am I to them?"

"A knight who remembered his vows," the smith said.

They found Raymun outside the challengers' paddock at the south end of the lists, waiting with his cousin's horse and Dunk's. Thunder tossed restlessly beneath the weight of crinet, chamfron, and blanket of heavy mail. Pate inspected the armor and pronounced it good work even though someone else had forged it. Wherever the armor had come from, Dunk was grateful.

Then he saw the others; the one-eyed man with the salt-and-pepper beard, the young knight in the striped yellow-and-black surcoat with the beehives on the shield. *Robyn Rhysling and Humfrey Beesbury*, he thought in astonishment. *And Ser Humfrey Hardyng as well.* Hardyng was mounted on Aerion's red charger, now barded in his red-and-white diamonds.

He went to them. "Sers, I am in your debt."

"The debt is Aerion's," Ser Humfrey Hardyng replied, "and we mean to collect it."

"I had heard your leg was broken."

"You heard the truth," Hardyng said. "I cannot walk. But so long as I can sit a horse, I can fight."

Raymun took Dunk aside. "I hoped Hardyng would want another chance at Aerion, and he did. As it happens, the other Humfrey is his brother by marriage. Egg is responsible for Ser Robyn, whom he knew from other tourneys. So you are five."

"Six," said Dunk in wonder, pointing. A knight was entering the paddock, his squire leading his charger behind him. "The Laughing Storm." A head taller than Ser Raymun and almost of a height with Dunk, Ser Lyonel wore a cloth-of-gold surcoat bearing the crowned stag of House Baratheon, and carried his antlered helm under his arm. Dunk reached for his hand. "Ser Lyonel, I cannot thank you enough for coming, nor Ser Steffon for bringing you."

"Ser Steffon?" Ser Lyonel gave him a puzzled look. "It was your squire who came to me. The boy, Aegon. My own lad tried to chase him off, but he slipped between his legs and turned a flagon of wine over my head." He laughed. "There has not been a trial of seven for more than a hundred years, do you know that? I was not about to miss a chance to fight the Kingsguard knights and tweak Prince Maekar's nose in the bargain."

"Six," Dunk said hopefully to Raymun Fossoway as Ser Lyonel joined the others. "Your cousin will bring the last, surely."

A roar went up from the crowd. At the north end of the meadow, a column of knights came trotting out of the river mist. The three Kingsguard came first, like ghosts in their gleaming, white enamel armor, long white cloaks trailing behind them. Even their shields were white, blank and clean as a field of newfallen snow. Behind rode Prince Maekar and his sons. Aerion was mounted on a dapple grey, orange and red flickering through the slashes in the horse's caparison at each stride. His brother's destrier was a smaller bay, armored in overlapping black and gold scales. A green silk plume trailed from Daeron's helm. It was their father who made the most fearsome appearance, however. Black curved dragon teeth ran across his shoulders, along the crest of his helm, and down his back, and the huge, spiked mace strapped to his saddle was as deadly-looking a weapon as any Dunk had ever seen.

"Six," Raymun exclaimed suddenly. "They are only six."

It was true, Dunk saw. *Three black knights and three white. They are a man short as well.* Was it possible that Aerion had not been able to find a seventh man? What would that mean? Would they fight six against six if neither found a seventh?

Egg slipped up beside him as he was trying to puzzle it out. "Ser, it's time you donned your armor."

"Thank you, squire. If you would be so good?"

Steely Pate lent the lad a hand. Hauberk and gorget, greaves and gauntlet, coif and codpiece, they turned him into steel, checking each buckle and each clasp thrice. Ser Lyonel sat sharpening his sword on a whet-stone while the Humfreys talked quietly, Ser Robyn prayed, and Ray-mun Fossoway paced back and forth, wondering where his cousin had got to.

Dunk was fully armored by the time Ser Steffon finally appeared. "Raymun," he called, "my mail, if you please." He had changed into a padded doublet to wear beneath his steel.

"Ser Steffon," said Dunk, "what of your friends? We need another knight to make our seven."

"You need two, I fear," Ser Steffon said. Raymun laced up the back of the hauberk.

"M'lord?" Dunk did not understand. "Two?"

Ser Steffon picked up a gauntlet of fine, lobstered steel and slid his left hand into it, flexing his fingers. "I see five here," he said while Raymun fastened his sword belt. "Beesbury, Rhysling, Hardyng, Baratheon, and yourself."

"And you," said Dunk. "You're the sixth."

"I am the seventh," said Ser Steffon, smiling, "but for the other side. I fight with Prince Aerion and the accusers."

Raymun had been about to hand his cousin his helm. He stopped as if struck. "No."

"Yes." Ser Steffon shrugged. "Ser Duncan understands, I am sure. I have a duty to my prince."

"You told him to rely on you." Raymun had gone pale.

"Did I?" He took the helm from his cousin's hands. "No doubt I was sincere at the time. Bring me my horse."

"Get him yourself," said Raymun angrily. "If you think I wish any part of this, you're as thick as you are vile."

"Vile?" Ser Steffon *tsk*ed. "Guard your tongue, Raymun. We're both apples from the same tree. And you are my squire. Or have you forgotten your vows?"

"No. Have you forgotten yours? You swore to be a knight."

"I shall be more than a knight before this day is done. *Lord* Fossoway. I like the sound of that." Smiling, he pulled on his other gauntlet, turned away, and crossed the paddock to his horse. Though the other defenders stared at him with contemptuous eyes, no one made a move to stop him.

Dunk watched Ser Steffon lead his destrier back across the field. His hands coiled into fists, but his throat felt too raw for speech. *No words would move the likes of him anyway.*

"Knight me." Raymun put a hand on Dunk's shoulder and turned him. "I will take my cousin's place. Ser Duncan, knight me." He went to one knee.

Frowning, Dunk moved a hand to the hilt of his longsword, then hesitated. "Raymun, I ... I should not."

"You must. Without me, you are only five."

"The lad has the truth of it," said Ser Lyonel Baratheon. "Do it, Ser Duncan. Any knight can make a knight."

"Do you doubt my courage?" Raymun asked.

"No," said Dunk. "Not that, but ..." Still he hesitated.

A fanfare of trumpets cut the misty-morning air. Egg came running up to them. "Ser, Lord Ashford summons you."

The Laughing Storm gave an impatient shake of the head. "Go to him, Ser Duncan. I'll give squire Raymun his knighthood." He slid his sword out of his sheath and shouldered Dunk aside. "Raymun of House Fossoway," he began solemnly, touching the blade to the squire's right shoulder, "in the name of the Warrior I charge you to be brave." The sword moved from his right shoulder to his left. "In the name of the Father I charge you to be just." Back to the right. "In the name of the Mother I charge you to defend the young and innocent." The left. "In the name of the Maiden I charge you to protect all women ..."

Dunk left them there, feeling as relieved as he was guilty. *We are still one short,* he thought as Egg held Thunder for him. *Where will I find another man?* He turned the horse and rode slowly toward the viewing stand, where Lord Ashford stood waiting. From the north end of the lists, Prince Aerion advanced to meet him. "Ser Duncan," he said cheerfully, "it would seem you have only five champions."

"Six," said Dunk. "Ser Lyonel is knighting Raymun Fossoway. We will fight you six against seven." Men had won at far worse odds, he knew.

But Lord Ashford shook his head. "That is not permitted, ser. If you cannot find another knight to take your side, you must be declared guilty of the crimes of which you stand accused."

Guilty, thought Dunk. *Guilty of loosening a tooth, and for that I must die.* "M'lord, I beg a moment."

"You have it."

Dunk rode slowly along the fence. The viewing stand was crowded with knights. "M'lords," he called to them, "do none of you remember Ser Arlan of Pennytree? I was his squire. We served many of you. Ate at your tables and slept in your halls." He saw Manfred Dondarrion seated in the highest tier. "Ser Arlan took a wound in your lord father's service." The knight said something to the lady beside him, paying no heed. Dunk was forced to move on. "Lord Lannister, Ser Arlan unhorsed you once in tourney." The Grey Lion examined his gloved hands, studiedly refusing to raise his eyes. "He was a good man, and he taught me how to be a knight. Not only sword and lance, but honor. A knight defends the innocent, he said. That's all I did. I need one more knight to fight beside me. One, that's all. Lord Caron? Lord Swann?" Lord Swann laughed softly as Lord Caron whispered in his ear.

Dunk reined up before Ser Otho Bracken, lowering his voice. "Ser Otho, all know you for a great champion. Join us, I beg you. In the names of the old gods and the new. My cause is just."

"That may be," said the Brute of Bracken, who had at least the grace to reply, "but it is your cause, not mine. I know you not, boy."

Heartsick, Dunk wheeled Thunder and raced back and forth before the tiers of pale, cold men. Despair made him shout. *"ARE THERE NO TRUE KNIGHTS AMONG YOU?"*

Only silence answered.

Across the field, Prince Aerion laughed. "The dragon is not mocked," he called out.

Then came a voice. "I will take Ser Duncan's side."

A black stallion emerged from out of the river mists, a black knight on his back. Dunk saw the dragon shield, and the red enamel crest upon his helm with its three roaring heads. *The Young Prince. Gods be good, is it truly him?*

Lord Ashford made the same mistake. "Prince Valarr?"

"No." The black knight lifted the visor of his helm. "I did not think to enter the lists at Ashford, my lord, so I brought no armor. My son was good enough to lend me his." Prince Baelor smiled almost sadly.

The accusers were thrown into confusion, Dunk could see. Prince Maekar spurred his mount forward. "Brother, have you taken leave of your senses?" He pointed a mailed finger at Dunk. "This man attacked my son."

"This man protected the weak, as every true knight must," replied Prince Baelor. "Let the gods determine if he was right or wrong." He

gave a tug on his reins, turned Valarr's huge black destrier, and trotted to the south end of the field.

Dunk brought Thunder up beside him, and the other defenders gathered round them; Robyn Rhysling and Ser Lyonel, the Humfreys. *Good men all, but are they good enough?* "Where is Raymun?"

"*Ser* Raymun, if you please." He cantered up, a grim smile lighting his face beneath his plumed helm. "My pardons, ser. I needed to make a small change to my sigil, lest I be mistaken for my dishonorable cousin." He showed them all his shield. The polished golden field remained the same, and the Fossoway apple, but this apple was green instead of red. "I fear I am still not ripe ... but better green than wormy, eh?"

Ser Lyonel laughed, and Dunk grinned despite himself. Even Prince Baelor seemed to approve.

Lord Ashford's septon had come to the front of the viewing stand and raised his crystal to call the throng to prayer.

"Attend me, all of you," Baelor said quietly. "The accusers will be armed with heavy war lances for the first charge. Lances of ash, eight feet long, banded against splitting and tipped with a steel point sharp enough to drive through plate with the weight of a warhorse behind it."

"We shall use the same," said Ser Humfrey Beesbury. Behind him, the septon was calling on the Seven to look down and judge this dispute, and grant victory to the men whose cause was just.

"No," Baelor said. "We will arm ourselves with tourney lances instead."

"Tourney lances are made to break," objected Raymun.

"They are also made twelve feet long. If our points strike home, theirs cannot touch us. Aim for helm or chest. In a tourney it is a gallant thing to break your lance against a foe's shield, but here it may well mean death. If we can unhorse them and keep our own saddles, the advantage is ours." He glanced to Dunk. "If Ser Duncan is killed, it is considered that the gods have judged him guilty, and the contest is over. If both of his accusers are slain, or withdraw their accusations, the same is true. Elsewise, all seven of one side or the other must perish or yield for the trial to end."

"Prince Daeron will not fight," Dunk said.

"Not well, anyway," laughed Ser Lyonel. "Against that, we have three of the White Swords to contend with."

Baelor took that calmly. "My brother erred when he demanded that the Kingsguard fight for his son. Their oath forbids them to harm a prince of the blood. Fortunately, I am such." He gave them a faint smile. "Keep the others off me long enough, and I shall deal with the Kingsguard."

"My prince, is that chivalrous?" asked Ser Lyonel Baratheon as the septon was finishing his invocation.

"The gods will let us know," said Baelor Breakspear.

A deep expectant silence had fallen across Ashford Meadow.

Eighty yards away, Aerion's grey stallion trumpeted with impatience and pawed the muddy ground. Thunder was very still by comparison; he was an older horse, veteran of half a hundred fights, and he knew what was expected of him. Egg handed Dunk up his shield. "May the gods be with you, ser," the boy said.

The sight of his elm tree and shooting star gave him heart. Dunk

slid his left arm through the strap and tightened his fingers around the grip. *Oak and iron, guard me well, or else I'm dead, and doomed to hell.* Steely Pate brought his lance to him, but Egg insisted that it must be he who put it into Dunk's hand.

To either side, his companions took up their own lances and spread out in a long line. Prince Baelor was to his right and Ser Lyonel to his left, but the narrow eyeslit of the greathelm limited Dunk's vision to what was directly ahead of him. The viewing stand was gone, and likewise the smallfolk crowding the fence; there was only the muddy field, the pale, blowing mist, the river, town, and castle to the north, and the princeling on his grey charger with flames on his helm and a dragon on his shield. Dunk watched Aerion's squire hand him a war lance, eight feet long and black as night. *He will put that through my heart if he can.*

A horn sounded.

For a heartbeat Dunk sat as still as a fly in amber, though all the horses were moving. A stab of panic went through him. *I have forgotten,* he thought wildly, *I have forgotten all, I will shame myself, I will lose everything.*

Thunder saved him. The big brown stallion knew what to do even if his rider did not. He broke into a slow trot. Dunk's training took over then. He gave the warhorse a light touch of spur and couched his lance. At the same time he swung his shield until it covered most of the left side of his body. He held it at an angle, to deflect blows away from him. *Oak and iron guard me well, or else I'm dead, and doomed to hell.*

The noise of the crowd was no more than the crash of distant waves. Thunder slid into a gallop. Dunk's teeth jarred together with the violence of the pace. He pressed his heels down, tightening his legs with all his strength and letting his body become part of the motion of the horse beneath. *I am Thunder and Thunder is me, we are one beast, we are joined, we are one.* The air inside his helm was already so hot he could scarce breathe.

In a tourney joust, his foe would be to his left across the tilting barrier, and he would need to swing his lance across Thunder's neck. The angle made it more likely that the wood would split on impact. But this was a deadlier game they played today. With no barriers dividing them, the destriers charged straight at one another. Prince Baelor's huge black was much faster than Thunder, and Dunk glimpsed him pounding ahead through the corner of his eyeslit. He sensed more than saw the others. *They do not matter, only Aerion matters, only he.*

He watched the dragon come. Spatters of mud sprayed back from the hooves of Prince Aerion's grey, and Dunk could see the horse's nostrils flaring. The black lance still angled upward. A knight who holds his lance high and brings it on line at the last moment always risks lowering it too far, the old man had told him. He brought his own point to bear on the center of the princeling's chest. *My lance is part of my arm*, he told himself. *It's my finger, a wooden finger. All I need do is touch him with my long wooden finger.*

He tried not to see the sharp iron point at the end of Aerion's black lance, growing larger with every stride. *The dragon, look at the dragon,* he thought. The great three-headed beast covered the prince's shield, red wings and gold fire. *No, look only where you mean to strike,* he remembered suddenly, but his lance had already begun to slide off line. Dunk tried to correct, but it was too late. He saw his point strike Aerion's shield, taking the dragon between two of its heads, gouging into a gout of painted flame. At the muffled *crack,* he felt Thunder recoil under him, trembling with the force of the impact, and half a heartbeat later something smashed into his side with awful force. The horses slammed together violently, armor crashing and clanging as Thunder stumbled and Dunk's lance fell from his hand. Then he was past his foe, clutching at his saddle in a desperate effort to keep his seat. Thunder lurched sideways in the sloppy mud and Dunk felt his rear legs slip out from under. They were sliding, spinning, and then the stallion's hindquarters slapped down hard. *"Up!"* Dunk roared, lashing out with his spurs. *"Up, Thunder!"* And somehow the old warhorse found his feet again.

He could feel a sharp pain under his rib, and his left arm was being pulled down. Aerion had driven his lance through oak, wool, and steel; three feet of splintered ash and sharp iron stuck from his side. Dunk reached over with his right hand, grasped the lance just below the head, clenched his teeth, and pulled it out of him with one savage yank. Blood followed, seeping through the rings of his mail to redden his surcoat. The world swam and he almost fell. Dimly, through the pain, he could hear voices calling his name. His beautiful shield was useless now. He tossed it aside, elm tree, shooting star, broken lance, and all, and drew his sword, but he hurt so much he did not think he could swing it.

Turning Thunder in a tight circle, he tried to get a sense of what was happening elsewhere on the field. Ser Humfrey Hardyng clung to the neck of his mount, obviously wounded. The other Ser Humfrey lay motionless in a lake of bloodstained mud, a broken lance protruding from his groin. He saw Prince Baelor gallop past, lance still intact, and drive one of the Kingsguard from his saddle. Another of the white knights was already down, and Maekar had been unhorsed as well. The third of the Kingsguard was fending off Ser Robyn Rhysling.

Aerion, where is Aerion? The sound of drumming hooves behind him made Dunk turn his head sharply. Thunder bugled and reared, hooves lashing out futilely as Aerion's grey stallion barreled into him at full gallop.

This time there was no hope of recovery. His longsword went spinning from his grasp, and the ground rose up to meet him. He landed with a bruising impact that jarred him to the bone and drove the breath from his lungs. Pain stabbed through him, so sharp he sobbed. For a moment it was all he could do to lie there. The taste of blood filled his mouth. *Dunk the lunk, thought he could be a knight.* He knew he had to find his feet again, or die. Groaning, he forced himself to hands and knees. He could not breathe, nor could he see. The eye-slit of his helm was packed with mud. Lurching blindly to his feet, Dunk scraped at the mud with a mailed finger. *There, that's . . .*

Through his fingers, he glimpsed a dragon flying, and a spiked morningstar whirling on the end of a chain. Then his head seemed to burst to pieces.

When his eyes opened he was on the ground again, sprawled on his back. The mud had all been knocked from his helm, but now one eye was closed by blood. Above was nothing was dark grey sky. His face throbbed, and he could feel cold wet metal pressing in against cheek and temple. *He broke my head, and I'm dying.* What was worse was the others who would die with him, Raymun and Prince Baelor and the rest. *I've failed them. I am no champion. I'm not even a hedge knight. I am nothing.* He remembered Prince Daeron boasting that no one could lie insensible in the mud as well as he did. *He never saw Dunk the lunk though, did he?* The shame was worse than the pain.

The dragon appeared above him.

Three heads it had, and wings bright as flame, red and yellow and orange. It was laughing. "Are you dead yet, hedge knight?" it asked. "Cry for quarter and admit your guilt, and perhaps I'll only claim a hand and a foot. Oh, and those teeth, but what are a few teeth? A man like you can live years on pease porridge." The dragon laughed again. "No? Eat *this,* then." The spiked ball whirled round and round the sky, and fell toward his head as fast as a shooting star.

Dunk rolled.

Where he found the strength he did not know, but he found it. He rolled into Aerion's legs, threw a steel-clad arm around his thigh, dragged him cursing into the mud, and rolled on top of him. *Let him swing his bloody morningstar now.* The prince tried forcing the lip of his shield up at Dunk's head, but his battered helm took the brunt of the impact. Aerion was strong, but Dunk was stronger, and larger and heavier as well. He grabbed hold of the shield with both hands and twisted until the straps broke. Then he brought it down on the top of the princeling's helm, again and again and again, smashing the enameled flames of his crest. The shield was thicker than Dunk's had been, solid oak banded with iron. A flame broke off. Then another. The prince ran out of flames long before Dunk ran out of blows.

Aerion finally let go the handle of his useless morningstar and clawed for the poniard at his hip. He got it free of its sheath, but when Dunk whanged his hand with the shield the knife sailed off into the mud.

He could vanquish Ser Duncan the Tall, but not Dunk of Flea Bottom. The old man had taught him jousting and swordplay, but this sort of fighting he had learned earlier, in shadowy wynds and crooked alleys behind the city's winesinks. Dunk flung the battered shield away and wrenched up the visor of Aerion's helm. *A visor is a weak point,* he remembered Steely Pate saying. The prince had all but ceased to struggle. His eyes were purple and full of terror. Dunk had a sudden urge to grab one and pop it like a grape between two steel fingers, but that would not be knightly. *"YIELD!"* he shouted.

"I yield," the dragon whispered, pale lips barely moving.

Dunk blinked down at him. For a moment he could not credit what his ears had heard. *Is it done, then?* He turned his head slowly from side to side, trying to see. His vision slit was partly closed by the blow that had smashed in the left side of his face. He glimpsed Prince Maekar, mace in hand, trying to fight his way to his son's side. Baelor Breakspear was holding him off.

Dunk lurched to his feet and pulled Prince Aerion up after him. Fumbling at the lacings of his helm, he tore it off and flung it away. At once he was drowned in sights and sounds; grunts and curses, the shouts of the crowd, one stallion screaming while another raced rid-erless across the field. Everywhere steel rang on steel. Raymun and his cousin were slashing at each other in front of the viewing stand, both afoot. Their shields were splintered ruins, the green apple and the red both hacked to tinder. One of the Kingsguard knights was carrying a wounded brother from the field. They both looked alike in their white armor and white cloaks. The third of the white knights was down, and the Laughing Storm had joined Prince Baelor against Prince Maekar. Mace, battle-axe, and longsword clashed and *clang*ed, ringing against helm and shield. Maekar was taking three blows for every one he landed, and Dunk could see that it would be over soon. *I must make an end to it before more of us are killed.*

Prince Aerion made a sudden dive for his morningstar. Dunk kicked him in the back and knocked him facedown, then grabbed ahold of one of his legs and dragged him across the field. By the time he reached the viewing stand where Lord Ashford sat, the Bright Prince was brown as a privy. Dunk hauled him onto his feet and rat-tled him, shaking some of the mud onto Lord Ashford and the fair maid. "Tell him!"

Aerion Brightflame spit out a mouthful of grass and dirt. "I with-draw my accusation."

Afterward Dunk could not have said whether he walked from the field under his own power or had required help. He hurt everywhere, and some places worse than others. *I am a knight now in truth?* he re-membered wondering. *Am I a champion?*

Egg helped him remove his greaves and gorget, and Raymun as well, and even Steely Pate. He was too dazed to tell them apart. They were fingers and thumbs and voices. Pate was the one complaining, Dunk knew. "Look what he's done to me armor," he said. "All dinted and banged and scratched. Aye, I ask you, why do I bother? I'll have to cut that mail off him, I fear."

"Raymun," Dunk said urgently, clutching at his friend's hands. "The others. How did they fare?" He had to know. "Has anyone died?"

"Beesbury," Raymun said. "Slain by Donnel of Duskendale in the first charge. Ser Humfrey is gravely wounded as well. The rest of us are bruised and bloody, no more. Save for you."

"And them? The accusers?"

"Ser Willem Wylde of the Kingsguard was carried from the field insensate, and I think I cracked a few of my cousin's ribs. At least I hope so."

"And Prince Daeron?" Dunk blurted. "Did he survive?"

"Once Ser Robyn unhorsed him, he lay where he fell. He may have a broken foot. His own horse trod on him while running loose about the field."

Dazed and confused as he was, Dunk felt a huge sense of relief. "His dream was wrong, then. The dead dragon. Unless Aerion died. He didn't though, did he?"

"No," said Egg. "You spared him. Don't you remember?"

"I suppose." Already his memories of the fight were becoming con-fused and vague. "One moment I feel drunk. The next it hurts so bad I know I'm dying."

They made him lie down on his back and talked over him as he gazed up into the roiling grey sky. It seemed to Dunk that it was still morning. He wondered how long the fight had taken.

"Gods be good, the lance point drove the rings deep into his flesh," he heard Raymun saying. "It will mortify unless . . ."

"Get him drunk and pour some boiling oil into it," someone sug-gested. "That's how the maesters do it."

"Wine." The voice had a hollow metallic ring to it. "*Not* oil, that will kill him, boiling wine. I'll send Maester Yormwell to have a look at him when he's done tending my brother."

A tall knight stood above him, in black armor dinted and scarred by many blows. *Prince Baelor.* The scarlet dragon on his helm had lost a head, both wings, and most of its tail. "Your Grace," Dunk said, "I am your man. Please. Your man."

"My man." The black knight put a hand on Raymun's shoulder to steady himself. "I need good men, Ser Duncan. The realm ..." His voice sounded oddly slurred. Perhaps he'd bit his tongue.

Dunk was very tired. It was hard to stay awake. "Your man," he murmured once more.

The prince moved his head slowly from side to side. "Ser Raymun ... my helm, if you'd be so kind. Visor ... visor's cracked, and my fingers ... fingers feel like wood ..."

"At once, Your Grace." Raymun took the prince's helm in both hands and grunted. "Goodman Pate, a hand."

Steely Pate dragged over a mounting stool. "It's crushed down at the back, Your Grace, toward the left side. Smashed into the gorget. Good steel, this, to stop such a blow."

"Brother's mace, most like," Baelor said thickly. "He's strong." He winced. "That ... feels queer, I ..."

"Here it comes." Pate lifted the battered helm away. "Gods be good. *Oh gods oh gods oh gods preserve ...* "

Dunk saw something red and wet fall out of the helm. Someone was screaming, high and terrible. Against the bleak grey sky swayed a tall tall prince in black armor with only half a skull. He could see red blood and pale bone beneath and something else, something blue-grey and pulpy. A queer troubled look passed across Baelor Breakspear's face, like a cloud passing before a sun. He raised his hand and touched the back of his head with two fingers, oh so lightly. And then he fell.

Dunk caught him. "Up," they say he said, just as he had with Thunder in the melee, "up, up." But he never remembered that afterward, and the prince did not rise.

* * *

Baelor of House Targaryen, Prince of Dragonstone, Hand of the King, Protector of the Realm, and heir apparent to the Iron Throne of the Seven Kingdoms of Westeros, went to the fire in the yard of Ashford Castle on the north bank of river Cockleswent. Other great houses might choose to bury their dead in the dark earth or sink them in the cold green sea, but the Targaryens were the blood of the dragon, and their ends were writ in flame.

He had been the finest knight of his age, and some argued that he should have gone to face the dark clad in mail and plate, a sword in his hand. In the end though, his royal father's wishes prevailed, and Daeron II had a peaceable nature. When Dunk shuffled past Baelor's bier, the prince wore a black velvet tunic with the three-headed dragon picked out in scarlet thread upon his breast. Around his throat was a heavy gold chain. His sword was sheathed by his side, but he did wear a helm, a thin golden helm with an open visor so men could see his face.

Valarr, the Young Prince, stood vigil at the foot of the bier while his father lay in state. He was a shorter, slimmer, handsomer version of his sire, without the twice-broken nose that had made Baelor seem more human than royal. Valarr's hair was brown, but a bright streak of silver-gold ran through it. The sight of it reminded Dunk of Aerion, but he knew that was not fair. Egg's hair was growing back as bright as his brother's, and Egg was a decent enough lad, for a prince.

When he stopped to offer awkward sympathies, well larded with thanks, Prince Valarr blinked cool blue eyes at him and said, "My father was only nine-and-thirty. He had it in him to be a great king, the greatest since Aegon the Dragon. Why would the gods take him, and leave *you*?" He shook his head. "Begone with you, Ser Duncan. Begone."

Wordless, Dunk limped from the castle, down to the camp by the green pool. He had no answer for Valarr. Nor for the questions he asked himself. The maesters and the boiling wine had done their work, and his wound was healing cleanly though there would be a deep, puckered scar between his left arm and his nipple. He could not see the wound without thinking of Baelor. *He saved me once with his sword, and once with a word even though he was a dead man as he stood there.* The world made no sense when a great prince died so a hedge knight might live.

Dunk sat beneath his elm and stared morosely at his foot.

When four guardsmen in the royal livery appeared in his camp late one day, he was sure they had come to kill him after all. Too weak and weary to reach for a sword, he sat with his back to the elm, waiting.

"Our prince begs the favor of a private word."

"Which prince?" asked Dunk, wary.

"This prince," a brusque voice said before the captain could answer. Maekar Targaryen walked out from behind the elm.

Dunk got slowly to his feet. *What would he have of me now?*

Maekar motioned, and the guards vanished as suddenly as they had appeared. The prince studied him a long moment, then turned and paced away from him to stand beside the pool, gazing down at his reflection in the water. "I have sent Aerion to Lys," he announced abruptly. "A few years in the Free Cities may change him for the better."

Dunk had never been to the Free Cities, so he did not know what to say to that. He was pleased that Aerion was gone from the Seven Kingdoms, and hoped he never came back, but that was not a thing you told a father of his son. He stood silent.

Prince Maekar turned to face him. "Some men will say I meant to kill my brother. The gods know it is a lie, but I will hear the whispers till the day I die. And it was my mace that dealt the fatal blow, I have no doubt. The only other foes he faced in the melee were three Kingsguard, whose vows forbade them to do any more than defend themselves. So it was me. Strange to say, I do not recall the blow that broke his skull. Is that a mercy or a curse? Some of both, I think."

From the way he looked at Dunk, it seemed the prince wanted an answer. "I could not say, Your Grace." Perhaps he should have hated Maekar, but instead he felt a queer sympathy for the man. "You swung the mace, m'lord, but it was for me Prince Baelor died. So I killed him too, as much as you."

"Yes," the prince admitted. "You'll hear them whisper as well. The king is old. When he dies, Valarr will climb the Iron Throne in place of his father. Each time a battle is lost or a crop fails, the fools will say, 'Baelor would not have let it happen, but the hedge knight killed him.'"

Dunk could see the truth in that. "If I had not fought, you would have had my hand off. And my foot. Sometimes I sit under that tree there and look at my feet and ask if I couldn't have spared one. How could my foot be worth a prince's life? And the other two as well, the Humfreys, they were good men too." Ser Humfrey Hardyng had succumbed to his wounds only last night.

"And what answer does your tree give you?"

"None that I can hear. But the old man, Ser Arlan, every day at evenfall he'd say, 'I wonder what the morrow will bring.' He never knew, no more than we do. Well, mighten it be that some morrow will come when I'll have need of that foot? When the *realm* will need that foot, even more than a prince's life?"

Maekar chewed on that a time, mouth clenched beneath the silvery-pale beard that made his face seem so square. "It's not bloody likely," he said harshly. "The realm has as many hedge knights as hedges, and all of them have feet."

"If Your Grace has a better answer, I'd want to hear it."

Maekar frowned. "It may be that the gods have a taste for cruel japes. Or perhaps there are no gods. Perhaps none of this had any meaning. I'd ask the High Septon, but the last time I went to him he told me that no man can truly understand the workings of the gods. Perhaps he should try sleeping under a tree." He grimaced. "My youngest son seems to have grown fond of you, ser. It is time he was a squire, but he tells me he will serve no knight but you. He is an unruly boy, as you will have noticed. Will you have him?"

"Me?" Dunk's mouth opened and closed and opened again. "Egg . . . Aegon, I mean . . . he is a good lad, but, Your Grace, I know you honor me, but . . . I am only a hedge knight."

"That can be changed," said Maekar. "Aegon is to return to my castle at Summerhall. There is a place there for you, if you wish. A knight of my household. You'll swear your sword to me, and Aegon can squire for you. While you train him, my master-at-arms will finish your own training." The prince gave him a shrewd look. "Your Ser Arlan did all he could for you, I have no doubt, but you still have much to learn."

"I know, m'lord." Dunk looked about him. At the green grass and the reeds, the tall elm, the ripples dancing across the surface of the sunlit pool. Another dragonfly was moving across the water, or perhaps it was the same one. *What shall it be, Dunk?* he asked himself. *Dragonflies or dragons?* A few days ago he would have answered at once. It was all he had ever dreamed, but now that the prospect was at hand it frightened him. "Just before Prince Baelor died, I swore to be his man."

"Presumptuous of you," said Maekar. "What did he say?"

"That the realm needed good men."

"That's true enough. What of it?"

"I will take your son as squire, Your Grace, but not at Summerhall. Not for a year or two. He's seen sufficient of castles, I would judge. I'll have him only if I can take him on the road with me." He pointed to old Chestnut. "He'll ride my stot, wear my old cloak, and he'll keep my sword sharp and my mail scoured. We'll sleep in inns and stables, and now and again in the halls of some landed knight or lesser lordling, and maybe under trees when we must."

Prince Maekar gave him an incredulous look. "Did the trial addle your wits, man? Aegon is a prince of the realm. The blood of the dragon. Princes are not made for sleeping in ditches and eating hard salt beef." He saw Dunk hesitate. "What is it you're afraid to tell me? Say what you will, ser."

"Daeron never slept in a ditch, I'll wager," Dunk said, very quietly, "and all the beef that Aerion ever ate was thick and rare and bloody, like as not."

Maekar Targaryen, Prince of Summerhall, regarded Dunk of Flea Bottom for a long time, his jaw working silently beneath his silvery beard. Finally he turned and walked away, never speaking a word. Dunk heard him riding off with his men. When they were gone, there was no sound but the faint thrum of the dragonfly's wings as it skimmed across the water.

The boy came the next morning, just as the sun was coming up. He wore old boots, brown breeches, a brown wool tunic, and an old traveler's cloak. "My lord father says I am to serve you."

"Serve you, *ser*," Dunk reminded him. "You can start by saddling the horses. Chestnut is yours, treat her kindly. I don't want to find you on Thunder unless I put you there."

Egg went to get the saddles. "Where are we going, ser?"

Dunk thought for a moment. "I have never been over the Red Mountains. Would you like to have a look at Dorne?"

Egg grinned. "I hear they have good puppet shows," he said.

THE
SWORN SWORD

I n an iron cage at the crossroads, two dead men were rotting in the
summer sun. Egg stopped below to have a look at them. "Who do
you think they were, ser?" His mule, Maester, grateful for the respite,
began to crop the dry brown devil grass along the verges, heedless of
the two huge wine casks on his back.

"Robbers," Dunk said. Mounted atop Thunder, he was much closer
to the dead men. "Rapers. Murderers." Dark circles stained his old
green tunic under both arms. The sky was blue and the sun was blazing hot, and he had sweated gallons since breaking camp this morning.

Egg took off his wide-brimmed, floppy straw hat. Beneath, his
head was bald and shiny. He used the hat to fan away the flies. There
were hundreds crawling on the dead men, and more drifting lazily
through the still, hot air. "It must have been something bad, for them
to be left to die inside a crow cage."

Sometimes Egg could be as wise as any maester, but other times he was still a boy of ten. "There are lords and lords," Dunk said. "Some don't need much reason to put a man to death."

The iron cage was barely big enough to hold one man, yet two had been forced inside it. They stood face-to-face, with their arms and legs in a tangle and their backs against the hot black iron of the bars. One had tried to eat the other, gnawing at his neck and shoulder. The crows had been at both of them. When Dunk and Egg had come around the hill, the birds had risen like a black cloud, so thick that Maester spooked.

"Whoever they were, they look half-starved," Dunk said. *Skeletons in skin, and the skin is green and rotting.* "Might be they stole some bread, or poached a deer in some lord's wood." With the drought entering its second year, most lords had become less tolerant of poaching, and they hadn't been very tolerant to begin with.

"It could be they were in some outlaw band." At Dosk, they'd heard a harper sing "The Day They Hanged Black Robin." Ever since, Egg had been seeing gallant outlaws behind every bush.

Dunk had met a few outlaws while squiring for the old man. He was in no hurry to meet any more. None of the ones he'd known had been especially gallant. He remembered one outlaw Ser Arlan had helped hang, who'd been fond of stealing rings. He would cut off a man's fingers to get at them, but with women he preferred to bite. There were no songs about him that Dunk knew. *Outlaws or poachers, makes no matter. Dead men make poor company.* He walked Thunder slowly around the cage. The empty eyes seemed to follow him. One of the dead men had his head down and his mouth gaping open. *He has no tongue,* Dunk observed. He supposed the crows might have eaten it. Crows always pecked a corpse's eyes out first, he had heard, but maybe the tongue went second. *Or maybe a lord had it torn out, for something that he said.*

Dunk pushed his fingers through his mop of sun-streaked hair. The dead were beyond his help, and they had casks of wine to get to Standfast. "Which way did we come?" he asked, looking from one road to the other. "I'm turned around."

"Standfast is that way, ser." Egg pointed.

"That's for us, then. We could be back by evenfall, but not if we sit here all day counting flies." He touched Thunder with his heels and turned the big destrier toward the left-hand fork.

Egg put his floppy hat back on and tugged sharply at Maester's lead. The mule left off cropping at the devil grass and came along without an argument for once. *He's hot as well,* Dunk thought, *and those wine casks must be heavy.*

The summer sun had baked the road as hard as brick. Its ruts were deep enough to break a horse's leg, so Dunk was careful to keep Thunder to the higher ground between them. He had twisted his own ankle the day they left Dosk, walking in the black of night when it was cooler. A knight had to learn to live with aches and pains, the old man used to say. *Aye, lad, and with broken bones and scars. They're as much a part of knighthood as your swords and shields.* If Thunder were to break a leg, though ... well, a knight without a horse was no knight at all.

Egg followed five yards behind him, with Maester and the wine casks. The boy was walking with one bare foot in a rut and one out, so he rose and fell with every step. His dagger was sheathed on one hip, his boots slung over his backpack, his ragged brown tunic rolled up and knotted round his waist. Beneath his wide-brimmed straw hat, his face was smudged and dirty, his eyes large and dark. He was ten, not quite five feet tall. Of late he had been sprouting fast though he had a long long way to grow before he'd be catching up to Dunk. He looked just like the stableboy he wasn't, and not at all like who he really was.

The dead men soon disappeared behind them, but Dunk found himself thinking about them all the same. The realm was full of lawless men these days. The drought showed no signs of ending, and smallfolk by the thousands had taken to the roads, looking for some place where the rains still fell. Lord Bloodraven had commanded them to return to their own lands and lords, but few obeyed. Many blamed Bloodraven and King Aerys for the drought. It was a judgment from the gods, they said, for the kinslayer is accursed. If they were wise, though, they did not say it loudly. *How many eyes does Lord Bloodraven have?* ran the riddle Egg had heard in Oldtown. *A thousand eyes, and one.*

Six years ago in King's Landing, Dunk had seen him with his own two eyes, as he rode a pale horse up the Street of Steel with fifty Ra-

ven's Teeth behind him. That was before King Aerys had ascended to
the Iron Throne and made him the Hand, but even so he cut a striking figure, garbed in smoke and scarlet with Dark Sister on his hip.
His pallid skin and bone-white hair made him look a living corpse.
Across his cheek and chin spread a winestain birthmark that was
supposed to resemble a red raven, though Dunk only saw an odd-
shaped blotch of discolored skin. He stared so hard that Bloodraven
felt it. The king's sorcerer had turned to study him as he went by. He
had one eye, and that one red. The other was an empty socket, the gift
Bittersteel had given him upon the Redgrass Field. Yet it seemed to
Dunk that both eyes had looked right through his skin, down to his
very soul.

Despite the heat, the memory made him shiver. "Ser?" Egg called.
"Are you unwell?"

"No," said Dunk. "I'm as hot and thirsty as them." He pointed toward the field beyond the road, where rows of melons were shriveling
on the vines. Along the verges goat's heads and tufts of devil grass
still clung to life, but the crops were not faring near as well. Dunk
knew just how the melons felt. Ser Arlan used to say that no hedge
knight need ever go thirsty. "Not so long as he has a helm to catch the
rain in. Rainwater is the best drink there is, lad." The old man never
saw a summer like this one, though. Dunk had left his helm at Standfast. It was too hot and heavy to wear, and there had been precious
little rain to catch in it. *What's a hedge knight to do when even the hedges
are brown and parched and dying?*

Maybe when they reached the stream he'd have a soak. He smiled,
thinking how good that would feel, to jump right in and come up
sopping wet and grinning, with water cascading down his cheeks and
through his tangled hair and his tunic clinging sodden to his skin.
Egg might want a soak as well, though the boy looked cool and dry,
more dusty than sweaty. He never sweated much. He liked the heat.
In Dorne he went about bare-chested, and turned brown as a Dornishmen. *It is his dragon blood,* Dunk told himself. *Whoever heard of a
sweaty dragon?* He would gladly have pulled his own tunic off, but it
would not be fitting. A hedge knight could ride bare naked if he chose;
he had no one to shame but himself. It was different when your sword
was sworn. *When you accept a lord's meat and mead, all you do reflects on*

him, Ser Arlan used to say. *Always do more than he expects of you, never less. Never flinch at any task or hardship. And above all, never shame the lord you serve.* At Standfast, "meat and mead" meant chicken and ale, but Ser Eustace ate the same plain fare himself.

Dunk kept his tunic on and sweltered.

Ser Bennis of the Brown Shield was waiting at the old plank bridge. "So you come back," he called out. "You were gone so long I thought you run off with the old man's silver." Bennis was sitting on his shaggy garron, chewing a wad of sourleaf that made it look as if his mouth was full of blood.

"We had to go all the way to Dosk to find some wine," Dunk told him. "The krakens raided Little Dosk. They carried off the wealth and women and burned half of what they did not take."

"That Dagon Greyjoy wants for hanging," Bennis said. "Aye, but who's to hang him? You see old Pinchbottom Pate?"

"They told us he was dead. The ironmen killed him when he tried to stop them taking off his daughter."

"Seven bloody hells." Bennis turned his head and spat. "I seen that daughter once. Not worth dying for, you ask me. That fool Pate owed me half a silver." The brown knight looked just as he had when they left; worse, he smelled the same as well. He wore the same garb every day: brown breeches, a shapeless roughspun tunic, horsehide boots. When armored he donned a loose brown surcoat over a shirt of rusted mail.

His sword belt was a cord of boiled leather, and his seamed face might have been made of the same thing. *His head looks like one of those shriveled melons that we passed.* Even his teeth were brown, under the red stains left by the sourleaf he liked to chew. Amidst all that brownness, his eyes stood out; they were a pale green, squinty small, close set, and shiny bright with malice. "Only two casks," he observed. "Ser Useless wanted four."

"We were lucky to find two," said Dunk. "The drought reached the Arbor too. We heard the grapes are turning into raisins on the vines, and the ironmen have been pirating—"

"Ser?" Egg broke in. "The water's gone."

Dunk had been so intent on Bennis that he hadn't noticed. Beneath the warped wooden planks of the bridge only sand and stones remained. *That's queer. The stream was running low when we left, but it was running.*

Bennis laughed. He had two sorts of laughs. Sometimes he cackled like a chicken, and sometimes he brayed louder than Egg's mule. This was his chicken laugh. "Dried up while you was gone, I guess. A drought'll do that."

Dunk was dismayed. *Well, I won't be soaking now.* He swung down to the ground. *What's going to happen to the crops?* Half the wells in the Reach had gone dry, and all the rivers were running low, even the Blackwater Rush and the mighty Mander.

"Nasty stuff, water," Bennis said. "Drank some once, and it made me sick as a dog. Wine's better."

"Not for oats. Not for barleycorn. Not for carrots, onions, cabbages.

Even grapes need water." Dunk shook his head. "How could it go dry so quick? We've only been gone six days."

"Wasn't much water in there to start with, Dunk. Time was, I could piss me bigger streams than this one."

"Not *Dunk*," said Dunk. "I told you that." He wondered why he bothered. Bennis was a mean-mouthed man, and it pleased him to make mock. "I'm called Ser Duncan the Tall."

"By who? Your bald pup?" He looked at Egg and laughed his chicken laugh. "You're taller than when you did for Pennytree, but you still look a proper *Dunk* to me."

Dunk rubbed the back of his neck and stared down at the rocks. "What should we do?"

"Fetch home the wines, and tell Ser Useless his stream's gone dry. The Standfast well still draws, he won't go thirsty."

"Don't call him Useless." Dunk was fond of the old knight. "You sleep beneath his roof, give him some respect."

"You respect him for the both o' us, Dunk," said Bennis. "I'll call him what I will."

The silvery grey planks creaked heavily as Dunk walked out onto the bridge, to frown down at the sand and stones below. A few small brown pools glistened amongst the rocks, he saw, none larger than his hand. "Dead fish, there and there, see?" The smell of them reminded him of the dead men at the crossroads.

"I see them, ser," said Egg.

Dunk hopped down to the streambed, squatted on his heels, and turned over a stone. *Dry and warm on top, moist and muddy underneath.* "The water can't have been gone long." Standing, he flicked the stone sidearm at the bank, where it crashed through a crumbling overhang in a puff of dry, brown earth. "The soil's cracked along the banks, but soft and muddy in the middle. Those fish were alive yesterday."

"Dunk the lunk, Pennytree used to call you, I recall." Ser Bennis spat a wad of sourleaf onto the rocks. It glistened red and slimy in the sunlight. "Lunks shouldn't try and think, their heads is too bloody thick for such."

Dunk the lunk, thick as a castle wall. From Ser Arlan the words had been affectionate. He had been a kindly man, even in his scolding. In the mouth of Ser Bennis of the Brown Shield, they sounded different.

"Ser Arlan's two years dead," Dunk said, "and I'm called Ser Duncan the Tall." He was sorely tempted to put his fist through the brown knight's face, and smash those red and rotten teeth to splinters. Bennis of the Brown Shield might be a nasty piece of work, but Dunk had a good foot and a half on him, and four stone as well. He might be a lunk, but he was big. Sometimes it seemed as though he'd thumped his head on half the doors in Westeros, not to mention every beam in every inn from Dorne up to the Neck. Egg's brother Aemon had measured him in Oldtown, and found he lacked an inch of seven feet, but that was half a year ago. He might have grown since. Growing was the one thing that Dunk did really well, the old man used to say.

He went back to Thunder and mounted up again. "Egg, get on back to Standfast with the wine. I'm going to see what's happened to the water."

"Streams dry up all the time," said Bennis.

"I just want to have a look—"

"Like how you looked under that rock? Shouldn't go turning over rocks, lunk. Never know what might crawl out. We got us nice straw pallets back at Standfast. There's eggs more days than not, and not much to do but listen to Ser Useless go on about how great he used to be. Leave it be, I say. The stream went dry, that's all."

Dunk was nothing if not stubborn. "Ser Eustace is waiting on his wine," he told Egg. "Tell him where I went."

"I will, ser." Egg gave a tug on Maester's lead. The mule twitched his ears, but started off again at once. *He wants to get those wine casks off his back.* Dunk could not blame him.

The stream flowed north and east when it was flowing, so he turned Thunder south and west. He had not ridden a dozen yards before Bennis caught him. "I best come see you don't get hanged." He pushed a fresh sourleaf into his mouth. "Past that clump o' sandwillows, the whole right bank is spider land."

"I'll stay on our side." Dunk wanted no trouble with the Lady of the Coldmoat. At Standfast you heard ill things of her. *The Red Widow,* she was called, for the husbands she had put into the ground. Old Sam Stoops said she was a witch, a poisoner, and worse. Two years ago she had sent her knights across the stream to seize an Osgrey man for stealing sheep. "When m'lord rode to Coldmoat to demand him back, he was told to look for him at the bottom of the moat," Sam had said. "She'd sewn poor Dake in a bag o' rocks and sunk him. 'Twas after that Ser Eustace took Ser Bennis into service, to keep them spiders off his lands."

Thunder kept a slow, steady pace beneath the broiling sun.

The sky was blue and hard, with no hint of cloud anywhere to be seen. The course of the stream meandered around rocky knolls and forlorn willows, through bare, brown hills and fields of dead and dying grain. An hour upstream from the bridge, they found themselves riding on the edge of the small Osgrey forest called Wat's Wood. The greenery looked inviting from afar and filled Dunk's head with thoughts of shady glens and chuckling brooks, but when they reached the trees they found them thin and scraggly, with drooping limbs. Some of the great oaks were shedding leaves, and half the pines had turned as brown as Ser Bennis, with rings of dead needles girdling their trunks. *Worse and worse,* thought Dunk. *One spark, and this will all go up like tinder.*

For the moment, though, the tangled underbrush along the Chequy Water was still thick with thorny vines, nettles, and tangles of briarwhite and young willow. Rather than fight through it, they crossed the dry streambed to the Coldmoat side, where the trees had been cleared away for pasture. Amongst the parched brown grasses and faded wildflowers, a few black-nosed sheep were grazing. "Never knew an animal stupid as a sheep," Ser Bennis commented. "Think they're kin to you, lunk?" When Dunk did not reply, he laughed his chicken laugh again.

Half a league farther south, they came upon the dam.

It was not large as such things went, but it looked strong. Two stout wooden barricades had been thrown across the stream from bank to bank, made from the trunks of trees with the bark still on. The space between them was filled with rocks and earth and packed down hard. Behind the dam the flow was creeping up the banks and spilling off into a ditch that had been cut through Lady Webber's fields. Dunk stood in his stirrups for a better look. The glint of sun off water betrayed a score of lesser channels, running off in all directions like a spider's web. *They are stealing our stream.* The sight filled him with indignation, especially when it dawned on him that the trees must surely have been taken from Wat's Wood.

"See what you went and did, lunk," said Bennis. "Couldn't have it that the stream dried up, no. Might be this starts with water, but it'll end with blood. Yours and mine, most like." The brown knight drew his sword. "Well, no help for it now. There's your thrice-damned diggers. Best we put some fear in them." He raked his garron with his spurs and galloped through the grass.

Dunk had no choice but to follow. Ser Arlan's longsword rode his hip, a good straight piece of steel. *If these ditch diggers have a lick of sense, they'll run.* Thunder's hooves kicked up clods of dirt.

One man dropped his shovel at the sight of the oncoming knights, but that was all. There were a score of the diggers, short and tall, old and young, all baked brown by the sun. They formed a ragged line as Bennis slowed, clutching their spades and picks. "This is Coldmoat land," one shouted.

"And that's an Osgrey stream." Bennis pointed with his longsword. "Who put that damned dam up?"

"Maester Cerrick made it," said one young digger.

"No," an older man insisted. "The grey pup pointed some and said do this and do that, but it were us who made it."

"Then you can bloody well unmake it."

The diggers' eyes were sullen and defiant. One wiped the sweat off his brow with the back of his hand. No one spoke.

"You lot don't hear so good," said Bennis. "Do I need to lop me off an ear or two? Who's first?"

"This is Webber land." The old digger was a scrawny fellow, stooped and stubborn. "You got no right to be here. Lop off any ears and m'lady will drown you in a sack."

Bennis rode closer. "Don't see no ladies here, just some mouthy peasant." He poked the digger's bare brown chest with the point of his sword, just hard enough to draw a bead of blood.

He goes too far. "Put up your steel," Dunk warned him. "This is not his doing. This maester set them to the task."

"It's for the crops, ser," a jug-eared digger said. "The wheat was dying, the maester said. The pear trees too."

"Well, maybe them pear trees die, or maybe you do."

"Your talk don't frighten us," said the old man.

"No?" Bennis made his longsword whistle, opening the old man's cheek from ear to jaw. "I said, them pear trees die, or you do." The digger's blood ran red down one side of his face.

He should not have done that. Dunk had to swallow his rage. Bennis was on his side in this. "Get away from here," he shouted at the diggers. "Go back to your lady's castle."

"Run," Ser Bennis urged.

Three of them let go of their tools and did just that, sprinting through the grass. But another man, sunburned and brawny, hefted a pick and said, "There's only two of them."

"Shovels against swords is a fool's fight, Jorgen," the old man said, holding his face. Blood trickled through his fingers. "This won't be the end of this. Don't think it will."

"One more word, and I might be the end o' you."

"We meant no harm to you," Dunk said, to the old man's bloody face. "All we want is our water. Tell your lady that."

"Oh, we'll tell her, ser," promised the brawny man, still clutching his pick. "That we will."

On the way home they cut through the heart of Wat's Wood, grateful for the small measure of shade provided by the trees. Even so, they cooked. Supposedly there were deer in the wood, but the only living things they saw were flies. They buzzed about Dunk's face as he rode, and crept round Thunder's eyes, irritating the big warhorse no end. The air was still, suffocating. *At least in Dorne the days were dry, and at night it grew so cold I shivered in my cloak.* In the Reach the nights were hardly cooler than the days, even this far north.

When ducking down beneath an overhanging limb, Dunk plucked a leaf and crumpled it between his fingers. It fell apart like thousand-year-old parchment in his hand. "There was no need to cut that man," he told Bennis.

"A tickle on the cheek was all it was, to teach him to mind his tongue. I should've cut his bloody throat for him, only then the rest would've run like rabbits, and we'd've had to ride down the lot o' them."

"You'd kill twenty men?" Dunk said, incredulous.

"Twenty-two. That's two more'n all your fingers and your toes, lunk. You have to kill them all, else they go telling tales." They circled round a deadfall. "We should've told Ser Useless the drought dried up his little pissant stream."

"Ser *Eustace.* You would have lied to him."

"Aye, and why not? Who's to tell him any different? The flies?" Bennis grinned a wet, red grin. "Ser Useless never leaves the tower except to see the boys down in the blackberries."

"A sworn sword owes his lord the truth."

"There's truths and truths, lunk. Some don't serve." He spat. "The gods make droughts. A man can't do a bloody buggering thing about the gods. The Red Widow, though ... we tell Useless that bitch dog took his water, he'll feel honor-bound to take it back. Wait and see. He'll think he's got to *do something.*"

"He should. Our smallfolk need that water for their crops."

"*Our* smallfolk?" Ser Bennis brayed his laughter. "Was I off having a squat when Ser Useless made you his heir? How many smallfolk you figure you got? Ten? And that's counting Squinty Jeyne's half-wit son that don't know which end o' the axe to hold. Go make knights o' every one, and we'll have half as many as the Widow, and never mind her squires and her archers and the rest. You'd need both hands and both feet to count all them, and your baldhead boy's fingers and toes too."

"I don't need toes to count." Dunk was sick of the heat, the flies, and the brown knight's company. *He may have ridden with Ser Arlan once, but that was years and years ago. The man has grown mean and false and craven.* He put his heels into his horse and trotted on ahead, to put the smell behind him.

Standfast was a castle only by courtesy. Though it stood bravely atop a rocky hill and could be seen for leagues around, it was no more than a towerhouse. A partial collapse a few centuries ago had required some rebuilding, so the north and west faces were pale grey stone above the windows and the old black stone below. Turrets had been added to the roofline during the repair, but only on the sides that were rebuilt; at the other two corners crouched ancient stone grotesques, so badly abraded by wind and weather that it was hard to say what they had been. The pinewood roof was flat but badly warped and prone to leaks.

A crooked path led from the foot of the hill up to the tower, so narrow it could only be ridden single file. Dunk led the way on the ascent, with Bennis just behind. He could see Egg above them, standing on a jut of rock in his floppy straw hat.

They reined up in front of the little daub-and-wattle stable that nestled at the tower's foot, half-hidden under a misshapen heap of purple moss. The old man's grey gelding was in one of the stalls, next to Maester. Egg and Sam Stoops had gotten the wine inside, it seemed. Hens were wandering the yard. Egg trotted over. "Did you find what happened to the stream?"

"The Red Widow's dammed it up." Dunk dismounted and gave Thunder's reins to Egg. "Don't let him drink too much at once."

"No, ser. I won't."

"Boy," Ser Bennis called. "You can take my horse as well."

Egg gave him an insolent look. "I'm not your squire."

That tongue of his will get him hurt one day, Dunk thought. "You'll take his horse, or you'll get a clout in the ear."

Egg made a sullen face but did as he was bid. As he reached for the bridle, though, Ser Bennis hawked and spat. A glob of glistening red phlegm struck the boy between two toes. He gave the brown knight an icy look. "You spit on my foot, ser."

Bennis clambered to the ground. "Aye. Next time I'll spit in your face. I'll have none o' your bloody tongue."

Dunk could see the anger in the boy's eyes. "Tend to the horses, Egg," he said, before things got any worse. "We need to speak with Ser Eustace."

The only entrance into Standfast was through an oak-and-iron door twenty feet above them. The bottom steps were blocks of smooth black stone, so worn they were bowl-shaped in the middle. Higher up, they gave way to a steep wooden stair that could be swung up like a drawbridge in times of trouble. Dunk shooed the hens aside and climbed two steps at a time.

Standfast was bigger than it appeared. Its deep vaults and cellars occupied a good part of the hill on which it perched. Aboveground, the tower boasted four stories. The upper two had windows and balconies, the lower two only arrow slits. It was cooler inside, but so dim that Dunk had to let his eyes adjust. Sam Stoops's wife was on her knees by the hearth, sweeping out the ashes. "Is Ser Eustace above or below?" Dunk asked her.

"Up, ser." The old woman was so hunched that her head was lower than her shoulders. "He just come back from visiting the boys, down in the blackberries."

The boys were Eustace Osgrey's sons: Edwyn, Harrold, Addam. Edwyn and Harrold had been knights, Addam a young squire. They had died on the Redgrass Field fifteen years ago, at the end of the Blackfyre Rebellion. "They died good deaths, fighting bravely for the king," Ser Eustace told Dunk, "and I brought them home and buried them among the blackberries." His wife was buried there as well. Whenever the old man breached a new cask of wine, he went down the hill to pour each of his boys a libation. "To the king!" he would call out loudly, just before he drank.

Ser Eustace's bedchamber occupied the fourth floor of the tower, with his solar just below. That was where he would be found, Dunk knew, puttering amongst the chests and barrels. The solar's thick grey walls were hung with rusted weaponry and captured banners, prizes from battles fought long centuries ago and now remembered by no one but Ser Eustace. Half the banners were mildewed, and all were badly faded and covered with dust, their once-bright colors gone to grey and green.

Ser Eustace was scrubbing the dirt off a ruined shield with a rag when Dunk came up the steps. Bennis followed fragrant at his heels. The old knight's eyes seemed to brighten a little at the sight of Dunk. "My good giant," he declared, "and brave Ser Bennis. Come have a look at this. I found it in the bottom of that chest. A treasure, though fearfully neglected."

It was a shield, or what remained of one. That was little enough. Almost half of it had been hacked away, and the rest was grey and splintered. The iron rim was solid rust, and the wood was full of wormholes. A few flakes of paint still clung to it, but too few to suggest a sigil.

"M'lord," said Dunk. The Osgreys had not been lords for centuries, yet it pleased Ser Eustace to be styled so, echoing as it did the past glories of his house. "What is it?"

"The Little Lion's shield." The old man rubbed at the rim, and some flakes of rust came off. "Ser Wilbert Osgrey bore this at the battle where he died. I am sure you know the tale."

"No, m'lord," said Bennis. "We don't, as it happens. The *Little* Lion, did you say? What, was he a dwarf or some such?"

"Certainly not." The old knight's mustache quivered. "Ser Wilbert was a tall and powerful man, and a great knight. The name was given him in childhood, as the youngest of five brothers. In his day there were still seven kings in the Seven Kingdoms, and Highgarden and the Rock were oft at war. The green kings ruled us then, the Gardeners. They were of the blood of old Garth Greenhand, and a green hand

upon a white field was their kingly banner. Gyles the Third took his banners
east, to war against the Storm King,
and Wilbert's brothers all went
with him, for in those days the
chequy lion always flew beside
the green hand when the King of
the Reach went forth to battle.

"Yet it happened that while
King Gyles was away, the
King of the Rock saw his
chance to tear a bite out of
the Reach, so he gathered
up a host of westermen and
came down upon us. The
Osgreys were the Marshals
of the Northmarch, so it
fell to the Little Lion to
meet them. It was the fourth
King Lancel who led the Lannisters, it seems to me, or mayhaps
the fifth. Ser Wilbert blocked King Lancel's path, and bid him halt.
'Come no farther,' he said. *'You are not wanted here. I forbid you to set foot
upon the Reach.'* But the Lannister ordered all his banners forward.

"They fought for half a day, the gold lion and the chequy. The Lannister was armed with a Valyrian sword that no common steel can
match, so the Little Lion was hard-pressed, his shield in ruins. In the
end, bleeding from a dozen grievous wounds, with his own blade broken in his hand, he threw himself headlong at his foe. King Lancel cut
him near in half, the singers say, but as he died the Little Lion found
the gap in the king's armor beneath his arm and plunged his dagger
home. When their king died, the westermen turned back, and the
Reach was saved." The old man stroked the broken shield as tenderly
as if it had been a child.

"Aye, m'lord," Bennis croaked, "we could use a man like that today.
Dunk and me had a look at your stream, m'lord. Dry as a bone, and
not from no drought."

The old man set the shield aside. "Tell me." He took a seat and in-dicated that they should do the same. As the brown knight launched into the tale, he sat listening intently, with his chin up and his shoul-ders back, as upright as a lance.

In his youth, Ser Eustace Osgrey must have been the very picture of chivalry, tall and broad and handsome. Time and grief had worked their will on him, but he was still unbent, a big-boned, broad-shouldered, barrel-chested man with features as strong and sharp as some old eagle. His close-cropped hair had gone white as milk, but the thick mustache that hid his mouth remained an ashy grey. His eyebrows were the same color, the eyes beneath a paler shade of grey, and full of sadness.

They seemed to grow sadder still when Bennis touched upon the dam. "That stream has been known as the Chequy Water for a thou-sand years or more," the old knight said. "I caught fish there as a boy, and my sons all did the same. Alysanne liked to splash in the shallows on hot summer days like this." Alysanne had been his daughter, who had perished in the spring. "It was on the banks of the Chequy Water that I kissed a girl for the first time. A cousin, she was, my uncle's youngest daughter, of the Osgreys of Leafy Lake. They are all gone now, even her." His mustache quivered. "This cannot be borne, sers. The woman will not have my water. She will not have my *chequy* water."

"Dam's built strong, m'lord," Ser Bennis warned. "Too strong for me and Ser Dunk to pull down in an hour, even with the baldhead boy to help. We'll need ropes and picks and axes, and a dozen men. And that's just for the work, not for the fighting."

Ser Eustace stared at the Little Lion's shield. Dunk cleared his throat. "M'lord, as to that, when we came upon the diggers, well ..."

"Dunk, don't trouble m'lord with trifles," said Bennis. "I taught one fool a lesson, that was all."

Ser Eustace looked up sharply. "What sort of lesson?"

"With my sword, as it were. A little claret on his cheek, that's all it were, m'lord."

The old knight looked long at him. "That ... that was ill considered, ser. The woman has a spider's heart. She murdered three of her hus-bands. And all her brothers died in swaddling clothes. Five, there were. Or six, mayhaps, I don't recall. They stood between her and the castle. She would whip the skin off any peasant who displeased her, I do not doubt, but for *you* to cut one . . . no, she will not suffer such an insult. Make no mistake. She will come for you, as she came for Lem."

"Dake, m'lord," Ser Bennis said. "Begging your lordly pardon, you knew him and I never did, but his name were Dake."

"If it please m'lord, I could go to Goldengrove and tell Lord Rowan of this dam," said Dunk. Rowan was the old knight's liege lord. The Red Widow held her lands of him as well.

"Rowan? No, look for no help there. Lord Rowan's sister wed Lord Wyman's cousin Wendell, so he is kin to the Red Widow. Besides, he loves me not. Ser Duncan, on the morrow you must make the rounds of all my villages and roust out every able-bodied man of fighting age. I am old, but I am not dead. The woman will soon find that the chequy lion still has claws!"

Two, Dunk thought glumly, *and I am one of them.*

Ser Eustace's lands supported three small villages, none more than a handful of hovels, sheepfolds, and pigs. The largest boasted a thatched one-room sept with crude pictures of the Seven scratched upon the walls in charcoal. Mudge, a stoop-backed old swineherd who'd once been to Oldtown, led devotions there every seventh day. Twice a year a real septon came through to forgive sins in the Mother's name. The smallfolk were glad of the forgiveness, but hated the septon's visits all the same since they were required to feed him.

They seemed no more pleased by the sight of Dunk and Egg. Dunk was known in the villages, if only as Ser Eustace's new knight, but not so much as a cup of water was offered him. Most of the men were in the fields, so it was largely women and children who crept out of the hovels at their coming, along with a few grandfathers too infirm for work. Egg bore the Osgrey banner, the chequy lion green and gold, rampant upon its field of white. "We come from Standfast with Ser Eustace's summons," Dunk told the villagers. "Every able-bodied man between the ages of fifteen and fifty is commanded to assemble at the tower on the morrow."

"Is it war?" asked one thin woman, with two children hiding behind her skirts and a babe sucking at her breast. "Is the black dragon come again?"

"There are no dragons in this, black or red," Dunk told her. "This is between the chequy lion and the spiders. The Red Widow has taken your water."

The woman nodded though she looked askance when Egg took off his hat to fan his face. "That boy got no hair. He sick?"

"It's *shaven*," said Egg. He put the hat back on, turned Maester's head, and rode off slowly.

The boy is in a prickly mood today. He had hardly said a word since they set out. Dunk gave Thunder a touch of the spur and soon caught the mule. "Are you angry that I did not take your part against Ser Bennis yesterday?" he asked his sullen squire, as they made for the next village. "I like the man no more than you, but he *is* a knight. You should speak to him with courtesy."

"I'm your squire, not his," the boy said. "He's dirty and mean-mouthed, and he pinches me."

If he had an inkling who you were, he'd piss himself before he laid a finger on you. "He used to pinch me too." Dunk had forgotten that till Egg's words brought it back. Ser Bennis and Ser Arlan had been amongst a party of knights hired by a Dornish merchant to see him safe from Lannisport to the Prince's Pass. Dunk had been no older than Egg, though taller. *He would pinch me under the arm so hard he'd leave a bruise. His fingers felt like iron pincers, but I never told Ser Arlan.* One of the other knights had vanished near Stoney Sept, and it was bruited about that Bennis had gutted him in a quarrel. "If he pinches you again, tell me and I'll end it. Till then, it does not cost you much to tend his horse."

"Someone has to," Egg agreed. "Bennis never brushes him. He never cleans his stall. He hasn't even *named* him!"

"Some knights never name their horses," Dunk told him. "That way, when they die in battle, the grief is not so hard to bear. There are always more horses to be had, but it's hard to lose a faithful friend." *Or so the old man said, but he never took his own counsel. He named every horse he ever owned.* So had Dunk. "We'll see how many men turn up at the tower ... but whether it's five or fifty, you'll need to do for them as well."

Egg looked indignant. "I have to serve *smallfolk*?"

"Not serve. Help. We need to turn them into fighters." *If the widow gives us time enough.* "If the gods are good, a few will have done some soldiering before, but most will be green as summer grass, more used to holding hoes than spears. Even so, a day may come when our lives depend on them. How old were you when you first took up a sword?"

"I was little, ser. The sword was made from wood."

"Common boys fight with wooden swords too, only theirs are sticks and broken branches. Egg, these men may seem fools to you. They won't know the proper names for bits of armor, or the arms of the great houses, or which king it was who abolished the lord's right to the first night ... but treat them with respect all the same. You are a squire born of noble blood, but you are still a boy. Most of them will be men grown. A man has his pride, no matter how low-born he may be. You would seem just as lost and stupid in their villages. And if you doubt that, go hoe a row and shear a sheep, and tell me the names of all the weeds and wildflowers in Wat's Wood."

The boy considered for a moment. "I could teach them the arms of the great houses, and how Queen Alysanne convinced King Jaehaerys to abolish the first night. And they could teach me which weeds are best for making poisons, and whether those green berries are safe to eat."

"They could," Dunk agreed, "but before you get to King Jaehaerys, you'd best help us teach them how to use a spear. And don't go eating anything that Maester won't."

The next day a dozen would-be warriors found their way to Standfast to assemble among the chickens. One was too old, two were too young, and one skinny boy turned out to be a skinny girl. Those Dunk sent back to their villages, leaving eight: three Wats, two Wills, a Lem, a Pate, and Big Rob the lackwit. *A sorry lot,* he could not help but think. The strapping handsome peasant boys who won the hearts of highborn maidens in the songs were nowhere to be seen. Each man was dirtier than the last. Lem was fifty if he was a day, and Pate had weepy eyes; they were the only two who had ever soldiered before. Both had been gone with Ser Eustace and his sons to fight in the Blackfyre Rebellion. The other six were as green as Dunk had feared. All eight had lice. Two of the Wats were brothers. "Guess your mother didn't know no other name," Bennis said, cackling.

As far as arms went, they brought a scythe, three hoes, an old knife, some stout wooden clubs. Lem had a sharpened stick that might serve for a spear, and one of the Wills allowed that he was good at chucking rocks. "Well and good," Bennis said, "we got us a bloody trebuchet." After that the man was known as Treb.

"Are any of you skilled with a longbow?" Dunk asked them.

The men scuffed at the dirt while hens pecked the ground around them. Pate of the weepy eyes finally answered. "Begging your pardon, ser, but m'lord don't permit us longbows. Osgrey deers is for the chequy lions, not the likes o' us."

"We will get swords and helms and chain mail?" the youngest of the three Wats wanted to know.

"Why, sure you will," said Bennis, "just as soon as you kill one o' the widow's knights and strip his bloody corpse. Make sure you stick your arm up his horse's arse too, that's where you'll find his silver." He pinched young Wat beneath his arm until the lad squealed in pain, then marched the whole lot of them off to Wat's Wood to cut some spears.

When they came back, they had eight fire-hardened spears of wildly unequal length, and crude shields of woven branches. Ser Bennis had made himself a spear as well, and he showed them how to thrust with the point and use the shaft to parry . . . and where to put the point to kill. "The belly and the throat are best, I find." He pounded his fist against his chest. "Right there's the heart, that will do the job as well. Trouble is, the ribs is in the way. The belly's nice and soft. Gutting's slow, but certain. Never knew a man to live when his guts was hanging out. Now if some fool goes and turns his back on you, put your point between his shoulder blades or through his kidney. That's here. They don't live long once you prick 'em in the kidney."

Having three Wats in the company caused confusion when Bennis was trying to tell them what to do. "We should give them village names, ser," Egg suggested, "like Ser Arlan of Pennytree, your old master." That might have worked, only their villages had no names either. "Well," said Egg, "we could call them for their crops, ser." One village sat amongst beanfields, one planted mostly barleycorn, and the third cultivated rows of cabbages, carrots, onions, turnips, and melons. No one wanted to be a Cabbage or a Turnip, so the last lot became the Melons. They ended up with four Barleycorns, two Melons, and two Beans. As the brothers Wat were both Barleycorns, some further distinction was required. When the younger brother made mention of once having fallen down the village well, Bennis dubbed him "Wet Wat," and that was that. The men were thrilled to have been given "lord's names," save for Big Rob, who could not seem to remember whether he was a Bean or a Barleycorn.

Once all of them had names and spears, Ser Eustace emerged from Standfast to address them. The old knight stood outside the tower door, wearing his mail and plate beneath a long, woolen surcoat that age had turned more yellow than white. On front and back it bore the chequy lion, sewn in little squares of green and gold. "Lads," he said, "you all remember Dake. The Red Widow threw him in a sack and drowned him. She took his life, and now she thinks to take our water too, the Chequy Water that nourishes our crops … but she will not!" He raised his sword above his head. "For Osgrey!" he said ringingly. "For Standfast!"

"Osgrey!" Dunk echoed. Egg and the recruits took up the shout. *"Osgrey! Osgrey! For Standfast!"*

Dunk and Bennis drilled the little company amongst the pigs and chickens, while Ser Eustace watched from the balcony above. Sam Stoops had stuffed some old sacks with soiled straw. Those became their foes. The recruits began practicing their spear work as Bennis bellowed at them. "Stick and twist and rip it free. Stick and twist and rip, but *get the damn thing out*! You'll be wanting it soon enough for the next one. Too slow, Treb, too damn slow. If you can't do it quicker, go back to chucking rocks. Lem, get your weight behind your thrust. There's a boy. And in and out and in and out. Fuck 'em with it, that's the way, in and out, rip 'em, rip 'em, *rip 'em*."

When the sacks had been torn to pieces by half a thousand spear thrusts and all the straw spilled out onto the ground, Dunk donned his mail and plate and took up a wooden sword to see how the men would fare against a livelier foe.

Not too well, was the answer. Only Treb was quick enough to get a spear past Dunk's shield, and he only did it once. Dunk turned one clumsy lurching thrust after another, pushed their spears aside, and bulled in close. If his sword had been steel instead of pine, he would have slain each of them half a dozen times. "You're *dead* once I get past your point," he warned them, hammering at their legs and arms to drive the lesson home. Treb and Lem and Wet Wat soon learned how to give ground, at least. Big Rob dropped his spear and ran, and Bennis had to chase him down and drag him back in tears. The end of the afternoon saw the lot of them all bruised and battered, with fresh blisters rising on their callused hands from where they gripped the spears. Dunk bore no marks himself, but he was half-drowned in sweat by the time Egg helped him peel his armor off.

As the sun was going down, Dunk marched their little company down into the cellar and forced them all to have a bath, even those who'd had one just last winter. Afterward Sam Stoops's wife had bowls of stew for all, thick with carrots, onions, and barley. The men were bone tired, but to hear them talk, every one of them would soon be twice as deadly as a Kingsguard knight. They could hardly wait to prove their valor. Ser Bennis egged them on by telling them of the joys of the soldier's life—loot and women, chiefly. The two old hands agreed with him. Lem had brought back a knife and a pair of fine boots from the Blackfyre Rebellion, to hear him tell it; the boots were too small for him to wear, but he had them hanging on his wall. And Pate could not say enough about some of the camp followers he'd known following the dragon.

Sam Stoops had set them up with eight straw pallets in the undercroft, so once their bellies were filled they all went off to sleep. Bennis lingered long enough to give Dunk a look of disgust. "Ser Useless should have fucked a few more peasant wenches while he still had a bit o' sap left in them old sad balls o' his," he said. "If he'd sowed himself a nice crop o' bastard boys back then, might be we'd have some soldiers now."

"They seem no worse than any other peasant levy." Dunk had marched with a few such while squiring for Ser Arlan.

"Aye," Ser Bennis said. "In a fortnight they might stand their own, 'gainst some other lot o' peasants. Knights, though?" He shook his head and spat.

Standfast's well was in the undercellar, in a dank chamber walled in stone and earth. It was there that Sam Stoops's wife soaked and scrubbed and beat the clothes before carrying them up to the roof to dry. The big stone washtub was also used for baths. Bathing required drawing water from the well bucket by bucket, heating it over the hearth in a big, iron kettle, emptying the kettle into the tub, then starting the whole process once again. It took four buckets to fill the kettle, and three kettles to fill the tub. By the time the last kettle was hot, the water from the first had cooled to lukewarm. Ser Bennis had been heard to say that the whole thing was too much bloody bother, which was why he crawled with lice and fleas and smelled like a bad cheese.

Dunk at least had Egg to help him when he felt in dire need of a good wash, as he did tonight. The lad drew the water in a glum silence and hardly spoke as it was heating. "Egg?" Dunk asked as the last kettle was coming to a boil. "Is aught amiss?" When Egg made no reply, he said, "Help me with the kettle."

Together they wrestled it from hearth to tub, taking care not to splash themselves. "Ser," the boy asked, "what do you think Ser Eustace means to do?"

"Tear down the dam, and fight off the widow's men if they try to stop us." He spoke loudly, so as to be heard above the splashing of the bathwater. Steam rose in a white curtain as they poured, bringing a flush to his face.

"Their shields are woven wood, ser. A lance could punch right through them, or a crossbow bolt."

"We may find some bits of armor for them, when they're ready." That was the best they could hope for.

"They might be killed, ser. Wet Wat is still half a boy. Will Barleycorn is to be married the next time the septon comes. And Big Rob doesn't even know his left foot from his right."

Dunk let the empty kettle thump down onto the hard-packed earthen floor. "Roger of Pennytree was younger than Wet Wat when he died on the Redgrass Field. There were men in your father's host who'd just been married too, and other men who'd never even kissed a girl. There were hundreds who didn't know their left foot from their right, maybe thousands."

"That was *different*," Egg insisted. "That was war."

"So is this. The same thing, only smaller."

"Smaller and *stupider*, ser."

"That's not for you or me to say," Dunk told him. "It's their duty to go to war when Ser Eustace summons them ... and to die, if need be."

"Then we shouldn't have named them, ser. It will only make the grief harder for us when they die." He screwed up his face. "If we used my boot—"

"No." Dunk stood on one leg to pull his own boot off.

"Yes, but my father—"

"No." The second boot went the way of the first.

"We—"

"No." Dunk pulled his sweat-stained tunic up over his head and tossed it at Egg. "Ask Sam Stoops's wife to wash that for me."

"I will, ser, but—"

"No, I said. Do you need a clout in the ear to help you hear better?" He unlaced his breeches. Underneath was only him; it was too hot for smallclothes. "It's good that you're concerned for Wat and Wat and Wat and the rest of them, but the boot is only meant for dire need." *How many eyes does Lord Bloodraven have? A thousand eyes, and one.* "What did your father tell you when he sent you off to squire for me?"

"To keep my hair shaved or dyed, and tell no man my true name," the boy said, with obvious reluctance.

Egg had served Dunk for a good year and a half, though some days it seemed like twenty. They had climbed the Prince's Pass together and crossed the deep sands of Dorne, both red and white. A poleboat had taken them down the Greenblood to the Planky Town, where they took passage for Oldtown on the galleas *White Lady*. They had slept in stables, inns, and ditches, broken bread with holy brothers, whores, and mummers, and chased down a hundred puppet shows. Egg had kept Dunk's horse groomed, his longsword sharp, his mail free of rust. He had been as good a companion as any man could wish for, and the hedge knight had come to think of him almost as a little brother.

He isn't, though. This egg had been hatched of dragons, not of chickens. *Egg* might be a hedge knight's squire, but Aegon of House Targaryen was the fourth and youngest son of Maekar, Prince of Summerhall, himself the fourth son of the late King Daeron the Good, the Second of His Name, who'd sat the Iron Throne for five-and-twenty years until the Great Spring Sickness took him off.

"So far as most folk are concerned, Aegon Targaryen went back to Summerhall with his brother Daeron after the tourney at Ashford Meadow," Dunk reminded the boy. "Your father did not want it known that you were wandering the Seven Kingdoms with some hedge knight. So let's hear no more about your boot."

A look was all the answer that he got. Egg had big eyes, and somehow his shaven head made them look even larger. In the dimness of the lamplit cellar they looked black, but in better light their true color could be seen—deep and dark and purple.

Valyrian eyes, thought Dunk. In Westeros, few but the blood of the dragon had eyes that color or hair that shone like beaten gold and strands of silver woven all together.

When they'd been poling down the Greenblood, the orphan girls had made a game of rubbing Egg's shaven head for luck. It made the boy blush redder than a pomegranate. "Girls are so *stupid,*" he would say. "The next one who touches me is going into the river." Dunk had to tell him, "Then *I'll* be touching you. I'll give you such a clout in the ear you'll be hearing bells for a moon's turn." That only goaded the boy to further insolence. "Better bells than stupid *girls,*" he insisted, but he never threw anyone into the river.

Dunk stepped into the tub and eased himself down until the water covered him up to his chin. It was still scalding hot on top, though cooler farther down. He clenched his teeth to keep from yelping. If he did the boy would laugh. Egg *liked* his bathwater scalding hot.

"Do you need more water boiled, ser?"

"This will serve." Dunk rubbed at his arms and watched the dirt come off in long grey clouds. "Fetch me the soap. Oh, and the long-handled scrub brush too." Thinking about Egg's hair had made him remember that his own was filthy. He took a deep breath and slid beneath the water to give it a good soak. When he emerged again, sloshing, Egg was standing beside the tub with the soap and long-handled horsehair brush in hand. "You have hairs on your cheek," Dunk observed, as he took the soap from him. "Two of them. There, below your ear. Make sure you get them the next time you shave your head."

"I will, ser." The boy seemed pleased by the discovery.

No doubt he thinks a bit of beard makes him a man. Dunk had thought the same when he first found some fuzz growing on his upper lip. *I tried to shave with my dagger, and almost nicked my nose off.* "Go and get some sleep now," he told Egg. "I won't have any more need of you till morning."

It took a long while to scrub all the dirt and sweat away. Afterward, he put the soap aside, stretched out as much as he was able, and closed his eyes. The water had cooled by then. After the savage heat of the day, it was a welcome relief. He soaked till his feet and fingers were all wrinkled up and the water had gone grey and cold, and only then reluctantly climbed out.

Though he and Egg had been given thick straw pallets down in the cellar, Dunk preferred to sleep up on the roof. The air was fresher there, and sometimes there was a breeze. It was not as though he need have much fear of rain. The next time it rained on them up there would be the first.

Egg was asleep by the time Dunk reached the roof. He lay on his back with his hands behind his head and stared up at the sky. The stars were everywhere, thousands and thousands of them. It reminded him of a night at Ashford Meadow, before the tourney started. He had seen a falling star that night. Falling stars were supposed to bring you luck, so he'd told Tanselle to paint it on his shield, but Ashford had been anything but lucky for him. Before the tourney ended, he had almost lost a hand and a foot, and three good men had lost their lives. *I gained a squire, though. Egg was with me when I rode away from Ashford. That was the only good thing to come of all that happened.*

He hoped that no stars fell tonight.

* * *

There were red mountains in the distance and white sands beneath his feet. Dunk was digging, plunging a spade into the hot, dry earth and flinging the fine sand back over his shoulder. He was making a hole. *A grave,* he thought, *a grave for hope.* A trio of Dornish knights stood watching, making mock of him in quiet voices. Farther off the merchants waited with their mules and wayns and sand sledges. They wanted to be off, but he could not leave until he'd buried Chestnut. He would not leave his old friend to the snakes and scorpions and sand dogs.

The stot had died on the long, thirsty crossing between the Prince's Pass and Vaith, with Egg upon his back. His front legs just seemed to fold up under him, and he knelt right down, rolled onto his side, and died. His carcass sprawled beside the hole. Already it was stiff. Soon it would begin to smell.

Dunk was weeping as he dug, to the amusement of the Dornish knights. "Water is precious in the waste," one said, "you ought not to waste it, ser." The other chuckled and said, "Why do you weep? It was only a horse, and a poor one."

Chestnut, Dunk thought, digging, *his name was Chestnut, and he bore me on his back for years, and never bucked or bit.* The old stot had looked a sorry thing beside the sleek sand steeds that the Dornishmen were riding, with their elegant heads, long necks, and flowing manes, but he had given all he had to give.

"Weeping for a swaybacked stot?" Ser Arlan said, in his old man's voice. "Why, lad, you never wept for me, who put you on his back." He gave a little laugh, to show he meant no harm by the reproach. "That's Dunk the lunk, thick as a castle wall."

"He shed no tears for me, either," said Baelor Breakspear from the grave, "though I was his prince, the hope of Westeros. The gods never meant for me to die so young."

"My father was only nine-and-thirty," said Prince Valarr. "He had it in him to be a great king, the greatest since Aegon the Dragon." He looked at Dunk with cool blue eyes. "Why would the gods take him, and leave *you*?" The Young Prince had his father's light brown hair, but a streak of silver-gold ran through it.

You are dead, Dunk wanted to scream, *you are all three dead, why won't you leave me be?* Ser Arlan had died of a chill, Prince Baelor of the blow his brother dealt him during Dunk's trial of seven, his son Valarr during the Great Spring Sickness. *I am not to blame for that. We were in Dorne, we never even knew.*

"You are mad," the old man told him. "We will dig no hole for you, when you kill yourself with this folly. In the deep sands a man must hoard his water."

"Begone with you, Ser Duncan," Valarr said. "Begone."

Egg helped him with the digging. The boy had no spade, only his hands, and the sand flowed back into the grave as fast as they could fling it out. It was like trying to dig a hole in the sea. *I have to keep digging,* Dunk told himself, though his back and shoulders ached from the effort. *I have to bury him down deep where the sand dogs cannot find him. I have to . . .*

". . . die?" said Big Rob the simpleton from the bottom of the grave. Lying there, so still and cold, with a ragged red wound gaping in his belly, he did not look very big at all.

Dunk stopped and stared at him. "You're not dead. You're down sleeping in the cellar." He looked to Ser Arlan for help. "Tell him, ser," he pleaded, "tell him to get out of the grave."

Only it was not Ser Arlan of Pennytree standing over him at all, it was Ser Bennis of the Brown Shield. The brown knight only cackled. "Dunk the lunk," he said, "gutting's slow, but certain. Never knew a man to live with his entrails hanging out." Red froth bubbled on his lips. He turned and spat, and the white sands drank it down. Treb was standing behind him with an arrow in his eye, weeping slow, red tears. And there was Wet Wat too, his head cut near in half, with old Lem and red-eyed Pate and all the rest. They had all been chewing sourleaf with Bennis, Dunk thought at first, but then he realized that it was blood trickling from their mouths. *Dead,* he thought, *all dead,* and the brown knight brayed. "Aye, so best get busy. You've more graves to dig, lunk. Eight for them and one for me and one for old Ser Useless, and one last one for your baldhead boy."

The spade slipped from Dunk's hands. "Egg," he cried, "run! We have to *run!*" But the sands were giving way beneath their feet. When the boy tried to scramble from the hole, its crumbling sides gave way and collapsed. Dunk saw the sands wash over Egg, burying him as he opened his mouth to shout. He tried to fight his way to him, but the sands were rising all around him, pulling him down into the grave, filling his mouth, his nose, his eyes ...

Come the break of day, Ser Bennis set about teaching their recruits to form a shield wall. He lined the eight of them up shoulder to shoulder, with their shields touching and their spear points poking through like long, sharp, wooden teeth. Then Dunk and Egg mounted up and charged them.

Maester refused to go within ten feet of the spears and stopped abruptly, but Thunder had been trained for this. The big warhorse pounded straight ahead, gathering speed. Hens ran beneath his legs and flapped away screeching. Their panic must have been contagious. Once more Big Rob was the first to drop his spear and run, leaving a gap in the middle of the wall. Instead of closing up, Standfast's other warriors joined the flight. Thunder trod upon their discarded shields before Dunk could rein him up. Woven branches cracked and splintered beneath his iron-shod hooves. Ser Bennis rattled off a pungent string of curses as chickens and peasants scattered in all directions. Egg fought manfully to hold his laughter in but finally lost the battle.

"Enough of that." Dunk drew Thunder to a halt, unfastened his helm, and tore it off. "If they do that in a battle, it will get the whole lot of them killed." *And you and me as well, most like.* The morning was already hot, and he felt as soiled and sticky as if he'd never bathed at all. His head was pounding, and he could not forget the dream he dreamed the night before. *It never happened that way,* he tried to tell himself. *It wasn't like that.* Chestnut had died on the long dry ride to Vaith, that part was true. He and Egg rode double until Egg's brother gave them Maester. The rest of it, though ...

I never wept. I might have wanted to, but I never did. He had wanted to bury the horse as well, but the Dornishmen would not wait. "Sand dogs must eat and feed their pups," one of the Dornish knights told him as he helped Dunk strip the stot of saddle and bridle. "His flesh will feed the dogs or feed the sands. In a year, his bones will be scoured clean. This is Dorne, my friend." Remembering, Dunk could not help but wonder who would feed on Wat's flesh, and Wat's, and Wat's. *Maybe there are chequy fish down beneath the Chequy Water.*

He rode Thunder back to the tower and dismounted. "Egg, help Ser Bennis round them up and get them back here." He shoved his helm at Egg and strode to the steps.

Ser Eustace met him in the dimness of his solar. "That was not well-done."

"No, m'lord," said Dunk. "They will not serve." *A sworn sword owes his liege service and obedience, but this is madness.*

"It was their first time. Their fathers and brothers were as bad or worse when they began their training. My sons worked with them, before we went to help the king. Every day, for a good fortnight. They made soldiers of them."

"And when the battle came, m'lord?" Dunk asked. "How did they fare then? How many of them came home with you?"

The old knight looked long at him. "Lem," he said at last, "and Pate, and Dake. Dake foraged for us. He was as fine a forager as I ever knew. We never marched on empty bellies. Three came back, ser. Three and me." His mustache quivered. "It may take longer than a fortnight."

"M'lord," said Dunk, "the woman could be here upon the morrow, with all her men." *They are good lads,* he thought, *but they will soon be dead lads if they go up against the knights of Coldmoat.* "There must be some other way."

"Some other way." Ser Eustace ran his fingers lightly across the Little Lion's shield. "I will have no justice from Lord Rowan, nor this king ..." He grasped Dunk by the forearm. "It comes to me that in days gone by, when the green kings ruled, you could pay a man a blood price if you had slain one of his animals or peasants."

"A blood price?" Dunk was dubious.

"Some other way, you said. I have some coin laid by. It was only a little claret on the cheek, Ser Bennis says. I could pay the man a silver stag, and three to the woman for the insult. I could, and would ... if she would take the dam down." The old man frowned. "I cannot go to her, however. Not at Coldmoat." A fat black fly buzzed around his head and lighted on his arm. "The castle was ours once. Did you know that, Ser Duncan?"

"Aye, m'lord." Sam Stoops had told him.

"For a thousand years before the Conquest, we were the Marshals of the Northmarch. A score of lesser lordlings did us fealty, and a hundred landed knights. We had four castles then, and watchtowers on the hills to warn of the coming of our enemies. Coldmoat was the greatest of our seats. Lord Perwyn Osgrey raised it. Perwyn the Proud, they called him.

"After the Field of Fire, Highgarden passed from kings to stewards and the Osgreys dwindled and diminished. 'Twas Aegon's son King Maegor who took Coldmoat from us, when Lord Ormond Osgrey spoke out against his supression of the Stars and Swords, as the Poor Fellows and the Warrior's Sons were called." His voice had grown hoarse. "There is a chequy lion carved into the stone above the gates of Coldmoat. My father showed it to me, the first time he took me with him to call on old Reynard Webber. I showed it to my own sons in turn. Addam ... Addam served at Coldmoat, as a page and squire, and a ... a certain ... fondness grew up between him and Lord Wyman's daughter. So one winter day I donned my richest raiment and went to Lord Wyman to propose a marriage. His refusal was courteous, but as I left I heard him laughing with Ser Lucas Inchfield. I never returned to Coldmoat after that, save once, when that woman presumed to carry off one of mine own. When they told me to seek for poor Lem at the bottom of the moat—"

"Dake," said Dunk. "Bennis says his name was Dake."

"Dake?" The fly was creeping down his sleeve, pausing to rub its legs together the way flies do. Ser Eustace shooed it away and rubbed his lip beneath his mustache. "Dake. That was what I said. A staunch fellow, I recall him well. He foraged for us, during the war. We never marched on empty bellies. When Ser Lucas informed me of what had been done to my poor Dake, I swore a holy vow that I would never again set foot inside that castle, unless to take possession. So you see, I cannot go there, Ser Duncan. Not to pay the blood price, nor for any other reason. I *cannot.*"

Dunk understood. "I could go, m'lord. I swore no vows."

"You are a good man, Ser Duncan. A brave knight, and true." Ser Eustace gave Dunk's arm a squeeze. "Would that the gods had spared my Alysanne. You are the sort of man I had always hoped that she might marry. A true knight, Ser Duncan. A true knight."

Dunk was turning red. "I will tell Lady Webber what you said, about the blood price, but ..."

"You will save Ser Bennis from Dake's fate. I know it. I am no mean judge of men, and you are the true steel. You will give them pause, ser. The very sight of you. When that woman sees that Standfast has such a champion, she may well take down that dam of her own accord."

Dunk did not know what to say to that. He knelt. "M'lord. I will go upon the morrow, and do the best I can."

"On the morrow." The fly came circling back and lit upon Ser Eustace's left hand. He raised his right and smashed it flat. "Yes. On the morrow."

"*Another* bath?" Egg said, dismayed. "You washed yesterday."

"And then I spent a day in armor, swimming in my sweat. Close your lips and fill the kettle."

"You washed the night Ser Eustace took us into service," Egg pointed out. "And last night, and now. That's *three times,* ser."

"I need to treat with a highborn lady. Do you want me to turn up before her high seat smelling like Ser Bennis?"

"You would have to roll in a tub of Maester's droppings to smell as bad as that, ser." Egg filled the kettle. "Sam Stoops says the castellan at Coldmoat is as big as you are. Lucas Inchfield is his name, but he's called the Longinch for his size. Do you think he's as big as you are, ser?"

"No." It had been years since Dunk had met anyone as tall as he was. He took the kettle and hung it above the fire.

"Will you fight him?"

"No." Dunk almost wished it had been otherwise. He might not be the greatest fighter in the realm, but size and strength could make up for many lacks. *Not for a lack of wits, though.* He was no good with words, and worse with women. This giant Lucas Longinch did not daunt him half so much as the prospect of facing the Red Widow. "I'm going to talk to the Red Widow, that's all."

"What will you tell her, ser?"

"That she has to take the dam down." *You must take down your dam, m'lady, or else . . .* "Ask her to take down the dam, I mean." *Please give back our Chequy Water.* "If it pleases her." *A little water, m'lady, if it please you.* Ser Eustace would not want him to beg. *How do I say it, then?*

The water soon began to steam and bubble. "Help me lug this to the tub," Dunk told the boy. Together they lifted the kettle from the hearth and crossed the cellar to the big wooden tub. "I don't know how to talk with highborn ladies," he confessed as they were pouring. "We both might have been killed in Dorne, on account of what I said to Lady Vaith."

"Lady Vaith was mad," Egg reminded him, "but you could have been more gallant. Ladies like it when you're gallant. If you were to rescue the Red Widow the way you rescued that puppet girl from Aerion . . ."

"Aerion's in Lys, and the widow's not in want of rescuing." He did not want to talk of Tanselle. *Tanselle Too-Tall was her name, but she was not too tall for me.*

"Well," the boy said, "some knights sing gallant songs to their ladies, or play them tunes upon a lute."

"I have no lute." Dunk looked morose. "And that night I drank too much in the Planky Town, you told me I sang like an ox in a mud wallow."

"I had forgotten, ser."

"How could you forget?"

"You told me to forget, ser," said Egg, all innocence. "You told me I'd get a clout in the ear the next time I mentioned it."

"There will be no singing." Even if he had the voice for it, the only song Dunk knew all the way through was "The Bear, the Bear, and the Maiden Fair." He doubted that would do much to win over Lady Webber. The kettle was steaming once again. They wrestled it over to the tub and upended it.

Egg drew water to fill it for the third time, then clambered back onto the well. "You'd best not take any food or drink at Coldmoat, ser. The Red Widow poisoned all her husbands."

"I'm not like to marry her. She's a highborn lady, and I'm Dunk of Flea Bottom, remember?" He frowned. "Just how many husbands has she had, do you know?"

"Four," said Egg, "but no children. Whenever she gives birth, a demon comes by night to carry off the issue. Sam Stoops's wife says she sold her babes unborn to the Lord of the Seven Hells, so he'd teach her his black arts."

"Highborn ladies don't meddle with the black arts. They dance and sing and do embroidery."

"Maybe she dances with demons and embroiders evil spells," Egg said with relish. "And how would you know what highborn ladies do, ser? Lady Vaith is the only one you ever knew."

That was insolent, but true. "Might be I don't know any highborn ladies, but I know a boy who's asking for a good clout in the ear." Dunk rubbed the back of his neck. A day in chain mail always left it hard as wood. "You've known queens and princesses. Did they dance with demons and practice the black arts?"

"Lady Shiera does. Lord Bloodraven's paramour. She bathes in blood to keep her beauty. And once my sister Rhae put a love potion in my drink, so I'd marry her instead of my sister Daella."

Egg spoke as if such incest was the most natural thing in the world. *For him it is.* The Targaryens had been marrying brother to sister for hundreds of years, to keep the blood of the dragon pure. Though the last actual dragon had died before Dunk was born, the dragonkings went on. *Maybe the gods don't mind them marrying their sisters.* "Did the potion work?" Dunk asked.

"It would have," said Egg, "but I spit it out. I don't want a wife, I want to be a knight of the Kingsguard and live only to serve and defend the king. The Kingsguard are sworn not to wed."

"That's a noble thing, but when you're older you may find you'd

"Wear the one you wore today. I'll bring the other, and you can change when you reach the castle."

"*Before* I reach the castle. I'd look a fool, changing clothes on the drawbridge. And who said you were coming with me?"

"A knight is more impressive with a squire in attendance."

That was true. The boy had a good sense of such things. *He should. He served two years as a page at King's Landing.* Even so, Dunk was reluctant to take him into danger. He had no notion what sort of welcome awaited him at Coldmoat. If this Red Widow was as dangerous as they said, he could end up in a crow cage, like those two men they had seen upon the road. "You will stay and help Bennis with the smallfolk," he told Egg. "And don't give me that sullen look." He kicked his breeches off and climbed into the tub of steaming water. "Go on and get to sleep now, and let me have my bath. You're not going, and that's the end of it."

Egg was up and gone when Dunk awoke, with the light of the morning sun in his face. *Gods be good, how can it be so hot so soon?* He sat up and stretched, yawning, then climbed to his feet and stumbled sleepily down to the well, where he lit a fat tallow candle, splashed some cold water on his face, and dressed.

When he stepped out into the sunlight, Thunder was waiting by the stable, saddled and bridled. Egg was waiting too, with Maester, his mule.

The boy had put his boots on. For once he looked a proper squire, in a handsome doublet of green-and-gold checks and a pair of tight white woolen breeches. "The breeches were torn in the seat, but Sam Stoops's wife sewed them up for me," he announced.

"The clothes were Addam's," said Ser Eustace, as he led his own grey gelding from his stall. A chequy lion adorned the frayed silk cloak that flowed from the old man's shoulders. "The doublet is a trifle musty from the trunk, but it should serve. A knight is more impressive with a squire in attendance, so I have decided that Egg should accompany you to Coldmoat."

Outwitted by a boy of ten. Dunk looked at Egg and silently mouthed the words *clout in the ear.* The boy grinned.

"I have something for you as well, Ser Duncan. Come." Ser Eustace produced a cloak and shook it out with a flourish.

It was white wool, bordered with squares of green satin and cloth-of-gold. A woolen cloak was the last thing he needed in such heat, but when Ser Eustace draped it about his shoulders, Dunk saw the pride on his face, and found himself unable to refuse. "Thank you, m'lord."

"It suits you well. Would that I could give you more." The old man's mustache twitched. "I sent Sam Stoops down into the cellar to search through my sons' things, but Edwyn and Harrold were smaller men, thinner in the chest and much shorter in the leg. None of what they left would fit you, sad to say."

"The cloak is enough, m'lord. I won't shame it."

"I do not doubt that." He gave his horse a pat. "I thought I'd ride with you part of the way if you have no objection."

"None, m'lord."

Egg led them down the hill, sitting tall on Maester. "Must he wear that floppy straw hat?" Ser Eustace asked Dunk. "He looks a bit foolish, don't you think?"

"Not so foolish as when his head is peeling, m'lord." Even at this hour, with the sun barely above the horizon, it was hot. *By afternoon the saddles will be hot enough to raise blisters.* Egg might look elegant in the dead boy's finery, but he would be a boiled Egg by nightfall. Dunk at least could change; he had his good tunic in his saddlebag and his old green one on his back.

"We'll take the west way," Ser Eustace announced. "It is little used these past years but still the shortest way from Standfast to Coldmoat Castle." The path took them around back of the hill, past the graves where the old knight had laid his wife and sons to rest in a thicket of blackberry bushes. "They loved to pick the berries here, my boys. When they were little they would come to me with sticky faces and scratches on their arms, and I'd know just where they'd been." He smiled fondly. "Your Egg reminds me of my Addam. A brave boy, for one so young. Addam was trying to protect his wounded brother Harrold when the battle washed over them. A riverman with six acorns on his shield took his arm off with an axe." His sad grey eyes found Dunk's. "This old master of yours, the knight of Pennytree ... did he fight in the Blackfyre Rebellion?"

"He did, m'lord. Before he took me on." Dunk had been no more than three or four at the time, running half-naked through the alleys of Flea Bottom, more animal than boy.

"Was he for the red dragon or the black?"

Red or black? was a dangerous question, even now. Since the days of Aegon the Conqueror, the arms of House Targaryen had borne a three-headed dragon, red on black. Daemon the Pretender had reversed those colors on his own banners, as many bastards did. *Ser Eustace is my liege lord,* Dunk reminded himself. *He has a right to ask.* "He fought beneath Lord Hayford's banner, m'lord."

"Green fretty over gold, a green pale wavy?"

"It might be, m'lord. Egg would know." The lad could recite the arms of half the knights in Westeros.

"Lord Hayford was a noted *loyalist.* King Daeron made him his Hand just before the battle. Butterwell had done such a dismal job that many questioned his loyalty, but Lord Hayford had been stalwart from the first."

"Ser Arlan was beside him when he fell. A lord with three castles on his shield cut him down."

"Many good men fell that day, on both sides. The grass was not red before the battle. Did your Ser Arlan tell you that?"

"Ser Arlan never liked to speak about the battle. His squire died there too. Roger of Pennytree was his name, Ser Arlan's sister's son." Even saying the name made Dunk feel vaguely guilty. *I stole his place.* Only princes and great lords had the means to keep two squires. If Aegon the Unworthy had given his sword to his heir Daeron instead of his bastard Daemon, there might never have been a Blackfyre Rebellion, and Roger of Pennytree might be alive today. *He would be a knight someplace, a truer knight than me. I would have ended on the gallows, or been sent off to the Night's Watch to walk the Wall until I died.*

"A great battle is a terrible thing," the old knight said, "but in the midst of blood and carnage, there is sometimes also beauty, beauty that could break your heart. I will never forget the way the sun looked when it set upon the Redgrass Field ... ten thousand men had died, and the air was thick with moans and lamentations, but above us the sky turned gold and red and orange, so beautiful it made me weep to know that my sons would never see it." He sighed. "It was a closer thing than they would have you believe, these days. If not for Bloodraven ..."

"I'd always heard that it was Baelor Breakspear who won the battle," said Dunk. "Him and Prince Maekar."

"The hammer and the anvil?" The old man's mustache gave a twitch. "The singers leave out much and more. Daemon was the Warrior himself that day. No man could stand before him. He broke Lord Arryn's van to pieces and slew the Knight of Ninestars and Wild Wyl Waynwood before coming up against Ser Gwayne Corbray of the Kingsguard. For near an hour they danced together on their horses, wheeling and circling and slashing as men died all around them. It's said that whenever Blackfyre and Lady Forlorn clashed, you could hear the sound for a league around. It was half a song and half a scream, they say. But when at last the Lady faltered, Blackfyre clove through Ser Gwayne's helm and left him blind and bleeding.

"Daemon dismounted to see that his fallen foe was not trampled, and commanded Redtusk to carry him back to the maesters in the rear. And there was his mortal error, for the Raven's Teeth had gained the top of Weeping Ridge, and Bloodraven saw his half brother's royal standard three hundred yards away, and Daemon and his sons beneath it. He slew Aegon first, the elder of the twins, for he knew that Daemon would never leave the boy while warmth lingered in his body, though white shafts fell like rain. Nor did he, though seven arrows pierced him, driven as much by sorcery as by Bloodraven's bow. Young Aemon took up Blackfyre when the blade slipped from his dying father's fingers, so Bloodraven slew him too, the younger of the twins. Thus perished the black dragon and his sons.

"There was much and more afterward, I know. I saw a bit of it myself ... the rebels running, Bittersteel turning the rout and leading his mad charge ... his battle with Bloodraven, second only to the one Daemon fought with Gwayne Corbray ... Prince Baelor's hammerblow against the rebel rear, the Dornishmen all screaming as they filled the air with spears ... but at the end of the day, it made no matter. The war was done when Daemon died.

"So close a thing ... if Daemon had ridden over Gwayne Corbray and left him to his fate, he might have broken Maekar's left before Bloodraven could take the ridge. The day would have belonged to the black dragons then, with the Hand slain and the road to King's Landing open before them. Daemon might have been sitting on the Iron Throne by the time Prince Baelor could come up with his stormlords and his Dornishmen.

"The singers can go on about their hammer and their anvil, ser, but it was the kinslayer who turned the tide with a white arrow and a black spell. He rules us now as well, make no mistake. King Aerys is his creature. It would not surprise me to learn that Bloodraven had ensorcelled His Grace, to bend him to his will. Small wonder we are cursed." Ser Eustace shook his head, and lapsed into a brooding silence. Dunk wondered how much Egg had overheard, but there was no way to ask him. *How many eyes does Lord Bloodraven have?* he thought.

Already the day was growing hotter. *Even the flies have fled,* Dunk noted. *Flies have better sense than knights. They stay out of the sun.* He wondered whether he and Egg would be offered hospitality at Coldmoat. A tankard of cool brown ale would go down well. Dunk was considering that prospect with pleasure when he remembered what Egg had said about the Red Widow poisoning her husbands. His thirst fled at once. There were worse things than dry throats.

"There was a time when House Osgrey held all the lands for many leagues around, from Nunny in the east to Cobble Cove," Ser Eustace said. "Coldmoat was ours, and the Horseshoe Hills, the caves at Derring Downs, the villages of Dosk and Little Dosk and Brandybottom, both sides of Leafy Lake ... Osgrey maids wed Florents, Swanns, and Tarbecks, even Hightowers and Blackwoods."

The edge of Wat's Wood had come in sight. Dunk shielded his eyes with one hand and squinted at the greenery. For once he envied Egg his floppy hat. *At least we'll have some shade.*

"Wat's Wood once extended all the way to Coldmoat," Ser Eustace said. "I do not recall who Wat was. Before the Conquest you could find aurochs in his wood, though, and great elks of twenty hands and more. There were more red deer than any man could take in a lifetime, for none but the king and the chequy lion were allowed to hunt here. Even in my father's day, there were trees on both sides of the stream, but the spiders cleared the woods away to make pasture for their cows and sheep and horses."

A thin finger of sweat crept down Dunk's chest. He found himself wishing devoutly that his liege lord would keep quiet. *It is too hot for talk. It is too hot for riding. It is just too bloody hot.*

In the woods they came upon the carcass of a great brown tree cat, crawling with maggots. "Eew," Egg said, as he walked Maester wide around it, "that stinks worse than Ser Bennis."

Ser Eustace reined up. "A tree cat. I had not known there were any left in this wood. I wonder what killed him." When no one answered, he said, "I will turn back here. Just continue on the west way and it will take you straight to Coldmoat. You have the coin?" Dunk nodded.

"Good. Come home with my water, ser." The old knight trotted off, back the way they'd come.

When he was gone, Egg said, "I thought how you should speak to Lady Webber, ser. You should win her to your side with gallant compliments." The boy looked as cool and crisp in his chequy tunic as Ser Eustace had in his cloak.

Am I the only one who sweats? "Gallant compliments," Dunk echoed. "What sort of gallant compliments?"

"You know, ser. Tell her how fair and beautiful she is."

Dunk had doubts. "She's outlived four husbands, she must be as old as Lady Vaith. If I say she's fair and beautiful when she's old and warty, she will take me for a liar."

"You just need to find something true to say about her. That's what my brother Daeron does. Even ugly old whores can have nice hair or well-shaped ears, he says."

"Well-shaped ears?" Dunk's doubts were growing.

"Or pretty eyes. Tell her that her gown brings out the color of her eyes." The lad reflected for a moment. "Unless she only has the one eye, like Lord Bloodraven."

My lady, that gown brings out the color of your eye. Dunk had heard knights and lordlings mouth such gallantries at other ladies. They never put it quite so baldly, though. *Good lady, that gown is beautiful. It brings out the color of both your lovely eyes.* Some of the ladies had been old and scrawny, or fat and florid, or pox-scarred and homely, but all wore gowns and had two eyes, and as Dunk recalled, they'd been well pleased by the flowery words. *What a lovely gown, my lady. It brings out the lovely beauty of your beautiful-colored eyes.* "A hedge knight's life is simpler," Dunk said glumly. "If I say the wrong thing, she's like to sew me in a sack of rocks and throw me in her moat."

"I doubt she'll have that big a sack, ser," said Egg. "We could use my boot instead."

"No," Dunk growled, "we couldn't."

When they emerged from Wat's Wood, they found themselves well upstream of the dam. The waters had risen high enough for Dunk to take that soak he'd dreamed of. *Deep enough to drown a man,* he thought. On the far side, the bank had been cut through and a ditch dug to divert some of the flow westward. The ditch ran along the road, feeding a myriad of smaller channels that snaked off through the fields. *Once we cross the stream, we are in the Widow's power.* Dunk wondered what he was riding into. He was only one man, with a boy of ten to guard his back.

Egg fanned his face. "Ser? Why are we stopped?"

"We're not." Dunk gave his mount his heels and splashed down into the stream. Egg followed on the mule. The water rose as high as Thunder's belly before it began to fall again. They emerged dripping on the Widow's side. Ahead, the ditch ran straight as a spear, shining green and golden in the sun.

When they spied the towers of Coldmoat several hours later, Dunk stopped to change to his good Dornish tunic and loosen his long-sword in its scabbard. He did not want the blade sticking should he need to pull it free. Egg gave his dagger's hilt a shake as well, his face solemn beneath his floppy hat. They rode on side by side, Dunk on the big destrier, the boy upon his mule, the Osgrey banner flapping listlessly from its staff.

Coldmoat came as somewhat of a disappointment after all that Ser Eustace had said of it. Compared to Storm's End or Highgarden and other lordly seats that Dunk had seen, it was a modest castle ... but it *was* a castle, not a fortified watchtower. Its crenellated outer walls stood thirty feet high, with towers at each corner, each one half again the size of Standfast. From every turret and spire the black banners of Webber hung heavy, each emblazoned with a spotted spider upon a silvery web.

"Ser?" Egg said. "The water. Look where it goes."

The ditch ended under Coldmoat's eastern walls, spilling down into the moat from which the castle took its name. The gurgle of the falling water made Dunk grind his teeth. *She will not have my chequy water.* "Come," he said to Egg.

Over the arch of the main gate a row of spider banners drooped in the still air, above the older sigil carved deep into the stone. Centuries of wind and weather had worn it down, but the shape of it was still distinct: a rampant lion made of checkered squares. The gates beneath were open. As they clattered across the drawbridge, Dunk made note of how low the moat had fallen. *Six feet at least,* he judged.

Two spearmen barred their way at the portcullis. One had a big black beard and one did not. The beard demanded to know their purpose here. "My lord of Osgrey sent me to treat with Lady Webber," Dunk told him. "I am called Ser Duncan the Tall."

"Well, I knew you wasn't Bennis," said the beardless guard. "We would have smelled him coming." He had a missing tooth and a spotted spider badge sewn above his heart.

The beard was squinting suspiciously at Dunk. "No one sees her ladyship unless the Longinch gives his leave. You come with me. Your stableboy can stay with the horses."

"I'm a squire, not a stableboy," Egg insisted. "Are you blind, or only stupid?"

The beardless guard broke into laughter. The beard put the point of his spear to the boy's throat. "Say that again."

Dunk gave Egg a clout in the ear. "No, shut your mouth and tend the horses." He dismounted. "I'll see Ser Lucas now."

The beard lowered his spear. "He's in the yard."

They passed beneath the spiked iron portcullis and under a murder hole before emerging in the outer ward. Hounds were barking in the kennels, and Dunk could hear singing coming from the leaded-glass windows of a seven-sided wooden sept. In front of the smithy, a blacksmith was shoeing a warhorse, with a 'prentice boy assisting. Nearby a squire was loosing shafts at the archery butts, while a freckled girl with a long braid matched him shot for shot. The quintain was spinning too, as half a dozen knights in quilted padding took their turns knocking it around.

They found Ser Lucas Longinch amongst the watchers at the quintain, speaking with a great fat septon who was sweating worse than Dunk, a round white pudding of a man in robes as damp as if he'd worn them in his bath. Inchfield was a lance beside him, stiff and straight and very tall ... though not so tall as Dunk. *Six feet and seven inches,* Dunk judged, *and each inch prouder than the last.* Though he wore black silk and cloth-of-silver, Ser Lucas looked as cool as if he were walking on the Wall.

"My lord," the guard hailed him. "This one comes from the chicken tower for an audience with her ladyship."

The septon turned first, with a hoot of delight that made Dunk wonder if he were drunk. "And what is this? A hedge knight? You have large hedges in the Reach." The septon made a sign of blessing. "May the Warrior fight ever at your side. I am Septon Sefton. An unfortunate name, but mine own. And you?"

"Ser Duncan the Tall."

"A modest fellow, this one," the septon said to Ser Lucas. "Were I as large as him, I'd call myself Ser Sefton the Immense. Ser Sefton the Tower. Ser Sefton With the Clouds About His Ears." His moon face was flushed, and there were wine stains on his robe.

Ser Lucas studied Dunk. He was an older man; forty at the least, perhaps as old as fifty, sinewy rather than muscular, with a remarkably ugly face. His lips were thick, his teeth a yellow tangle, his nose broad and fleshy, his eyes protruding. *And he is angry,* Dunk sensed, even before the man said, "Hedge knights are beggars with blades at best, outlaws at worst. Be gone with you. We want none of your sort here."

Dunk's face darkened. "Ser Eustace Osgrey sent me from Standfast to treat with the lady of the castle."

"Osgrey?" The septon glanced at Longinch. "Osgrey of the chequy lion? I thought House Osgrey was extinguished."

"Near enough as makes no matter. The old man is the last of them. We let him keep a crumbling towerhouse a few leagues east." Ser Lucas frowned at Dunk. "If Ser Eustace wants to talk with her ladyship, let him come himself." His eyes narrowed. "You were the one with Bennis at the dam. Don't trouble to deny it. I ought to hang you."

"Seven save us." The septon dabbed sweat from his brow with his sleeve. "A brigand, is he? And a big one. Ser, repent your evil ways, and the Mother will have mercy." The septon's pious plea was undercut when he farted. "Oh, dear. Forgive my wind, ser. That's what comes of beans and barley bread."

"I am not a brigand," Dunk told the two of them, with all the dignity that he could muster.

The Longinch was unmoved by the denial. "Do not presume upon my patience, ser ... if you are a *ser.* Run back to your chicken tower and tell Ser Eustace to deliver up Ser Bennis Brownstench. If he spares us the trouble of winkling him out of Standfast, her ladyship might be more inclined to clemency."

"I will speak with her ladyship about Ser Bennis and the trouble at the dam, and about the stealing of our water too."

"Stealing?" said Ser Lucas. "Say that to our lady, and you'll be swimming in a sack before the sun has set. Are you quite certain that you wish to see her?"

The only thing that Dunk was certain of was that he wanted to drive his fist through Lucas Inchfield's crooked yellow teeth. "I've told you what I want."

"Oh, let him speak with her," the septon urged. "What harm could it do? Ser Duncan has had a long ride beneath this beastly sun, let the fellow have his say."

Ser Lucas studied Dunk again. "Our septon is a godly man. Come. I will thank you to be brief." He strode across the yard, and Dunk was forced to hurry after him.

The doors of the castle sept had opened, and worshippers were streaming down the steps. There were knights and squires, a dozen children, several old men, three septas in white robes and hoods ...

and one soft, fleshy lady of high birth, garbed in a gown of dark blue damask trimmed with Myrish lace, so long its hems were trailing in the dirt. Dunk judged her to be forty. Beneath a spun-silver net her auburn hair was piled high, but the reddest thing about her was her face.

"My lady," Ser Lucas said, when they stood before her and her sep-tas, "this hedge knight claims to bring a message from Ser Eustace Osgrey. Will you hear it?"

"If you wish it, Ser Lucas." She peered at Dunk so hard that he could not help but recall Egg's talk of sorcery. *I don't think this one bathes in blood to keep her beauty.* The widow was stout and square, with an oddly pointed head that her hair could not quite conceal. Her nose was too big, and her mouth too small. She did have two eyes, he was relieved to see, but all thought of gallantry had abandoned Dunk by then. "Ser Eustace bid me talk with you concerning the recent trouble at your dam."

She blinked. "The ... dam, you say?"

A crowd was gathering about them. Dunk could feel unfriendly eyes upon him. "The stream," he said, "the Chequy Water. Your lady-ship built a dam across it ..."

"Oh, I am quite sure I haven't," she replied. "Why, I have been at my devotions all morning, ser."

Dunk heard Ser Lucas chuckle. "I did not mean to say that your ladyship built the dam herself, only that ... without that water, all our crops will die ... the smallfolk have beans and barley in the fields, and melons ..."

"Truly? I am very fond of melons." Her small mouth made a happy bow. "What sort of melons are they?"

Dunk glanced uneasily at the ring of faces, and felt his own face growing hot. *Something is amiss here. Longinch is playing me for a fool.* "M'lady, could we continue our discussion in some ... more private place?"

"A silver says the great oaf means to *bed her*!" someone japed, and a roar of laughter went up all around him. The lady cringed away, half in terror, and raised both hands to shield her face. One of the septas moved quickly to her side and put a protective arm around her shoul-ders.

sooner have a girl than a white cloak." Dunk was thinking of Tanselle Too-Tall, and the way she'd smiled at him at Ashford. "Ser Eustace said I was the sort of man he'd hoped to have his daughter wed. Her name was Alysanne."

"She's dead, ser."

"I know she's dead," said Dunk, annoyed. "If she was alive, he said. If she was, he'd like her to marry me. Or someone like me. I never had a lord offer me his daughter before."

"His *dead* daughter. And the Osgreys might have been lords in the old days, but Ser Eustace is only a landed knight."

"I know what he is. Do you want a clout in the ear?"

"Well," said Egg, "I'd sooner have a clout than a *wife*. Especially a dead wife, ser. The kettle's steaming."

They carried the water to the tub, and Dunk pulled his tunic over his head. "I will wear my Dornish tunic to Coldmoat." It was sandsilk, the finest garment that he owned, painted with his elm and falling star.

"If you wear it for the ride, it will get all sweaty, ser," Egg said.

"And what is all this merriment?" The voice cut through the laughter, cool and firm. "Will no one share the jape? Ser knight, why are you troubling my good-sister?"

It was the girl he had seen earlier at the archery butts. She had a quiver of arrows on one hip and held a longbow that was just as tall as she was, which wasn't very tall. If Dunk was shy an inch of seven feet, the archer was shy an inch of five. He could have spanned her waist with his two hands. Her red hair was bound up in a braid so long it brushed past her thighs, and she had a dimpled chin, a snub nose, and a light spray of freckles across her cheeks.

"Forgive us, Lady Rohanne." The speaker was a pretty young lord with the Caswell centaur embroidered on his doublet. "This great oaf took the Lady Helicent for you."

Dunk looked from one lady to the other. "*You* are the Red Widow?" he heard himself blurt out. "But you're too—"

"Young?" The girl tossed her longbow to the lanky lad he'd seen her shooting with. "I am five-and-twenty, as it happens. Or was it *small* you meant to say?"

"—pretty. It was pretty." Dunk did not know where that came from, but he was glad it came. He liked her nose, and the strawberry-blond color of her hair, and the small but well-shaped breasts beneath her leather jerkin. "I thought that you'd be . . . I mean . . . they said you were four times a widow, so . . ."

"My first husband died when I was ten. He was twelve, my father's squire, ridden down upon the Redgrass Field. My husbands seldom linger long, I fear. The last died in the spring."

That was what they always said of those who had perished during the Great Spring Sickness two years past. *He died in the spring.* Many tens of thousands had died in the spring, amongst them a wise old king and two young princes full of promise. "I . . . I am sorry for all your losses, m'lady." *A gallantry, you lunk, give her a gallantry.* "I want to say . . . your gown . . ."

"Gown?" She glanced down at her boots and breeches, loose linen tunic and leather jerkin. "I wear no gown."

"Your hair, I meant . . . it's soft and . . ."

"And how would you know that, ser? If you had ever touched my hair, I should think that I might remember."

"Not soft," Dunk said miserably. "Red, I meant to say. Your hair is very red."

"*Very* red, ser? Oh, not as red as your face, I hope." She laughed, and the onlookers laughed with her.

All but Ser Lucas Longinch. "My lady," he broke in, "this man is one of Standfast's sellswords. He was with Bennis of the Brown Shield when he attacked your diggers at the dam and carved up Wolmer's face. Old Osgrey sent him to treat with you."

"He did, m'lady. I am called Ser Duncan the Tall."

"Ser Duncan the Dim, more like," said a bearded knight who wore the threefold thunderbolt of Leygood. More guffaws sounded. Even Lady Helicent had recovered herself enough to give a chuckle.

"Did the courtesy of Coldmoat die with my lord father?" the girl asked. *No, not a girl, a woman grown.* "How did Ser Duncan come to make such an error, I wonder?"

Dunk gave Inchfield an evil look. "The fault was mine."

"Was it?" The Red Widow looked Dunk over from his heels up to his head though her gaze lingered longest on his chest. "A tree and shooting star. I have never seen those arms before." She touched his tunic, tracing a limb of his elm tree with two fingers. "And painted, not sewn. The Dornish paint their silks, I've heard, but you look too big to be a Dornishman."

"Not all Dornishmen are small, m'lady." Dunk could feel her fingers through the silk. Her hand was freckled too. *I'll bet she's freckled all over.* His mouth was oddly dry. "I spent a year in Dorne."

"Do all the oaks grow so tall there?" she said, as her fingers traced a tree limb round his heart.

"It's meant to be an elm, m'lady."

"I shall remember." She drew her hand back, solemn. "The ward is too hot and dusty for a conversation. Septon, show Ser Duncan to my audience chamber."

"It would be my great pleasure, good-sister."

"Our guest will have a thirst. You may send for a flagon of wine as well."

"Must I?" The fat man beamed. "Well, if it please you."

"I will join you as soon as I have changed." Unhooking her belt and

quiver, she handed them to her companion. "I'll want Maester Cerrick as well. Ser Lucas, go ask him to attend me."

"I will bring him at once, my lady," said Lucas Longinch.

The look she gave her castellan was cool. "No need. I know you have many duties to perform about the castle. It will suffice if you send Maester Cerrick to my chambers."

"M'lady," Dunk called after her. "My squire was made to wait by the gates. Might he join us as well?"

"Your squire?" When she smiled, she looked a girl of five-and-ten, not a woman five-and-twenty. *A pretty girl full of mischief and laughter.* "If it please you, certainly."

"Don't drink the wine, ser," Egg whispered to him, as they waited with the septon in her audience chamber. The stone floors were covered with sweet-smelling rushes, the walls hung with tapestries of tourney scenes and battles.

Dunk snorted. "She has no need to poison me," he whispered back. "She thinks I'm some great lout with pease porridge between his ears."

"As it happens, my good-sister likes pease porridge," said Septon Sefton, as he reappeared with a flagon of wine, a flagon of water, and three cups. "Yes, yes, I heard. I'm fat, not deaf." He filled two cups with wine and one with water. The third he gave to Egg, who gave it a long, dubious look and put it aside. The septon took no notice. "This is an Arbor vintage," he was telling Dunk. "Very fine, and the poison gives it a special piquancy." He winked at Egg. "I seldom touch the grape myself, but I have heard." He handed Dunk a cup.

The wine was lush and sweet, but Dunk sipped it gingerly, and only after the septon had quaffed down half of his in three big, lip-smacking gulps. Egg crossed his arms and continued to ignore his water.

"She does like pease porridge," the septon said, "and you as well, ser. I know my own good-sister. When I first saw you in the yard, I half hoped you were some suitor, come from King's Landing to seek my lady's hand."

Dunk furrowed his brow. "How did you know I was from King's Landing, septon?"

"Kingslanders have a certain way of speaking." The septon took a gulp of wine, sloshed it about his mouth, swallowed, and sighed with pleasure. "I have served there many years, attending our High Septon in the Great Sept of Baelor." He sighed. "You would not know the city since the spring. The fires changed it. A quarter of the houses gone, and another quarter empty. The rats are gone as well. That is the queerest thing. I never thought to see a city without rats."

Dunk had heard that too. "Were you there during the Great Spring Sickness?"

"Oh, indeed. A dreadful time, ser, dreadful. Strong men would wake healthy at the break of day and be dead by evenfall. So many died so quickly there was no time to bury them. They piled them in the Dragonpit instead, and when the corpses were ten feet deep, Lord Rivers commanded the pyromancers to burn them. The light of the fires shone through the windows, as it did of yore when living dragons still nested beneath the dome. By night you could see the glow all through the city, the dark green glow of wildfire. The color green still haunts me to this day. They say the spring was bad in Lannisport and worse in Oldtown, but in King's Landing it cut down four of ten. Neither young nor old were spared, nor rich nor poor, nor great nor humble. Our good High Septon was taken, the gods' own voice on earth, with a third of the Most Devout and near all our silent sisters. His Grace King Daeron, sweet Matarys and bold Valarr, the Hand ... oh, it was a dreadful time. By the end, half the city was praying to the Stranger." He had another drink. "And where were you, ser?"

"In Dorne," said Dunk.

"Thank the Mother for her mercy, then." The Great Spring Sickness had never come to Dorne, perhaps because the Dornish had closed their borders and their ports, as had the Arryns of the Vale, who had also been spared. "All this talk of death is enough to put a man off wine, but cheer is hard to come by in such times as we are living. The drought endures, for all our prayers. The kingswood is one great tinder box, and fires rage there night and day. Bittersteel and the sons of Daemon Blackfyre are hatching plots in Tyrosh, and Dagon Greyjoy's krakens prowl the sunset sea like wolves, raiding as far south as the Arbor. They carried off half the wealth of Fair Isle, it's said, and a hundred women too. Lord Farman is repairing his defenses, though that strikes me as akin to the man who claps his pregnant daughter in a chastity belt when her belly's big as mine. Lord Bracken is dying slowly on the Trident, and his eldest son perished in the spring. That means Ser Otho must succeed. The Blackwoods will never stomach the Brute of Bracken as a neighbor. It will mean war."

Dunk knew about the ancient enmity between the Blackwoods and the Brackens. "Won't their liege lord force a peace?"

"Alas," said Septon Sefton, "Lord Tully is a boy of eight, surrounded by women. Riverrun will do little, and King Aerys will do less. Unless some maester writes a book about it, the whole matter may escape his royal notice. Lord Rivers is not like to let any Brackens in to see him. Pray recall, our Hand was born half-Blackwood. If he acts at all, it will be only to help his cousins bring the Brute to bay. The Mother marked Lord Rivers on the day that he was born, and Bittersteel marked him once again upon the Redgrass Field."

Dunk knew he meant Bloodraven. Brynden Rivers was the Hand's true name. His mother had been a Blackwood, his father King Aegon the Fourth.

The fat man drank his wine and rattled on. "As for Aerys, His Grace cares more for old scrolls and dusty prophecies than for lords and laws. He will not even bestir himself to sire an heir. Queen Aelinor prays daily at the Great Sept, beseeching the Mother Above to bless her with a child, yet she remains a maid. Aerys keeps his own apartments, and it is said that he would sooner take a book to bed than any woman." He filled his cup again. "Make no mistake, 'tis Lord Rivers who rules us, with his spells and spies. There is no one to oppose him. Prince Maekar sulks at Summerhall, nursing his grievances against his royal brother. Prince Rhaegel is as meek as he is mad, and his children are ... well, children. Friends and favorites of Lord Rivers fill every office, the lords of the small council lick his hand, and this new Grand Maester is as steeped in sorcery as he is. The Red Keep is garrisoned by Raven's Teeth, and no man sees the king without his leave."

Dunk shifted uncomfortably in his seat. *How many eyes does Lord Bloodraven have? A thousand eyes, and one.* He hoped the King's Hand did not have a thousand ears and one as well. Some of what Septon Sefton was saying sounded treasonous. He glanced at Egg, to see how he was taking all of this. The boy was struggling with all his might to hold his tongue.

The septon pushed himself to his feet. "My good-sister will be a while yet. As with all great ladies, the first ten gowns she tries will be found not to suit her mood. Will you take more wine?" Without waiting for an answer, he refilled both cups.

"The lady I mistook," said Dunk, anxious to speak of something else, "is she your sister?"

"We are all children of the Seven, ser, but apart from that ... dear me, no. Lady Helicent was sister to Ser Rolland Uffering, Lady Rohanne's fourth husband, who died in the spring. My brother was his predecessor, Ser Simon Staunton, who had the great misfortune to choke upon a chicken bone. Coldmoat crawls with revenants, it must be said. The husbands die yet their kin remain, to drink my lady's wines and eat her sweetmeats, like a plague of plump pink locusts done up in silk and velvet." He wiped his mouth. "And yet she must wed again, and soon."

"Must?" said Dunk.

"Her lord father's will demands it. Lord Wyman wanted grandsons to carry on his line. When he sickened he tried to wed her to the Longinch, so he might die knowing that she had a strong man to protect her, but Rohanne refused to have him. His lordship took his vengeance in his will. If she remains unwed on the second anniversary of her father's passing, Coldmoat and its lands pass to his cousin Wendell. Perhaps you glimpsed him in the yard. A short man with a goiter on his neck, much given to flatulence. Though it is small of me to say so. I am cursed with excess wind myself. Be that as it may. Ser Wendell is grasping and stupid, but his lady wife is Lord Rowan's sister ... and damnably fertile, that cannot be denied. She whelps as often as he farts. Their sons are quite as bad as he is, their daughters worse, and all of them have begun to count the days. Lord Rowan has upheld the will, so her ladyship has only till the next new moon."

"Why has she waited so long?" Dunk wondered aloud.

The septon shrugged. "If truth be told, there has been a dearth of suitors. My good-sister is not hard to look upon, you will have noticed, and a stout castle and broad lands add to her charms. You would think that younger sons and landless knights would swarm about her ladyship like flies. You would be wrong. The four dead husbands make them wary, and there are those who will say that she is barren too ... though never in her hearing unless they yearn to see the inside of a crow cage. She has carried two children to term, a boy and a girl, but neither lived to see a name day. Those few who are not put off by talk of poisonings and sorcery want no part of the Longinch. Lord Wyman charged him on his deathbed to protect his daughter from unworthy suitors, which he has taken to mean *all* suitors. Any man who means to have her hand would need to face his sword first." He finished his wine and set the cup aside. "That is not to say there has been no one. Cleyton Caswell and Simon Leygood have been the most persistent, though they seem more interested in her lands than in her person. Were I given to wagering, I should place my gold on Gerold Lannister. He has yet to put in an appearance, but they say he is golden-haired and quick of wit, and more than six feet tall ..."

"... and Lady Webber is much taken with his letters." The lady in question stood in the doorway, beside a homely young maester with a great, hooked nose. "You would lose your wager, good-brother. Gerold will never willingly forsake the pleasures of Lannisport and the splendor of Casterly Rock for some little lordship. He has more influence as Lord Tybolt's brother and advisor than he could ever hope for as my husband. As for the others, Ser Simon would need to sell off half my land to pay his debts and Ser Cleyton trembles like a leaf whenever the Longinch deigns to look his way. Besides, he is prettier than I am. And you, septon, have the biggest mouth in Westeros."

"A large belly requires a large mouth," said Septon Sefton, utterly unabashed. "Else it soon becomes a small one."

"Are *you* the Red Widow?" Egg asked, astonished. "I'm near as tall as you are!"

"Another boy made that same observation not half a year ago. I sent him to the rack to make him taller." When Lady Rohanne settled onto the high seat on the dais, she pulled her braid forward over her left shoulder. It was so long that the end of it lay coiled in her lap, like a sleeping cat. "Ser Duncan, I should not have teased you in the yard, when you were trying so hard to be gracious. It was only that you blushed so red ... was there no girl to tease you, in the village where you grew so tall?"

"The village was King's Landing." He did not mention Flea Bottom. "There were girls, but ..." The sort of teasing that went on in Flea Bottom sometimes involved cutting off a toe.

"I expect they were afraid to tease you." Lady Rohanne stroked her braid. "No doubt they were frightened of your size. Do not think ill of

Lady Helicent, I pray you. My good-sister is a simple creature, but she has no harm in her. For all her piety, she could not dress herself without her septas."

"It was not her doing. The mistake was mine."

"You lie most gallantly. I know it was Ser Lucas. He is a man of cruel humors, and you offended him on sight."

"How?" Dunk said, puzzled. "I never did him any harm."

She smiled a smile that made him wish that she was plainer. "I saw you standing with him. You're taller by a hand, or near enough. It has been a long while since Ser Lucas met anyone he could not look down on. How old are you, ser?"

"Near twenty, if it please m'lady." Dunk liked the ring of *twenty,* though most like he was a year younger, maybe two. No one knew for certain, least of all him. He must have had a mother and a father like everybody else, but he'd never known them, not even their names, and no one in Flea Bottom had ever cared much when he'd been born, or to whom.

"Are you as strong as you appear?"

"How strong do I appear, m'lady?"

"Oh, strong enough to annoy Ser Lucas. He is my castellan, though not by choice. Like Coldmoat, he is a legacy of my father. Did you come to knighthood on some battlefield, Ser Duncan? Your speech suggests that you were not born of noble blood, if you will forgive my saying so."

I was born of gutter blood. "A hedge knight named Ser Arlan of Pennytree took me on to squire for him when I was just a boy. He taught me chivalry and the arts of war."

"And this same Ser Arlan knighted you?"

Dunk shuffled his feet. One of his boots was half-unlaced, he saw. "No one else was like to do it."

"Where is Ser Arlan now?"

"He died." He raised his eyes. He could lace his boot up later. "I buried him on a hillside."

"Did he fall valiantly in battle?"

"There were rains. He caught a chill."

"Old men are frail, I know. I learned that from my second husband. I was thirteen when we wed. He would have been five-and-fifty on his next name day, had he lived long enough to see it. When he was half a year in the ground, I gave him a little son, but the Stranger came for him as well. The septons said his father wanted him beside him. What do you think, ser?"

"Well," Dunk said hesitantly, "that might be, m'lady."

"Nonsense," she said, "the boy was born too weak. Such a tiny thing. He scarce had strength enough to nurse. Still. The gods gave his father five-and-fifty years. You would think they might have granted more than three days to the son."

"You would." Dunk knew little and less about the gods. He went to sept sometimes, and prayed to the Warrior to lend strength to his arms, but elsewise he let the Seven be.

"I am sorry your Ser Arlan died," she said, "and sorrier still that you took service with Ser Eustace. All old men are not the same, Ser Duncan. You would do well to go home to Pennytree."

"I have no home but where I swear my sword." Dunk had never seen Pennytree; he couldn't even say if it was in the Reach.

"Swear it here, then. The times are uncertain. I have need of knights. You look as though you have a healthy appetite, Ser Duncan. How many chickens can you eat? At Coldmoat you would have your fill of warm pink meat and sweet fruit tarts. Your squire looks in need of sustenance as well. He is so scrawny that all his hair has fallen out. We'll have him share a cell with other boys of his own age, he'll like that. My master-at-arms can train him in all the arts of war."

"I train him," said Dunk defensively.

"And who else? Bennis? Old Osgrey? The chickens?"

There had been days when Dunk had set Egg to chasing chickens.

It helps make him quicker, he thought, but he knew that if he said it, she would laugh. She was distracting him, with her snub nose and her freckles. Dunk had to remind himself of why Ser Eustace had sent him here. "My sword is sworn to my lord of Osgrey, m'lady," he said, "and that's the way it is."

"So be it, ser. Let us speak of less pleasant matters." Lady Rohanne gave her braid a tug. "We do not suffer attacks on Coldmoat or its people. So tell me why I should not have you sewn in a sack."

"I came to parley," he reminded her, "and I have drunk your wine." The taste still lingered in his mouth, rich and sweet. So far it had not poisoned him. Perhaps it was the wine that made him bold. "And you don't have a sack big enough for me."

To his relief, Egg's jape made her smile. "I have several that are big enough for Bennis, though. Maester Cerrick says Wolmer's face was sliced open almost to the bone."

"Ser Bennis lost his temper with the man, m'lady. Ser Eustace sent me here to pay the blood price."

"The blood price?" She laughed. "He is an old man, I know, but I had not realized that he was so old as that. Does he think we are living in the Age of Heroes, when a man's life was reckoned to be worth no more than a sack of silver?"

"The digger was not killed, m'lady," Dunk reminded her. "No one was killed that I saw. His face was cut, is all."

Her fingers danced idly along her braid. "How much does Ser Eustace reckon Wolmer's cheek to be worth, pray?"

"One silver stag. And three for you, m'lady."

"Ser Eustace sets a niggard's price upon my honor, though three silvers are better than three chickens, I grant you. He would do better to deliver Bennis up to me for chastisement."

"Would this involve that sack you mentioned?"

"It might." She coiled her braid around one hand. "Osgrey can keep his silver. Only blood can pay for blood."

"Well," said Dunk, "it may be as you say, m'lady, but why not send for that man that Bennis cut, and ask him if he'd sooner have a silver stag or Bennis in a sack?"

"Oh, he'd pick the silver if he couldn't have both. I don't doubt that, ser. It is not his choice to make. This is about the lion and the spider now, not some peasant's cheek. It is Bennis I want, and Bennis I shall have. No one rides onto my lands, does harm to one of mine, and escapes to laugh about it."

"Your ladyship rode onto Standfast land, and did harm to one of Ser Eustace's," Dunk said, before he stopped to think about it.

"Did I?" She tugged her braid again. "If you mean the sheep-stealer, the man was notorious. I had twice complained to Osgrey, yet he did nothing. I do not ask thrice. The king's law grants me the power of pit and gallows."

It was Egg who answered her. "On your own lands," the boy insisted. "The king's law gives lords the power of pit and gallows on their own lands."

"Clever boy," she said. "If you know that much, you will also know that landed knights have no right to punish without their liege lord's leave. Ser Eustace holds Standfast of Lord Rowan. Bennis broke the king's peace when he drew blood and must answer for it." She looked to Dunk. "If Ser Eustace will deliver Bennis to me, I'll slit his nose, and that will be the end of it. If I must come and take him, I make no such promise."

Dunk had a sudden sick feeling in the pit of his stomach. "I will tell him, but he won't give up Ser Bennis." He hesitated. "The dam was the cause of all the trouble. If your ladyship would consent to take it down—"

"Impossible," declared the young maester by Lady Rohanne's side. "Coldmoat supports twenty times as many smallfolk as does Standfast. Her ladyship has fields of wheat and corn and barley, all dying from the drought. She has half a dozen orchards, apples and apricots and three kinds of pears. She has cows about to calf, five hundred head of black-nosed sheep, and she breeds the finest horses in the Reach. We have a dozen mares about to foal."

"Ser Eustace has sheep too," Dunk said. "He has melons in the fields, beans and barleycorn, and . . ."

"You were taking water for the *moat*!" Egg said loudly.

I was getting to the moat, Dunk thought.

"The moat is essential to Coldmoat's defenses," the maester insisted. "Do you suggest that Lady Rohanne leave herself open to attack, in such uncertain times as these?"

"Well," Dunk said slowly, "a dry moat is still a moat. And m'lady has strong walls, with ample men to defend them."

"Ser Duncan," Lady Rohanne said, "I was ten years old when the black dragon rose. I begged my father not to put himself at risk, or at least to leave my husband. Who would protect me, if both my men were gone? So he took me up onto the ramparts, and pointed out Coldmoat's strong points. 'Keep them strong,' he said, 'and they will keep you safe. If you see to your defenses, no man may do you harm.' The first thing he pointed at was the moat." She stroked her cheek with the tail of her braid. "My first husband perished on the Redgrass Field. My father found me others, but the Stranger took them too. I no longer trust in men, no matter how *ample* they may seem. I trust in stone and steel and water. I trust in moats, ser, and mine will *not* go dry."

"What your father said, that's well and good," said Dunk, "but it doesn't give you the right to take Osgrey water."

She tugged her braid. "I suppose Ser Eustace told you that the stream was his."

"For a thousand years," said Dunk. "It's *named* the Chequy Water. That's plain."

"So it is." She tugged again; once, twice, thrice. "As the river is called the Mander, though the Manderlys were driven from its banks a thousand years ago. Highgarden is still Highgarden, though the last Gardener died on the Field of Fire. Casterly Rock teems with Lannisters, and nowhere a Casterly to be found. The world changes, ser. This Chequy Water rises in the Horseshoe Hills, which were wholly mine when last I looked. The water is mine as well. Maester Cerrick, show him."

The maester descended from the dais. He could not have been much older than Dunk, but in his grey robes and chain collar he had an air of somber wisdom that belied his years. In his hands was an old parchment. "See for yourself, ser," he said as he unrolled it, and offered it to Dunk.

Dunk the lunk, thick as a castle wall. He felt his cheeks reddening again. Gingerly he took parchment from the maester and scowled at the writing. Not a word of it was intelligible to him, but he knew the wax seal beneath the ornate signature; the three-headed dragon of House Targaryen. *The king's seal.* He was looking at a royal decree of some sort. Dunk moved his head from side to side so they would think that he was reading. "There's a word here I can't make out," he muttered, after a moment. "Egg, come have a look, you have sharper eyes than me."

The boy darted to his side. "Which word, ser?" Dunk pointed. "That one? Oh." Egg read quickly, then raised his eyes to Dunk's and gave a little nod.

It is her stream. She has a paper. Dunk felt as though he'd been punched in the stomach. *The king's own seal.* "This ... there must be some mistake. The old man's sons died in service to the king. Why would His Grace take his stream away?"

"If King Daeron had been a less forgiving man, he should have lost his head as well."

For half a heartbeat Dunk was lost. "What do you mean?"

"She means," said Maester Cerrick, "that Ser Eustace Osgrey is a rebel and a traitor."

"Ser Eustace chose the black dragon over the red, in hopes that a Blackfyre king might restore the lands and castles that the Osgreys had lost under the Targaryens," Lady Rohanne said. "Chiefly he wanted Coldmoat. His sons paid for his treason with their life's blood. When he brought their bones home and delivered his daughter to the king's men for a hostage, his wife threw herself from the top of Stand-fast tower. Did Ser Eustace tell you that?" Her smile was sad. "No, I did not think so."

"The black dragon." *You swore your sword to a traitor, lunk. You ate a traitor's bread and slept beneath a rebel's roof.* "M'lady," he said, groping, "the black dragon ... that was fifteen years ago. This is now, and there's a drought. Even if he was a rebel once, Ser Eustace still needs water."

The Red Widow rose, and smoothed her skirts. "He had best pray for rain, then."

That was when Dunk recalled Osgrey's parting words in the wood. "If you will not grant him a share of the water for his own sake, do it for his son."

"His son?"

"Addam. He served here as your father's page and squire."

Lady Rohanne's face was stone. "Come closer."

He did not know what else to do, but to obey. The dais added a good foot to her height, yet even so Dunk towered over her. "Kneel," she said. He did.

The slap she gave him had all her strength behind it, and she was stronger than she looked. His cheek burned, and he could taste blood in his mouth from a broken lip, but she hadn't truly hurt him. For a moment all Dunk could think of was grabbing her by that long red braid and pulling her across his lap to slap her arse, as you would a spoiled child. *If I do, she'll scream, though, and twenty knights will come bursting in to kill me.*

"You dare appeal to me in *Addam's* name?" Her nostrils flared. "Remove yourself from Coldmoat, ser. At once."

"I never meant—"

"*Go,* or I will find a sack large enough for you if I have to sew one up myself. Tell Ser Eustace to bring me Bennis of the Brown Shield by the morrow, else I will come for him myself with fire and sword. Do you understand me? *Fire and sword!*"

Septon Sefton took Dunk's arm and pulled him quickly from the room. Egg followed close behind them. "That was most unwise, ser," the fat septon whispered, and he led them to the steps. "*Most* unwise. To mention Addam Osgrey . . ."

"Ser Eustace told me she was fond of the boy."

"Fond?" The septon huffed heavily. "She loved the boy, and him her. It never went beyond a kiss or two, but . . . it was Addam she wept for after the Redgrass Field, not the husband she hardly knew. She blames Ser Eustace for his death, and rightly so. The boy was twelve."

Dunk knew what it was to bear a wound. Whenever someone spoke of Ashford Meadow, he thought of the three good men who'd died to save his foot, and it never failed to hurt. "Tell m'lady that it was not my wish to hurt her. Beg her pardon."

"I shall do all I can, ser," Septon Sefton said, "but tell Ser Eustace to bring her Bennis, and *quickly*. Elsewise it will go hard on him. It will go very hard."

Not until the walls and towers of Coldmoat had vanished in the west behind them did Dunk turn to Egg and say, "What words were written on that paper?"

"It was a grant of rights, ser. To Lord Wyman Webber, from the king. For his leal service in the late rebellion, Lord Wyman and his descendants were granted all rights to the Chequy Water, from where it rises in the Horseshoe Hills to the shores of Leafy Lake. It also said that Lord Wyman and his descendants should have the right to take red deer and boar and rabbits in Wat's Wood when e'er it pleased them, and to cut twenty trees from the wood each year." The boy cleared his throat. "The grant was only for a time, though. The paper said that if Ser Eustace were to die without a male heir of his body, Standfast would revert to the crown, and Lord Webber's privileges would end."

They were the Marshals of the Northmarch for a thousand years. "All they left the old man was a tower to die in."

"And his head," said Egg. "His Grace did leave him his head, ser. Even though he was a rebel."

Dunk gave the boy a look. "Would you have taken it?"

Egg had to think about it. "Sometimes at court I would serve the king's small council. They used to fight about it. Uncle Baelor said that clemency was best when dealing with an honorable foe. If a defeated man believes he will be pardoned, he may lay down his sword and bend the knee. Elsewise he will fight on to the death and slay more loyal men and innocents. But Lord Bloodraven said that when you pardon rebels, you only plant the seeds of the next rebellion." His voice was full of doubts. "Why would Ser Eustace rise against King

Daeron? He was a good king, everybody says so. He brought Dorne into the realm and made the Dornishmen our friends."

"You would have to ask Ser Eustace, Egg." Dunk thought he knew the answer, but it was not one the boy would want to hear. *He wanted a castle with a lion on the gatehouse, but all he got were graves amongst the blackberries.* When you swore a man your sword, you promised to serve and obey, to fight for him at need, not to pry into his affairs and question his allegiances . . . but Ser Eustace had played him for a fool. *He said his sons died fighting for the king and let me believe the stream was his.*

Night caught them in Wat's Wood.

That was Dunk's fault. He should have gone the straight way home, the way they'd gone, but instead he'd taken them north for another look at the dam. He had half a thought to try and tear the thing apart with his bare hands. But the Seven and Ser Lucas Longinch did not prove so obliging. When they reached the dam they found it guarded by a pair of crossbowmen with spider badges sewn on their jerkins. One sat with his bare feet in the stolen water. Dunk could gladly have throttled him for that alone, but the man heard them coming and was quick to snatch up his bow. His fellow, even quicker, had a quarrel nocked and ready. The best that Dunk could do was scowl at them threateningly.

After that, there was naught to do but retrace their steps. Dunk did not know these lands as well as Ser Bennis did; it would have been humiliating to get lost in a wood as small as Wat's. By the time they splashed across the stream, the sun was low on the horizon and the first stars were coming out, along with clouds of mites. Amongst the tall black trees, Egg found his tongue again. "Ser? That fat septon said my father sulks in Summerhall."

"Words are wind."

"My father doesn't sulk."

"Well," said Dunk, "he might. *You* sulk."

"I do not. Ser." He frowned. "Do I?"

"Some. Not too often, though. Elsewise I'd clout you in the ear more than I do."

"You clouted me in the ear at the gate."

"That was half a clout at best. If I ever give you a whole clout, you'll know it."

"The Red Widow gave *you* a whole clout."

Dunk touched his swollen lip. "You don't need to sound so pleased about it." *No one ever clouted your father in the ear, though. Maybe that's why Prince Maekar is the way he is.* "When the king named Lord Bloodraven his Hand, your lord father refused to be part of his council and departed King's Landing for his own seat," he reminded Egg. "He has been at Summerhall for a year, and half of another. What do you call that, if not sulking?"

"I call it being wroth," Egg declared loftily. "His Grace should have made my father Hand. He's his *brother,* and the finest battle commander in the realm since Uncle Baelor died. Lord Bloodraven's not even a real lord, that's just some stupid *courtesy.* He's a sorcerer, and baseborn besides."

"Bastard born, not baseborn." Bloodraven might not be a real lord, but he was noble on both sides. His mother had been one of the many mistresses of King Aegon the Unworthy. Aegon's bastards had been the bane of the Seven Kingdoms ever since the old king died. He had legitimized the lot upon his deathbed; not only the Great Bastards like Bloodraven, Bittersteel, and Daemon Blackfyre, whose mothers had been ladies, but even the lesser ones he'd fathered on whores and tavern wenches, merchant's daughters, mummer's maidens, and every pretty peasant girl who chanced to catch his eye. *Fire and Blood* were the words of House Targaryen, but Dunk once heard Ser Arlan say that Aegon's should have been, *Wash Her and Bring Her to My Bed.*

"King Aegon washed Bloodraven clean of bastardy," he reminded Egg, "the same as he did the rest of them."

"The old High Septon told my father that king's laws are one thing, and the laws of the gods another," the boy said stubbornly. "Trueborn children are made in a marriage bed and blessed by the Father and the Mother, but bastards are born of lust and weakness, he said. King Aegon decreed that his bastards were not bastards, but he could not change their nature. The High Septon said all bastards are born to betrayal ... Daemon Blackfyre, Bittersteel, even Bloodraven. Lord Rivers was more cunning than the other two, he said, but in the end he would prove himself a traitor too. The High Septon counseled my father never to put any trust in him, nor in any other bastards, great or small."

Born to betrayal, Dunk thought. *Born of lust and weakness. Never to be trusted, great or small.* "Egg," he said, "didn't you ever think that I might be a bastard?"

"You, ser?" That took the boy aback. "You are not."

"I might be. I never knew my mother, or what became of her. Maybe I was born too big and killed her. Most like she was some whore or tavern girl. You don't find highborn ladies down in Flea Bottom. And if she ever wed my father ... well, what became of *him,* then?" Dunk did not like to be reminded of his life before Ser Arlan found him. "There was a pot shop in King's Landing where I used to sell them rats and cats and pigeons for the brown. The cook always claimed my father was some thief or cutpurse. 'Most like I saw him hanged,' he used to tell me, 'but maybe they just sent him to the Wall.' When I was squiring for Ser Arlan, I would ask him if we couldn't go up that way someday, to take service at Winterfell or some other northern castle. I had this notion that if I could only reach the Wall, might be I'd come on some old man, a real tall man who looked like me. We never went, though. Ser Arlan said there were no hedges in the north, and all the woods were full of wolves." He shook his head. "The long and short of it is, most like you're squiring for a bastard."

For once Egg had nothing to say. The gloom was deepening around them. Lantern bugs moved slowly through the trees, their little lights like so many drifting stars. There were stars in the sky as well, more stars than any man could ever hope to count, even if he lived to be as old as King Jaehaerys.

Dunk need only lift his eyes to find familiar friends: the Stallion and the Sow, the King's Crown and the Crone's Lantern, the Galley, Ghost, and Moonmaid. But there were clouds to the north, and the blue eye of the Ice Dragon was lost to him, the blue eye that pointed north.

The moon had risen by the time they came to Standfast, standing dark and tall atop its hill. A pale yellow light was spilling from the tower's upper windows, he saw. Most nights Ser Eustace sought his bed as soon as he had supped, but not tonight, it seemed. *He is waiting for us,* Dunk knew.

Bennis of the Brown Shield was waiting up as well. They found him sitting on the tower steps, chewing sourleaf and honing his longsword in the moonlight. The slow scrape of stone on steel carried a long way. However much Ser Bennis might neglect his clothes and person, he kept his weapons well.

"The lunk comes back," Bennis said. "Here I was sharpening my steel to go rescue you from that Red Widow."

"Where are the men?"

"Treb and Wet Wat are on the roof standing watch, case the widow comes to call. The rest crawled into bed whimpering. Sore as sin, they are. I worked them hard. Drew a little blood off that big lackwit, just to make him mad. He fights better when he's mad." He smiled his brown and red smile. "Nice bloody lip you got. Next time, don't go turning over rocks. What did the woman say?"

"She means to keep the water. And she wants you as well, for cutting that digger by the dam."

"Thought she might." Bennis spat. "Lot o' bother for some peasant. He ought to thank me. Women like a man with scars."

"You won't mind her slitting your nose, then."

"Bugger that. If I wanted my nose slit, I'd slit it for myself." He jerked a thumb up. "You'll find Ser Useless in his chambers, brooding on how great he used to be."

Egg spoke up. "He fought for the black dragon."

Dunk could have given the boy a clout, but the brown knight only laughed. " 'Course he did. Just look at him. He strike you as the kind who picks the winning side?"

"No more than you. Else you wouldn't be here with us." Dunk turned to Egg. "Tend to Thunder and Maester, then come up and join us."

When Dunk came up through the trap, the old knight was sitting by the hearth in his bedrobe, though no fire had been laid. His father's cup was in his hand, a heavy silver cup that had been made for some Lord Osgrey back before the Conquest. A chequy lion adorned the bowl, done in flakes of jade and gold, though some of the jade flakes had gone missing. At the sound of Dunk's footsteps, the old knight looked up and blinked like a man waking from a dream. "Ser Duncan. You are back. Did the sight of you give Lucas Inchfield pause, ser?"

"Not as I saw, m'lord. More like, it made him wroth." Dunk told it all as best he could, though he omitted the part about Lady Helicent, which made him look an utter fool. He would have left out the clout too, but his broken lip had puffed up twice its normal size, and Ser Eustace could not help but notice.

When he did, he frowned. "Your lip . . ."

Dunk touched it gingerly. "Her ladyship gave me a slap."

"She *struck* you?" His mouth opened and closed. "She struck my envoy, who came to her beneath the chequy lion? She dared lay hands upon your person?"

"Only the one hand, ser. It stopped bleeding before we even left the castle." He made a fist. "She wants Ser Bennis, not your silver, and she won't take down the dam. She showed me a parchment with some writing on it, and the king's own seal. It said the stream is hers. And . . ." He hesitated. "She said that you were . . . that you had . . ."

". . . risen with the black dragon?" Ser Eustace seemed to slump. "I feared she might. If you wish to leave my service, I will not stop you." The old knight gazed into his cup though what he might be looking for Dunk could not say.

"You told me your sons died fighting for the king."

"And so they did. The *rightful* king, Daemon Blackfyre. The King Who Bore the Sword." The old man's mustache quivered. "The men of the red dragon call themselves the *loyalists,* but we who chose the black were just as loyal, once. Though now ... all the men who marched beside me to seat Prince Daemon on the Iron Throne have melted away like morning dew. Mayhaps I dreamed them. Or more like, Lord Bloodraven and his Raven's Teeth have put the fear in them. They cannot all be dead."

Dunk could not deny the truth of that. Until this moment, he had never met a man who'd fought for the Pretender. *I must have, though. There were thousands of them. Half the realm was for the red dragon, and half was for the black.* "Both sides fought valiantly, Ser Arlan always said." He thought the old knight would want to hear that.

Ser Eustace cradled his wine cup in both hands. "If Daemon had ridden over Gwayne Corbray ... if Fireball had not been slain on the eve of battle ... if Hightower and Tarbeck and Oakheart and Butterwell had lent us their full strength instead of trying to keep one foot in each camp ... if Manfred Lothston had proved true instead of treacherous ... if storms had not delayed Lord Bracken's sailing with the Myrish crossbowmen ... if Quickfinger had not been caught with the stolen dragon's eggs ... so many *ifs*, ser ... had any one come out differently, it could all have turned t'other way. Then we would be called the loyalists, and the red dragons would be remembered as men who fought to keep the usurper Daeron the Falseborn upon his stolen throne, and failed."

"That's as it may be, m'lord," said Dunk, "but things went the way they went. It was all years ago, and you were pardoned."

"Aye, we were pardoned. So long as we bent the knee and gave him a hostage to ensure our future loyalty, Daeron forgave the traitors and the rebels." His voice was bitter. "I bought my head back with my daughter's life. Alysanne was seven when they took her off to King's Landing and twenty when she died, a silent sister. I went to King's Landing once to see her, and she would not even speak to me, her own father. A king's mercy is a poisoned gift. Daeron Targaryen left me life, but took my pride and dreams and honor." His hand trembled, and wine spilled red upon his lap, but the old man took no notice of it. "I should have gone with Bittersteel into exile, or died beside my sons and my sweet king. That would have been a death worthy of a chequy lion descended from so many proud lords and mighty warriors. Daeron's mercy made me smaller."

In his heart the black dragon never died, Dunk realized.

"My lord?"

It was Egg's voice. The boy had come in as Ser Eustace was speaking of his death. The old knight blinked at him as if he were seeing him for the first time. "Yes, lad? What is it?"

"If it please you ... the Red Widow says you rebelled to get her castle. That isn't true, is it?"

"The castle?" He seemed confused. "Coldmoat ... Coldmoat was promised me by Daemon, yes, but ... it was not for gain, no ..."

"Then why?" asked Egg.

"Why?" Ser Eustace frowned.

"Why were you a traitor? If it wasn't just the castle."

Ser Eustace looked at Egg a long time before replying. "You are only a young boy. You would not understand."

"Well," said Egg, "I might."

"*Treason* ..." is only a word. When two princes fight for a chair where only one may sit, great lords and common men alike must choose. And when the battle's done, the victors will be hailed as loyal men and true, whilst those who were defeated will be known forevermore as rebels and traitors. That was my fate."

Egg thought about it for a time. "Yes, my lord. Only ... King Daeron was a good man. Why would you choose Daemon?"

"Daeron ..." Ser Eustace almost slurred the word, and Dunk realized he was half-drunk. "Daeron was spindly and round of shoulder, with a little belly that wobbled when he walked. Daemon stood straight and proud, and his stomach was flat and hard as an oaken shield. And he could *fight*. With axe or lance or flail, he was as good as any knight I ever saw, but with *the sword* he was the Warrior himself. When Prince Daemon had Blackfyre in his hand, there was not a man to equal him ... not Ulrick Dayne with Dawn, no, nor even the Dragonknight with Dark Sister.

"You can know a man by his friends, Egg. Daeron surrounded himself with maesters, septons, and singers. Always there were women whispering in his ear, and his court was full of Dornishmen. How not, when he had taken a Dornishwoman into his bed and sold his own sweet sister to the Prince of Dorne, though it was Daemon that she loved? Daeron bore the same name as the Young Dragon, but when his Dornish wife gave him a son he named the child Baelor, after the feeblest king who ever sat the Iron Throne.

"Daemon, though ... Daemon was no more pious than a king need be, and all the great knights of the realm gathered to him. It would suit Lord Bloodraven if their names were all forgotten, so he has forbidden us to sing of them, but *I* remember. Robb Reyne, Gareth the Grey, Ser Aubrey Ambrose, Lord Gormon Peake, Black Byren Flowers, Redtusk, Fireball ... *Bittersteel*! I ask you, has there ever been such a noble company, such a roll of heroes?

"*Why*, lad? You ask me why? Because Daemon was the better man. The old king saw it too. He gave the sword to Daemon. *Blackfyre*, the sword of Aegon the Conqueror, the blade that every Targaryen king had wielded since the Conquest ... he put that sword in Daemon's hand the day he knighted him, a boy of twelve."

"My father says that was because Daemon was a swordsman, and Daeron never was," said Egg. "Why give a horse to a man who cannot ride? The sword was not the kingdom, he says."

The old knight's hand jerked so hard that wine spilled from his silver cup. "Your father is a fool."

"He is *not*," the boy said.

Osgrey's face twisted in anger. "You asked a question and I answered it, but I will not suffer insolence. Ser Duncan, you should beat this boy more often. His courtesy leaves much to be desired. If I must needs do it myself, I will—"

"No," Dunk broke in. "You won't. Ser." He had made up his mind. "It is dark. We will leave at first light."

Ser Eustace stared at him, stricken. "Leave?"

"Standfast. Your service." *You lied to us. Call it what you will, there was no honor in it.* He unfastened his cloak, rolled it up, and put it in the old man's lap.

Osgrey's eyes grew narrow. "Did that woman offer to take you into service? Are you leaving me for that whore's bed?"

"I don't know that she is a whore," Dunk said, "or a witch or a poi-soner or none of that. But whatever she may be makes no matter. We're leaving for the hedges, not for Coldmoat."

"The ditches, you mean. You're leaving me to prowl in the woods like wolves, to waylay honest men upon the roads." His hand was shaking. The cup fell from his fingers, spilling wine as it rolled along the floor. "Go, then. Go. I want none of you. I should never have taken you on. *Go!*"

"As you say, ser." Dunk beckoned, and Egg followed.

That last night Dunk wanted to be as far from Eustace Osgrey as he could, so they slept down in the cellar, amongst the rest of Standfast's meager host. It was a restless night. Lem and red-eyed Pate both snored, the one loudly and the other constantly. Dank vapors filled the cellar, rising through the trap from the deeper vaults below. Dunk tossed and turned on the scratchy bed, drifting off into a half sleep only to wake suddenly in darkness. The bites he'd gotten in the woods were itching fiercely, and there were fleas in the straw as well. *I will be well rid of this place, well rid of the old man, and Ser Bennis, and the rest of them.* Maybe it was time that he took Egg back to Summerhall to see his father. He would ask the boy about that in the morning, when they were well away.

Morning seemed a long way off, though. Dunk's head was full of dragons, red and black ... full of chequy lions, old shields, battered boots ... full of streams and moats and dams, and papers stamped with the king's great seal that he could not read.

And *she* was there as well, the Red Widow, Rohanne of the Cold-moat. He could see her freckled face, her slender arms, her long red braid. It made him feel guilty. *I should be dreaming of Tanselle. Tanselle Too-Tall, they called her, but she was not too tall for me.* She had painted arms upon his shield and he had saved her from the Bright Prince, but she vanished even before the trial of seven. *She could not bear to see me die,* Dunk often told himself, but what did he know? He was as thick as a castle wall. Just thinking of the Red Widow was proof enough of that. *Tanselle smiled at me, but we never held each other, never kissed, not even lips to cheek.* Rohanne at least had touched him; he had the swollen lip to prove it. *Don't be daft. She's not for the likes of you. She is too small, too clever, and much too dangerous.*

Drowsing at long last, Dunk dreamed. He was running through a glade in the heart of Wat's Wood, running toward Rohanne, and she was shooting arrows at him. Each shaft she loosed flew true, and pierced him through the chest, yet the pain was strangely sweet. He should have turned and fled, but he ran toward her instead, running slowly as you always did in dreams, as if the very air had turned to honey. Another arrow came, and yet another. Her quiver seemed to have no end of shafts. Her eyes were grey and green and full of mischief. *Your gown brings out the color of your eyes,* he meant to say to her, but she was not wearing any gown, or any clothes at all. Across her small breasts was a faint spray of freckles, and her nipples were red and hard as little berries. The arrows made him look like some great porcupine as he went stumbling to her feet, but somehow he still found the strength to grab her braid. With one hard yank he pulled her down on top of him and kissed her.

He woke suddenly, at the sound of a shout.

In the darkened cellar, all was confusion. Curses and complaints echoed back and forth, and men were stumbling over one another as they fumbled for their spears or breeches. No one knew what was happening. Egg found the tallow candle and got it lit, to shed some light upon the scene. Dunk was the first one up the steps. He almost collided with Sam Stoops rushing down, puffing like a bellows and babbling incoherently. Dunk had to hold him by both shoulders to keep him from falling. "Sam, what's wrong?"

"The sky," the old man whimpered. "The *sky*!" No more sense could be got from him, so they all went up to the roof for a look. Ser Eustace was there before them, standing by the parapets in his bedrobe, staring off into the distance.

The sun was rising in the west.

It was a long moment before Dunk realized what that meant. "Wat's Wood is afire," he said in a hushed voice. From down at the base of the tower came the sound of Bennis cursing, a stream of such surpassing filth that it might have made Aegon the Unworthy blush. Sam Stoops began to pray.

They were too far away to make out flames, but the red glow engulfed half the western horizon, and above the light the stars were vanishing. The King's Crown was half gone already, obscured behind a veil of the rising smoke.

Fire and sword, she said.

The fire burned all through the night. No one in Standfast slept tonight. Before long they could smell the smoke, and see flames dancing in the distance like girls in scarlet skirts. They all wondered if the fire would engulf them. Dunk stood behind the parapets, his eyes burning, watching for riders in the night. "Bennis," he said, when the brown knight came up, chewing on his sourleaf, "it's you she wants. Might be you should go."

"What, run?" He brayed. "On *my* horse? Might as well try to fly off on one o' these damn chickens."

"Then give yourself up. She'll only slit your nose."

"I like my nose how it is, lunk. Let her try and take me, we'll see what gets slit open." He sat cross-legged with his back against a merlon and took a whetstone from his pouch to sharpen his sword. Ser Eustace stood above him. In low voices, they spoke of how to fight the war. "The Longinch will expect us at the dam," Dunk heard the old knight say, "so we will burn her crops instead. Fire for fire." Ser Bennis thought that would be just the thing, only maybe they should put her mill to the torch as well. "It's six leagues on t'other side o' the castle, the Longinch won't be looking for us there. Burn the mill and kill the miller, that'll cost her dear."

Egg was listening too. He coughed, and looked at Dunk with wide white eyes. "Ser, you have to stop them."

"How?" Dunk asked. *The Red Widow will stop them. Her, and that Lucas Longinch.* "They're only making noise, Egg. It's that, or piss their breeches. And it's naught to do with us now."

Dawn came with hazy grey skies and air that burned the eyes. Dunk meant to make an early start; though after their sleepless night he did not know how far they'd get. He and Egg broke their fast on boiled eggs while Bennis was rousting the others outside for more drill. *They are Osgrey men and we are not,* he told himself. He ate four of the eggs. Ser Eustace owed him that much, as he saw it. Egg ate two. They washed them down with ale.

"We could go to Fair Isle, ser," the boy said, as they were gathering up their things. "If they're being raided by the ironmen, Lord Farman might be looking for some swords."

It was a good thought. "Have you ever been to Fair Isle?"

"No, ser," Egg said, "but they say it's fair. Lord Farman's seat is fair too. It's called Faircastle."

Dunk laughed. "Faircastle it shall be." He felt as if a great weight had been lifted off his shoulders. "I'll see to the horses," he said, when he'd tied his armor up in a bundle, secured with hempen rope. "Go to the roof and get our bedrolls, squire." The last thing he wanted this morning was another confrontation with the chequy lion. "If you see Ser Eustace, let him be."

"I will, ser."

Outside, Bennis had his recruits lined up with their spears and shields and was trying to teach them to advance in unison. The brown knight paid Dunk not the slightest heed as he crossed the yard. *He will lead the whole lot of them to their deaths. The Red Widow could be here any moment.* Egg came bursting from the tower door and clattered down the wooden steps with their bedrolls. Above him, Ser Eustace stood stiffly on the balcony, his hands resting on the parapet. When his eyes met Dunk's his mustache quivered, and he quickly turned away. The air was hazy with blowing smoke.

Bennis had his shield slung across his back, a tall kite shield of unpainted wood, dark with countless layers of old varnish and girded all about with iron. It bore no blazon, only a center bosse that reminded Dunk of some great eye, shut tight. *As blind as he is.* "How do you mean to fight her?" Dunk asked.

Ser Bennis looked at his soldiers, his mouth running red with sourleaf. "Can't hold the hill with so few spears. Got to be the tower. We all hole up inside." He nodded at the door. "Only one way in. Haul up them wooden steps, and there's no way they can reach us."

"Until they build some steps of their own. They might bring ropes and grapnels too, and swarm down on you through the roof. Unless they just stand back with their crossbows and fill you full of quarrels while you're trying to hold the door."

The Melons, Beans, and Barleycorns were listening to all they said.

All their brave talk had blown away though there was no breath of wind. They stood clutching their sharpened sticks, looking at Dunk and Bennis and each other.

"This lot won't do you a lick of good," Dunk said with a nod at the ragged Osgrey army. "The Red Widow's knights will cut them to pieces if you leave them in the open, and their spears won't be any use inside that tower."

"They can chuck things off the roof," said Bennis. "Treb is good at chucking rocks."

"He could chuck a rock or two, I suppose," said Dunk, "until one of the widow's crossbowmen puts a bolt through him."

"Ser?" Egg stood beside him. "Ser, if we mean to go, we'd best be gone, in case the widow comes."

The boy was right. *If we linger, we'll be trapped here.* Yet still Dunk hesitated. "Let them go, Bennis."

"What, lose our valiant lads?" Bennis looked at the peasants and brayed laughter. "Don't you lot be getting any notions," he warned them. "I'll gut any man who tries to run."

"Try, and I'll gut you." Dunk drew his sword. "Go home, all of you," he told the smallfolk. "Go back to your villages, and see if the fire's spared your homes and crops."

No one moved. The brown knight stared at him, his mouth working. Dunk ignored him. "Go," he told the smallfolk once again. It was as if some god had put the word into his mouth. *Not the Warrior. Is there a god for fools?* "GO!" he said again, roaring it this time.

"Take your spears and shields, but *go*, or you won't live to see the morrow. Do you want to kiss your wives again? Do you want to hold your children? *Go home!* Have you all gone deaf?"

They hadn't. A mad scramble ensued amongst the chickens. Big Rob trod on a hen as he made his dash, and Pate came within half a foot of disemboweling Will Bean when his own spear tripped him up, but off they went, running. The Melons went one way, the Beans another, the Barleycorns a third. Ser Eustace was shouting down at them from above, but no one paid him any mind. *They are deaf to him at least,* Dunk thought.

By the time the old knight emerged from his tower and came scrambling down the steps, only Dunk and Egg and Bennis remained amongst the chickens. "Come back," Ser Eustace shouted at his fast-fleeing host. "You do not have my leave to go. *You do not have my leave!*"

"No use, m'lord," said Bennis. "They're gone."

Ser Eustace rounded on Dunk, his mustache quivering with rage. "You had no right to send them away. *No right!* I told them not to go, I *forbade* it. I *forbade* you to dismiss them."

"We never heard you, my lord." Egg took off his hat to fan away the smoke. "The chickens were cackling too loud."

The old man sank down onto Standfast's lowest step. "What did that woman offer you to deliver me to her?" he asked Dunk in a bleak voice. "How much gold did she give you to betray me, to send my lads away and leave me here alone?"

"You're not alone, m'lord." Dunk sheathed his sword. "I slept beneath your roof and ate your eggs this morning. I owe you some service still. I won't go slinking off with my tail between my legs. My sword's still here." He touched the hilt.

"One sword." The old knight got slowly to his feet. "What can one sword hope to do against that woman?"

"Try and keep her off your land, to start with." Dunk wished he was as certain as he sounded.

The old knight's mustache trembled every time he took a breath. "Yes," he said at last. "Better to go boldly than hide behind stone walls. Better to die a lion than a rabbit. We were the Marshals of the North-march for a thousand years. I must have my armor." He started up the steps.

Egg was looking up at Dunk. "I never knew you had a tail, ser," the boy said.

"Do you want a clout in the ear?"

"No, ser. Do you want your armor?"

"That," Dunk said, "and one thing more."

There was talk of Ser Bennis coming with them, but in the end Ser Eustace commanded him to stay and hold the tower. His sword would be of little use against the odds that they were like to face, and the sight of him would inflame the widow further.

The brown knight did not require much convincing. Dunk helped him knock loose the iron pegs that held the upper steps in place. Bennis clambered up them, untied the old grey hempen rope, and hauled on it with all his strength. Creaking and groaning, the wooden stair swung upward, leaving ten feet of air between the top stone step and the tower's only entrance. Sam Stoops and his wife were both inside. The chickens would need to fend for themselves. Sitting below on his grey gelding, Ser Eustace called up to say, "If we have not returned by nightfall . . ."

"... I'll ride for Highgarden, m'lord, and tell Lord Tyrell how that woman burned your wood and murdered you."

Dunk followed Egg and Maester down the hill. The old man came after, his armor rattling softly. For once a wind was rising, and he could hear the flapping of his cloak.

Where Wat's Wood had stood they found a smoking wasteland. The fire had largely burned itself out by the time they reached the wood, but here and there a few patches were still burning, fiery islands in a sea of ash and cinders. Elsewhere the trunks of burned trees thrust like blackened spears into the sky. Other trees had fallen and lay athwart the west way with limbs charred and broken, dull red fires smoldering inside their hollow hearts. There were hot spots on the forest floor as well, and places where the smoke hung in the air like a hot grey haze. Ser Eustace was stricken with a fit of coughing, and for a few moments Dunk feared the old man would need to turn back, but finally it passed.

They rode past the carcass of a red deer, and later on what might have been a badger. Nothing lived, except the flies. Flies could live through anything, it seemed. "The Field of Fire must have looked like this," Ser Eustace said. "It was there our woes began, two hundred years ago. The last of the green kings perished on that field, with the finest flowers of the Reach around him. My father said the dragonfire burned so hot that their swords melted in their hands. Afterward the blades were gathered up, and went to make the Iron Throne. Highgarden passed from kings to stewards, and the Osgreys dwindled and diminished, until the Marshals of the Northmarch were no more than landed knights bound in fealty to the Rowans."

Dunk had nothing to say to that, so they rode in silence for a time, till Ser Eustace coughed, and said, "Ser Duncan, do you remember the story that I told you?"

"I might, ser," said Dunk. "Which one?"

"The Little Lion."

"I remember. He was the youngest of five sons."

"Good." He coughed again. "When he slew Lancel Lannister, the westermen turned back. Without the king there was no war. Do you understand what I am saying?"

"Aye," Dunk said reluctantly. *Could I kill a woman?* For once Dunk wished he *were* as thick as that castle wall. *It must not come to that. I must not let it come to that.*

A few green trees still stood where the west way crossed the Chequy Water; their trunks were charred and blackened on one side. Just beyond, the water glimmered darkly. *Blue and green,* Dunk thought, *but all the gold is gone.* The smoke had veiled the sun.

Ser Eustace halted when he reached the water's edge. "I took a holy vow. I will not cross that stream. Not so long as the land beyond is *hers.*" The old knight wore mail and plate beneath his yellowed surcoat. His sword was on his hip.

"What if she never comes, ser?" Egg asked.

With fire and sword, Dunk thought. "She'll come."

She did, and within the hour. They heard her horses first, then the faint metallic sound of clinking armor, growing louder. The drifting smoke made it hard to tell how far off they were until her banner-bearer pushed through the ragged grey curtain. His staff was crowned by an iron spider painted white and red, with the black banner of the Webbers hanging listlessly beneath. When he saw them across the water, he halted on the bank. Ser Lucas Inchfield appeared half a heartbeat later, armored head to heel.

Only then did Lady Rohanne herself appear, astride a coal-black mare decked out in strands of silverly silk, like unto a spider's web. The widow's cloak was made of the same stuff. It billowed from her shoulders and her wrists, as light as air. She was armored too, in a suit of green enamel scale chased with gold and silver. It fit her figure like a glove and made her look as if she were garbed in summer leaves. Her long red braid hung down behind her, bouncing as she rode. Septon

Sefton rode red-faced at her side, atop a big grey gelding. On her other side was her young maester, Cerrick, mounted on a mule.

More knights came after, half a dozen of them, attended by as many esquires. A column of mounted crossbowmen brought up the rear and fanned out to either side of the road when they reached the Chequy Water and saw Dunk waiting on the other side. There were three-and-thirty fighting men all told, excluding the septon, the maester, and the widow herself. One of the knights caught Dunk's eye—a squat, bald keg of a man in mail and leather, with an angry face and an ugly goiter on his neck.

The Red Widow walked her mare to the edge of the water. "Ser Eustace, Ser Duncan," she called across the stream, "we saw your fire burning in the night."

"Saw it?" Ser Eustace shouted back. "Aye, you saw it . . . after you made it."

"That is a vile accusation."

"For a vile act."

"I was asleep in my bed last night, with my ladies all around me. The shouts from the walls awoke me, as they did most everyone. Old men climbed up steep tower steps to look, and babes at the breast saw the red light and wept in fear. And that is all I know of your fire, ser."

"It was your fire, woman," insisted Ser Eustace. "My wood is gone. *Gone*, I say!"

Septon Sefton cleared his throat. "Ser Eustace," he boomed, "there are fires in the kingswood too, and even in the rainwood. The drought has turned all our woods to kindling."

Lady Rohanne raised an arm and pointed. "Look at my fields,

Osgrey. How dry they are. I would have been a fool to set a fire. Had the wind changed direction, the flames might well have leapt the stream and burned out half my crops."

"Might have?" Ser Eustace shouted. "It was my woods that burned, and you that burned them. Most like you cast some witch's spell to drive the wind, just as you used your dark arts to slay your husbands and your brothers!"

Lady Rohanne's face grew harder. Dunk had seen that look at Cold-moat, just before she slapped him. "Prattle," she told the old man. "I will waste no more words on you, ser. Produce Bennis of the Brown Shield or we will come and take him."

"That you shall not do," Ser Eustace declared in ringing tones. "That you shall *never* do." His mustache twitched. "Come no farther. This side of the stream is mine, and you are not wanted here. You shall have no hospitality from me. No bread and salt, not even shade and water. You come as an intruder. I forbid you to set foot on Osgrey land."

Lady Rohanne drew her braid over her shoulder. "Ser Lucas," was all she said. The Longinch made a gesture, the crossbowmen dismounted, winched back their bowstrings with the help of hook and stirrup, and plucked quarrels from their quivers. "Now, ser," her lady-ship called out, when every bow was nocked and raised and ready, "what was it you forbade me?"

Dunk had heard enough. "If you cross the stream without leave, you are breaking the king's peace."

Septon Sefton urged his horse forward a step. "The king will nei-ther know nor care," he called. "We are all the Mother's children, ser. For her sake, stand aside."

Dunk frowned. "I don't know much of gods, septon ... but aren't we the Warrior's children, too?" He rubbed the back of his neck. "If you try to cross, I'll stop you."

Ser Lucas the Longinch laughed. "Here's a hedge knight who yearns to be a hedgehog, my lady," he said to the Red Widow. "Say the word, and we'll put a dozen quarrels in him. At this distance they will punch through that armor like it was made of spit."

"No. Not yet, ser." Lady Rohanne studied him from across the stream. "You are two men and a boy. We are three-and-thirty. How do you propose to stop us crossing?"

"Well," said Dunk, "I'll tell you. But only you."

"As you wish." She pressed her heels into her horse and rode her out into the stream. When the water reached the mare's belly, she halted, waiting. "Here I am. Come closer, ser. I promise not to sew you in a sack."

Ser Eustace grasped Dunk by the arm before he could respond. "Go to her," the old knight said, "but remember the Little Lion."

"As you say, m'lord." Dunk walked Thunder down into the water. He drew up beside her, and said, "M'lady."

"Ser Duncan." She reached up and laid two fingers on his swollen lip. "Did I do this, ser?"

"No one else has slapped my face of late, m'lady."

"That was bad of me. A breach of hospitality. The good septon has been scolding me." She gazed across the water at Ser Eustace. "I scarce remember Addam any longer. It was more than half my life ago. I remember that I loved him, though. I have not loved any of the others."

"His father put him in the blackberries, with his brothers," Dunk said. "He was fond of blackberries."

"I remember. He used to pick them for me, and we'd eat them in a bowl of cream."

"The king pardoned the old man for Daemon," said Dunk. "It is past time you pardoned him for Addam."

"Give me Bennis and I'll consider that."

"Bennis is not mine to give."

She sighed. "I would as lief not have to kill you."

"I would as lief not die."

"Then give me Bennis. We'll cut his nose off and hand him back, and that will be the end of that."

"It won't, though," Dunk said. "There's still the dam to deal with, and the fire. Will you give us the men who set it?"

"There were lantern bugs in that wood," she said. "It may be they set the fire off, with their little lanterns."

"No more teasing now, m'lady," Dunk warned her. "This is no time for it. Tear down the dam and let Ser Eustace have the water to make up for the wood. That's fair, is it not?"

"It might be if I had burned the wood. Which I did not. I was at Coldmoat, safe abed." She looked down at the water. "What is there to prevent us from riding right across the stream? Have you scattered caltrops amongst the rocks? Hidden archers in the ashes? Tell me what you think is going to stop us."

"Me." He pulled one gauntlet off. "In Flea Bottom I was always bigger and stronger than the other boys, so I used to beat them bloody and steal from them. The old man taught me not to do that. It was wrong, he said, and besides, sometimes little boys have great big brothers. Here, have a look at this." Dunk twisted the ring off his finger and held it out to her. She had to let loose of her braid to take it.

"Gold?" she said, when she felt the weight of it. "What is this, ser?" She turned it over in her hand. "A signet. Gold and onyx." Her green eyes narrowed as she studied the seal. "Where did you find this, ser?"

"In a boot. Wrapped in rags and stuffed up in the toe."

Lady Rohanne's fingers closed around it. She glanced at Egg and old Ser Eustace. "You took a great risk in showing me this ring, ser. But how does it avail us? If I should command my men to cross ..."

"Well," said Dunk, "that would mean I'd have to fight."

"And die."

"Most like," he said, "and Egg would go back where he comes from, and tell what happened here."

"Not if he died as well."

"I don't think you'd kill a boy of ten," he said, hoping he was right. "Not *this* boy of ten, you wouldn't. You got three-and-thirty men there, like you said. Men talk. That fat one there especially. No matter how deep you dug the graves, the tale would out. And then, well ... might be a spotted spider's bite can kill a lion, but a dragon is a different sort of beast."

"I would sooner be the dragon's friend." She tried the ring on her finger. It was too big even for her thumb. "Dragon or no, I must have Bennis of the Brown Shield."

"No."

"You are seven feet of stubborn."

"Less an inch."

She gave him back the ring. "I cannot return to Coldmoat empty-handed. They will say the Red Widow has lost her bite, that she was too weak to do justice, that she could not protect her smallfolk. You do not understand, ser."

"I might." *Better than you know.* "I remember once some little lord in the stormlands took Ser Arlan into service, to help him fight some other little lord. When I asked the old man what they were fighting over, he said, 'Nothing, lad. It's just some pissing contest.'"

Lady Rohanne gave him a shocked look but could sustain it no more than half a heartbeat before it turned into a grin. "I have heard a thousand empty courtesies in my time, but you are the first knight who ever said *pissing* in my presence." Her freckled face went somber. "Those pissing contests are how lords judge one another's strength, and woe to any man who shows his weakness. A woman must needs piss twice as hard, if she hopes to rule. And if that woman should happen to be *small* ... Lord Stackhouse covets my Horseshoe Hills, Ser Clifford Conklyn has an old claim to Leafy Lake, those dismal Durwells live by stealing cattle ... and beneath mine own roof I have the Longinch. Every day I wake wondering if this might be the day he marries me by force." Her hand curled tight around her braid, as hard as if it were a rope, and she was dangling over a precipice. "He wants to, I know. He holds back for fear of my wroth, just as Conklyn and Stackhouse and the Durwells tread carefully where the Red Widow is concerned. If any of them thought for a moment that I had turned weak and soft ..."

Dunk put the ring back on his finger, and drew his dagger.

The widow's eyes went wide at the sight of naked steel. "What are you doing?" she said. "Have you lost your *wits*? There are a dozen crossbows trained on you."

"You wanted blood for blood." He laid the dagger against his cheek. "They told you wrong. It wasn't Bennis cut that digger, it was me." He pressed the edge of the steel into his face, slashed downward. When he shook the blood off the blade some spattered on her face. *More freckles,* he thought. "There, the Red Widow has her due. A cheek for a cheek."

"You are quite mad." The smoke had filled her eyes with tears. "If you were better born, I'd marry you."

"Aye, m'lady. And if pigs had wings and scales and breathed flame, they'd be as good as dragons." Dunk slid the knife back in its sheath. His face had begun to throb. The blood ran down his cheek and dripped onto his gorget. The smell made Thunder snort and paw the water. "Give me the men who burned the wood."

"No one burned the wood," she said, "but if some man of mine had done so, it must have been to please me. How could I give such a man to you?" She glanced back at her escort. "It would be best if Ser Eustace were just to withdraw his accusation."

"Those pigs will be breathing fire first, m'lady."

"In that case, I must assert my innocence before the eyes of gods and men. Tell Ser Eustace that I demand an apology . . . or a trial. The choice is his." She wheeled her horse about to ride back to her men.

The stream would be their battleground.

Septon Sefton waddled out and said a prayer, beseeching the Father Above to look down on these two men and judge them justly, asking the Warrior to lend his strength to the man whose cause was just and true, begging the Mother's mercy for the liar, that he might be forgiven for his sins. When the praying was over and done with, he turned to Ser Eustace Osgrey one last time. "Ser," he said, "I beg you once again, withdraw your accusation."

"I will not," the old man said, his mustache trembling.

The fat septon turned to Lady Rohanne. "Good-sister, if you did this thing, confess your guilt, and offer good Ser Eustace some restitution for his wood. Elsewise blood must flow."

"My champion will prove my innocence before the eyes of gods and men."

"Trial by battle is not the only way," said the septon, waist deep in the water. "Let us go to Goldengrove, I implore you both, and place the matter before Lord Rowan for his judgment."

"*Never,*" said Ser Eustace. The Red Widow shook her head.

Ser Lucas Inchfield looked at Lady Rohanne, his face dark with fury. "You *will* marry me when this mummer's farce is done. As your lord father wished."

"My lord father never knew you as I do," she gave back.

220 † *George R.R. Martin*

Dunk went to one knee beside Egg and put the signet back in the boy's hand—four three-headed dragons, two and two, the arms of Maekar, Prince of Summerhall. "Back in the boot," he said, "but if it happens that I die, go to the nearest of your father's friends and have him take you back to Summerhall. Don't try to cross the whole Reach on your own. See you don't forget, or my ghost will come and clout you in the ear."

"Yes, ser," said Egg, "but I'd sooner you didn't die."

"It's too hot to die." Dunk donned his helm, and Egg helped him

fasten it tightly to his gorget. The blood was sticky on his face though Ser Eustace had torn a piece off his cloak to help stop the gash from bleeding. He rose and went to Thunder. Most of the smoke had blown away, he saw as he swung up onto the saddle, but the sky was still dark. *Clouds,* he thought, *dark clouds.* It had been so long. *Maybe it's an omen. But is it his omen, or mine?* Dunk was no good with omens.

Across the stream, Ser Lucas had mounted up as well. His horse was a chestnut courser; a splendid animal, swift and strong, but not as large as Thunder. What the horse lacked in size he made up for in armor, though; he was clad in crinet, chanfron, and a coat of light chain. The Longinch himself wore black enameled plate and silvery ringmail. An onyx spider squatted malignantly atop his helmet, but his shield displayed his own arms: a bend sinister, chequy black and white, on a pale grey field. Dunk watched Ser Lucas hand it to a squire. *He does not mean to use it.* When another squire delivered him a poleaxe, he knew why. The axe was long and lethal, with a banded haft, a heavy head, and a wicked spike on its back, but it was a two-handed weapon. The Longinch would need to trust in his armor to protect him. *I need to make him rue that choice.*

His own shield was on his left arm, the shield Tanselle had painted with his elm and falling star. The old shield rhyme echoed in his head. *Oak and iron, guard me well, or else I'm dead, and doomed to hell.* He slid his longsword from its scabbard. The weight of it felt good in his hand.

He put his heels into Thunder's flanks and walked the big destrier down into the water. Across the stream, Ser Lucas did the same. Dunk pressed right, so as to present the Longinch with his left side, protected by his shield. That was not something Ser Lucas was willing to concede him. He turned his courser quickly, and they came together in a tumult of grey steel and green spray. Ser Lucas struck with his poleaxe. Dunk had to twist in the saddle to catch it on his shield. The force of it shot down his arm and jarred his teeth together. He swung his sword in answer, a sideways cut that took the other knight beneath his upraised arm. Steel screamed on steel, and it was on.

The Longinch spurred his courser in a circle, trying to get around to Dunk's unprotected side,

but Thunder wheeled to meet him, snapping at the other horse. Ser Lucas delivered one crashing blow after another, standing in his stirrups to get all his weight and strength behind the axehead. Dunk shifted his shield to catch each blow as it came. Half-crouched beneath its oak, he hacked at Inchfield's arms and side and legs, but his plate turned every stroke. Round they went, and round again, the water lapping at their legs. The Longinch attacked, and Dunk defended, watching for a weakness.

Finally he saw it. Every time Ser Lucas lifted his axe for another blow, a gap appeared beneath his arm. There was mail and leather there, and padding underneath, but no steel plate. Dunk kept his shield up, trying to time his attack. *Soon. Soon.* The axe crashed down, wrenched free, came up. *Now!* He slammed his spurs into Thunder, driving him closer, and thrust with his longsword, to drive his point through the opening.

But the gap vanished as quick as it had appeared. His swordpoint scraped a rondel, and Dunk, overextended, almost lost his seat. The axe descended with a crash, slanting off the iron rim of Dunk's shield, crunching against the side of his helm, and striking Thunder a glancing blow along the neck.

The destrier screamed and reared up on two legs, his eye rolling white in pain as the sharp, coppery smell of blood filled the air. He lashed out with his iron hooves just as Longinch was moving in. One caught Ser Lucas in the face, the other on a shoulder. Then the heavy warhorse came down atop his courser.

It all happened in a heartbeat. The two horses went down in a tangle, kicking and biting at each other, churning up the water and the mud below. Dunk tried to throw himself from the saddle, but one foot tangled in a stirrup. He fell face-first, sucking down one desperate gulp of air before the stream came rushing into the helm through the eyeslit. His foot was still caught up, and he felt a savage yank as Thunder's struggles almost pulled his leg out of its socket. Just as quickly he was free, turning, sinking. For a moment he flailed helplessly in the water. The world was blue and green and brown.

The weight of his armor pulled him down until his shoulder bumped the streambed. *If that is down the other way is up.* Dunk's steel-clad hands fumbled at the stones and sands, and somehow he gathered his legs up under him and stood. He was reeling, dripping mud, with water pouring from the breath holes in his dinted helm, but he was standing. He sucked down air.

His battered shield still clung to his left arm, but his scabbard was empty and his sword was gone. There was blood inside his helm as well as water. When he tried to shift his weight, his ankle sent a lance of pain right up his leg. Both horses had struggled back to their feet, he saw. He turned his head, squinting one-eyed through a veil of blood, searching for his foe. *Gone,* he thought, *he's drowned, or Thunder crushed his skull in.*

Ser Lucas burst up out of the water right in front of him, sword in hand. He struck Dunk's neck a savage blow, and only the thickness of his gorget kept his head upon his shoulders. He had no blade to answer with, only his shield.

He gave ground, and the Longinch came after, screaming and slashing. Dunk's upraised arm took a numbing blow above the elbow. A cut to his hip made him grunt in pain. As he backed away, a rock turned beneath his foot, and he went down to one knee, chest high in the water. He got his shield up, but this time Ser Lucas struck so hard he split the thick oak right down the middle and drove the remnants back into Dunk's face. His ears were ringing and his mouth was full of blood, but somewhere far away he heard Egg screaming. "Get him, ser, get him, get him, he's *right there!*"

Dunk dove forward. Ser Lucas had wrenched his sword free for another cut. He slammed into him waist high and knocked him off his feet. The stream swallowed both of them again, but this time Dunk was ready. He kept one arm around the Longinch and forced him to the bottom. Bubbles came streaming out from behind Inchfield's battered, twisted visor, but still he fought. He found a rock at the bottom of the stream and began hammering at Dunk's head and hands. Dunk fumbled at his sword belt. *Have I lost the dagger too?* he wondered. No, there it was. His hand closed round the hilt and he wrenched it free, and drove it slowly through the churning water, through the iron rings and boiled leather beneath the arm of Lucas the Longinch, turning it as he pushed. Ser Lucas jerked and twisted, and the strength left him. Dunk shoved away and floated. His chest was on fire. A fish flashed past his face, long and white and slender. *What's that?* he wondered. *What's that? What's that?*

He woke in the wrong castle.

When his eyes opened, he did not know where he was. It was blessedly cool. The taste of blood was in his mouth and he had a cloth across his eyes, a heavy cloth fragrant with some unguent. It smelled of cloves, he thought.

Dunk groped at his face, pulled the cloth away. Above him torchlight played against a high ceiling. Ravens were walking on the rafters overhead, peering down with small black eyes and *quork*ing at him. *I am not blind, at least.* He was in a maester's tower. The walls were lined with racks of herbs and potions in earthen jars and vessels of green glass. A long trestle table nearby was covered with parchments, books, and queer bronze instruments, all spattered with droppings from the ravens in the rafters. He could hear them muttering at one another.

He tried to sit. It proved a bad mistake. His head swam, and his left leg screamed in agony when he put the slightest weight upon it. His ankle was wrapped in linen, he saw, and there were linen strips around his chest and shoulders too.

"Be still." A face appeared above him, young and pinched, with dark brown eyes on either side of a hooked nose. Dunk knew that face. The man who owned it was all in grey, with a chain collar hanging loose about his neck, a maester's chain of many metals. Dunk grabbed him by the wrist. "Where . . . ?"

"Coldmoat," said the maester. "You were too badly injured to return to Standfast, so Lady Rohanne commanded us to bring you here. Drink this." He raised a cup of . . . something . . . to Dunk's lips. The potion had a bitter taste, like vinegar, but at least it washed away the taste of blood.

Dunk made himself drink it all. Afterward he flexed the fingers of his sword hand, and then the other. *At least my hands still work, and my arms.* "What . . . what did I hurt?"

"What not?" The maester snorted. "A broken ankle, a sprained knee, a broken collarbone, bruising . . . your upper torso is largely green and yellow and your right arm is a purply black. I thought your skull was cracked as well, but it appears not. There is that gash in your face, ser. You will have a scar, I fear. Oh, and you had drowned by the time we pulled you from the water."

"Drowned?" said Dunk.

"I never suspected that one man could swallow so much water, not even a man as large as you, ser. Count yourself fortunate that I am ironborn. The priests of the Drowned God know how to drown a man and bring him back, and I have made a study of their beliefs and customs."

I drowned. Dunk tried to sit again, but the strength was not in him. *I drowned in water that did not even come up to my neck.* He laughed, then groaned in pain. "Ser Lucas?"

"Dead. Did you doubt it?"

No. Dunk doubted many things, but not that. He remembered how the strength had gone out of the Longinch's limbs, all at once. "Egg," he got out. "I want Egg."

"Hunger is a good sign," the maester said, "but it is sleep you need just now, not food."

Dunk shook his head, and regretted it at once. "Egg is my squire..."

"Is he? A brave lad, and stronger than he looks. He was the one to pull you from the stream. He helped us get that armor off you too, and rode with you in the wayn when we brought you here. He would not sleep himself, but sat by your side with your sword across his lap, in case someone tried to do you harm. He even suspected *me,* and insisted that I taste anything I meant to feed you. A queer child, but devoted."

"Where is he?"

"Ser Eustace asked the boy to attend him at the wedding feast. There was no one else on his side. It would have been discourteous for him to refuse."

"Wedding feast?" Dunk did not understand.

"You would not know, of course. Coldmoat and Standfast were reconciled after your battle. Lady Rohanne begged leave of old Ser Eustace to cross his land and visit Addam's grave, and he granted her that right. She knelt before the blackberries and began to weep, and he was so moved that he went to comfort her. They spent the whole night talking of young Addam and my lady's noble father. Lord Wyman and Ser Eustace were fast friends, until the Blackfyre Rebellion. His lordship and my lady were wed this morning, by our good Septon Sefton. Eustace Osgrey is the Lord of Coldmoat, and his chequy lion flies beside the Webber spider on every tower and wall."

Dunk's world was spinning slowly all around him. *That potion. He's put me back to sleep.* He closed his eyes and let all the pain drain out of him. He could hear the ravens *quork*ing and screaming at each other, and the sound of his own breath, and something else as well ... a softer sound, steady, heavy, somehow soothing. "What's that?" he murmured sleepily. "That sound ... ?"

"That?" The maester listened. "That's just rain."

*   *   *

He did not see her till the day they took their leave.

"This is folly, ser," Septon Sefton complained, as Dunk limped heavily across the yard, swinging his splinted foot and leaning on a crutch. "Maester Cerrick says you are not half-healed as yet, and this rain ... you're like to catch a chill, if you do not drown again. At least wait for the rain to stop."

"That may be years." Dunk was grateful to the fat septon, who had visited him near every day ... to pray for him, ostensibly, though more time seemed to be taken up with tales and gossip. He would miss his loose and lively tongue and cheerful company, but that changed nothing. "I need to go."

The rain was lashing down around them, a thousand cold grey whips upon his back. His cloak was already sodden. It was the white wool cloak Ser Eustace had given him, with the green-and-gold-checkered border. The old knight had pressed it on him once again, as a parting gift. "For your courage and leal service, ser," he said. The brooch that pinned the cloak at his shoulder was a gift as well; an ivory spider brooch with silver legs. Clusters of crushed garnets made spots upon its back.

"I hope this is not some mad quest to hunt down Bennis," Septon Sefton said. "You are so bruised and battered that I would fear for you if that one found you in such a state."

Bennis, Dunk thought bitterly, *bloody Bennis.* While Dunk had been making his stand at the stream, Bennis had tied up Sam Stoops and his wife, ransacked Standfast from top to bottom, and made off with every item of value he could find, from candles, clothes, and weaponry to Osgrey's old silver cup and a small cache of coins the old man had hidden in his solar behind a mildewed tapestry. One day Dunk hoped to meet Ser Bennis of the Brown Shield again, and when he did ... "Bennis will keep."

"Where will you go?" The septon was panting heavily. Even with Dunk on a crutch, he was too fat to match his pace.

"Fair Isle. Harrenhal. The Trident. There are hedges everywhere." He shrugged. "I've always wanted to see the Wall."

"The Wall?" The septon jerked to a stop. "I despair of you, Ser Duncan!" he shouted, standing in the mud with outspread hands as the rain came down around him. "Pray, ser, pray for the Crone to light your way!" Dunk kept walking.

She was waiting for him inside the stables, standing by the yellow bales of hay in a gown as green as summer. "Ser Duncan," she said when he came pushing through the door. Her red braid hung down in front, the end of it brushing against her thighs. "It is good to see you on your feet."

You never saw me on my back, he thought. "M'lady. What brings you to the stables? It's a wet day for a ride."

"I might say the same to you."

"Egg told you?" *I owe him another clout in the ear.*

"Be glad he did, or I would have sent men after you to drag you back. It was cruel of you to try to steal away without so much as a farewell."

She had never come to see him while he was in Maester Cerrick's care, not once. "That green becomes you well, m'lady," he said. "It brings out the color of your eyes." He shifted his weight awkwardly on the crutch. "I'm here for my horse."

"You do not need to go. There is a place for you here, when you're recovered. Captain of my guards. And Egg can join my other squires. No one need ever know who he is."

"Thank you, m'lady, but no." Thunder was in a stall a dozen places down. Dunk hobbled toward him.

"Please reconsider, ser. These are perilous times, even for dragons and their friends. Stay until you've healed." She walked along beside him. "It would please Lord Eustace too. He is very fond of you."

"Very fond," Dunk agreed. "If his daughter wasn't dead, he'd want me to marry her. Then you could be my lady mother. I never had a mother, much less a *lady* mother."

For half a heartbeat Lady Rohanne looked as though she was going to slap him again. *Maybe she'll just kick my crutch away.*

"You are angry with me, ser," she said instead. "You must let me make amends."

"Well," he said, "you could help me saddle Thunder."

"I had something else in mind." She reached out her hand for his, a freckled hand, her fingers strong and slender. *I'll bet she's freckled all over.* "How well do you know horses?"

"I ride one."

"An old destrier bred for battle, slow-footed and ill-tempered. Not a horse to ride from place to place."

"If I need to get from place to place, it's him or these." Dunk pointed at his feet.

"You have large feet," she observed. "Large hands as well. I think you must be large all over. Too large for most palfreys. They'd look like ponies with you perched upon their backs. Still, a swifter mount would serve you well. A big courser, with some Dornish sand steed for endurance." She pointed to the stall across from Thunder's. "A horse like her."

She was a blood bay with a bright eye and a long, fiery mane. Lady Rohanne took a carrot from her sleeve and stroked her head as she took it. "The carrot, not the fingers," she told the horse, before she turned again to Dunk. "I call her Flame, but you may name her as you please. Call her Amends, if you like."

For a moment he was speechless. He leaned on the crutch and looked at the blood bay with new eyes. She was magnificent. A better mount than any the old man had ever owned. You had only to look at those long, clean limbs to see how swift she'd be.

"I bred her for beauty and for speed."

He turned back to Thunder. "I cannot take her."

"Why not?"

"She is too good a horse for me. Just look at her."

A flush crept up Rohanne's face. She clutched her braid, twisting it between her fingers. "I had to marry, you know that. My father's will ... oh, don't be such a fool."

"What else should I be? I'm thick as a castle wall and bastard-born as well."

"Take the horse. I refuse to let you go without something to remember me by."

"I will remember you, m'lady. Have no fear of that."

"Take her!"

Dunk grabbed her braid and pulled her face to his. It was awkward with the crutch and the difference in their heights. He almost fell before he got his lips on hers. He kissed her hard. One of her hands went round his neck, and one around his chest. He learned more about kissing in a moment than he had ever known from watching. But when they finally broke apart, he drew his dagger. "I know what I want to re-member you by, m'lady."

Egg was waiting for him at the gatehouse, mounted on a handsome new sorrel palfrey and holding Mae-ster's lead. When Dunk trot-ted up to them on Thunder, the boy looked surprised. "She said she wanted to give you a new horse, ser."

"Even highborn ladies don't get all they want," Dunk said, as they rode out across the drawbridge. "It wasn't a horse I wanted." The moat was so high it was threatening to overflow its banks. "I took something else to remember her by in-stead. A lock of that red hair." He reached under his cloak, brought out the braid, and smiled.

In the iron cage at the crossroads, the corpses still embraced. They looked lonely, forlorn. Even the flies had abandoned them, and the crows as well. Only some scraps of skin and hair remained upon the dead men's bones.

Dunk halted, frowning. His ankle was hurting from the ride, but it made no matter. Pain was as much a part of knighthood as were swords and shields. "Which way is south?" he asked Egg. It was hard to know, when the world was all rain and mud and the sky was grey as a granite wall.

"That's south, ser." Egg pointed. "That's north."

"Summerhall is south. Your father."

"The Wall is north."

Dunk looked at him. "That's a long way to ride."

"I have a new horse, ser."

"So you do." Dunk had to smile. "And why would you want to see the Wall?"

"Well," said Egg, "I hear it's tall."

THE
MYSTERY KNIGHT

A light summer rain was falling as Dunk and Egg took their leave of Stoney Sept.

Dunk rode his old warhorse Thunder, with Egg beside him on the spirited young palfrey he'd named Rain, leading their mule, Maester. On Maester's back were bundled Dunk's armor and Egg's books, their bedrolls, tent, and clothing, several slabs of hard salt beef, half a flagon of mead, and two skins of water. Egg's old straw hat, wide-brimmed and floppy, kept the rain off the mule's head. The boy had cut holes for Maester's ears. Egg's new straw hat was on his own head. Except for the ear holes, the two hats looked much the same to Dunk.

As they neared the town gates, Egg reined up sharply. Up above the gateway a traitor's head had been impaled upon an iron spike. It was fresh from the look of it, the flesh more pink than green, but the carrion crows had already gone to work on it. The dead man's lips and cheeks were torn and ragged; his eyes were two brown holes weeping slow red tears as raindrops mingled with the crusted blood. The dead man's mouth sagged open, as if to harangue travelers passing through the gate below.

Dunk had seen such sights before. "Back in King's Landing when I was a boy, I stole a head right off its spike once," he told Egg. Actually it had been Ferret who scampered up the wall to snatch the head, after Rafe and Pudding said he'd never dare, but when the guards came running he'd tossed it down, and Dunk was the one who'd caught it. "Some rebel lord or robber knight, it was. Or maybe just a common murderer. A head's a head. They all look the same after a few days on a spike." He and his three friends had used the head to terrorize the girls of Flea Bottom. They'd chase them through the alleys and make them give the head a kiss before they'd let them go. That head got kissed a lot, as he recalled. There wasn't a girl in King's Landing who could run as fast as Rafe. Egg was better off not hearing that part, though. *Ferret, Rafe, and Pudding. Little monsters, those three, and me the worst of all.* His friends and he had kept the head until the flesh turned black and began to slough away. That took the fun out of chasing girls, so one night they burst into a pot shop and tossed what was left into the kettle. "The crows always go for the eyes," he told Egg. "Then the cheeks cave in, the flesh turns green ..." He squinted. "Wait. I know that face."

"You do, ser," said Egg. "Three days ago. The hunchbacked septon we heard preaching against Lord Bloodraven."

He remembered then. *He was a holy man sworn to the Seven, even if he did preach treason.* "His hands are scarlet with a brother's blood, and the blood of his young nephews too," the hunchback had declared to the crowd that had gathered in the market square. "A shadow came at his command to strangle brave Prince Valarr's sons in their mother's womb. Where is our Young Prince now? Where is his brother, sweet Matarys? Where has Good King Daeron gone, and fearless Baelor Breakspear? The grave has claimed them, every one, yet *he* endures, this pale bird with bloody beak who perches on King Aerys's shoulder and caws into his ear. The mark of hell is on his face and in his empty eye, and he has brought us drought and pestilence and murder. Rise up, I say, and remember our true king across the water. Seven gods there are, and seven kingdoms, and the Black Dragon sired seven sons! Rise up, my lords and ladies. Rise up, you brave knights and sturdy yeomen, and cast down Bloodraven, that foul sorcerer, lest your children and your children's children be cursed forevermore."

Every word was treason. Even so, it was a shock to see him here, with holes where his eyes had been. "That's him, aye," Dunk said, "and another good reason to put this town behind us." He gave Thunder a touch of the spur, and he and Egg rode through the gates of Stoney Sept, listening to the soft sound of the rain.

How many eyes does Lord Bloodraven have? the riddle ran. *A thousand eyes, and one.* Some claimed the King's Hand was a student of the dark arts who could change his face, put on the likeness of a one-eyed dog, even turn into a mist. Packs of gaunt grey wolves hunted down his foes, men said, and carrion crows spied for him and whispered secrets in his ear. Most of the tales were only tales, Dunk did not doubt, but no one could doubt that Bloodraven had informers everywhere.

He had seen the man once with his own two eyes, back in King's Landing. White as bone were the skin and hair of Brynden Rivers, and his eye—he only had the one, the other having been lost to his half brother Bittersteel on the Redgrass Field—was red as blood. On cheek and neck he bore the winestain birthmark that had given him his name.

When the town was well behind them Dunk cleared his throat, and said, "Bad business, cutting off the heads of septons. All he did was talk. Words are wind."

"Some words are wind, ser. Some are treason." Egg was skinny as a stick, all ribs and elbows, but he did have a mouth.

"Now you sound a proper princeling."

Egg took that for an insult, which it was. "He might have been a septon, but he was preaching lies, ser. The drought wasn't Lord Bloodraven's fault, nor the Great Spring Sickness either."

"Might be that's so, but if we start cutting off the heads of all the fools and liars, half the towns in the Seven Kingdoms will be empty."

Six days later, the rain was just a memory.

Dunk had stripped off his tunic to enjoy the warmth of sunlight on his skin. When a little breeze came up, cool and fresh and fragrant as a maiden's breath, he sighed. "Water," he announced. "Smell it? The lake can't be far now."

"All I can smell is Maester, ser. He stinks." Egg gave the mule's lead a savage tug. Maester had stopped to crop at the grass beside the road, as he did from time to time.

"There's an old inn by the lakeshore." Dunk had stopped there once when he was squiring for the old man. "Ser Arlan said they brewed a fine brown ale. Might be we could have a taste while we waited for the ferry."

Egg gave him a hopeful look. "To wash the food down, ser?"

"What food would that be?"

"A slice off the roast?" the boy said. "A bit of duck, a bowl of stew? Whatever they have, ser."

Their last hot meal had been three days ago. Since then, they had been living on windfalls and strips of old salt beef as hard as wood. *It would be good to put some real food in our bellies before we start north. That Wall's a long way off.*

"We could spend the night as well," suggested Egg.

"Does m'lord want a feather bed?"

"Straw will serve me well enough, ser," said Egg, offended.

"We have no coin for beds."

"We have twenty-two pennies, three stars, one stag, and that old chipped garnet, ser."

Dunk scratched at his ear. "I thought we had two silvers."

"We did, until you bought the tent. Now we have the one."

"We won't have any if we start sleeping at inns. You want to share a bed with some peddler and wake up with his fleas?" Dunk snorted. "Not me. I have my own fleas, and they are not fond of strangers. We'll sleep beneath the stars."

"The stars are good," Egg allowed, "but the ground is hard, ser, and sometimes it's nice to have a pillow for your head."

"Pillows are for princes." Egg was as good a squire as a knight could want, but every so often he would get to feeling princely. *The lad has dragon blood, never forget.* Dunk had beggar's blood himself ... or so they used to tell him back in Flea Bottom, when they weren't telling him that he was sure to hang. "Might be we can afford some ale and a hot supper, but I'm not wasting good coin on a bed. We need to save our pennies for the ferryman." The last time he had crossed the lake, the ferry only cost a few coppers, but that had been six years ago, or maybe seven. Everything had grown more costly since then.

"Well," said Egg, "we could use my boot to get across."

"We could," said Dunk, "but we won't." Using the boot was dangerous. *Word would spread. Word always spreads.* His squire was not bald by chance. Egg had the purple eyes of old Valyria, and hair that shone like beaten gold and strands of silver woven together. He had as well wear a three-headed dragon as a brooch as let that hair grow out. These were perilous times in Westeros, and . . . well, it was best to take no chances. "Another word about your bloody boot, and I'll clout you in the ear so hard you'll *fly* across the lake."

"I'd sooner swim, ser." Egg swam well, and Dunk did not. The boy turned in the saddle. "Ser? Someone's coming up the road behind us. Hear the horses?"

"I'm not deaf." Dunk could see their dust as well. "A large party. And in haste."

"Do you think they might be outlaws, ser?" Egg rose in the stirrups, more eager than afraid. The boy was like that.

"Outlaws would be quieter. Only lords make so much noise." Dunk rattled his sword hilt to loosen the blade in its scabbard. "Still, we'll get off the road and let them pass. There are lords and lords." It never hurt to be a little wary. The roads were not as safe as when Good King Daeron sat the Iron Throne.

He and Egg concealed themselves behind a thornbush. Dunk unslung his shield and slipped it onto his arm. It was an old thing, tall and heavy, kite-shaped, made of pine and rimmed with iron.

He had bought it in Stoney Sept to replace the shield the Longinch had hacked to splinters when they fought. Dunk had not had time to have it painted with his elm and shooting star, so it still bore the arms of its last owner: a hanged man swinging grim and grey beneath a gallows tree. It was not a sigil that he would have chosen for himself, but the shield had come cheap.

The first riders galloped past within moments: two young lordlings mounted on a pair of coursers. The one on the bay wore an openfaced helm of gilded steel with three tall-feathered plumes—one white, one red, one gold. Matching plumes adorned his horse's crinet.

The black stallion beside him was barded in blue and gold. His trappings rippled with the wind of his passage as he thundered past. Side by side the riders streaked on by, whooping and laughing, their long cloaks streaming behind.

A third lord followed more sedately, at the head of a long column. There were two dozen in the party, grooms and cooks and serving men, all to attend three knights, plus men-at-arms and mounted crossbowmen, and a dozen drays heavy laden with their armor, tents, and provisions. Slung from the lord's saddle was his shield, dark orange and charged with three black castles.

Dunk knew those arms, but from where? The lord who bore them was an older man, sour-mouthed and saturnine, with a close-cropped salt-and-pepper beard. *He might have been at Ashford Meadow,* Dunk thought. *Or maybe we served at his castle when I was squiring for Ser Arlan.* The old hedge knight had done service at so many different keeps and castles through the years that Dunk could not recall the half of them.

The lord reined up abruptly, scowling at the thornbush. "You. In the bush. Show yourself." Behind him two crossbowmen slipped quarrels into the notch. The rest continued on their way.

Dunk stepped through the tall grass, his shield upon his arm, his right hand resting on the pommel of his longsword. His face was a red-brown mask from the dust the horses had kicked up, and he was naked from the waist up. He looked a scruffy sight, he knew, though it was like to be the size of him that gave the other pause. "We want no quarrel, m'lord. There's only the two of us, me and my squire." He beckoned Egg forward.

"Squire? Do you claim to be a knight?"

Dunk did not like the way the man was looking at him. *Those eyes could flay a man.* It seemed prudent to remove his hand from his sword. "I am a hedge knight, seeking service."

"Every robber knight I've ever hanged has said the same. Your device may be prophetic, ser ... if *ser* you are. A gallows and a hanged man. These are your arms?"

"No, m'lord. I need to have the shield repainted."

"Why? Did you rob it off a corpse?"

"I bought it, for good coin." *Three castles, black on orange ... where have I seen those before?* "I am no robber."

The lord's eyes were chips of flint. "How did you come by that scar upon your cheek? A cut from a whip?"

"A dagger. Though my face is none of your concern, m'lord."

"I'll be the judge of what is my concern."

By then the two younger knights had come trotting back to see what had delayed their party. "There you are, Gormy," called the rider on the black, a young man lean and lithe, with a comely clean-shaven face and fine features. Black hair fell shining to his collar. His doublet was made of dark blue silk edged in gold satin. Across his chest an engrailed cross had been embroidered in gold thread, with a golden fiddle in the first and third quarters, a golden sword in the second and the fourth. His eyes caught the deep blue of his doublet and sparkled with amusement. "Alyn feared you'd fallen from your horse. A palpable excuse, it seems to me, I was about to leave him in my dust."

"Who are these two brigands?" asked the rider on the bay.

Egg bristled at the insult. "You have no call to name us brigands, my lord. When we saw your dust we thought *you* might be outlaws, that's the only reason that we hid. This is Ser Duncan the Tall, and I'm his squire."

The lordlings paid no more heed to that than they would have paid the croaking of a frog. "I believe that is the largest lout that I have ever seen," declared the knight of three feathers. He had a pudgy face beneath a head of curly hair the color of dark honey. "Seven feet if he's an inch, I'd wager. What a mighty crash he'll make when he comes tumbling down."

Dunk felt color rising to his face. *You'd lose your wager,* he thought. The last time he had been measured, Egg's brother Aemon pronounced him an inch shy of seven feet.

"Is that your warhorse, Ser Giant?" said the feathered lordling. "I suppose we could butcher it for the meat."

"Lord Alyn oft forgets his courtesies," the black-haired knight said. "Please forgive his churlish words, ser. Alyn, you will ask Ser Duncan for his pardon."

"If I must. Will you forgive me, ser?" He did not wait for reply, but turned his bay about and trotted down the road.

The other lingered. "Are you bound for the wedding, ser?"

Something in his tone made Dunk want to tug his forelock. He resisted the impulse, and said, "We're for the ferry, m'lord."

"As are we ... but the only lords hereabouts are Gormy and that wastrel who just left us, Alyn Cockshaw. I am a vagabond hedge knight like yourself. Ser John the Fiddler, I am called."

That was the sort of name a hedge knight might choose, but Dunk had never seen any hedge knight garbed or armed or mounted in such splendor. *The knight of the golden hedge,* he thought. "You know my name. My squire is called Egg."

"Well met, ser. Come, ride with us to Whitewalls and break a few lances to help Lord Butterwell celebrate his new marriage. I'll wager you could give a good account of yourself."

Dunk had not done any jousting since Ashford Meadow. *If I could win a few ransoms, we'd eat well on the ride north,* he thought, but the lord with the three castles on his shield said, "Ser Duncan needs to be about his journey, as do we."

John the Fiddler paid the older man no mind. "I would love to cross swords with you, ser. I've tried men of many lands and races, but never one your size. Was your father large as well?"

"I never knew my father, ser."

"I am sad to hear it. Mine own sire was taken from me too soon." The Fiddler turned to the lord of the three castles. "We should ask Ser Duncan to join our jolly company."

"We do not need his sort."

Dunk was at a loss for words. Penniless hedge knights were not oft asked to ride with highborn lords. *I would have more in common with their servants.* Judging from the length of their column, Lord Cockshaw and the Fiddler had brought grooms to tend their horses, cooks to feed them, squires to clean their armor, guards to defend them. Dunk had Egg.

"His sort?" The Fiddler laughed. "What sort is that? The big sort? Look at the *size* of him. We want strong men. Young swords are worth more than old names, I've oft heard it said."

"By fools. You know little and less about this man. He might be a brigand, or one of Lord Bloodraven's spies."

"I'm no man's spy," said Dunk. "And m'lord has no call to speak of me as if I were deaf or dead or down in Dorne."

Those flinty eyes considered him. "Down in Dorne would be a good place for you, ser. You have my leave to go there."

"Pay him no mind," the Fiddler said. "He's a sour old soul, he suspects everyone. Gormy, I have a good feeling about this fellow. Ser Duncan, will you come with us to Whitewalls?"

"M'lord, I . . ." How could he share a camp with such as these? Their serving men would raise their pavilions, their grooms would curry their horses, their cooks would serve them each a capon or a joint of beef, whilst Dunk and Egg gnawed on strips of hard salt beef. "I couldn't."

"You see," said the lord of the three castles. "He knows his place, and it is not with us." He turned his horse back toward the road. "By now Lord Cockshaw is half a league ahead."

"I suppose I must chase him down again." The Fiddler gave Dunk an apologetic smile. "Perchance we'll meet again someday. I hope so. I should love to try my lance on you."

Dunk did not know what to say to that. "Good fortune in the lists, ser," he finally managed, but by then Ser John had wheeled about to chase the column. The older lord rode after him. Dunk was glad to see his back. He had not liked his flinty eyes, nor Lord Alyn's arrogance. The Fiddler had been pleasant enough, but there was something odd about him as well.

"Two fiddles and two swords, a cross engrailed," he said to Egg as they watched the dust of their departure. "What house is that?"

"None, ser. I never saw that shield in any roll of arms."

Perhaps he is a hedge knight after all. Dunk had devised his own arms at Ashford Meadow, when a puppeteer called Tanselle Too-Tall asked him what he wanted painted on his shield. "Was the older lord some kin to House Frey?" The Freys bore castles on their shields, and their holdings were not far from here.

Egg rolled his eyes. "The Frey arms are two blue *towers* connected by a bridge, on a grey field. Those were three *castles*, black on orange, ser. Did you see a bridge?"

"No." *He just does that to annoy me.* "And next time you roll your eyes at me, I'll clout you on the ear so hard they'll roll back into your head for good."

Egg looked chastened. "I never meant—"

"Never mind what you meant. Just tell me who he was."

"Gormon Peake, the Lord of Starpike."

"That's down in the Reach, isn't it? Does he really have three castles?"

"Only on his shield, ser. House Peake did hold three castles once, but two of them were lost."

"How do you lose two castles?"

"You fight for the black dragon, ser."

"Oh." Dunk felt stupid. *That again.*

For two hundred years the realm had been ruled by the descendants of Aegon the Conqueror and his sisters, who had made the Seven Kingdoms one and forged the Iron Throne. Their royal banners bore the three-headed dragon of House Targaryen, red on black. Sixteen years ago, a bastard son of King Aegon IV named Daemon Blackfyre had risen in revolt against his trueborn brother. Daemon had used the three-headed dragon on his banners too, but he reversed the colors, as many bastards did. His revolt had ended on the Redgrass Field, where Daemon and his twin sons died beneath a rain of Lord Bloodraven's arrows. Those rebels who survived and bent the knee were pardoned, but some lost land, some titles, some gold. All gave hostages to ensure their future loyalty.

Three castles, black on orange. "I remember now. Ser Arlan never liked to talk about the Redgrass Field, but once in his cups he told me how his sister's son had died." He could almost hear the old man's voice again, smell the wine upon his breath. "Roger of Pennytree, that was his name. His head was smashed in by a mace wielded by a lord with three castles on his shield." *Lord Gormon Peake. The old man never knew his name. Or never wanted to.* By that time Lord Peake and John the Fiddler and their party were no more than a plume of red dust in the distance. *It was sixteen years ago. The Pretender died, and those who followed him were exiled or forgiven. Anyway, it has naught to do with me.*

For a while they rode along without talking, listening to the plaintive cries of birds. Half a league on, Dunk cleared his throat, and said, "'Butterwell,' he said. His lands are near?"

"On the far side of the lake, ser. Lord Butterwell was the master of coin when King Aegon sat the Iron Throne. King Daeron made him Hand, but not for long. His arms are undy green and white and yellow, ser." Egg loved showing off his heraldry.

"Is he a friend of your father?"

Egg made a face. "My father never liked him. In the Rebellion, Lord Butterwell's second son fought for the pretender and his eldest for the king. That way he was certain to be on the winning side. Lord Butterwell didn't fight for anyone."

"Some might call that prudent."

"My father calls it craven."

Aye, he would. Prince Maekar was a hard man, proud and full of scorn. "We have to go by Whitewalls to reach the kingsroad. Why not fill our bellies?" Just the thought was enough to cause his guts to rumble. "Might be that one of the wedding guests will need an escort back to his own seat."

"You said that we were going north."

"The Wall has stood eight thousand years, it will last a while longer. It's a thousand leagues from here to there, and we could do with some more silver in our purse." Dunk was picturing himself atop Thunder, riding down that sour-faced old lord with the three castles on his shield. *That would be sweet. 'It was old Ser Arlan's squire who defeated you,' I could tell him when he came to ransom back his arms and armor. 'The boy who replaced the boy you killed.' The old man would like that.*

"You're not thinking of entering the lists, are you, ser?"

"Might be it's time."

"It's not, ser."

"Maybe it's time I gave you a good clout in the ear." *I'd only need to win two tilts. If I could collect two ransoms and pay out only one, we'd eat like kings for a year.* "If there was a melee, I might enter that." Dunk's size and strength would serve him better in a melee than in the lists.

"It's not customary to have a melee at a marriage, ser."

"It's customary to have a feast, though. We have a long way to go. Why not set out with our bellies full for once?"

The sun was low in the west by the time they saw the lake, its waters glimmering red and gold, bright as a sheet of beaten copper. When they glimpsed the turrets of the inn above some willows, Dunk donned his sweaty tunic once again and stopped to splash some water on his face. He washed off the dust of the road as best he could and ran wet fingers through his thick mop of sun-streaked hair. There was nothing to be done for his size, or the scar that marked his cheek, but he wanted to make himself appear somewhat less the wild-robber knight.

The inn was bigger than he'd expected, a great grey sprawl of a place, timbered and turreted, half of it built on pilings out over the water. A road of rough-cut planks had been laid down over the muddy lakeshore to the ferry landing, but neither the ferry nor the ferry-men were in evidence. Across the road stood a stable with a thatched roof. A drystone wall enclosed the yard, but the gate was open. Within, they found a well and a watering trough. "See to the animals," Dunk told Egg, "but see that they don't drink too much. I'll ask about some food."

He found the innkeep sweeping off the steps. "Are you come for the ferry?" the woman asked him. "You're too late. The sun's going down, and Ned don't like to cross by night unless the moon is full. He'll be back first thing in the morning."

"Do you know how much he asks?"

"Three pennies for each of you, and ten for your horses."

"We have two horses and a mule."

"It's ten for mules as well."

Dunk did the sums in his head, and came up with six-and-thirty, more than he had hoped to spend. "Last time I came this way it was only two pennies, and six for horses."

"Take that up with Ned, it's naught to me. If you're looking for a bed, I've none to offer. Lord Shawney and Lord Costayne brought their retinues. I'm full to bursting."

"Is Lord Peake here as well?" *He killed Ser Arlan's squire.* "He was with Lord Cockshaw and John the Fiddler."

"Ned took them across on his last run." She looked Dunk up and down. "Were you part of their company?"

"We met them on the road, is all." A good smell was drifting out the windows of the inn, one that made Dunk's mouth water. "We might like some of what you're roasting, if it's not too costly."

"It's wild boar," the woman said, "well peppered, and served with onions, mushrooms, and mashed neeps."

"We could do without the neeps. Some slices off the boar and a tankard of your good brown ale would do for us. How much would you ask for that? And maybe we could have a place on your stable floor to bed down for the night?"

That was a mistake. "The stables are for horses. That's why we call them stables. You're big as a horse, I'll grant you, but I only see two legs." She swept her broom at him to shoo him off. "I can't be expected to feed all the Seven Kingdoms. The boar is for my guests. So is my ale. I won't have lords saying that I run short of food or drink before they were surfeit. The lake is full of fish, and you'll find some other rogues camped down by the stumps. Hedge knights, if you believe them." Her tone made it quite clear that she did not. "Might be they'd have food to share. It's naught to me. Away with you now, I've work to do." The door closed with a solid *thump* behind her, before Dunk could even think to ask where he might find these stumps.

He found Egg sitting on the horse trough, soaking his feet in the water and fanning his face with his big floppy hat. "Are they roasting pig, ser? I smell pork."

"Wild boar," said Dunk in a glum tone, "but who wants boar when we have good salt beef?"

Egg made a face. "Can I please eat my boots instead, ser? I'll make a new pair out of the salt beef. It's tougher."

"No," said Dunk, trying not to smile. "You can't eat your boots. One more word and you'll eat my fist, though. Get your feet out of that trough." He found his greathelm on the mule and slung it underhand at Egg. "Draw some water from the well and soak the beef." Unless you soaked it for a good long time, the salt beef was like to break your teeth. It tasted best when soaked in ale, but water would serve. "Don't use the trough either, I don't care to taste your feet."

"My feet could only improve the taste, ser," Egg said, wriggling his toes. But he did as he was bid.

* * *

The hedge knights did not prove hard to find. Egg spied their fire flickering in the woods along the lakeshore, so they made for it, leading the animals behind them. The boy carried Dunk's helm beneath one arm, sloshing with each step he took. By then the sun was a red memory in the west. Before long the trees opened up, and they found themselves in what must once have been a weirwood grove. Only a ring of white stumps and a tangle of bone-pale roots remained to show where the trees had stood, when the children of the forest ruled in Westeros.

Amongst the weirwood stumps, they found two men squatting near a cookfire, passing a skin of wine from hand to hand. Their horses were cropping at the grass beyond the grove, and they had stacked their arms and armor in neat piles. A much younger man sat apart from the other two, his back against a chestnut tree. "Well met, sers," Dunk called out in a cheerful voice. It was never wise to take armed men unawares. "I am called Ser Duncan the Tall. The lad is Egg. May we share your fire?"

A stout man of middling years rose to greet them, garbed in tattered finery. Flamboyant ginger whiskers framed his face. "Well met, Ser Duncan. You are a large one ... and most welcome, certainly, as is your lad. *Egg,* was it? What sort of name is that, pray?"

"A short one, ser." Egg knew better than to admit that *Egg* was short for *Aegon.* Not to men he did not know.

"Indeed. What happened to your hair?"

Rootworms, Dunk thought. *Tell him it was rootworms, boy.* That was the safest story, the tale they told most often ... though sometimes Egg took it in his head to play some childish game.

"I shaved it off, ser. I mean to stay shaven until I earn my spurs."

"A noble vow. I am Ser Kyle, the Cat of Misty Moor. Under yonder chestnut sits Ser Glendon, ah, Ball. And here you have the good Ser Maynard Plumm."

Egg's ears pricked up at that name. "Plumm ... are you kin to Lord Viserys Plumm, ser?"

"Distantly," confessed Ser Maynard, a tall, thin, stoop-shouldered man with long, straight, flaxen hair, "though I doubt that his lordship would admit to it. One might say that he is of the sweet Plumms, whilst I am of the sour." Plumm's cloak was as purple as his name, though frayed about the edges and badly dyed. A moonstone brooch big as a hen's egg fastened it at the shoulder. Elsewise he wore dun-colored roughspun and stained brown leather.

"We have salt beef," said Dunk.

"Ser Maynard has a bag of apples," said Kyle the Cat. "And I have pickled eggs and onions. Why, together we have the makings of a feast! Be seated, ser. We have a fine choice of stumps for your comfort. We will be here until midmorning, unless I miss my guess. There is only the one ferry, and it is not big enough to take us all. The lords and their tails must cross first."

"Help me with the horses," Dunk told Egg. Together the two of them unsaddled Thunder, Rain, and Maester.

Only when the animals had been fed and watered and hobbled for the night did Dunk accept the wineskin that Ser Maynard offered him. "Even sour wine is better than none," said Kyle the Cat. "We'll drink finer vintages at Whitewalls. Lord Butterwell is said to have the best wines north of the Arbor. He was once the King's Hand, as his father's father was before him, and he is said to be a pious man besides, and very rich."

"His wealth is all from cows," said Maynard Plumm. "He ought to take a swollen udder for his arms. These Butterwells have milk running in their veins, and the Freys are no better. This will be a marriage of cattle thieves and toll collectors, one lot of coin clinkers joining with another. When the Black Dragon rose, this lord of cows sent one son to Daemon and one to Daeron, to make certain there was a Butterwell on the winning side. Both perished on the Redgrass Field, and his youngest died in the spring. That's why he's making this new marriage. Unless this new wife gives him a son, Butterwell's name will die with him."

"As it should." Ser Glendon Ball gave his sword another stroke with the whetstone. "The Warrior hates cravens."

The scorn in his voice made Dunk give the youth a closer look. Ser Glendon's clothes were of good cloth, but well-worn and ill matched, with the look of hand-me-downs. Tufts of dark brown hair stuck out from beneath his iron halfhelm. The lad himself was short and chunky, with small, close-set eyes, thick shoulders, and muscular arms. His eyebrows were shaggy as two caterpillars after a wet spring, his nose bulbous, his chin pugnacious. And he was young. *Sixteen, might be. No more than eighteen.* Dunk might have taken him for a squire if Ser Kyle had not named him with a *ser.* The lad had pimples on his cheeks in place of whiskers.

"How long have you been a knight?" Dunk asked him.

"Long enough. Half a year when the moon turns. I was knighted by Ser Morgan Dunstable of Tumbler's Falls, two dozen people saw it, but I have been training for knighthood since I was born. I rode before I walked, and knocked a grown man's tooth out of his head before I lost any of my own. I mean to make my name at Whitewalls and claim the dragon's egg."

"The dragon's egg? Is that the champion's prize? Truly?" The last dragon had perished half a century ago. Ser Arlan had once seen a clutch of her eggs, though. *They were hard as stone, but beautiful to look upon,* the old man had told Dunk. "How could Lord Butterwell come by a dragon's egg?"

"King Aegon presented the egg to his father's father after guesting for a night at his old castle," said Ser Maynard Plumm.

"Was it a reward for some act of valor?" asked Dunk.

Ser Kyle chuckled. "Some might call it that. Supposedly old Lord Butterwell had three young maiden daughters when His Grace came calling. By morning, all three had royal bastards in their little bellies. A hot night's work, that was."

Dunk had heard such talk before. Aegon the Unworthy had bedded half the maidens in the realm and fathered bastards on the lot of them, supposedly. Worse, the old king had legitimized them all upon his deathbed; the baseborn ones born of tavern wenches, whores, and shepherd girls, and the Great Bastards whose mothers had been high-born. "We'd all be bastard sons of old King Aegon if half these tales were true."

"And who's to say we're not?" Ser Maynard quipped.

"You ought to come with us to Whitewalls, Ser Duncan," urged Ser Kyle. "Your size is sure to catch some lordling's eye. You might find good service there. I know I shall. Joffrey Caswell will be at this wedding, the Lord of Bitterbridge. When he was three I made him his first sword. I carved it out of pine, to fit his hand. In my greener days my sword was sworn to his father."

"Was that one carved from pine as well?" Ser Maynard asked.

Kyle the Cat had the grace to laugh. "That sword was good steel, I assure you. I should be glad to ply it once again in the service of the centaur. Ser Duncan, even if you do not choose to tilt, do join us for the wedding feast. There will be singers and musicians, jugglers and tumblers, and a troupe of comic dwarfs."

Dunk frowned. "Egg and I have a long journey before us. We're headed north to Winterfell. Lord Beron Stark is gathering swords to drive the krakens from his shores for good."

"Too cold up there for me," said Ser Maynard. "If you want to kill krakens, go west. The Lannisters are building ships to strike back at the ironmen on their home islands. That's how you put an end to Dagon Greyjoy. Fighting him on land is fruitless, he just slips back to sea. You have to beat him on the water."

That had the ring of truth, but the prospect of fighting ironmen at sea was not one that Dunk relished. He'd had a taste of that on the

White Lady, sailing from Dorne to Oldtown, when he'd donned his armor to help the crew repel some raiders. The battle had been desperate and bloody, and once he'd almost fallen in the water. That would have been the end of him.

"The throne should take a lesson from Stark and Lannister," declared Ser Kyle the Cat. "At least they fight. What do the Targaryens do? King Aerys hides amongst his books, Prince Rhaegel prances naked through the Red Keep's halls, and Prince Maekar broods at Summerhall."

Egg was prodding at the fire with a stick to send sparks floating up into the night. Dunk was pleased to see him ignoring the mention of his father's name. *Perhaps he's finally learned to hold that tongue of his.*

"Myself, I blame Bloodraven," Ser Kyle went on. "He is the King's Hand, yet he does nothing, whilst the krakens spread flame and terror up and down the sunset sea."

Ser Maynard gave a shrug. "His eye is fixed on Tyrosh, where Bittersteel sits in exile, plotting with the sons of Daemon Blackfyre. So he keeps the king's ships close at hand, lest they attempt to cross."

"Aye, that may well be," Ser Kyle said, "but many would welcome the return of Bittersteel. Bloodraven is the root of all our woes, the white worm gnawing at the heart of the realm."

Dunk frowned, remembering the hunchbacked septon at Stoney Sept. "Words like that can cost a man his head. Some might say you're talking treason."

"How can the truth be treason?" asked Kyle the Cat. "In King Daeron's day, a man did not have to fear to speak his mind, but now?" He made a rude noise. "Bloodraven put King Aerys on the Iron Throne, but for how long? Aerys is weak, and when he dies it will be bloody war between Lord Rivers and Prince Maekar for the crown, the Hand against the heir."

"You have forgotten Prince Rhaegel, my friend," Ser Maynard objected, in a mild tone. "He comes next in line to Aerys, not Maekar, and his children after him."

"Rhaegel is feeble-minded. Why, I bear him no ill will, but the man is good as dead, and those twins of his as well, though whether they will die of Maekar's mace or Bloodraven's spells ..."

Seven save us, Dunk thought, as Egg spoke up shrill and loud. "Prince Maekar is Prince Rhaegel's *brother.* He loves him well. He'd never do harm to him or his."

"Be quiet, boy," Dunk growled at him. "These knights want none of your opinions."

"I can talk if I want."

"No," said Dunk. "You can't." *That mouth of yours will get you killed someday. And me as well, most like.* "That salt beef's soaked long enough, I think. A strip for all our friends, and be quick about it."

Egg flushed, and for half a heartbeat Dunk feared the boy might talk back. Instead he settled for a sullen look, seething as only a boy of eleven years can seethe. "Aye, ser," he said, fishing in the bottom of

Dunk's helm. His shaven head shone redly in the firelight as he passed out the salt beef.

Dunk took his piece and worried at it. The soak had turned the meat from wood to leather, but that was all. He sucked on one corner, tasting the salt and trying not to think about the roast boar at the inn, crackling on its spit and dripping fat.

As dusk deepened, flies and stinging midges came swarming off the lake. The flies preferred to plague their horses, but the midges had a taste for man flesh. The only way to keep from being bitten was to sit close to the fire, breathing smoke. *Cook or be devoured,* Dunk thought glumly, *now there's a beggar's choice.* He scratched at his arms and edged closer to the fire.

The wineskin soon came round again. The wine was sour and strong. Dunk drank deep, and passed along the skin, whilst the Cat of Misty Moor began to talk of how he had saved the life of the Lord of Bitterbridge during the Blackfyre Rebellion. "When Lord Armond's banner-bearer fell, I leapt down from my horse with traitors all around us—"

"Ser," said Glendon Ball. "Who were these *traitors*?"

"The Blackfyre men, I meant."

Firelight glimmered off the steel in Ser Glendon's hand. The pockmarks on his face flamed as red as open sores, and his every sinew was wound as tight as a crossbow. "My father fought for the black dragon."

This again. Dunk snorted. *Red or black?* was not a thing you asked a man. It always made for trouble. "I am sure Ser Kyle meant no insult to your father."

"None," Ser Kyle agreed. "It's an old tale, the red dragon and the black. No sense for us to fight about it now, lad. We are all brothers of the hedges here."

Ser Glendon seemed to weigh the Cat's words to see if he was being mocked. "Daemon Blackfyre was no traitor. The old king gave *him* the sword. He saw the worthiness in Daemon, even though he was born bastard. Why else would he put Blackfyre into his hand in place of Daeron's? He meant for him to have the kingdom too. Daemon was the better man."

A hush fell. Dunk could hear the soft crackle of the fire. He could feel midges crawling on the back of his neck. He slapped at them, watching Egg, willing him to be still. "I was just a boy when they fought the Redgrass Field," he said, when it seemed that no one else would speak, "but I squired for a knight who fought with the red dragon, and later served another who fought for the black. There were brave men on both sides."

"Brave men," echoed Kyle the Cat, a bit feebly.

"Heroes." Glendon Ball turned his shield about, so all of them could see the sigil painted there, a fireball blazing red and yellow across a night-black field. "I come from hero's blood."

"You're *Fireball's* son," Egg said.

That was the first time they saw Ser Glendon smile.

Ser Kyle the Cat studied the boy closely. "How can that be? How old are you? Quentyn Ball died—"

"—before I was born," Ser Glendon finished, "but in me, he lives again." He slammed his sword back into its scabbard. "I'll show you all at Whitewalls, when I claim the dragon's egg."

The next day proved the truth of Ser Kyle's prophecy. Ned's ferry was nowise large enough to accommodate all those who wished to cross, so Lords Costayne and Shawney must go first, with their tails. That required several trips, each taking more than an hour. There were the mudflats to contend with, horses and wagons to be gotten down the planks, loaded on the boat, and unloaded again across the lake. The two lords slowed matters even further when they got into a shouting match over precedence. Shawney was the elder, but Costayne held himself to be better born.

There was naught that Dunk could do but wait and swelter. "We could go first if you let me use my boot," Egg said.

"We could," Dunk answered, "but we won't. Lord Costayne and Lord Shawney were here before us. Besides, they're lords."

Egg made a face. "Rebel lords."

Dunk frowned down at him. "What do you mean?"

"They were for the black dragon. Well, Lord Shawney was, and Lord Costayne's father. Aemon and I used to fight the battle on Maester Melaquin's green table with painted soldiers and little banners. Costayne's arms quarter a silver chalice on black with a black rose on gold. That banner was on the left of Daemon's host. Shawney was with Bittersteel on the right, and almost died of his wounds."

"Old dead history. They're here now, aren't they? So they bent the knee, and King Daeron gave them pardon."

"Yes, but—"

Dunk pinched the boy's lips shut. "Hold your tongue."

Egg held his tongue.

No sooner had the last boatload of Shawney men pushed off than Lord and Lady Smallwood turned up at the landing with their own tail, so they must needs wait again.

The fellowship of the hedge had not survived the night, it was plain to see. Ser Glendon kept his own company, prickly and sullen. Kyle the Cat judged that it would be midday before they were allowed to board the ferry, so he detached himself from the others to try and ingratiate himself with Lord Smallwood, with whom he had some slight acquaintance. Ser Maynard spent his time gossiping with the innkeep.

"Stay well away from that one," Dunk warned Egg. There was something about Plumm that troubled him. "He could be a robber knight, for all we know."

The warning only seemed to make Ser Maynard more interesting to Egg. "I never knew a robber knight. Do you think he means to steal the dragon's egg?"

"Lord Butterwell will have the egg well guarded, I'm sure." Dunk scratched the midge bites on his neck. "Do you think he might display it at the feast? I'd like to get a look at one."

"I'd show you mine, ser, but it's at Summerhall."

"Yours? Your *dragon's* egg?" Dunk frowned down at the boy, wondering if this was some jape. "Where did it come from?"

"From a dragon, ser. They put it in my cradle."

"Do you want a clout in the ear? There are no dragons."

"No, but there are eggs. The last dragon left a clutch of five, and they have more on Dragonstone, old ones from before the Dance. My brothers all have them too. Aerion's looks as though it's made of gold and silver, with veins of fire running through it. Mine is white and green, all swirly."

"Your dragon's egg." *They put it in his cradle.* Dunk was so used to Egg that sometimes he forgot Aegon was a prince. *Of course they'd put a dragon egg inside his cradle.* "Well, see that you don't go mentioning this egg where anyone is like to hear."

"I'm not *stupid,* ser." Egg lowered his voice. "Someday the dragons will return. My brother Daeron's dreamed of it, and King Aerys read it in a prophecy. Maybe it will be my egg that hatches. That would be *splendid*."

"Would it?" Dunk had his doubts.

Not Egg. "Aemon and I used to pretend that our eggs would be the ones to hatch. If they did, we could fly through the sky on dragon-back, like the first Aegon and his sisters."

"Aye, and if all the other knights in the realm should die, I'd be the

Lord Commander of the Kingsguard. If these eggs are so bloody precious, why is Lord Butterwell giving his away?"

"To show the realm how rich he is?"

"I suppose." Dunk scratched his neck again and glanced over at Ser Glendon Ball, who was tightening the cinches on his saddle as he waited for the ferry. *That horse will never serve.* Ser Glendon's mount was a swaybacked stot, undersized and old. "What do you know about his sire? Why did they call him Fireball?"

"For his hot head and red hair. Ser Quentyn Ball was the master-at-arms at the Red Keep. He taught my father and my uncles how to fight. The Great Bastards too. King Aegon promised to raise him to the Kingsguard, so Fireball made his wife join the silent sisters, only by the time a place came open King Aegon was dead and King Daeron named Ser Willam Wylde instead. My father says that it was Fireball as much as Bittersteel who convinced Daemon Blackfyre to claim the crown and rescued him when Daeron sent the Kingsguard to arrest him. Later on, Fireball killed Lord Lefford at the gates of Lannisport and sent the Grey Lion running back to hide inside the Rock. At the crossing of the Mander he cut down the sons of Lady Penrose one by one. They say he spared the life of the youngest one as a kindness to his mother."

"That was chivalrous of him," Dunk had to admit. "Did Ser Quentyn die upon the Redgrass Field?"

"Before, ser," Egg replied. "An archer put an arrow through his throat as he dismounted by a stream to have a drink. Just some common man, no one knows who."

"Those common men can be dangerous when they get it in their heads to start slaying lords and heroes." Dunk saw the ferry creeping slowly across the lake. "Here it comes."

"It's slow. Are we going to go to Whitewalls, ser?"

"Why not? I want to see this dragon's egg." Dunk smiled. "If I win the tourney, we'd *both* have dragon's eggs."

Egg gave him a doubtful look.

"What? Why are you looking at me that way?"

"I could tell you, ser," the boy said solemnly, "but I need to learn to hold my tongue."

* * *

They seated the hedge knights well below the salt, closer to the doors than to the dais.

Whitewalls was almost new as castles went, having been raised a mere forty years ago by the grandsire of its present lord. The smallfolk hereabouts called it the Milkhouse, for its walls and keeps and towers were made of finely dressed white stone, quarried in the Vale and brought over the mountains at great expense. Inside were floors and pillars of milky white marble veined with gold; the rafters overhead were carved from the bone-pale trunks of weirwoods. Dunk could not begin to imagine what all of that had cost.

The hall was not so large as some others he had known, though. *At least we were allowed beneath the roof,* Dunk thought, as he took his place on the bench between Ser Maynard Plumm and Kyle the Cat. Though uninvited, the three of them had been welcomed to the feast quick enough; it was ill luck to refuse a knight hospitality on your wedding day.

Young Ser Glendon had a harder time, however. "Fireball never had a son," Dunk heard Lord Butterwell's steward tell him, loudly. The stripling answered heatedly, and the name of Ser Morgan Dunstable was mentioned several times, but the steward had remained adamant. When Ser Glendon touched his sword hilt, a dozen men-at-arms appeared with spears in hand, and for a moment it looked as though there might be bloodshed. It was only the intervention of a big blond knight named Kirby Pimm that saved the situation. Dunk was too far away to hear, but he saw Pimm clasp an arm around the steward's shoulders and murmur in his ear, laughing. The steward frowned, and said something to Ser Glendon that turned the boy's face dark red. *He looks as if he's about to cry,* Dunk thought, watching. *That, or kill someone.* After all of that, the young knight was finally admitted to the castle hall.

Poor Egg was not so fortunate. "The great hall is for the lords and knights," an understeward had informed them haughtily when Dunk had tried to bring the boy inside. "We have set up tables in the inner yard for squires, grooms, and men-at-arms."

If you had an inkling who he was, you would seat him on the dais on a cushioned throne. Dunk had not much liked the look of the other squires. A few were lads of Egg's own age, but most were older, seasoned fighters who long ago had made the choice to serve a knight rather than become one. *Or did they have a choice?* Knighthood required more than chivalry and skill at arms; it required horse and sword and armor too, and all of that was costly. "Watch your tongue," he told Egg before he left him in that company. "These are grown men, they won't take kindly to your insolence. Sit and eat and listen, might be you'll learn some things."

For his own part, Dunk was just glad to be out of the hot sun, with a wine cup before him and a chance to fill his belly. Even a hedge knight grows weary of chewing every bite of food for half an hour. Down here below the salt, the fare would be more plain than fancy,

but there would be no lack of it. Below the salt was good enough for Dunk.

But peasant's pride is lordling's shame, the old man used to say. "This cannot be my proper place," Ser Glendon Ball told the understeward hotly. He had donned a clean doublet for the feast, a handsome old garment with gold lace at the cuffs and collar and the red chevron and white plates of House Ball sewn across the chest. "Do you know who my father was?"

"A noble knight and mighty lord, I have no doubt," said the understeward, "but the same is true of many here. Please take your seat or take your leave, ser. It is all the same to me."

In the end the boy took his place below the salt with the rest of them, his mouth sullen. The long white hall was filling up as more knights crowded onto the benches. The crowd was larger than Dunk had anticipated, and from the looks of it some of the guests had come a very long way. He and Egg had not been around so many lords and knights since Ashford Meadow, and there was no way to guess who else might turn up next. *We should have stayed out in the hedges, sleeping under trees. If I am recognized . . .*

When a serving man placed a loaf of black bread on the cloth in front of each of them, Dunk was grateful for the distraction. He sawed the loaf open lengthwise, hollowed out the bottom half for a trencher, and ate the top. It was stale, but compared to his salt beef it was custard. At least it did not have to be soaked in ale or milk or water to make it soft enough to chew.

"Ser Duncan, you appear to attracting a deal of attention," Ser Maynard Plumm observed, as Lord Vyrwel and his party went parading past them toward places of high honor at the top of the hall. "Those girls up on the dais cannot seem to take their eyes off you. I'll wager they have never seen a man so big. Even seated, you are half a head taller than any man in the hall."

Dunk hunched his shoulders. He was used to being stared at, but that did not mean he liked it. "Let them look."

"That's the Old Ox down there beneath the dais," Ser Maynard said. "They call him a huge man, but seems to me his belly is the biggest thing about him. You're a bloody giant next to him."

"Indeed, ser," said one of their companions on the bench, a sallow man, saturnine, clad in grey and green. His eyes were small and shrewd, set close together beneath thin, arching brows. A neat black beard framed his mouth, to make up for his receding hair. "In such a field as this, your size alone should make you one of the most formidable competitors."

"I had heard the Brute of Bracken might be coming," said another man, farther down the bench.

"I think not," said the man in green and grey. "This is only a bit of jousting to celebrate his lordship's nuptials. A tilt in the yard to mark the tilt between the sheets. Hardly worth the bother for the likes of Otho Bracken."

Ser Kyle the Cat took a drink of wine. "I'll wager my lord of Butterwell does not take the field either. He will cheer on his champions from his lord's box in the shade."

"Then he'll see his champions fall," boasted Ser Glendon Ball, "and in the end, he'll hand his egg to me."

"Ser Glendon is the son of Fireball," Ser Kyle explained to the new man. "Might we have the honor of your name, ser?"

"Ser Uthor Underleaf. The son of no one of importance."

Underleaf's garments were of good cloth, clean and well cared for but simply cut. A silver clasp in the shape of a snail fastened his cloak. "If your lance is the equal of your tongue, Ser Glendon, you may even give this big fellow here a contest."

Ser Glendon glanced at Dunk as the wine was being poured. "If we meet, he'll fall. I don't care how big he is."

Dunk watched a server fill his wine cup. "I am better with a sword than with a lance," he admitted, "and even better with a battle-axe. Will there be a melee here?" His size and strength would stand him in good stead in a melee, and he knew he could give as good as he got. Jousting was another matter.

"A melee? At a marriage?" Ser Kyle sounded shocked. "That would be unseemly."

Ser Maynard gave a chuckle. "A marriage *is* a melee, as any married man could tell you."

Ser Uthor chuckled. "There's just the joust, I fear, but besides the dragon's egg, Lord Butterwell has promised thirty golden dragons for the loser of the final tilt, and ten each for the knights defeated in the round before."

Ten dragons is not so bad. Ten dragons would buy a palfrey, so Dunk would not need to ride Thunder save in battle. Ten dragons would buy a suit of plate for Egg, and a proper knight's pavilion sewn with Dunk's tree and falling star. *Ten dragons would mean roast goose and ham and pigeon pie.*

"There are ransoms to be had as well, for those who win their matches," Ser Uthor said as he hollowed out his trencher, "and I have heard it rumored that some men place wagers on the tilts. Lord Butterwell himself is not fond of taking risks, but amongst his guests are some who wager heavily."

No sooner had he spoken than Ambrose Butterwell made his entrance, to a fanfare of trumpets from the minstrel's gallery. Dunk shoved to his feet with the rest as Butterwell escorted his new bride down a patterned Myrish carpet to the dais, arm in arm. The girl was fifteen and freshly flowered, her lord husband fifty and freshly widowed. She was pink and he was grey. Her bride's cloak trailed behind her, done in undy green and white and yellow. It looked so hot and heavy that Dunk wondered how she could bear to wear it. Lord Butterwell looked hot and heavy too, with his heavy jowls and thinning, flaxen hair.

The bride's father followed close behind her, hand in hand with his young son. Lord Frey of the Crossing was a lean man, elegant in blue and grey, his heir a chinless boy of four whose nose was dripping snot. Lords Costayne and Risley came next, with their lady wives, daughters of Lord Butterwell by his first wife. Frey's daughters followed with their own husbands. Then came Lord Gormon Peake; Lords Smallwood and Shawney; various lesser

lords and landed knights. Amongst them Dunk glimpsed John the Fiddler and Alyn Cockshaw. Lord Alyn looked to be in his cups, though the feast had not yet properly begun.

By the time all of them had sauntered to the dais, the high table was as crowded as the benches. Lord Butterwell and his bride sat on plump downy cushions in a double throne of gilded oak. The rest planted themselves in tall chairs with fancifully carved arms. On the wall behind them two huge banners hung from the rafters: the twin towers of Frey, blue on grey, and the green and white and yellow undy of the Butterwells.

It fell to Lord Frey to lead the toasts. *"The king!"* he began, simply. Ser Glendon held his wine cup out above the water basin. Dunk clanked his cup against it, and against Ser Uthor's and the rest as well. They drank.

"Lord Butterwell, our gracious host," Frey proclaimed next. "May the Father grant him long life and many sons."

They drank again.

"Lady Butterwell, the maiden bride, my darling daughter. May the Mother make her fertile." Frey gave the girl a smile. "I shall want a grandson before the year is out. Twins would suit me even better, so churn the butter well tonight, my sweet."

Laughter rang against the rafters, and the guests drank still once more. The wine was rich and red and sweet.

Then Lord Frey said, *"I give you the King's Hand, Brynden Rivers.* May the Crone's lamp light his path to wisdom." He lifted his goblet high and drank, together with Lord Butterwell and his bride and the others on the dais. Below the salt, Ser Glendon turned his cup over to spill its contents to the floor.

"A sad waste of good wine," said Maynard Plumm.

"I do not drink to kinslayers," said Ser Glendon. "Lord Bloodraven is a sorcerer and a bastard."

"Born bastard," Ser Uthor agreed mildly, "but his royal father made him legitimate as he lay dying." He drank deep, as did Ser Maynard and many others in the hall. Near as many lowered their cups, or turned them upside down as Ball had done. Dunk's own cup was heavy in his hand. *How many eyes does Lord Bloodraven have?* the riddle went. *A thousand eyes, and one.*

Toast followed toast, some proposed by Lord Frey and some by others. They drank to young Lord Tully, Lord Butterwell's liege lord, who had begged off from the wedding. They drank to the health of Leo Longthorn, Lord of Highgarden, who was rumored to be ailing. They drank to the memory of their gallant dead. *Aye,* thought Dunk, remembering. *I'll gladly drink to them.*

Ser John the Fiddler proposed the final toast. *"To my brave brothers!* I know that they are smiling tonight!"

Dunk had not intended to drink so much, with the jousting on the morrow, but the cups were filled anew after every toast, and he found he had a thirst. "Never refuse a cup of wine or a horn of ale," Ser Arlan had once told him, "it may be a year before you see another." *It would have been discourteous not to toast the bride and groom,* he told himself, *and dangerous not to drink to the king and his Hand, with strangers all about.*

Mercifully, the Fiddler's toast was the last. Lord Butterwell rose ponderously to thank them for coming and promise good jousting on the morrow. "Let the feast begin!"

Suckling pig was served at the high table; a peacock roasted in its plumage; a great pike crusted with crushed almonds. Not a bite of that made it down below the salt. Instead of suckling pig they got salt pork, soaked in almond milk and peppered pleasantly. In place of peacock they had capons, crisped up nice and brown and stuffed with onions, herbs, mushrooms, and roasted chestnuts. In place of pike they ate chunks of flaky white cod in a pastry coffyn, with some sort of tasty brown sauce that Dunk could not quite place. There was pease porridge besides; buttered turnips; carrots drizzled with honey; and a ripe white cheese that smelled as strong as Bennis of the Brown Shield. Dunk ate well, but all the while wondered what Egg was getting in the yard. Just in case, he slipped half a capon into the pocket of his cloak, with some hunks of bread and a little of the smelly cheese.

As they ate, pipes and fiddles filled the air with spritely tunes, and the talk turned to the morrow's jousting. "Ser Franklyn Frey is well regarded along the Green Fork," said Uthor Underleaf, who seemed to know these local heroes well. "That's him upon the dais, the uncle of the bride. Lucas Nayland is down from Hag's Mire, he should not be discounted. Nor should Ser Mortimer Boggs, of Crackclaw Point. Elsewise, this should be a tourney of household knights and village heroes. Kirby Pimm and Galtry the Green are the best of those, though neither is a match for Lord Butterwell's good-son, Black Tom Heddle. A nasty bit of business, that one. He won the hand of his lordship's eldest daughter by killing three of her other suitors, it's said, and once unhorsed the Lord of Casterly Rock."

"What, young Lord Tybolt?" asked Ser Maynard.

"No, the old Grey Lion, the one who died in the spring."

That was how men spoke of those who had perished during the Great Spring Sickness. *He died in the spring.* Tens of thousands had died in the spring, amongst them a king and two young princes.

"Do not slight Ser Buford Bulwer," said Kyle the Cat. "The Old Ox slew forty men upon the Redgrass Field."

"And every year his count grows higher," said Ser Maynard. "Bulwer's day is done. Look at him. Past sixty, soft and fat, and his right eye is good as blind."

"Do not trouble to search the hall for the champion," a voice behind Dunk said. "Here I stand, sers. Feast your eyes."

Dunk turned to find Ser John the Fiddler looming over him, a half smile on his lips. His white silk doublet had dagged sleeves lined with red satin, so long their points drooped down past his knees. A heavy silver chain looped across his chest, studded with huge, dark amethysts whose color matched his eyes. *That chain is worth as much as everything I own,* Dunk thought.

The wine had colored Ser Glendon's cheeks and inflamed his pimples. "Who are you, to make such boasts?"

"They call me John the Fiddler."

"Are you a musician or a warrior?"

"I can make sweet song with either lance or resined bow, as it happens. Every wedding needs a singer, and every tourney needs a mystery knight. May I join you? Butterwell was good enough to place me on the dais, but I prefer the company of my fellow hedge knights to fat pink ladies and old men." The Fiddler clapped Dunk upon the shoulder. "Be a good fellow and shove over, Ser Duncan."

Dunk shoved over. "You are too late for food, ser."

"No matter. I know where Butterwell's kitchens are. There is still some wine, I trust?" The Fiddler smelled of oranges and limes, with a hint of some strange eastern spice beneath. Nutmeg, perhaps. Dunk could not have said. What did he know of nutmeg?

"Your boasting is unseemly," Ser Glendon told the Fiddler.

"Truly? Then I must beg for your forgiveness, ser. I would never wish to give offense to any son of Fireball."

That took the youth aback. "You know who I am?"

"Your father's son, I hope."

"Look," said Ser Kyle the Cat. "The wedding pie."

Six kitchen boys were pushing it through the doors, upon a wide, wheeled cart. The pie was brown and crusty and immense, and there were noises coming from inside it, squeaks and squawks and thumps. Lord and Lady Butterwell descended from the dais to meet it, sword in hand. When they cut it open half a hundred birds burst forth to fly around the hall. In other wedding feasts Dunk had attended, the pies had been filled with doves or songbirds, but inside this one were bluejays and skylarks, pigeons and doves, mockingbirds and nightin- gales, small brown sparrows and a great red parrot. "One-and-twenty sorts of birds," said Ser Kyle.

"One-and-twenty sorts of bird droppings," said Ser Maynard.

"You have no poetry in your heart, ser."

"You have shit upon your shoulder."

"This is the proper way to fill a pie," Ser Kyle sniffed, cleaning off his tunic. "The pie is meant to be the marriage, and a true marriage has in it many sorts of things—joy and grief, pain and pleasure, love and lust and loyalty. So it is fitting that there be birds of many sorts. No man ever truly knows what a new wife will bring him."

"Her cunt," said Plumm, "or what would be the point?"

Dunk shoved back from the table. "I need a breath of air." It was a piss he needed, truth be told, but in fine company like this it was more courteous to talk of air. "Pray excuse me."

"Hurry back, ser," said the Fiddler. "There are jugglers yet to come, and you do not want to miss the bedding."

Outside, the night wind lapped at Dunk like the tongue of some great beast. The hard-packed earth of the yard seemed to move be- neath his feet . . . or it might be that he was swaying.

The lists had been erected in the center of the outer yard. A three- tiered wooden viewing stand had been raised beneath the walls, so Lord Butterwell and his highborn guests would be well shaded on their cushioned seats. There were tents at both ends of the lists where the knights could don their armor, with racks of tourney lances standing ready. When the wind lifted the banners for an instant, Dunk could smell the whitewash on the tilting barrier. He set off in search of the inner ward. He had to hunt up Egg and send the boy to the master of the games to enter him in the lists. That was a squire's duty.

Whitewalls was strange to him, however, and somehow Dunk got turned around. He found himself outside the kennels, where the hounds caught scent of him and began to bark and howl. *They want to tear my throat out,* he thought, *or else they want the capon in my cloak.* He doubled back the way he'd come, past the sept. A woman went running past, breathless with laughter, a bald knight in hard pursuit. The man kept falling, until finally the woman had to come back and help him up. *I should slip into the sept and ask the Seven to make that knight my first opponent,* Dunk thought, but that would have been impious. *What I really need is a privy, not a prayer.* There were some bushes near at hand, beneath a flight of pale stone steps. *Those will serve.* He groped his way behind them and unlaced his breeches. His bladder had been full to bursting. The piss went on and on.

Somewhere above, a door came open. Dunk heard footfalls on the steps, the scrape of boots on stone. "... beggar's feast you've laid before us. Without Bittersteel ..."

"Bittersteel be buggered," insisted a familiar voice. "No bastard can be trusted, not even him. A few victories will bring him over the water fast enough."

Lord Peake. Dunk held his breath ... and his piss.

"Easier to speak of victories than win them." This speaker had a deeper voice than Peake, a bass rumble with an angry edge to it. "Old Milkblood expected the boy to have it, and so will all the rest. Glib words and charm cannot make up for that."

"A dragon would. The prince insists the egg will hatch. He dreamed it, just as he once dreamed his brothers dead. A living dragon will win us all the swords that we would want."

"A dragon is one thing, a dream's another. I promise you, Bloodraven is not off dreaming. We need a warrior, not a dreamer. Is the boy his father's son?"

"Just do your part as promised and let me concern myself with that. Once we have Butterwell's gold and the swords of House Frey, Harrenhal will follow, then the Brackens. Otho knows he cannot hope to stand ..."

The voices were fading as the speakers moved away. Dunk's piss began to flow again. He gave his cock a shake, and laced himself back up. "His father's son," he muttered. Who were they speaking of? Fireball's son?

By the time he emerged from under the steps, the two lords were well across the yard. He almost shouted after them, to make them show their faces, but thought better of it. He was alone and unarmed, and half-drunk besides. *Maybe more than half.* He stood there frowning for a moment, then marched back to the hall.

Inside, the last course had been served and the frolics had begun. One of Lord Frey's daughters played "Two Hearts That Beat as One" on the high harp, very badly. Some jugglers flung flaming torches at each other for a while, and some tumblers did cartwheels in the air. Lord Frey's nephew began to sing "The Bear, the Bear, and the Maiden Fair" while Ser Kirby Pimm beat out time upon the table with a wooden spoon. Others joined in, until the whole hall was bellowing, "*A bear! A bear! All black and brown, and covered with hair!*" Lord Caswell passed out at the table with his face in a puddle of wine, and Lady Vyrwel began to weep, though no one was quite certain as to the cause of her distress.

All the while the wine kept flowing. The rich Arbor reds gave way to local vintages, or so the Fiddler said; if truth be told, Dunk could not tell the difference. There was hippocras as well, he had to try a cup of that. *It might be a year before I have another.* The other hedge knights, fine fellows all, had begun to talk of women they had known. Dunk found himself wondering where Tanselle was tonight. He *knew* where Lady Rohanne was—abed at Coldmoat Castle, with old Ser Eustace beside her, snoring through his mustache—so he tried not to think of her. *Do they ever think of me?* he wondered.

His melancholy ponderings were rudely interrupted when a troupe of painted dwarfs came bursting from the belly of a wheeled wooden pig to chase Lord Butterwell's fool about the tables, walloping him with inflated pig's bladders that made rude noises every time a blow was struck. It was the funniest thing Dunk had seen in years, and he laughed with all the rest. Lord Frey's son was so taken by their antics that he joined in, pummeling the wedding guests with a bladder borrowed from a dwarf. The child had the most irritating laugh Dunk had ever heard, a high, shrill hiccup of a laugh that made him want to take the boy over a knee, or throw him down a well. *If he hits me with that bladder, I may do it.* "There's the lad who made this marriage," Ser Maynard said, as the chinless urchin went screaming past.

"How so?" The Fiddler held up an empty wine cup, and a passing server filled it.

Ser Maynard glanced toward the dais, where the bride was feeding cherries to her husband. "His lordship will not be the first to butter that biscuit. His bride was deflowered by a scullion at the Twins, they say. She would creep down to the kitchens to meet him. Alas, one night that little brother of hers crept down after her. When he saw them making the two-backed beast, he let out a shriek, and cooks and guardsmen came running and found milady and her potboy coupling on the slab of marble where the cook rolls out the dough, both naked as their name day and floured up from head to heel."

That cannot be true, Dunk thought. Lord Butterwell had broad lands, and pots of yellow gold. Why would he wed a girl who'd been soiled by a kitchen scullion and give away his dragon's egg to mark the match? The Freys of the Crossing were no nobler than the Butterwells. They owned a bridge instead of cows, that was the only difference. *Lords. Who can ever understand them?* Dunk ate some nuts and pondered what he'd overheard whilst pissing. *Dunk the drunk, what is it that you think you heard?* He had another cup of hippocras, since the first had tasted good. Then he lay his head down atop his folded arms and closed his eyes just for a moment, to rest them from the smoke.

When he opened them again, half the wedding guests were on their feet and shouting, "Bed them! Bed them!" They were making such an uproar that they woke Dunk from a pleasant dream involving Tanselle Too-Tall and the Red Widow. *"Bed them! Bed them!"* the calls rang out. Dunk sat up and rubbed his eyes.

Ser Franklyn Frey had the bride in his arms and was carrying her down the aisle, with men and boys swarming all around him. The ladies at the high table had surrounded Lord Butterwell. Lady Vyrwel had recovered from her grief and was trying to pull his lordship from his chair, while one of his daughters unlaced his boots and some Frey woman pulled up his tunic. Butterwell was flailing at them ineffectually, and laughing. He was drunk, Dunk saw, and Ser Franklyn was a deal drunker ... so drunk he almost dropped the bride. Before Dunk quite realized what was happening, John the Fiddler had dragged him to his feet. "Here!" he cried out. "Let the giant carry her!"

The next thing he knew he was climbing a tower stair with the bride squirming in his arms. How he kept his feet was beyond him. The girl would not be still and the men were all around them, making ribald japes about flouring her up and kneading her well whilst they pulled off her clothes. The dwarfs joined in as well. They swarmed around Dunk's legs, shouting and laughing and smacking at his calves with their bladders. It was all he could do not to trip over them.

Dunk had no notion where Lord Butterwell's bedchamber was to be found, but the other men pushed and prodded him until he got there, by which time the bride was red-faced, giggling, and nearly naked, save for the stocking on her left leg, which had somehow survived the climb. Dunk was crimson too, and not from exertion.

His arousal would have been obvious if anyone had been looking, but fortunately all eyes were on the bride. Lady Butterwell looked nothing like Tanselle, but having the one squirming half-naked in his arms had started Dunk thinking about the other. *Tanselle Too-Tall, that was her name, but she was not too tall for me.* He wondered if he would ever find her again. There had been some nights when he thought he must have dreamed her. *No, lunk, you only dreamed she liked you.*

Lord Butterwell's bedchamber was large and lavish, once he found it. Myrish carpets covered the floors, a hundred scented candles burned in nooks and crannies, and a suit of plate inlaid with gold and gems stood beside the door. It even had its own privy set into a small stone alcove in the outer wall.

When Dunk finally plopped the bride onto her marriage bed, a dwarf leapt in beside her and seized one of her breasts for a bit of a fondle. The girl let out a squeal, the men roared with laughter, and Dunk seized the dwarf by his collar and hauled him kicking off m'lady. He was carrying the little man across the room to chuck him out the door when he saw the dragon's egg.

Lord Butterwell had placed it on a black velvet cushion atop a marble plinth. It was much bigger than a hen's egg, though not so big as he'd imagined. Fine red scales covered its surface, shining bright as jewels by the light of lamps and candles. Dunk dropped the dwarf and picked up the egg, just to feel it for a moment. It was heavier than he'd expected. *You could smash a man's head with this, and never crack the shell.* The scales were smooth beneath his fingers, and the deep, rich red seemed to shimmer as he turned the egg in his hands. *Blood and flame,* he thought, but there were gold flecks in it as well, and whorls of midnight black.

"Here, you! What do you think you're doing, ser?" A knight he did not know was glaring at him, a big man with a coal-black beard and boils, but it was the voice that made him blink, a deep voice, thick with anger. *It was him, the man with Peake,* Dunk realized, as the man said, "Put that down. I'll thank you to keep your greasy fingers off his lordship's treasures, or by the Seven, you shall wish you had."

The other knight was not near as drunk as Dunk, so it seemed wise to do as he said. He put the egg back on its pillow, very carefully, and wiped his fingers on his sleeve. "I meant no harm, ser." *Dunk the lunk, thick as a castle wall.* Then he shoved past the man with the black beard and out the door.

There were noises in the stairwell, glad shouts and girlish laughter. The women were bringing Lord Butterwell to his bride. Dunk had no wish to encounter them, so he went up instead of down, and found himself on the tower roof beneath the stars, with the pale castle glimmering in the moonlight all around him.

He was feeling dizzy from the wine, so he leaned against a parapet. *Am I going to be sick?* Why did he go and touch the dragon's egg? He remembered Tanselle's puppet show, and the wooden dragon that had started all the trouble there at Ashford. The memory made Dunk feel guilty, as it always did. *Three good men dead, to save a hedge knight's foot.* It made no sense, and never had. *Take a lesson from that, lunk. It is not for the likes of you to mess about with dragons or their eggs.*

"It almost looks as if it's made of snow."

Dunk turned. John the Fiddler stood behind him, smiling in his silk and cloth-of-gold. "What's made of snow?"

"The castle. All that white stone in the moonlight. Have you ever been north of the Neck, Ser Duncan? I'm told it snows there even in the summer. Have you ever seen the Wall?"

"No, m'lord." *Why he is going on about the Wall?* "That's where we were going, Egg and me. Up north, to Winterfell."

"Would that I could join you. You could show me the way."

"The way?" Dunk frowned. "It's right up the kingsroad. If you stay to the road and keep going north, you can't miss it."

The Fiddler laughed. "I suppose not ... though you might be surprised at what some men can miss." He went to the parapet and looked out across the castle. "They say those Northmen are a savage folk, and their woods are full of wolves."

"M'lord? Why did you come up here?"

"Alyn was seeking for me, and I did not care to be found. He grows tiresome when he drinks, does Alyn. I saw you slip away from that bedchamber of horrors and slipped out after you. I've had too much wine, I grant you, but not enough to face a naked Butterwell." He gave Dunk an enigmatic smile. "I dreamed of you, Ser Duncan. Before I even met you. When I saw you on the road, I knew your face at once. It was as if we were old friends."

Dunk had the strangest feeling then, as if he had lived this all before. *I dreamed of you, he said. My dreams are not like yours, Ser Duncan. Mine are true.* "You *dreamed* of me?" he said, in a voice made thick by wine. "What sort of dream?"

"Why," the Fiddler said, "I dreamed that you were all in white from head to heel, with a long pale cloak flowing from those broad shoulders. You were a White Sword, ser, a Sworn Brother of the Kingsguard, the greatest knight in all the Seven Kingdoms, and you lived for no other purpose but to guard and serve and please your king." He put a hand on Dunk's shoulder. "You have dreamed the same dream, I know you have."

He had, it was true. *The first time the old man let me hold his sword.* "Every boy dreams of serving in the Kingsguard."

"Only seven boys grow up to wear the white cloak, though. Would it please you to be one of them?"

"Me?" Dunk shrugged away the lordling's hand, which had begun to knead his shoulder. "It might. Or not." The knights of the Kingsguard served for life and swore to take no wife and hold no lands. *I might find Tanselle again someday. Why shouldn't I have a wife, and sons?* "It makes no matter what I dream. Only a king can make a Kingsguard knight."

"I suppose that means I'll have to take the throne, then. I would much rather be teaching you to fiddle."

"You're drunk." *And the crow once called the raven black.*

"Wonderfully drunk. Wine makes all things possible, Ser Duncan. You'd look a god in white, I think, but if the color does not suit you, perhaps you would prefer to be a lord?"

Dunk laughed in his face. "No, I'd sooner sprout big blue wings and fly. One's as likely as t'other."

"Now you mock me. A true knight would never mock his king."
The Fiddler sounded hurt. "I hope you will put more faith in what I
tell you when you see the dragon hatch."

"A dragon will hatch? A *living* dragon? What, here?"

"I dreamed it. This pale white castle, you, a dragon bursting from
an egg, I dreamed it all, just as I once dreamed of my brothers lying
dead. They were twelve and I was only seven, so they laughed at me,
and died. I am two-and-twenty now, and I trust my dreams."

Dunk was remembering another tourney, remembering how he
had walked through the soft spring rains with another princeling. *I
dreamed of you and a dead dragon,* Egg's brother Daeron said to him. *A
great beast, huge, with wings so large they could cover this meadow. It had
fallen on top of you, but you were alive and the dragon was dead.* And so he
was, poor Baelor. Dreams were a treacherous ground on which to
build. "As you say, m'lord," he told the Fiddler. "Pray excuse me."

"Where *are* you going, ser?"

"To my bed, to sleep. I'm drunk as a dog."

"Be my dog, ser. The night's alive with promise. We can howl together and wake the very gods."

"What do you want of me?"

"Your sword. I would make you mine own man, and raise you high. My dreams do not lie, Ser Duncan. You shall have that white cloak, and I must have the dragon's egg. I *must*, my dreams have made that plain. Perhaps the egg will hatch, or else ..."

Behind them, the door banged open violently. *"There he is, my lord."* A pair of men-at-arms stepped onto the roof. Lord Gormon Peake was just behind them.

"Gormy," the Fiddler drawled. "Why, what are you doing in my bedchamber, my lord?"

"It is a roof, ser, and you have had too much wine." Lord Gormon made a sharp gesture, and the guards moved forward. "Allow us to help you to that bed. You are jousting on the morrow, pray recall. Kirby Pimm can prove a dangerous foe."

"I had hoped to joust with good Ser Duncan here."

Peake gave Dunk an unsympathetic look. "Later, perhaps. For your first tilt, you have drawn Ser Kirby Pimm."

"Then Pimm must fall! So must they all! The mystery knight prevails against all challengers, and wonder dances in his wake." A guardsman took the Fiddler by the arm. "Ser Duncan, it seems that we must part," he called, as they helped him down the steps.

Only Lord Gormon remained upon the roof with Dunk. "Hedge knight," he growled, "did your mother never teach you not to reach your hand into the dragon's mouth?"

"I never knew my mother, m'lord."

"That would explain it. What did he promise you?"

"A lordship. A white cloak. Big blue wings."

"Here's *my* promise: three feet of cold steel through your belly if you speak a word of what just happened."

Dunk shook his head to clear his wits. It did not seem to help. He bent double at the waist, and retched.

Some of the vomit spattered Peake's boots. The lord cursed. "Hedge knights," he exclaimed in disgust. "You have no place here. No true knight would be so discourteous as to turn up uninvited, but you creatures of the hedge . . ."

"We are wanted nowhere and turn up everywhere, m'lord." The wine had made Dunk bold, else he would have held his tongue. He wiped his mouth with the back of his hand.

"Try and remember what I told you, ser. It will go ill for you if you do not." Lord Peake shook the vomit off his boot. Then he was gone. Dunk leaned against the parapet again. He wondered who was madder, Lord Gormon or the Fiddler.

By the time he found his way back to the hall, only Maynard Plumm remained of his companions. "Was there any flour on her teats when you got the smallclothes off her?" he wanted to know.

Dunk shook his head, poured himself another cup of wine, tasted it, and decided that he had drunk enough.

Butterwell's stewards had found rooms in the keep for the lords and ladies, and beds in the barracks for their retinues. The rest of the guests had their choice between a straw pallet in the cellar or a spot of ground beneath the western walls to raise their pavilions. The modest sailcloth tent Dunk had acquired in Stoney Sept was no pavilion, but it kept the rain and sun off.

Some of his neighbors were still awake, the silken walls of their pavilions glowing like colored lanterns in the night. Laughter came from inside a blue pavilion covered with sunflowers, and the sounds of love from one striped in white and purple. Egg had set up their own tent a bit apart from the others. Maester and the two horses were hobbled nearby, and Dunk's arms and armor had been neatly stacked against the castle walls. When he crept into the tent, he found his squire sitting cross-legged by a candle, his head shining as he peered over a book.

"Reading books by candlelight will make you blind." Reading remained a mystery to Dunk though the lad had tried to teach him.

"I need the candlelight to see the words, ser."

"Do you want a clout in the ear? What book is that?" Dunk saw bright colors on the page, little painted shields hiding in amongst the letters.

"A roll of arms, ser."

"Looking for the Fiddler? You won't find him. They don't put hedge knights in those rolls, just lords and champions."

"I wasn't looking for him. I saw some other sigils in the yard ...

Lord Sunderland is here, ser. He bears the heads of three pale ladies, on undy green and blue."

"A Sisterman? Truly?" The Three Sisters were islands in the Bite. Dunk had heard septons say that the isles were sinks of sin and avarice. Sisterton was the most notorious smugglers' den in all of Westeros. "He's come a long way. He must be kin to Butterwell's new bride."

"He isn't, ser."

"Then he's here for the feast. They eat fish on the Three Sisters, don't they? A man gets sick of fish. Did you get enough to eat? I brought you half a capon and some cheese." Dunk rummaged in the pocket of his cloak.

"They fed us ribs, ser." Egg's nose was deep in the book. "Lord Sunderland fought for the black dragon, ser."

"Like old Ser Eustace? He wasn't so bad, was he?"

"No, ser," Egg said, "but ..."

"I saw the dragon's egg." Dunk squirreled the food away with their hardbread and salt beef. "It was red, mostly. Does Lord Bloodraven own a dragon's egg as well?"

Egg lowered his book. "Why would he? He's baseborn."

"Bastard born, not baseborn." Bloodraven had been born on the wrong side of the blanket, but he was noble on both sides. Dunk was about to tell Egg about the men he'd overheard when he noticed his face. "What happened to your lip?"

"A fight, ser."

"Let me see it."

"It only bled a little. I dabbed some wine on it."

"Who were you fighting?"

"Some other squires. They said—"

"Never mind what they said. What did I tell you?"

"To hold my tongue and make no trouble." The boy touched his broken lip. "They called my father a *kinslayer,* though."

He is, lad, though I do not think he meant it. Dunk had told Egg half a hundred times not to take such words to heart. *You know the truth. Let that be enough.* They had heard such talk before, in winesinks and low taverns, and around campfires in the woods. The whole realm knew how Prince Maekar's mace had felled his brother Baelor Breakspear at Ashford Meadow. Talk of plots was only to be expected. "If they knew

Prince Maekar was your father, they would never have said such things." *Behind your back, yes, but never to your face.* "And what did *you* tell these other squires, instead of holding your tongue?"

Egg looked abashed. "That Prince Baelor's death was just a mishap. Only when I said Prince Maekar loved his brother Baelor, Ser Addam's squire said he loved him to death, and Ser Mallor's squire said he meant to love his brother Aerys the same way. That was when I hit him. I hit him good."

"I ought to hit you good. A fat ear to go with that fat lip. Your father would do the same if he were here. Do you think Prince Maekar needs a little boy to defend him? What did he tell you when he sent you off with me?"

"To serve you faithfully as your squire and not flinch from any task or hardship."

"And what else?"

"To obey the king's laws, the rules of chivalry, and you."

"And what else?"

"To keep my hair shaven or dyed," the boy said, with obvious reluctance, "and tell no man my true name."

Dunk nodded. "How much wine had this boy drunk?"

"He was drinking barley beer."

"You see? The barley beer was talking. Words are wind, Egg. Just let them blow on past you."

"*Some* words are wind." The boy was nothing if not stubborn. "Some words are treason. This is a traitors' tourney, ser."

"What, all of them?" Dunk shook his head. "If it was true, that was a long time ago. The black dragon's dead, and those who fought with him are fled or pardoned. And it's not true. Lord Butterwell's sons fought on both sides."

"That makes him *half* a traitor, ser."

"Sixteen years ago." Dunk's mellow, winey haze was gone. He felt angry, and near sober. "Lord Butterwell's steward is the master of the games, a man named Cosgrove. Find him and enter my name for the lists. No, wait ... hold back my name." With so many lords on hand, one of them might recall Ser Duncan the Tall from Ashford Meadow. "Enter me as the Gallows Knight." The smallfolk loved it when a mystery knight appeared at a tourney.

Egg fingered his fat lip. "The Gallows Knight, ser?"

"For the shield."

"Yes, but ..."

"Go do as I said. You have read enough for one night." Dunk pinched the candle out between his thumb and forefinger.

The sun rose hot and hard, implacable.

Waves of heat rose shimmering off the white stones of the castle. The air smelled of baked earth and torn grass, and no breath of wind stirred the banners that drooped atop the keep and gatehouse, green and white and yellow.

Thunder was restless, in a way that Dunk had seldom seen before. The stallion tossed his head from side to side as Egg was tightening his saddle cinch. He even bared his big square teeth at the boy. *It is so hot,* Dunk thought, *too hot for man or mount.* A warhorse does not have a placid disposition even at the best of times. *The Mother herself would be foul-tempered in this heat.*

In the center of the yard the jousters began another run. Ser Harbert rode a golden courser barded in black and decorated with the red and white serpents of House Paege, Ser Franklyn a sorrel whose grey silk trapper bore the twin towers of Frey. When they came together, the red and white lance cracked clean in two and the blue one exploded into splinters, but neither man lost his seat. A cheer went up from the viewing stand and the guardsmen on the castle walls, but it was short and thin and hollow. *It is too hot for cheering.* Dunk mopped sweat from his brow. *It is too hot for jousting.* His head was beating like a drum. *Let me win this tilt and one more, and I will be content.*

The knights wheeled their horses about at the end of the lists and tossed down the jagged remains of their lances, the fourth pair they had broken. *Three too many.* Dunk had put off donning his armor as long as he dared, yet already he could feel his smallclothes sticking to his skin beneath his steel. *There are worse things than being soaked with sweat,* he told himself, remembering the fight on the *White Lady,* when the ironmen had come swarming over her side. He had been soaked in blood by the time that day was done.

Fresh lances in hand, Paege and Frey put their spurs into their mounts once again. Clods of cracked, dry earth sprayed back from beneath their horses' hooves with every stride. The *crack* of the lances breaking made Dunk wince. *Too much wine last night, and too much food.* He had some vague memory of carrying the bride up the steps and meeting John the Fiddler and Lord Peake upon a roof. *What was I doing on a roof?* There had been talk of dragons, he recalled, or dragon's eggs, or something, but ...

A noise broke his reverie, part roar and part moan. Dunk saw the golden horse trotting riderless to the end of the lists, as Ser Harbert Paege rolled feebly on the ground. *Two more before my turn.* The sooner he unhorsed Ser Uthor, the sooner he could take his armor off, have a cool drink, and rest. He should have at least an hour before they called him forth again.

Lord Butterwell's portly herald climbed to the top of the viewing stand to summon the next pair of jousters. *"Ser Argrave the Defiant,"* he called, *"a knight of Nunny, in service to Lord Butterwell of Whitewalls. Ser Glendon Flowers, the Knight of the Pussywillows. Come forth and prove your valor."* A gale of laughter rippled through the viewing stands.

Ser Argrave was a spare, leathery man, a seasoned household knight in dinted grey armor riding an unbarded horse. Dunk had known his sort before; such men were tough as old roots and knew their business. His foe was young Ser Glendon, mounted on his wretched stot and armored in a heavy mail hauberk and open-faced iron halfhelm. On his arm his shield displayed his father's fiery sigil. *He needs a breastplate and a proper helm,* Dunk thought. *A blow to the head or chest could kill him, clad like that.*

Ser Glendon was plainly furious at his introduction. He wheeled his mount in an angry circle, and shouted, "I am Glendon *Ball*, not Glendon Flowers. Mock me at your peril, herald. I warn you, I have hero's blood." The herald did not deign to reply, but more laughter greeted the young knight's protest. "Why are they laughing at him?" Dunk wondered aloud. "Is he a bastard, then?" *Flowers* was the surname given to bastards born of noble parents in the Reach. "And what was all that about pussywillows?"

"I could find out, ser," said Egg.

"No. It is none of our concern. Do you have my helm?" Ser Argrave and Ser Glendon dipped their lances before Lord and Lady Butter-well. Dunk saw Butterwell lean over and whisper something in his bride's ear. The girl began to giggle.

"Yes, ser." Egg had donned his floppy hat, to shade his eyes and keep the sun off his shaven head. Dunk liked to tease the boy about that hat, but just now he wished he had one like it. *Better a straw hat than an iron one, beneath this sun.* He pushed his hair out of his eyes, eased the greathelm down into place with two hands, and fastened it to his gorget. The lining stank of old sweat, and he could feel the weight of all that iron on his neck and shoulders. His head throbbed from last night's wine.

"Ser," Egg said, "it is not too late to withdraw. If you lose Thunder and your armor . . . "

I would be done as a knight. "Why should I lose?" Dunk demanded. Ser Argrave and Ser Glendon had ridden to opposite ends of the lists. "It is not as if I face the Laughing Storm. Is there some knight here like to give me trouble?"

"Almost all of them, ser."

"I owe you a clout in the ear for that. Ser Uthor is ten years my senior and half my size." Ser Argrave lowered his visor. Ser Glendon did not have a visor to lower.

"You have not ridden in a tilt since Ashford Meadow, ser."

Insolent boy. "I've trained." Not as faithfully as he might have, to be sure. When he could, he took his turn riding at quintains or rings, where such were available. And sometimes he would command Egg to climb a tree and hang a shield or barrel stave beneath a well-placed limb for them to tilt at.

"You're better with a sword than with a lance," Egg said. "With an axe or a mace there are few to match your strength."

There was enough truth in that to annoy Dunk all the more. "There is no contest for swords or maces," he pointed out, as Fireball's son and Ser Argrave the Defiant began their charge. "Go get my shield."

Egg made a face, then went to fetch the shield.

Across the yard, Ser Argrave's lance struck Ser Glendon's shield and glanced off, leaving a gouge across the comet. But Ball's coronal found the center of his foe's breastplate with such force that it burst his saddle cinch. Knight and saddle both went tumbling to the dust. Dunk was impressed despite himself. *The boy jousts almost as well as he talks.* He wondered if that would stop their laughing at him.

A trumpet rang, loud enough to make Dunk wince. Once more the herald climbed his stand. *"Ser Joffrey of House Caswell, Lord of Bitter-bridge and Defender of the Fords. Ser Kyle, the Cat of Misty Moor. Come forth and prove your valor."*

Ser Kyle's armor was of good quality but old and worn, with many dints and scratches. "The Mother has been merciful to me, Ser Duncan," he told Dunk and Egg, on his way to the lists. "I am sent against Lord Caswell, the very man I came to see."

If any man upon the field felt worse than Dunk this morning it had to be Lord Caswell, who had drunk himself insensible at the feast. "It's a wonder he can sit ahorse after last night," said Dunk. "The victory is yours, ser."

"Oh, no." Ser Kyle smiled a silken smile. "The cat who wants his bowl of cream must know when to purr and when to show his claws, Ser Duncan. If his lordship's lance so much as scrapes against my shield, I shall go tumbling to the earth. Afterward, when I bring my horse and armor to him, I will compliment his lordship on how much his prowess has grown since I made him his first sword. That will recall me to him, and before the day is out I shall be a Caswell man again, a knight of Bitterbridge."

There is no honor in that, Dunk almost said, but he bit his tongue instead. Ser Kyle would not be the first hedge knight to trade his honor for a warm place by the fire. "As you say," he muttered. "Good fortune to you. Or bad, if you prefer."

Lord Joffrey Caswell was a weedy youth of twenty, though admittedly he looked rather more impressive in his armor than he had last night when he'd been facedown in a puddle of wine. A yellow centaur was painted on his shield, pulling on a longbow. The same centaur adorned the white silk trappings of his horse and gleamed atop his helm in yellow gold. *A man who has a centaur for his sigil should ride better than that.* Dunk did not know how well Ser Kyle wielded a lance, but from the way Lord Caswell sat his horse it looked as though a loud cough might unseat him. *All the Cat need do is ride past him very fast.*

Egg held Thunder's bridle as Dunk swung himself ponderously up into the high, stiff saddle. As he sat there waiting, he could feel the eyes upon him. *They are wondering if the big hedge knight is any good.* Dunk wondered that himself. He would find out soon enough.

The Cat of Misty Moor was true to his word. Lord Caswell's lance was wobbling all the way across the field, and Ser Kyle's was ill aimed. Neither man got his horse up past a trot. All the same, the Cat went tumbling when Lord Joffrey's coronal chanced to whack his shoulder. *I thought all cats landed gracefully upon their feet,* Dunk thought, as the hedge knight rolled in the dust. Lord Caswell's lance remained unbroken. As he brought his horse around, he thrust it high into the air repeatedly, as if he'd just unseated Leo Longthorn or the Laughing Storm. The Cat pulled off his helm and went chasing down his horse.

"My shield," Dunk said to Egg. The boy handed it up. He slipped his left arm through the strap and closed his hand around the grip. The weight of the kite shield was reassuring though its length made it awkward to handle, and seeing the hanged man once again gave him an uneasy feeling. *Those are ill-omened arms.* He resolved to get the shield repainted as soon as he could. *May the Warrior grant me a smooth course and a quick victory,* he prayed, as Butterwell's herald was clambering up the steps once more. *"Ser Uthor Underleaf,"* his voice rang out. *"The Gallows Knight. Come forth and prove your valor."*

"Be careful, ser," Egg warned as he handed Dunk a tourney lance, a tapered wooden shaft twelve feet long ending in a rounded iron coronal in the shape of a closed fist. "The other squires say Ser Uthor has a good seat. And he's quick."

"Quick?" Dunk snorted. "He has a snail on his shield. How quick can he be?" He put his heels into Thunder's flanks and walked the horse slowly forward, his lance upright. *One victory, and I am no worse than before. Two will leave us well ahead. Two is not too much to hope for, in this company.* He had been fortunate in the lots, at least. He could as easily have drawn the Old Ox or Ser Kirby Pimm or some other local hero. Dunk wondered if the master of games was deliberately matching the hedge knights against each other, so no lordling need suffer the ignominy of losing to one in the first round. *It does not matter. One foe at a time, that was what the old man always said. Ser Uthor is all that should concern me now.*

They met beneath the viewing stand where Lord and Lady Butterwell sat on their cushions in the shade of the castle walls. Lord
Frey was beside them, dandling his snot-nosed son on one knee. A
row of serving girls were fanning them, yet Lord Butterwell's damask
tunic was stained beneath the arms, and his lady's hair was limp from
perspiration. She looked hot, bored, and uncomfortable, but when she
saw Dunk she pushed out her chest in a way that turned him red
beneath his helm. He dipped his lance to her and her lord husband.
Ser Uthor did the same. Butterwell wished them both a good tilt. His
wife stuck out her tongue.

It was time. Dunk trotted back to the south end of the lists. Eighty
feet away, his opponent was taking up his position as well. His grey
stallion was smaller than Thunder but younger and more spirited.
Ser Uthor wore green enamel plate and silvery chain mail. Streamers
of green and grey silk flowed from his rounded bascinet, and his
green shield bore a silver snail. *Good armor and a good horse means a
good ransom if I unseat him.*

A trumpet sounded.

Thunder started forward at a slow trot. Dunk swung his lance to the left and brought it down, so it angled across the horse's head and the wooden barrier between him and his foe. His shield protected the left side of his body. He crouched forward, legs tightening as Thunder drove down the lists. *We are one. Man, horse, lance, we are one beast of blood and wood and iron.*

Ser Uthor was charging hard, clouds of dust kicking up from the hooves of his grey. With forty yards between them, Dunk spurred Thunder to a gallop, and aimed the point of his lance squarely at the silver snail. The sullen sun, the dust, the heat, the castle, Lord Butterwell and his bride, the Fiddler and Ser Maynard, knights, squires, grooms, smallfolk, all vanished. Only the foe remained. The spurs again. Thunder broke into a run.

The snail was rushing toward them, growing with every stride of the grey's long legs . . . but ahead came Ser Uthor's lance with its iron fist. *My shield is strong, my shield will take the blow. Only the snail matters. Strike the snail and the tilt is mine.*

When ten yards remained between them, Ser Uthor shifted the point of his lance upward.

A crack rang in Dunk's ears as his lance hit. He felt the impact in his arm and shoulder, but never saw the blow strike home. Uthor's iron fist took him square between his eyes, with all the force of man and horse behind it.

Dunk woke upon his back, staring up at the arches of a barrel-vaulted ceiling. For a moment he did not know where he was, or how he had arrived there. Voices echoed in his head, and faces drifted past him; old Ser Arlan, Tanselle Too-Tall, Bennis of the Brown Shield, the Red Widow, Baelor Breakspear, Aerion the Bright Prince, mad, sad Lady Vaith. Then all at once the joust came back to him: the heat, the snail, the iron fist coming at his face. He groaned, and rolled onto one elbow. The movement set his skull to pounding like some monstrous war drum.

Both of his eyes seemed to be working, at least. Nor could he feel a hole in his head, which was all to the good. He was in some cellar, he saw, with casks of wine and ale on every side. *At least it is cool here,* he thought, *and drink is close at hand.* The taste of blood was in his mouth. Dunk felt a stab of fear. If he had bitten off his tongue, he would be dumb as well as thick. "Good morrow," he croaked, just to hear his voice. The words echoed off the ceiling. Dunk tried to push himself onto his feet, but the effort set the cellar spinning.

"Slowly, slowly," said a quavery voice, close at hand. A stooped old man appeared beside the bed, clad in robes as grey as his long hair. About his neck was a maester's chain of many metals. His face was aged and lined, with deep creases on either side of a great beak of a nose. "Be still, and let me see your eyes." He peered in Dunk's left eye, then the right, holding them open between his thumb and forefinger.

"My head hurts."

The maester snorted. "Be grateful it still rests upon your shoulders, ser. Here, this may help somewhat. Drink."

Dunk made himself swallow every drop of the foul potion and managed not to spit it out. "The tourney," he said, wiping his mouth with the back of his hand. "Tell me. What's happened?"

"The same foolishness that always happens in these affrays. Men have been knocking each other off horses with sticks. Lord Small-wood's nephew broke his wrist and Ser Eden Risley's leg was crushed beneath his horse, but no one has been killed thus far. Though I had my fears for you, ser."

"Was I unhorsed?" His head still felt as though it were stuffed full of wool, else he would never have asked such a stupid question. Dunk regretted it the instant the words were out.

"With a crash that shook the highest ramparts. Those who had wagered good coin on you were most distraught, and your squire was beside himself. He would be sitting with you still if I had not chased him off. I need no children underfoot. I reminded him of his duty."

Dunk found that he needed reminding himself. "What duty?"

"Your mount, ser. Your arms and armor."

"Yes," Dunk said, remembering. The boy was a good squire; he knew what was required of him. *I have lost the old man's sword and the armor that Steely Pate forged for me.*

"Your fiddling friend was also asking after you. He told me you were to have the best of care. I threw him out as well."

"How long have you been tending me?" Dunk flexed the fingers of his sword hand. All of them still seemed to work. *Only my head's hurt, and Ser Arlan used to say I never used that anyway.*

"Four hours, by the sundial."

Four hours was not so bad. He had once heard tell of a knight struck so hard that he slept for forty years and woke to find himself old and withered. "Do you know if Ser Uthor won his second tilt?" Maybe the Snail would win the tourney. It would take some sting from the defeat if Dunk could tell himself that he had lost to the best knight in the field.

"That one? Indeed he did. Against Ser Addam Frey, a cousin to the bride, and a promising young lance. Her ladyship fainted when Ser Addam fell. She had to be helped back to her chambers."

Dunk forced himself to his feet, reeling as he rose, but the maester helped to steady him. "Where are my clothes? I must go. I have to ... I must..."

"If you cannot recall, it cannot be so very urgent." The maester made an irritated motion. "I would suggest that you avoid rich foods, strong drink, and further blows between your eyes ... but I learned long ago that knights are deaf to sense. Go, go. I have other fools to tend."

Outside, Dunk glimpsed a hawk soaring in wide circles through the bright blue sky. He envied him. A few clouds were gathering to the east, dark as Dunk's mood. As he found his way back to the tilting ground, the sun beat down on his head like a hammer on an anvil. The earth seemed to move beneath his feet ... or it might just be that he was swaying. He had almost fallen twice climbing the cellar steps. *I should have heeded Egg.*

He made his slow way across the outer ward, around the fringes of the crowd. Out on the field, plump Lord Alyn Cockshaw was limping off between two squires, the latest conquest of young Glendon Ball. A third squire held his helm, its three proud feathers broken. *"Ser John the Fiddler,"* the herald cried. *"Ser Franklyn of House Frey, a knight of the Twins, sworn to the Lord of the Crossing. Come forth and prove your valor."*

Dunk could only stand and watch as the Fiddler's big black trotted onto the field in a swirl of blue silk and golden swords and fiddles. His breastplate was enameled blue as well, as were his poleyns, couter, greaves, and gorget. The ringmail underneath was gilded. Ser Franklyn rode a dapple grey with a flowing silver mane, to match the grey of his silks and the silver of his armor. On shield and surcoat and horse trappings he bore the twin towers of Frey. They charged and charged again. Dunk stood watching but saw none of it. *Dunk the lunk, thick as a castle wall,* he chided himself. *He had a snail upon his shield. How could you lose to a man with a snail upon his shield?*

There was cheering all around him. When Dunk looked up, he saw that Franklyn Frey was down. The Fiddler had dismounted, to help his fallen foe back to his feet. *He is one step closer to his dragon's egg,* Dunk thought, *and where am I?*

As he approached the postern gate, Dunk came upon the company of dwarfs from last night's feast preparing to take their leave They were hitching ponies to their wheeled wooden pig, and a second wayn of more conventional design. There were six of them, he saw, each smaller and more malformed than the last. A few might have

been children, but they were all so short that it was hard to tell. In daylight, dressed in horsehide breeches and roughspun hooded cloaks, they seemed less jolly than they had in motley. "Good morrow to you," Dunk said, to be courteous. "Are you for the road? There's clouds to the east, could mean rain."

The only answer that he got was a glare from the ugliest dwarf. *Was he the one I pulled off Lady Butterwell last night?* Up close, the little man smelled like a privy. One whiff was enough to make Dunk hasten his steps.

The walk across the Milkhouse seemed to take Dunk as long as it had once taken him and Egg to cross the sands of Dorne. He kept a wall beside him, and from time to time he leaned on it. Every time he turned his head the world would swim. *A drink,* he thought. *I need a drink of water, or else I'm like to fall.*

A passing groom told him where to find the nearest well. It was there that he discovered Kyle the Cat, talking quietly with Maynard Plumm. Ser Kyle's shoulders were slumped in dejection, but he looked up at Dunk's approach. "Ser Duncan? We had heard that you were dead, or dying."

Dunk rubbed his temples. "I only wish I were."

"I know that feeling well." Ser Kyle sighed. "Lord Caswell did not know me. When I told him how I carved his first sword, he stared at me as if I'd lost my wits. He said there was no place at Bitterbridge for knights as feeble as I had shown myself to be." The Cat gave a bitter laugh. "He took my arms and armor, though. My mount as well. What will I do?"

Dunk had no answer for him. Even a freerider required a horse to ride; sellswords must have swords to sell. "You will find another horse," Dunk said as he drew the bucket up. "The Seven Kingdoms are full of horses. You will find some other lord to arm you." He cupped his hands, filled them with water, drank.

"Some other lord. Aye. Do you know of one? I am not so young and strong as you. Nor as big. Big men are always in demand. Lord Butterwell likes his knights large, for one. Look at that Tom Heddle. Have you seen him joust? He has overthrown every man he's faced. Fireball's lad has done the same, though. The Fiddler as well. Would that he had been the one to unhorse me. He refuses to take ransoms. He wants no more than the dragon's egg, he says ... that and the friendship of his fallen foes. The flower of chivalry, that one."

Maynard Plumm gave a laugh. "The fiddle of chivalry, you mean. That boy is fiddling up a storm, and all of us would do well to be gone from here before it breaks."

"He takes no ransoms?" said Dunk. "A gallant gesture."

"Gallant gestures come easy when your purse is fat with gold," said Ser Maynard. "There is a lesson here if you have the sense to take it, Ser Duncan. It is not too late for you to go."

"Go? Go where?"

Ser Maynard shrugged. "Anywhere. Winterfell, Summerhall, Asshai by the Shadow. It makes no matter, so long as it's not here. Take your horse and armor and slip out the postern gate. You won't be missed. The Snail's got his next tilt to think about, and the rest have eyes only for the jousting."

For half a heartbeat Dunk was tempted. So long as he was armed and horsed, he would remain a knight of sorts. Without them he was no more than a beggar. *A big beggar, but a beggar all the same.* But his arms and armor belonged to Ser Uthor now. So did Thunder. *Better a beggar than a thief.* He had been both in Flea Bottom, when he ran with Ferret, Rafe, and Pudding, but the old man had saved him from that life. He knew what Ser Arlan of Pennytree would have said to Plumm's suggestions. Ser Arlan being dead, Dunk said it for him. "Even a hedge knight has his honor."

"Would you rather die with honor intact or live with it besmirched? No, spare me, I know what you will say. Take your boy and flee, gallows knight. Before your arms become your destiny."

Dunk bristled. "How would you know my destiny? Did you have a dream, like John the Fiddler? What do you know of Egg?"

"I know that eggs do well to stay out of frying pans," said Plumm. "Whitewalls is not a healthy place for the boy."

"How did you fare in your own tilt, ser?" Dunk asked him.

"Oh, I did not chance the lists. The omens had gone sour. Who do you imagine is going to claim the dragon's egg, pray?"

Not me, Dunk thought. "The Seven know. I don't."

"Venture a guess, ser. You have two eyes."

He thought a moment. "The Fiddler?"

"Very good. Would you care to explain your reasoning?"

"I just ... I have a feeling."

"So do I," said Maynard Plumm. "A bad feeling, for any man or boy unwise enough to stand in our Fiddler's way."

Egg was brushing Thunder's coat outside their tent, but his eyes were far away. *The boy has taken my fall hard.* "Enough," Dunk called. "Any more and Thunder will be as bald as you."

"Ser?" Egg dropped the brush. "I *knew* no stupid snail could kill you, ser." He threw his arms around him.

Dunk swiped the boy's floppy straw hat and put it on his own head. "The maester said you made off with my armor."

Egg snatched back his hat indignantly. "I've scoured your mail and polished your greaves, gorget, and breastplate, ser, but your helm is cracked and dinted where Ser Uthor's coronal struck. You'll need to have it hammered out by an armorer."

"Let Ser Uthor have it hammered out. It's his now." *No horse, no sword, no armor. Perhaps those dwarfs would let me join their troupe. That would be a funny sight, six dwarfs pummeling a giant with pig bladders.* "Thunder is his too. Come. We'll take them to him and wish him well in the rest of his tilts."

"Now, ser? Aren't you going to ransom Thunder?"

"With what, lad? Pebbles and sheep pellets?"

"I thought about that, ser. If you could borrow—"

Dunk cut him off. "No one will lend me that much coin, Egg. Why should they? What am I but some great oaf who called himself a knight until some snail with a stick near stove his head in?"

"Well," said Egg, "you could have Rain, ser. I'll go back to riding Maester. We'll go to Summerhall. You can take service in my father's household. His stables are full of horses. You could have a destrier and a palfrey too."

Egg meant well, but Dunk could not go cringing back to Summerhall. Not that way, penniless and beaten, seeking service without so much as a sword to offer. "Lad," he said, "that's good of you, but I want no crumbs from your lord father's table, or from his stables neither. Might be it's time we parted ways." Dunk could always slink off to join the City Watch in Lannisport or Oldtown, they liked big men for that. *I've bumped my bean on every beam in every inn from Lannisport to King's Landing, might be it's time my size earned me a bit of coin instead of just a lumpy head.* But watchmen did not have squires. "I've taught you what I could, and that was little enough. You'll do better with a proper master-at-arms to see to your training, some fierce old knight who knows which end of the lance to hold."

"I don't want a proper master-at-arms," Egg said. "I want you. What if I used my—"

"No. None of that, I will not hear it. Go gather up my arms. We will present them to Ser Uthor with my compliments. Hard things only grow harder if you put them off."

Egg kicked the ground, his face as droopy as his big straw hat. "Aye, ser. As you say."

From the outside Ser Uthor's tent was very plain; a large square box of dun-colored sailcloth staked to the ground with hempen ropes. A silver snail adorned the center pole above a long grey pennon, but that was the only decoration.

"Wait here," Dunk told Egg. The boy had hold of Thunder's lead. The big brown destrier was laden with Dunk's arms and armor, even to his new old shield. *The Gallows Knight. What a dismal mystery knight I proved to be.* "I won't be long." He ducked his head and stooped to shoulder through the flap.

The tent's exterior left him ill prepared for the comforts he found within. The ground beneath his feet was carpeted in woven Myrish rugs, rich with color. An ornate trestle table stood surrounded by camp chairs. The feather bed was covered with soft cushions, and an iron brazier burned perfumed incense.

Ser Uthor sat at the table, a pile of gold and silver before him and a flagon of wine at his elbow, counting coins with his squire, a gawky fellow close in age to Dunk. From time to time the Snail would bite a coin, or set one aside. "I see I still have much to teach you, Will," Dunk heard him say. "This coin has been clipped, t'other shaved. And this one?" A gold piece danced across his fingers. "*Look* at the coins before taking them. Here, tell me what you see." The dragon spun through the air. Will tried to catch it, but it bounced off his fingers and fell to the ground. He had to get down on his knees to find it. When he did, he turned it over twice before saying, "This one's good, m'lord. There's a dragon on the one side and a king on t'other ..."

Underleaf glanced toward Dunk. "The Hanged Man. It is good to see you moving about, ser. I feared I'd killed you. Will you do me a kindness and instruct my squire as to the nature of dragons? Will, give Ser Duncan the coin."

Dunk had no choice but to take it. *He unhorsed me, must he make me caper for him too?* Frowning, he hefted the coin in his palm, examined both sides, tasted it. "Gold, not shaved or clipped. The weight feels right. I'd have taken it too, m'lord. What's wrong with it?"

"The king."

Dunk took a closer look. The face on the coin was young, clean-shaven, handsome. King Aerys was bearded on his coins, the same as old King Aegon. King Daeron, who'd come between them, had been clean-shaven, but this wasn't him. The coin did not appear worn enough to be from before Aegon the Unworthy. Dunk scowled at the word beneath the head. *Six letters.* They looked the same as he had seen on other dragons. *Daeron,* the letters read, but Dunk knew the face of Daeron the Good, and this wasn't him. When he looked again, he saw something odd about the shape of the fourth letter, it wasn't . . .

"Daemon," he blurted out. "It says *Daemon*. There never was any King Daemon, though, only—"

"—the Pretender. Daemon Blackfyre struck his own coinage during his rebellion."

"It's gold, though," Will argued. "If it's gold, it should be just as good as them other dragons, m'lord."

The Snail clouted him along the side of the head. "Cretin. Aye, it's gold. Rebel's gold. Traitor's gold. It's treasonous to own such a coin, and twice as treasonous to pass it. I'll need to have this melted down." He hit the man again. "Get out of my sight. This good knight and I have matters to discuss."

Will wasted no time in scrambling from the tent. "Have a seat," Ser Uthor said politely. "Will you take wine?" Here in his own tent, Underleaf seemed a different man than at the feast.

A snail hides in his shell, Dunk remembered. "Thank you, no." He flicked the gold coin back to Ser Uthor. *Traitor's gold. Blackfyre gold. Egg said this was a traitor's tourney, but I would not listen.* He owed the boy an apology.

"Half a cup," Underleaf insisted. "You sound in need of it." He filled two cups with wine and handed one to Dunk. Out of his armor, he looked more a merchant than a knight. "You've come about the forfeit, I assume."

"Aye." Dunk took the wine. Maybe it would help to stop his head from pounding. "I brought my horse, and my arms and armor. Take them, with my compliments."

Ser Uthor smiled. "And this is where I tell you that you rode a gallant course."

Dunk wondered if *gallant* was a chivalrous way of saying *clumsy*. "That is good of you to say, but—"

"I think you misheard me, ser. Would it be too bold of me to ask how you came to knighthood, ser?"

"Ser Arlan of Pennytree found me in Flea Bottom, chasing pigs. His old squire had been slain on the Redgrass Field, so he needed

someone to tend his mount and clean his mail. He promised he would teach me sword and lance and how to ride a horse if I would come and serve him, so I did."

"A charming tale ... though if I were you I would leave out the part about the pigs. Pray, where is your Ser Arlan now?"

"He died. I buried him."

"I see. Did you take him home to Pennytree?"

"I didn't know where it was." Dunk had never seen the old man's Pennytree. Ser Arlan seldom spoke of it, no more than Dunk was wont to speak of Flea Bottom. "I buried him on a hillside facing west, so he could see the sun go down." The camp chair creaked alarmingly beneath his weight.

Ser Uthor resumed his seat. "I have my own armor, and a better horse than yours. What do I want with some old done nag and a sack of dinted plate and rusty mail?"

"Steely Pate made that armor," Dunk said, with a touch of anger. "Egg has taken good care of it. There's not a spot of rust on my mail, and the steel is good and strong."

"Strong and heavy," Ser Uthor complained, "and too big for any man of normal size. You are uncommon large, Duncan the Tall. As for your horse, he is too old to ride and too stringy to eat."

"Thunder is not as young as he used to be," Dunk admitted, "and my armor is large, as you say. You could sell it though. In Lannisport and King's Landing there are plenty of smiths who will take it off your hands."

"For a tenth of what it's worth, perhaps," said Ser Uthor, "and only to melt down for the metal. No. It's sweet silver I require, not old iron. The coin of the realm. Now, do you wish to ransom back your arms, or no?"

Dunk turned the wine cup in his hands, frowning. It was solid silver, with a line of golden snails inlaid around the lip. The wine was gold as well, and heady on the tongue. "If wishes were fishes, aye, I'd pay. Gladly. Only—"

"—you don't have two stags to lock horns."

"If you would ... would lend my horse and armor back to me, I could pay the ransom later. Once I found the coin."

The Snail looked amused. "Where would you find it, pray?"

"I could take service with some lord, or ..." It was hard to get the words out. They made him feel a beggar. "It might take a few years, but I would pay you. I swear it."

"On your honor as a knight?"

Dunk flushed. "I could make my mark upon a parchment."

"A hedge knight's scratch upon a scrap of paper?" Ser Uthor rolled his eyes. "Good to wipe my arse. No more."

"You are a hedge knight too."

"Now you insult me. I ride where I will and serve no man but myself, true ... but it has been many a year since I last slept beneath a hedge. I find that inns are far more comfortable. I am a *tourney* knight, the best that you are ever like to meet."

"The best?" His arrogance made Dunk angry. "The Laughing Storm might not agree, ser. Nor Leo Longthorn, nor the Brute of Bracken. At Ashford Meadow no one spoke of snails. Why is that if you're such a famous tourney champion?"

"Have you heard me name myself a champion? That way lies renown. I would sooner have the pox. Thank you, but no. I shall win my next joust, aye, but in the final I shall fall. Butterwell has thirty drag-ons for the knight who comes second, that shall suffice for me ... along with some goodly ransoms and the proceeds of my wagers." He gestured at the piles of silver stags and golden dragons on the table. "You seem a healthy fellow, and very large. Size will always impress the fools though it means little and less in jousting. Will was able to get odds of three to one against me. Lord Shawney gave five to one, the fool." He picked up a silver stag and set it to spinning with a flick of his long fingers. "The Old Ox will be the next to tumble. Then the Knight of the Pussywillows, if he survives that long. Sentiment being what it is, I should get fine odds against them both. The commons love their village heroes."

"Ser Glendon has hero's blood," Dunk blurted out.

"Oh, I do hope so. Hero's blood should be good for two to one. Whore's blood draws poorer odds. Ser Glendon speaks about his pur-ported sire at every opportunity, but have you noticed that he never makes mention of his mother? For good reason. He was born of a camp follower. Jenny, her name was. Penny Jenny, they called her, until the Redgrass Field. The night before the battle, she fucked so many men that thereafter she was known as Redgrass Jenny. Fireball had her before that, I don't doubt, but so did a hundred other men. Our friend Glendon presumes quite a lot, it seems to me. He does not even have red hair."

Hero's blood, thought Dunk. "He says he is a knight."

"Oh, that much is true. The boy and his sister grew up in a brothel, called the Pussywillows. After Penny Jenny died, the other whores took care of them and fed the lad the tale his mother had concocted, about him being Fireball's seed. An old squire who lived nearby gave the boy his training, such that it was, in trade for ale and cunt, but being but a squire he could not knight the little bastard. Half a year ago, however, a party of knights chanced upon the brothel and a cer-tain Ser Morgan Dunstable took a drunken fancy to Ser Glendon's sister. As it happens, the sister was still virgin and Dunstable did not have the price of her maidenhead. So a bargain was struck. Ser Mor-gan dubbed her brother a knight, right there in the Pussywillows in front of twenty witnesses, and afterward little sister took him up-stairs and let him pluck her flower. And there you are."

Any knight could make a knight. When he was squiring for Ser Arlan, Dunk had heard tales of other men who'd bought their knighthood with a kindness or a threat or a bag of silver coins, but never with a sister's maidenhead. "That's just a tale," he heard himself say. "That can't be true."

"I had it from Kirby Pimm, who claims that he was there, a witness to the knighting." Ser Uthor shrugged. "Hero's son, whore's son, or both, when he faces me the boy will fall."

"The lots may give you some other foe."

Ser Uthor arched an eyebrow. "Cosgrove is as fond of silver as the next man. I promise you, I shall draw the Old Ox next, then the boy. Would you care to wager on it?"

"I have nothing left to wager." Dunk did not know what distressed him more: learning that the Snail was bribing the master of the games to get the pairings he desired, or realizing the man had desired *him*. He stood. "I have said what I came to say. My horse and sword are yours, and all my armor."

The Snail steepled his fingers. "Perhaps there is another way. You are not entirely without your talents. You fall most splendidly." Ser Uthor's lips glistened when he smiled. "I will lend you back your steed and armor ... if you enter my service."

"Service?" Dunk did not understand. "What sort of service? You have a squire. Do you need to garrison some castle?"

"I might if I had a castle. If truth be told, I prefer a good inn. Castles cost too much to maintain. No, the service I would require of you is that you face me in a few more tourneys. Twenty should suffice. You can do that, surely? You shall have a tenth part of my winnings, and in future I promise to strike that broad chest of yours and not your head."

"You'd have me travel about with you to be unhorsed?"

Ser Uthor chuckled pleasantly. "You are such a strapping specimen, no one will ever believe that some round-shouldered old man with a snail on his shield could put you down." He rubbed his chin. "You need a new device yourself, by the way. That hanged man is grim enough, I grant you, but ... well, he's *hanging*, isn't he? Dead and defeated. Something fiercer is required. A bear's head, mayhaps. A skull. Or three skulls, better still. A babe impaled upon a spear. And you should let your hair grow long and cultivate a beard, the wilder and more unkempt the better. There are more of these little tourneys than you know. With the odds I'd get we'd win enough to buy a dragon's egg before—"

"—it got about that I was hopeless? I lost my armor, not my honor. You'll have Thunder and my arms, no more."

"Pride ill becomes a beggar, ser. You could do much worse than ride with me. At the least I could teach you a thing or two of jousting, about which you are pig ignorant at present."

"You'd make a fool of me."

"I did that earlier. And even fools must eat."

Dunk wanted to smash that smile off his face. "I see why you have a snail on your shield. You are no true knight."

"Spoken like a true oaf. Are you so blind you cannot see your danger?" Ser Uthor put his cup aside. "Do you know why I struck you where I did, ser?" He got to his feet, and touched Dunk lightly in the center of his chest. "A coronal placed here would have put you on the ground just as quickly. The head is a smaller target, the blow is more difficult to land ... though more likely to be mortal. I was paid to strike you there."

"Paid?" Dunk backed away from him. "What do you mean?"

"Six dragons tendered in advance, four more promised when you died. A paltry sum for a knight's life. Be thankful for that. Had more been offered, I might have put the point of my lance through your eyeslit."

Dunk felt dizzy again. *Why would someone pay to have me killed? I've done no harm to any man at Whitewalls.* Surely no one hated him that much but Egg's brother Aerion, and the Bright Prince was in exile across the narrow sea. "Who paid you?"

"A serving man brought the gold at sunrise, not long after the master of the games nailed up the pairings. His face was hooded, and he did not speak his master's name."

"But why?" said Dunk.

"I did not ask." Ser Uthor filled his cup again. "I think you have more enemies than you know, Ser Duncan. How not? There are some who would say you were the cause of all our woes."

Dunk felt a cold hand on his heart. "Say what you mean."

The Snail shrugged. "I may not have been at Ashford Meadow, but jousting is my bread and salt. I follow tourneys from afar as faithfully as the maesters follow stars. I know how a certain hedge knight became the cause of a trial of seven at Ashford Meadow, resulting in the death of Baelor Breakspear at his brother Maekar's hand." Ser Uthor seated himself, and stretched his legs out. "Prince Baelor was well loved. The Bright Prince had friends as well, friends who will not have forgotten the cause of his exile. Think on my offer, ser. The snail may leave a trail of slime behind him, but a little slime will do a man no harm … while if you dance with dragons, you must expect to burn."

The day seemed darker when Dunk stepped from the Snail's tent. The clouds in the east had grown bigger and blacker, and the sun was sinking to the west, casting long shadows across the yard. Dunk found the squire Will inspecting Thunder's feet.

"Where's Egg?" he asked of him.

"The bald boy? How would I know? Run off somewhere."

He could not bear to say farewell to Thunder, Dunk decided. *He'll be back at the tent with his books.* He wasn't, though. The books were there, bundled neatly in a stack beside Egg's bedroll, but of the boy there was no sign. Something was wrong here. Dunk could feel it. It was not like Egg to wander off without his leave.

A pair of grizzled men-at-arms were drinking barley beer outside a striped pavilion a few feet away. "... well, bugger that, once was enough for me," one muttered. "The grass was green when the sun come up, aye ..." He broke off when the other man gave him a nudge, and only then took note of Dunk. "Ser?"

"Have you seen my squire? Egg, he's called."

The man scratched at the grey stubble underneath one ear. "I remember him. Less hair than me, and a mouth three times his size. Some o' the other lads shoved him about a bit, but that was last night. I've not seen him since, ser."

"Scared him off," said his companion.

Dunk gave that one a hard look. "If he comes back, tell him to wait for me here."

"Aye, ser. That we will."

Might be he just went to watch the jousts. Dunk headed back toward the tilting grounds. As he passed the stables he came on Ser Glendon Ball, brushing down a pretty sorrel charger. "Have you seen Egg?" he asked him.

"He ran past a few moments ago." Ser Glendon pulled a carrot from his pocket and fed it to the sorrel. "Do you like my new horse? Lord Costayne sent his squire to ransom her, but I told him to save his gold. I mean to keep her for my own."

"His lordship will not like that."

"His lordship said that I had no right to put a fireball upon my shield. He told me my device should be a clump of pussywillows. His lordship can go bugger himself."

Dunk could not help but smile. He had supped at that same table himself, choking down the same bitter dishes as served up by the likes of the Bright Prince and Ser Steffon Fossoway. He felt a certain kinship with the prickly young knight. *For all I know, my mother was a whore as well.* "How many horses have you won?"

Ser Glendon shrugged. "I lost count. Mortimer Boggs still owes me one. He said he'd rather eat his horse than have some whore's bastard riding her. And he took a hammer to his armor before sending it to me. It's full of holes. I suppose I can still get something for the metal." He sounded more sad than angry. "There was a stable by the ... the inn where I was raised. I worked there when I was a boy, and when I could I'd sneak the horses off while their owners were busy. I was always good with horses. Stots, rounseys, palfreys, drays, plowhorses, warhorses, I rode them all. Even a Dornish sand steed. This old man I knew taught me how to make my own lances. I thought if I showed them all how good I was, they'd have no choice but to admit I was my father's son. But they won't. Even now. They just won't."

"Some never will," Dunk told him. "It doesn't matter what you do. Others, though . . . they're not all the same. I've met some good ones." He thought a moment. "When the tourney's done, Egg and I mean to go north. Take service at Winterfell and fight for the Starks against the ironmen. You could come with us." The north was a world all its own, Ser Arlan always said. No one up there was like to know the tale of Penny Jenny and the Knight of the Pussywillows. *No one will laugh at you up there. They will know you only by your blade, and judge you by your worth.*

Ser Glendon gave him a suspicious look. "Why would I want to do that? Are you telling me I need to run away and hide?"

"No. I just thought . . . two swords instead of one. The roads are not as safe as they once were."

"That's true enough," the boy said grudgingly, "but my father was once promised a place amongst the Kingsguard. I mean to claim the white cloak that he never got to wear."

You have as much chance of wearing a white cloak as I do, Dunk almost said. *You were born of a camp follower, and I crawled out of the gutters of Flea Bottom. Kings do not heap honor on the likes of you and me.* The lad would not have taken kindly to that truth, however. Instead he said, "Strength to your arm, then."

He had not gone more than a few feet when Ser Glendon called after him. "Ser Duncan, wait. I . . . I should not have been so sharp. A knight must needs be courteous, my mother used to say." The boy seemed to be struggling for words. "Lord Peake came to see me after my last joust. He offered me a place at Starpike. He said there was a storm coming the likes of which Westeros had not seen for a genera-tion, that he would need swords and men to wield them. Loyal men, who knew how to obey."

Dunk could hardly believe it. Gormon Peake had made his scorn for hedge knights plain, both on the road and on the roof, but the

316 of George R.R. Martin

offer was a generous one. "Peake is a great lord," he said, wary, "but . . . but not a man that I would trust, I think."

"No." The boy flushed. "There was a price. He'd take me into his service, he said . . . but first I would have to prove my loyalty. He would see that I was paired against his friend the Fiddler next, and he wanted me to swear that I would lose."

Dunk believed him. He should have been shocked, he knew, and yet somehow he wasn't. "What did you say?"

"I said I might not be able to lose to the Fiddler even if I were trying, that I had already unhorsed much better men than him, that the dragon's egg would be mine before the day was done." Ball smiled feebly. "It was not the answer that he wanted. He called me a fool, then, and told me that I had best watch my back. The Fiddler had many friends, he said, and I had none."

Dunk put a hand upon his shoulder, and squeezed. "You have one, ser. Two, once I find Egg."

The boy looked him in the eye, and nodded. "It is good to know there are some true knights still."

Dunk got his first good look at Ser Tommard Heddle whilst searching for Egg amongst the crowds about the lists. Heavyset and broad, with a chest like a barrel, Lord Butterwell's good-son wore black plate over boiled leather and an ornate helm fashioned in the likeness of some demon, scaled and slavering. His horse was three hands taller than Thunder and two stone heavier, a monster of a beast armored in a coat of ringmail. The weight of all that iron made him slow, so Heddle never got up past a canter when the course was run, but that did not prevent him making short work of Ser Clarence Charlton. As Charlton was borne from the field upon a litter, Heddle removed his demonic helm. His head was broad and bald, his beard black and square. Angry red boils festered on his cheek and neck.

Dunk knew that face. Heddle was the knight who'd growled at him in the bedchamber when he touched the dragon's egg, the man with the deep voice that he'd heard talking with Lord Peake.

A jumble of words came rushing back to him. . . . *beggar's feast you've laid before us . . . is the boy his father's son . . . Bittersteel . . . need the* sword . . . *Old Milkblood expects . . . is the boy his father's son . . . I promise you, Bloodraven is not off dreaming . . . is the boy his father's son?*

He stared at the viewing stand, wondering if somehow Egg had contrived to take his rightful place amongst the notables. There was no sign of the boy, however. Butterwell and Frey were missing too, though Butterwell's wife was still in her seat, looking bored and restive. *That's queer,* Dunk reflected. This was Butterwell's castle, his wedding, and Frey was father to his bride. These jousts were in their honor. Where would they have gone?

"*Ser Uthor Underleaf,*" the herald boomed. A shadow crept across Dunk's face as the sun was swallowed by a cloud. "*Ser Theomore of House Bulwer, the Old Ox, a knight of Blackcrown. Come forth and prove your valor.*"

The Old Ox made a fearsome sight in his blood-red armor, with black bull's horns rising from his helm. He needed the help of a brawny squire to get onto his horse, though, and the way his head was always turning as he rode suggested that Ser Maynard had been right about his eye. Still, the man received a lusty cheer as he took the field.

Not so the Snail, no doubt just as he preferred. On the first pass, both knights struck glancing blows. On the second, the Old Ox snapped his lance on Ser Uthor's shield, while the Snail's blow missed entirely. The same thing happened on the third pass, and this time Ser Uthor swayed as if about to fall. *He is feigning,* Dunk realized. *He is drawing the contest out to fatten the odds for next time.* He had only to glance around to see Will at work, making wagers for his master. Only then did it occur to him that he might have fattened his own purse with a coin or two upon the Snail. *Dunk the lunk, thick as a castle wall.*

The Old Ox fell on the fifth pass, knocked sideways by a coronal that slipped deftly off his shield to take him in the chest. His foot tangled in his stirrup as he fell, and he was dragged forty yards across the field before his men could get his horse under control. Again the litter came out, to bear him to the maester. A few drops of rain began to fall as Bulwer was carried away, darkening his surcoat where they fell. Dunk watched without expression. He was thinking about Egg. *What if this secret enemy of mine has got his hands on him?* It made as much sense as anything else. *The boy is blameless. If someone has a quarrel with me, it should not be him who answers for it.*

* * *

Ser John the Fiddler was being armed for his next tilt when Dunk found him. No fewer than three squires were attending him, buckling on his armor and seeing to the trappings of his horse, whilst Lord Alyn Cockshaw sat nearby drinking watered wine and looking bruised and peevish. When he caught sight of Dunk, Lord Alyn sputtered, dribbling wine upon on his chest. "How is it that you're still walking about? The Snail stove your face in."

"Steely Pate made me a good strong helm, m'lord. And my head is hard as stone, Ser Arlan used to say."

The Fiddler laughed. "Pay no mind to Alyn. Fireball's bastard knocked him off his horse onto that plump little rump of his, so now he has decided that he hates all hedge knights."

"That wretched pimpled creature is no son of Quentyn Ball," insisted Alyn Cockshaw. "He should never have been allowed to compete. If this were my wedding, I should have had him whipped for his presumption."

"What maid would marry you?" Ser John said. "And Ball's presumption is a deal less grating than your pouting. Ser Duncan, are you perchance a friend of Galtry the Green? I must shortly part him from his horse."

Dunk did not doubt it. "I do not know the man, m'lord."

"Will you take a cup of wine? Some bread and olives?"

"Only a word, m'lord."

"You may have all the words you wish. Let us adjourn to my pavilion." The Fiddler held the flap for him. "Not you, Alyn. You could do with a few less olives if truth be told."

Inside, the Fiddler turned back to Dunk. "I knew Ser Uthor had not killed you. My dreams are never wrong. And the Snail must face me soon enough. Once I've unhorsed him, I shall demand your arms and armor back. Your destrier as well, though you deserve a better mount. Will you take one as my gift?"

"I ... no ... I couldn't do that." The thought made Dunk uncomfortable. "I do not mean to be ungrateful, but ..."

"If it is the debt that troubles you, put the thought from your mind. I do not need your silver, ser. Only your friendship. How can you be one of my knights without a horse?" Ser John drew on his gauntlets of lobstered steel and flexed his fingers.

"My squire is missing."

"Ran off with a girl, perhaps?"

"Egg's too young for girls, m'lord. He would never leave me of his own will. Even if I were dying, he would stay until my corpse was cold. His horse is still here. So is our mule."

"If you like, I could ask my men to look for him."

My men. Dunk did not like the sound of that. *A tourney for traitors,* he thought. "You are no hedge knight."

"No." The Fiddler's smile was full of boyish charm. "But you knew that from the start. You have been calling me *m'lord* since we met upon the road, why is that?"

"The way you talk. The way you look. The way you act." *Dunk the lunk, thick as a castle wall.* "Up on the roof last night, you said some things ..."

"Wine makes me talk too much, but I meant every word. We belong together, you and I. My dreams do not lie."

"Your dreams don't lie," said Dunk, "but you do. John is not your true name, is it?"

"No." The Fiddler's eyes sparkled with mischief.

He has Egg's eyes.

"His true name will be revealed soon enough, to those who need to know." Lord Gormon Peake had slipped into the pavilion, scowling. "Hedge knight, I warn you—"

"Oh, stop it, Gormy," said the Fiddler. "Ser Duncan is with us, or will be soon. I told you, I dreamed of him." Outside, a herald's trumpet blew. The Fiddler turned his head. "They are calling me to the lists. Pray excuse me, Ser Duncan. We can resume our talk after I dispose of Ser Galtry the Green."

"Strength to your arm," Dunk said. It was only courteous.

Lord Gormon remained after Ser John had gone. "His dreams will be the death of all of us."

"What did it take to buy Ser Galtry?" Dunk heard himself say. "Was silver sufficient, or does he require gold?"

"Someone has been talking, I see." Peake seated himself in a camp chair. "I have a dozen men outside. I ought to call them in and have them slit your throat, ser."

"Why don't you?"

"His Grace would take it ill."

His Grace. Dunk felt as though someone had punched him in the belly. *Another black dragon,* he thought. *Another Blackfyre Rebellion. And soon another Redgrass Field. The grass was not red when the sun came up.* "Why this wedding?"

"Lord Butterwell wanted a new young wife to warm his bed, and Lord Frey had a somewhat soiled daughter. Their nuptials provided a plausible pretext for some like-minded lords to gather. Most of those invited here fought for the black dragon once. The rest have reason to resent Bloodraven's rule, or nurse grievances and ambitions of their own. Many of us had sons and daughters taken to King's Landing to vouchsafe our future loyalty, but most of the hostages perished in the Great Spring Sickness. Our hands are no longer tied. Our time is come. Aerys is weak. A bookish man and no warrior. The commons hardly know him, and what they know they do not like. His lords love him even less. His father was weak as well, that is true, but when his throne was threatened he had sons to take the field for him. Baelor and Maekar, the hammer and the anvil ... but Baelor Breakspear is no more, and Prince Maekar sulks at Summerhall, at odds with king and Hand."

Aye, thought Dunk, *and now some fool hedge knight has delivered his favorite son into the hands of his enemies. How better to ensure that the prince never stirs from Summerhall?* "There is Bloodraven," he said. "He is not weak."

"No," Lord Peake allowed, "but no man loves a sorcerer, and kin-slayers are accursed in the sight of gods and men. At the first sign of weakness or defeat, Bloodraven's men will melt away like summer snows. And if the dream the prince has dreamed comes true, and a living dragon comes forth here at Whitewalls ..."

Dunk finished for him. "... the throne is yours."

"His," said Lord Gormon Peake. "I am but a humble servant." He rose. "Do not attempt to leave the castle, ser. If you do, I will take it as a proof of treachery, and you will answer with your life. We have gone too far to turn back now."

The leaden sky was spitting down rain in earnest as John the Fiddler and Ser Galtry the Green took up fresh lances at opposite ends of the lists. Some of the wedding guests were streaming off toward the great hall, huddled under cloaks.

Ser Galtry rode a white stallion. A drooping green plume adorned his helm, a matching plume his horse's crinet. His cloak was a patch-work of many squares of fabric, each a different shade of green. Gold inlay made his greaves and gauntlet glitter, and his shield showed nine jade mullets upon a leek-green field. Even his beard was dyed green, in the fashion of the men of Tyrosh across the narrow sea.

Nine times he and the Fiddler charged with leveled lances, the green patchwork knight and the young lordling of the golden swords and fiddles, and nine times their lances shattered. By the eighth run the ground had begun to soften, and the big destriers splashed through pools of rainwater. On the ninth the Fiddler almost lost his seat, but recovered before he fell. "Well struck," he called out, laugh-ing. "You almost had me down, ser."

"Soon enough," the green knight shouted through the rain.

"No, I think not." The Fiddler tossed his splintered lance away, and a squire handed him a fresh one.

The next run was their last. Ser Galtry's lance scraped ineffectually off the Fiddler's shield, whilst Ser John's took the green knight squarely in the center of his chest and knocked him from his saddle, to land with a great brown splash. In the east Dunk saw the flash of distant lightning.

The viewing stands were emptying out quickly, as smallfolk and lordlings alike scrambled to get out of the wet. "See how they run," murmured Alyn Cockshaw as he slid up beside Dunk. "A few drops of rain and all the bold lords go squealing for shelter. What will they do when the real storm breaks, I wonder?"

The real storm. Dunk knew Lord Alyn was not talking about the weather. *What does this one want? Has he suddenly decided to befriend me?*

The herald mounted his platform once again. *"Ser Tommard Heddle, a knight of Whitewalls, in service to Lord Butterwell,"* he shouted, as thunder rumbled in the distance. *"Ser Uthor Underleaf. Come forth and prove your valor."*

Dunk glanced over at Ser Uthor in time to see the Snail's smile go sour. *This is not the match he paid for.* The master of the games had crossed him up, but why? *Someone else has taken a hand, someone Cosgrove esteems more than Uthor Underleaf.* Dunk chewed on that for a moment. *They do not know that Uthor does not mean to win,* he realized all at once. *They see him as a threat, so they mean for Black Tom to remove him from the Fiddler's path.* Heddle himself was part of Peake's conspiracy, he could be relied on to lose when the need arose. Which left no one but...

And suddenly Lord Peake himself was storming across the muddy field to climb the steps to the herald's platform, his cloak flapping behind him. *"We are betrayed,"* he cried. "Bloodraven has a spy amongst us. The dragon's egg is stolen!"

Ser John the Fiddler wheeled his mount around. "My egg? How is that possible? Lord Butterwell keeps guards outside his bedchamber night and day."

"Slain," Lord Peake declared, "but one man named his killer before he died."

Does he mean to accuse me? Dunk wondered. A dozen men had seen him touch the dragon's egg last night, when he'd carried Lady Butterwell to her lord husband's bed.

Lord Gormon's finger stabbed down in accusation. "There he stands. The whore's son. Seize him."

At the far end of the lists, Ser Glendon Ball looked up in confusion. For a moment he did not appear to comprehend what was happening, until he saw men rushing at him from all directions. Then the boy moved more quickly than Dunk could have believed. He had his sword half out of its sheath when the first man threw an arm around his throat. Ball wrenched free of his grip, but by then two more of them were on him. They slammed into him and dragged him down into the mud. Other men swarmed over them, shouting and kicking. *That could have been me,* Dunk realized. He felt as helpless as he had at Ashford, the day they'd told him he must lose a hand and a foot.

Alyn Cockshaw pulled him back. "Stay out of this if you want to find that squire of yours."

Dunk turned on him. "What do you mean?"

"I may know where to find the boy."

"Where?" Dunk was in no mood for games.

At the far end of the field, Ser Glendon was yanked roughly back onto his feet, piniomed between two men-at-arms in mail and half-helms. He was brown with mud from waist to ankle, and blood and rain washed down his cheeks. *Hero's blood,* thought Dunk, as Black Tom dismounted before the captive. "Where is the egg?"

Blood dribbled from Ball's mouth. "Why would I steal the egg? I was about to win it."

Aye, thought Dunk, *and that they could not allow.*

Black Tom slashed Ball across the face with a mailed fist. "Search his saddlebags," Lord Peake commanded. "We'll find the dragon's egg wrapped up and hidden, I'll wager."

Lord Alyn lowered his voice. "And so they will. Come with me if you want to find your squire. There's no better time than now, whilst they're all occupied." He did not wait for a reply.

Dunk had to follow. Three long strides brought him abreast of the lordling. "If you have done Egg any harm—"

"Boys are not to my taste. This way. Step lively now."

Through an archway, down a set of muddy steps, around a corner, Dunk stalked after him, splashing through puddles as the rain fell around them. They stayed close to the walls, cloaked in shadows, finally stopping in a closed courtyard where the paving stones were smooth and slick. Buildings pressed close on every side. Above were windows, closed and shuttered. In the center of the courtyard was a well, ringed with a low stone wall.

A lonely place, Dunk thought. He did not like the feel of it. Old instinct made him reach for his sword hilt before he remembered that the Snail had won his sword. As he fumbled at his hip where his scabbard should have hung, he felt the point of a knife poke his lower back. "Turn on me, and I'll cut your kidney out and give it to Butterwell's cooks to fry up for the feast."

The knife pushed in through the back of Dunk's jerkin, insistent. "Over to the well. No sudden moves, ser."

If he has thrown Egg down that well, he will need more than some little toy knife to save him. Dunk walked forward slowly. He could feel the anger growing in his belly.

The blade at his back vanished. "You may turn and face me now, hedge knight."

Dunk turned. "M'lord. Is this about the dragon's egg?"

"No. This is about the dragon. Did you think I would stand by and let you steal him?" Ser Alyn grimaced. "I should have known better than to trust that wretched Snail to kill you. I'll have my gold back, every coin."

Him? Dunk thought. *This plump, pasty-faced, perfumed lordling is my secret enemy?* He did not know whether to laugh or weep. "Ser Uthor earned his gold. I have a hard head, is all."

"So it seems. Back away."

Dunk took a step backwards.

"Again. Again. Once more."

Another step, and he was flush against the well. Its stones pressed against his lower back.

"Sit down on the rim. Not afraid of a little bath, are you? You cannot get much wetter than you are right now."

"I cannot swim." Dunk rested a hand on the well. The stones were wet. One moved beneath the pressure of his palm.

"What a shame. Will you jump, or must I prick you?"

Dunk glanced down. He could see the raindrops dimpling the water, a good twenty feet below. The walls were covered with a slime of algae. "I never did you any harm."

"And never will. Daemon's mine. I will command his Kingsguard. You are not worthy of a white cloak."

"I never claimed I was." *Daemon.* The name rang in Dunk's head. *Not John. Daemon, after his father. Dunk the lunk, thick as a castle wall.*

"Daemon Blackfyre sired seven sons. Two died upon the Redgrass Field, twins . . ."

"Aemon and Aegon. Wretched witless bullies, just like you. When we were little, they took pleasure in tormenting me and Daemon both. I wept when Bittersteel carried him off to exile, and again when Lord Peake told me he was coming home. But then he saw *you* upon the road and forgot that I existed." Cockshaw waved his dagger threateningly. "You can go into the water as you are, or you can go in bleeding. Which will it be?"

Dunk closed his hand around the loose stone. It proved to be less loose than he had hoped. Before he could wrench it free Ser Alyn lunged. Dunk twisted sideways, so the point of the blade sliced through the meat of his shield arm. And then the stone popped free. Dunk fed it to his lordship, and felt his teeth crack beneath the blow. "The well, is it?" He hit the lordling in the mouth again, then dropped the stone, seized Cockshaw by the wrist, and twisted until a bone snapped and the dagger clattered to the stones. "After you, m'lord." Sidestepping, Dunk yanked at the lordling's arm and planted a kick in the small of his back. Lord Alyn toppled headlong into the well. There was a splash.

"Well done, ser."

Dunk whirled. Through the rain, all he could make out was a hooded shape and a single pale white eye. It was only when the man came forward that the shadowed face beneath the cowl took on the familiar features of Ser Maynard Plumm, the pale eye no more than the moonstone brooch that pinned his cloak at the shoulder.

Down in the well, Lord Alyn was thrashing and splashing and calling for help. "*Murder!* Someone help me."

"He tried to kill me," Dunk said.

"That would explain all the blood."

"Blood?" He looked down. His left arm was red from shoulder to elbow, his tunic clinging to his skin. "Oh."

Dunk did not remember falling, but suddenly he was on the ground, with raindrops running down his face. He could hear Lord Alyn whimpering from the well, but his splashing had grown feebler. "We need to have that arm bound up." Ser Maynard slipped his own arm under Dunk. "Up now. I cannot lift you by myself. Use your legs."

Dunk used his legs. "Lord Alyn. He's going to drown."

"He shan't be missed. Least of all by the Fiddler."

"He's not," Dunk gasped, pale with pain, "a fiddler."

"No. He is Daemon of House Blackfyre, the Second of His Name. Or so he would style himself if ever he achieves the Iron Throne. You would be surprised to know how many lords prefer their kings brave and stupid. Daemon is young and dashing and looks good on a horse."

The sounds from the well were almost too faint to hear. "Shouldn't we throw his lordship down a rope?"

"Save him now to execute him later? I think not. Let him eat the meal that he meant to serve to you. Come, lean on me." Plumm guided him across the yard. This close, there was something queer about the cast of Ser Maynard's features. The longer Dunk looked, the less he seemed to see. "I did urge you to flee, you will recall, but you esteemed your honor more than your life. An honorable death is well and good, but if the life at stake is not your own, what then? Would your answer be the same, ser?"

"Whose life?" From the well came one last splash. "Egg? Do you mean Egg?" Dunk clutched at Plumm's arm. *"Where is he?"*

"With the gods. And you will know why, I think."

The pain that twisted inside Dunk just then made him forget his arm. He groaned. "He tried to use the boot."

"So I surmise. He showed the ring to Maester Lothar, who delivered him to Butterwell, who no doubt pissed his breeches at the sight of it and started wondering if he had chosen the wrong side and how much Bloodraven knows of this conspiracy. The answer to that last is *'quite a lot.'* " Plumm chuckled.

"Who are you?"

"A friend," said Maynard Plumm. "One who has been watching you and wondering at your presence in this nest of adders. Now be quiet until we get you mended."

Staying in the shadows, the two of them made their way back to Dunk's small tent. Once inside, Ser Maynard lit a fire, filled a bowl with wine, and set it on the flames to boil. "A clean cut, and at least it is not your sword arm," he said, slicing through the sleeve of Dunk's bloodstained tunic. "The thrust appears to have missed the bone. Still, we will need to wash it out, or you could lose the arm."

"It doesn't matter." Dunk's belly was roiling, and he felt as if he might retch at any moment. "If Egg is dead—"

"—you bear the blame. You should have kept him well away from here. I never said the boy was dead, though. I said that he was with the gods. Do you have clean linen? Silk?"

"My tunic. The good one I got in Dorne. What do you mean, he's with the gods?"

"In good time. Your arm first."

The wine soon began to steam. Ser Maynard found Dunk's good silk tunic, sniffed at it suspiciously, then slid out a dagger and began to cut it up. Dunk swallowed his protest. "Ambrose Butterwell has never been what you might call *decisive*," Ser Maynard said, as he wadded up three strips of silk and dropped them in the wine. "He had doubts about this plot from the beginning, doubts that were inflamed when he learned that the boy did not bear the sword. And this morning his dragon's egg vanished, and with it the last dregs of his courage."

"Ser Glendon did not steal the egg," Dunk said. "He was in the yard all day, tilting or watching others tilt."

"Peake will find the egg in his saddlebags all the same." The wine was boiling. Plumm drew on a leather glove, and said, "Try not to scream." Then he pulled a strip of silk out of the boiling wine, and began to wash the cut.

Dunk did not scream. He gnashed his teeth and bit his tongue and smashed his fist against his thigh hard enough to leave bruises, but he did not scream. Ser Maynard used the rest of his good tunic to make a bandage and tied it tight around his arm. "How does that feel?" he asked when he was done.

"Bloody awful." Dunk shivered. *"Where's Egg?"*

"With the gods. I told you."

Dunk reached up and wrapped his good hand around Plumm's neck. "Speak plain. I am sick of hints and winks. Tell me where to find the boy, or I will snap your bloody neck, friend or no."

"The sept. You would do well to go armed." Ser Maynard smiled. "Is that plain enough for you, Dunk?"

* * *

His first stop was Ser Uthor Underleaf's pavilion.

When Dunk slipped inside, he found only the squire Will bent over a washtub, scrubbing out his master's smallclothes. "You again? Ser Uthor is at the feast. What do you want?"

"My sword and shield."

"Have you brought the ransom?

"No."

"Then why would I let you take your arms?"

"I have need of them."

"That's no good reason."

"How about, try and stop me and I'll kill you."

Will gaped. "They're over there."

Dunk paused outside the castle sept. *Gods grant I am not too late.* His sword belt was back in its accustomed place, cinched tight about his waist. He had strapped the gallows shield to his wounded arm, and the weight of it was sending throbs of pain through him with every step. If anyone brushed up against him, he feared that he might scream. He pushed the doors open with his good hand.

Within, the sept was dim and hushed, lit only by the candles that twinkled on the altars of the Seven. The Warrior had the most candles burning, as might be expected during a tourney; many a knight would have come here to pray for strength and courage before chancing the lists. The Stranger's altar was shrouded in shadow, with but a single candle burning. The Mother and the Father each had dozens, the Smith and Maiden somewhat fewer. And beneath the shining lantern of the Crone knelt Lord Ambrose Butterwell, head bowed, praying silently for wisdom.

He was not alone. No sooner had Dunk started for him than two men-at-arms moved to cut him off, faces stern beneath their half-helms. Both wore mail beneath surcoats striped in the green, white, and yellow undy of House Butterwell. "Hold, ser," one said. "You have no business here."

"Yes, he does. I *warned* you he would find me."

The voice was Egg's.

When he stepped out from the shadows beneath the Father, his shaven head shining in the candlelight, Dunk almost rushed to the boy, to pluck him up with a glad cry and crush him in his arms. Something in Egg's tone made him hesitate. *He sounds more angry than afraid, and I have never seen him look so stern. And Butterwell on his knees. Something is queer here.*

Lord Butterwell pushed himself back to his feet. Even in the dim light of the candles, his flesh looked pale and clammy. "Let him pass," he told his guardsmen. When they stepped back, he beckoned Dunk closer. "I have done the boy no harm. I knew his father well, when I was the King's Hand. Prince Maekar needs to know, none of this was my idea."

"He shall," Dunk promised. *What is happening here?*

"Peake. This was all his doing, I swear it by the Seven." Lord Butterwell put one hand on the altar. "May the gods strike me down if I am false. He told me who I must invite and who must be excluded, and he brought this boy pretender here. I never wanted to be part of any treason, you must believe me. Tom Heddle now, he urged me on, I will not deny it. My good-son, married to my eldest daughter, but I will not lie, he was part of this."

"He is your champion," said Egg. "If he was in this, so were you."

Be quiet, Dunk wanted to roar. *That loose tongue of yours will get us killed.* Yet Butterwell seemed to quail. "My lord, you do not understand. Heddle commands my garrison."

"You must have *some* loyal guardsmen," said Egg.

"These men here," said Lord Butterwell. "A few more. I've been too lax, I will allow, but I have never been a traitor. Frey and I harbored doubts about Lord Peake's pretender since the beginning. *He does not bear the sword!* If he were his father's son, Bittersteel would have armed him with Blackfyre. And all this talk about a dragon ... madness, madness and folly." His lordship dabbed the sweat from his face with his sleeve. "And now they have taken the egg, the dragon's egg my grandsire had from the king himself as a reward for leal service. It was there this morning when I woke, and my guards swear no one entered or left the bedchamber. It may be that Lord Peake bought them, I cannot say, but *the egg is gone*. They must have it, or else ..."

Or else the dragon's hatched, thought Dunk. If a living dragon appeared again in Westeros, the lords and smallfolk alike would flock to whichever prince could lay claim to it. "My lord," he said, "a word with my ... my squire, if you would be so good."

"As you wish, ser." Lord Butterwell knelt to pray again. Dunk drew Egg aside and went down upon one knee to speak with him face-to-face. "I am going to clout you in the ear so hard your head will turn around backwards, and you'll spend the rest of your life looking at where you've been."

"You should, ser." Egg had the grace to look abashed. "I'm sorry. I just meant to send a raven to my father."

So I could stay a knight. The boy meant well. Dunk glanced over to where Butterwell was praying. "What did you do to him?"

"Scared him, ser."

"Aye, I can see that. He'll have scabs on his knees before the night is done."

"I didn't know what else to do, ser. The maester brought me to them once he saw my father's ring."

"Them?"

"Lord Butterwell and Lord Frey, ser. Some guards were there as well. Everyone was upset. Someone stole the dragon's egg."

"Not you, I hope?"

Egg shook his head. "No, ser. I knew I was in trouble when the maester showed Lord Butterwell my ring. I thought about saying that I'd stolen it, but I didn't think he would believe me. Then I remembered this one time I heard my father talking about something

Lord Bloodraven said, about how it was better to be frightening than frightened, so I told them that my father had sent us here to spy for him, that he was on his way here with an army, that his lordship had best release me and give up this treason or it would mean his head." He smiled a shy smile. "It worked better than I thought it would, ser."

Dunk wanted to take the boy by the shoulders and shake him until his teeth rattled. *This is no game,* he might have roared. *This is life and death.* "Did Lord Frey hear all this as well?"

"Yes. He wished Lord Butterwell happiness in his marriage and announced that he was returning to the Twins forthwith. That was when his lordship brought us here to pray."

Frey could flee, Dunk thought, *but Butterwell does not have that option, and soon or late he will begin to wonder why Prince Maekar and his army have not turned up.* "If Lord Peake should learn that you are in the castle—"

The sept's outer doors opened with a crash. Dunk turned to see Black Tom Heddle glowering in mail and plate, with rainwater dripping off his sodden cloak to puddle by his feet. A dozen men-at-arms stood with him, armed with spears and axes. Lightning flashed blue and white across the sky behind them, etching sudden shadows across the pale stone floor. A gust of wet wind set all the candles in the sept to dancing.

Oh, seven bloody hells was all that Dunk had time enough to think before Heddle said, "There's the boy. Take him."

Lord Butterwell had risen to his feet. "No. Halt. The boy's not to be molested. Tommard, what is the meaning of this?"

Heddle's face twisted in contempt. "Not all of us have milk running in our veins, your lordship. I'll have the boy."

"You do not understand." Butterwell's voice had turned into a high, thin quaver. "We are undone. Lord Frey is gone, and others will follow. Prince Maekar is coming with an army."

"All the more reason to take the boy as hostage."

"No, no," said Butterwell, "I want no more part of Lord Peake or his pretender. I will not fight."

Black Tom looked coldly at his lord. "Craven." He spat. "Say what you will. You'll fight or die, my lord." He pointed at Egg. "A stag to the first man to draw blood."

"No, no." Butterwell turned to his own guards. "Stop them, do you hear me? I command you. Stop them." But all the guards had halted in confusion, at a loss as to whom they should obey.

"Must I do it myself, then?" Black Tom drew his longsword.

Dunk did the same. "Behind me, Egg."

"Put up your steel, the both of you!" Butterwell screeched. "I'll have no bloodshed in the sept! Ser Tommard, this man is the prince's sworn shield. He'll kill you!"

"Only if he falls on me." Black Tom showed his teeth in a hard grin. "I saw him try to joust."

"I am better with a sword," Dunk warned him.

Heddle answered with a snort, and charged.

Dunk shoved Egg roughly backwards and turned to meet his blade. He blocked the first cut well enough, but the jolt of Black Tom's sword biting into his shield and the bandaged cut behind it sent a jolt of pain crackling up his arm. He tried a slash at Heddle's head in answer, but Black Tom slid away from it and hacked at him again. Dunk barely got his shield around in time. Pine chips flew and Heddle laughed, pressing his attack, low and high and low again. Dunk took each cut with his shield, but every blow was agony, and he found himself giving ground.

"Get him, ser," he heard Egg call. "Get him, get him, he's *right there.*" The taste of blood was in Dunk's mouth, and worse, his wound had opened once again. A wave of dizziness washed over him. Black Tom's blade was turning the long kite shield to splinters. *Oak and iron guard me well, or else I'm dead and doomed to hell,* Dunk thought, before he remembered that this shield was made of pine. When his back came up hard against an altar, he stumbled to one knee and realized he had no more ground left to give.

"You are no knight," said Black Tom. "Are those tears in your eyes, oaf?"

Tears of pain. Dunk pushed up off his knee, and slammed shield first into his foe.

Black Tom stumbled backwards, yet somehow kept his balance. Dunk bulled right after him, smashing him with the shield again and again, using his size and strength to knock Heddle halfway across the sept. Then he swung the shield aside and slashed out with his long-

sword, and Heddle screamed as the steel bit through wool and muscle deep into his thigh. His own sword swung wildly, but the blow was desperate and clumsy. Dunk let his shield take it one more time and put all his weight into his answer.

Black Tom reeled back a step and stared down in horror at his fore-arm flopping on the floor beneath the Stranger's altar. "You," he gasped, "you, you …"

"I told you." Dunk stabbed him through the throat. "I'm better with a sword."

* * *

Two of the men-at-arms fled back into the rain as a pool of blood spread out from Black Tom's body. The others clutched their spears and hesitated, casting wary glances toward Dunk as they waited for their lord to speak.

"This ... this was ill done," Butterwell finally managed. He turned to Dunk and Egg. "We must be gone from Whitewalls before those two bring word of this to Gormon Peake. He has more friends amongst the guests than I do. The postern gate in the north wall, we'll slip out there ... come, we must make haste."

Dunk slammed his sword into its scabbard. "Egg, go with Lord Butterwell." He put an arm around the boy, and lowered his voice. "Don't stay with him any longer than you need to. Give Rain his head and get away before his lordship changes sides again. Make for Maiden-pool, it's closer than King's Landing."

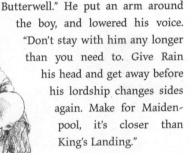

"What about you, ser?"

"Never mind about me."

"I'm your squire."

"Aye," said Dunk, "and you'll do as I tell you, or you'll get a good clout in the ear."

A group of men were leaving the great hall, pausing long enough to pull up their hoods before venturing out into the rain. The Old Ox was amongst them, and weedy Lord Caswell, once more in his cups. Both gave Dunk a wide berth. Ser Mortimer Boggs favored him with a curious stare but thought better of speaking to him. Uthor Underleaf was not so shy. "You come late to the feast, ser," he said as he was pulling on his gloves. "And I see you wear a sword again."

"You'll have your ransom for it, if that's all that concerns you." Dunk had left his battered shield behind and draped his cloak across his wounded arm to hide the blood. "Unless I die. Then you have my leave to loot my corpse."

Ser Uthor laughed. "Is that gallantry I smell, or just stupidity? The two scents are much alike, as I recall. It is not too late to accept my offer, ser."

"It is later than you think," Dunk warned him. He did not wait for Underleaf to answer but pushed past him, through the double doors. The great hall smelled of ale and smoke and wet wool. In the gallery above, a few musicians played softly. Laughter echoed from the high tables, where Ser Kirby Pimm and Ser Lucas Nayland were playing a drinking game. Up on the dais Lord Peake was speaking earnestly with Lord Costayne, while Ambrose Butterwell's new bride sat abandoned in her high seat.

Down below the salt, Dunk found Ser Kyle drowning his woes in Lord Butterwell's ale. His trencher was filled with a thick stew made with food left over from the night before. *A bowl o' brown,* they called such fare in the pot shops of King's Landing. Ser Kyle plainly had no stomach for it. Untouched, the stew had grown cold, and a film of grease glistened atop the brown.

Dunk slipped onto the bench beside him. "Ser Kyle."

The Cat nodded. "Ser Duncan. Will you have some ale?"

"No." Ale was the last thing that he needed.

"Are you unwell, ser? Forgive me, but you look—"

—better than I feel. "What was done with Glendon Ball?"

"They took him to the dungeons." Ser Kyle shook his head. "Whore's get or no, the boy never struck me as a thief."

"He isn't."

Ser Kyle squinted at him. "Your arm . . . how did . . ."

"A dagger." Dunk turned to face the dais, frowning. He had escaped death twice today. That would suffice for most men, he knew. *Dunk the lunk, thick as a castle wall.* He pushed to his feet. "Your Grace," he called.

A few men on nearby benches put down their spoons, broke off their conversations, and turned to look at him.

"*Your Grace,*" Dunk said again, more loudly. He strode up the Myrish carpet toward the dais. "*Daemon.*"

Now half the hall grew quiet. At the high table, the man who'd called himself the Fiddler turned to smile at him. He had donned a purple tunic for the feast, Dunk saw. *Purple, to bring out the color of his eyes.* "Ser Duncan. I am pleased that you are with us. What would you have of me?"

"Justice," said Dunk, "for Glendon Ball."

The name echoed off the walls, and for half a heartbeat it was as if every man, woman, and boy in the hall had turned to stone.

Then Lord Costayne slammed a fist upon a table, and shouted, "It's death that one deserves, not justice." A dozen other voices echoed his, and Ser Harbert Paege declared, "He's bastard born. All bastards are thieves, or worse. Blood will tell."

For a moment Dunk despaired. *I am alone here.* But then Ser Kyle the Cat pushed himself to his feet, swaying only slightly. "The boy may be a bastard, my lords, but he's *Fireball's* bastard. It's like Ser Harbert said. Blood will tell."

Daemon frowned. "No one honors Fireball more than I do," he said. "I will not believe this false knight is his seed. He stole the dragon's egg and slew three good men in the doing."

"He stole nothing and killed no one," Dunk insisted. "If three men were slain, look elsewhere for their killer. Your Grace knows as well as I that Ser Glendon was in the yard all day, riding one tilt after t'other."

"Aye," Daemon admitted. "I wondered at that myself. But the dragon's egg was found amongst his things."

"Was it? Where is it now?"

Lord Gormon Peake rose cold-eyed and imperious. "Safe, and well guarded. And why is that any concern of yours, ser?"

"Bring it forth," said Dunk. "I'd like another look at it, m'lord. T'other night, I only saw it for a moment."

Peake's eyes narrowed. "Your Grace," he said to Daemon, "it comes to me that this hedge knight arrived at Whitewalls with Ser Glendon, uninvited. He may well be part of this."

Dunk ignored that. "Your Grace, the dragon's egg that Lord Peake found amongst Ser Glendon's things was the one he placed there. Let him bring it forth if he can. Examine it yourself. I'll wager you it's no more than a painted stone."

The hall erupted into chaos. A hundred voices began to speak at once, and a dozen knights leapt to their feet. Daemon looked near as young and lost as Ser Glendon had when he had been accused. "Are you drunk, my friend?"

Would that I were. "I've lost some blood," Dunk allowed, "but not my wits. Ser Glendon has been wrongfully accused."

"Why?" Daemon demanded, baffled. "If Ball did no wrong, as you insist, why would his lordship say he did and try to prove it with some painted rock?"

"To remove him from your path. His lordship bought your other foes with gold and promises, but Ball was not for sale."

The Fiddler flushed. *"That is not true."*

"It is true. Send for Ser Glendon and ask him yourself."

"I will do just that. Lord Peake, have the bastard fetched up at once. And bring the dragon's egg as well. I wish to have a closer look at it."

Gormon Peake gave Dunk a look of loathing. "Your Grace, the bastard boy is being questioned. A few more hours, and we will have a confession for you, I do not doubt."

"By *questioned,* m'lord means *tortured,*" said Dunk. "A few more hours, and Ser Glendon will confess to having killed Your Grace's father and both your brothers too."

"Enough!" Lord Peake's face was almost purple. "One more word, and I will rip your tongue out by the roots."

"You lie," said Dunk. "That's two words."

"And you will rue the both of them," Peake promised. "Take this man and chain him in the dungeons."

"No." Daemon's voice was dangerously quiet. "I want the truth of this. Sunderland, Vyrwel, Smallwood, take your men and go find Ser Glendon in the dungeons. Bring him up forthwith and see that no harm comes to him. If any man should try to hinder you, tell him you are about the king's business."

"As you command," Lord Vyrwel answered.

"I will settle this as my father would," the Fiddler said. "Ser Glendon stands accused of grievous crimes. As a knight, he has a right to defend himself by strength of arms. I shall meet him in the lists, and let the gods determine guilt and innocence."

Hero's blood or whore's blood, Dunk thought, when two of Lord Vyrwel's men dumped Ser Glendon naked at his feet, *he has a deal less of it than he did before.*

The boy had been savagely beaten. His face was bruised and swollen, several of his teeth were cracked or missing, his right eye was weeping blood, and up and down his chest his flesh was red and cracking where they'd burned him with hot irons.

"You're safe now," murmured Ser Kyle. "There's no one here but hedge knights, and the gods know that we're a harmless lot." Daemon had given them the maester's chambers and commanded them to dress any hurts Ser Glendon might have suffered and see that he was ready for the lists. Three fingernails had been pulled from Ball's left hand, Dunk saw, as he washed the blood from the boy's face and hands. That worried him more than all the rest. "Can you hold a lance?"

"A lance?" Blood and spit dribbled from Ser Glendon's mouth when he tried to speak. "Do I have all my fingers?"

"Ten," said Dunk, "but only seven fingernails."

Ball nodded. "Black Tom was going to cut my fingers off, but he was called away. Is it him that I'm to fight?"

"No. I killed him."

That made him smile. "Someone had to."

"You're to tilt against the Fiddler, but his real name—"

"—is Daemon, aye. They told me. The Black Dragon." Ser Glendon laughed. "My father died for his. I would have been his man, and gladly. I would have fought for him, killed for him, died for him, but I could not lose for him." He turned his head and spat out a broken tooth. "Could I have a cup of wine?"

"Ser Kyle, get the wineskin."

The boy drank long and deep, then wiped his mouth. "Look at me. I'm shaking like a girl."

Dunk frowned. "Can you still sit a horse?"

"Help me wash and bring me my shield and lance and saddle," Ser Glendon said, "and you will see what I can do."

It was almost dawn before the rain let up enough for the combat to take place. The castle yard was a morass of soft mud, glistening wetly by the light of a hundred torches. Beyond the field a grey mist was rising, sending ghostly fingers up the pale stone walls to grasp the castle battlements. Many of the wedding guests had vanished during the intervening hours, but those who remained climbed the viewing stand again and settled themselves on planks of rain-soaked pine. Amongst them stood Ser Gormon Peake, surrounded by a knot of lesser lords and household knights.

It had only been a few years since Dunk had squired for old Ser Arlan. He had not forgotten how. He cinched the buckles on Ser Glendon's ill-fitting armor, fastened his helm to his gorget, helped him mount, and handed him his shield. Earlier contests had left deep gouges in the wood, but the blazing fireball could still be seen. *He looks as young as Egg,* Dunk thought. *A frightened boy, and grim.* His sorrel mare was unbarded and skittish as well. *He should have stayed with his own mount. The sorrel may be better bred and swifter, but a rider rides best on a horse that he knows well, and this one is a stranger to him.*

"I'll need a lance," Ser Glendon said. "A war lance."

Dunk went to the racks. War lances were shorter and heavier than the tourney lances that had been used in all the earlier tilts; eight feet of solid ash ending in an iron point. Dunk chose one and pulled it out, running his hand along its length to make sure it had no cracks.

At the far end of the lists, one of Daemon's squires was offering him a matching lance. He was a fiddler no more. In place of swords and fiddles, the trappings of his warhorse now displayed the three-headed dragon of House Blackfyre, black on a field of red. The prince had washed the black dye from his hair as well, so it flowed down to his collar in a cascade of silver and gold that glimmered like beaten metal in the torchlight. *Egg would have hair like that if he ever let it grow,* Dunk realized. He found it hard to picture him that way, but one day he knew he must if the two of them should live so long.

The herald climbed his platform once again. *"Ser Glendon the Bastard stands accused of theft and murder,"* he proclaimed, *"and now comes forth to prove his innocence at the hazard of his body. Daemon of House Blackfyre, the Second of His Name, rightborn King of the Andals and the Rhoynar and the First Men, Lord of the Seven Kingdoms and Protector of the Realm, comes forth to prove the truth of the accusations against the bastard Glendon."*

And all at once the years fell away, and Dunk was back at Ashford Meadow once again, listening to Baelor Breakspear just before they went forth to battle for his life. He slipped the war lance back in place, plucked a tourney lance from the next rack—twelve feet long, slender, elegant. "Use this," he told Ser Glendon. "It's what we used at Ashford, at the trial of seven."

"The Fiddler chose a war lance. He means to kill me."

"First he has to strike you. If your aim is true, his point will never touch you."

"I don't know."

"I do."

Ser Glendon snatched the lance from him, wheeled about, and trotted toward the lists. "Seven save us both, then."

Somewhere in the east, lightning cracked across a pale pink sky. Daemon raked his stallion's side with golden spurs and leapt forward like a thunderclap, lowering his war lance with its deadly iron point. Ser Glendon raised his shield and raced to meet him, swinging his own longer lance across his mare's head to bear upon the young pretender's chest. Mud sprayed back from their horses' hooves, and the torches seemed to burn the brighter as the two knights went pounding past.

Dunk closed his eyes. He heard a *crack,* a shout, a *thump.*

"No," he heard Lord Peake cry out, in anguish. *"Noooooo."* For half a heartbeat, Dunk almost felt sorry for him. He opened his eyes again. Riderless, the big black stallion was slowing to a trot. Dunk jumped out and grabbed him by the reins. At the far end of the lists, Ser Glendon Ball wheeled his mare and raised his splintered lance. Men rushed onto the field, to where the Fiddler lay unmoving, facedown in a puddle. When they helped him to his feet, he was mud from head to heel.

"The Brown Dragon," someone shouted. Laughter rippled through the yard, as the dawn washed over Whitewalls.

It was only a few heartbeats later, as Dunk and Ser Kyle were helping Glendon Ball off his horse, that the first trumpet blew, and the sentries on the walls raised the alarm. An army had appeared outside the castle, rising from the morning mists. "Egg wasn't lying after all," Dunk told Ser Kyle, astonished.

From Maidenpool had come Lord Mooton, from Raventree Lord Blackwood, from Duskendale Lord Darklyn. The royal demesnes about King's Landing sent forth Hayfords, Rosbys, Stokeworths, Masseys,

and the king's own sworn swords, led by three knights of the Kingsguard and stiffened by three hundred Raven's Teeth with tall white
weirwood bows. Mad Danelle Lothston herself rode forth in strength
from her haunted towers at Harrenhal, clad in black armor that fit her
like an iron glove, her long red hair streaming.

The light of the rising sun glittered off the points of five hundred
lances and ten times as many spears. The night's grey banners were
reborn in half a hundred gaudy colors. And above them all flew two
regal dragons on night-black fields: the great three-headed beast of
King Aerys I Targaryen, red as fire, and a white-winged fury breathing scarlet flame.

Not Maekar after all, Dunk knew, when he saw those banners. The
banners of the Prince of Summerhall showed four three-headed dragons, two and two, the arms of the fourth-born son of the late King
Daeron II Targaryen. A single white dragon announced the presence
of the King's Hand, Lord Brynden Rivers.

Bloodraven himself had come to Whitewalls.

The First Blackfyre Rebellion had perished on the Redgrass Field in
blood and glory. The Second Blackfyre Rebellion ended with a whim-
per. "They cannot cow us," Young Daemon proclaimed from the castle
battlements after he had seen the ring of iron that encircled them,
"for our cause is just. We'll slash through them and ride hell-bent for
King's Landing! Sound the trumpets!"

Instead, knights and lords and men-at-arms muttered quietly to
one another, and a few began to slink away, making for the stables or
a postern gate or some hidey-hole they hoped might keep them safe.
And when Daemon drew his sword and raised it above his head, every
man of them could see it was not Blackfyre. "We'll make another
Redgrass Field today," the pretender promised.

"Piss on that, fiddle boy," a grizzled squire shouted back at him. "I'd
sooner live."

In the end, the second Daemon Blackfyre rode forth alone, reined
up before the royal host, and challenged Lord Bloodraven to single
combat. "I will fight you, or the coward Aerys, or any champion you
care to name." Instead Lord Bloodraven's men surrounded him, pulled

him off his horse, and clasped him into golden fetters. The banner he had carried was planted in the muddy ground and set afire. It burned for a long time, sending up twisted a plume of smoke that could be seen for leagues around.

The only blood that was shed that day came when a man in service to Lord Vyrwel began to boast that he had been one of Bloodraven's eyes and would soon be well rewarded. "By the time the moon turns I'll be fucking whores and drinking Dornish red," he was purported to have said, just before one of Lord Costayne's knights slit his throat. "Drink that," he said, as Vyrwel's man drowned in his own blood. "It's not Dornish, but it's red."

Elsewise it was a sullen, silent column that trudged through the gates of Whitewalls to toss their weapons into a glittering pile before being bound and led away to await Lord Bloodraven's judgment. Dunk emerged with the rest of them, together with Ser Kyle the Cat and Glendon Ball. They had looked for Ser Maynard to join them, but Plumm had melted away sometime during the night.

It was late that afternoon before Ser Roland Crakehall of the Kingsguard found Dunk among the other prisoners. "Ser Duncan. Where in seven hells have you been hiding? Lord Rivers has been asking for you for hours. Come with me, if you please."

Dunk fell in beside him. Crakehall's long cloak flapped behind him with every gust of wind, as white as moonlight on snow. The sight of it made him think back on the words the Fiddler had spoken, up on the roof. *I dreamed that you were all in white from head to heel, with a long pale cloak flowing from those broad shoulders.* Dunk snorted. *Aye, and you dreamed of dragons hatching from stone eggs. One is likely as t'other.*

The Hand's pavilion was half a mile from the castle, in the shade of a spreading elm tree. A dozen cows were cropping at the grass nearby. *Kings rise and fall,* Dunk thought, *and cows and smallfolk go about their business.* It was something the old man used to say. "What will become of all of them?" he asked Ser Roland, as they passed a group of captives sitting on the grass.

"They'll be marched back to King's Landing for trial. The knights and men-at-arms should get off light enough. They were only following their liege lords."

"And the lords?"

"Some will be pardoned, so long as they tell the truth of what they know and give up a son or daughter to vouchsafe their future loyalty. It will go harder for those who took pardons after the Redgrass Field. They'll be imprisoned or attainted. The worst will lose their heads."

Bloodraven had made a start on that already, Dunk saw when they came up on his pavilion. Flanking the entrance, the severed heads of Gormon Peake and Black Tom Heddle had been impaled on spears, with their shields displayed beneath them. *Three castles, black on orange. The man who slew Roger of Pennytree.*

Even in death, Lord Gormon's eyes were hard and flinty. Dunk closed them with his fingers. "What did you do that for?" asked one of the guardsmen. "The crows'll have them soon enough."

"I owed him that much." If Roger had not died that day, the old man would never have looked twice at Dunk when he saw him chasing that pig through the alleys of King's Landing. *Some old dead king gave a sword to one son instead of another, that was the start of it. And now I'm standing here, and poor Roger's in his grave.*

"The Hand awaits," commanded Roland Crakehall.

Dunk stepped past him, into the presence of Lord Brynden Rivers, bastard, sorcerer, and Hand of the King.

Egg stood before him, freshly bathed and garbed in princely raiment, as would befit a nephew of the king. Nearby, Lord Frey was seated in a camp chair with a cup of wine to hand and his hideous little heir squirming in his lap. Lord Butterwell was there as well … on his knees, pale-faced and shaking.

"Treason is no less vile because the traitor proves a craven," Lord Rivers was saying. "I have heard your bleatings, Lord Ambrose, and I believe one word in ten. On that account I will allow you to retain a tenth part of your fortune. You may keep your wife as well. I wish you joy of her."

"And Whitewalls?" asked Butterwell, with quavering voice.

"Forfeit to the Iron Throne. I mean to pull it down stone by stone and sow the ground that it stands upon with salt. In twenty years, no one will remember it existed. Old fools and young malcontents still make pilgrimages to the Redgrass Field to plant flowers on the spot where Daemon Blackfyre fell. I will not suffer Whitewalls to become another monument to the black dragon." He waved a pale hand. "Now scurry away, roach."

"The Hand is kind." Butterwell stumbled off, so blind with grief that he did not even seem to recognize Dunk as he passed.

"You have my leave to go as well, Lord Frey," Rivers commanded. "We will speak again later."

"As my lord commands." Frey led his son from the pavilion.

Only then did the King's Hand turn to Dunk.

He was older than Dunk remembered him, with a lined, hard face, but his skin was still as pale as bone, and his cheek and neck still bore the ugly winestain birthmark that some people thought looked like a raven. His boots were black, his tunic scarlet. Over it he wore a cloak the color of smoke, fastened with a brooch in the shape of an iron hand. His hair fell to his shoulders, long and white and straight, brushed forward so as to conceal his missing eye, the one that Bittersteel had plucked from him on the Redgrass Field. The eye that remained was very red. *How many eyes has Bloodraven? A thousand eyes, and one.*

"No doubt Prince Maekar had some good reason for allowing his son to squire for a hedge knight," he said, "though I cannot imagine it included delivering him to a castle full of traitors plotting rebellion. How is it that I come to find my cousin in this nest of adders, ser? Lord Butterbutt would have me believe that Prince Maekar sent you here, to sniff out this rebellion in the guise of a mystery knight. Is that the truth of it?"

Dunk went to one knee. "No, m'lord. I mean, yes, m'lord. That's what Egg told him. Aegon, I mean. Prince Aegon. So that part's true. It isn't what you'd call the true truth, though."

"I see. So the two of you learned of this conspiracy against the crown and decided you would thwart it by yourselves, is that the way of it?

"That's not it either. We just sort of . . . blundered into it, I suppose you'd say."

Egg crossed his arms. "And Ser Duncan and I had matters well in hand before you turned up with your army."

"We had some help, m'lord," Dunk added.

"Hedge knights."

"Aye, m'lord. Ser Kyle the Cat, and Maynard Plumm. And Ser Glendon Ball. It was him unhorsed the Fidd ... the pretender."

"Yes, I've heard that tale from half a hundred lips already. The Bastard of the Pussywillows. Born of a whore and a traitor."

"Born of *heroes*," Egg insisted. "If he's amongst the captives, I want him found and released. And rewarded."

"And who are you to tell the King's Hand what to do?"

Egg did not flinch. "You know who I am, cousin."

"Your squire is insolent, ser," Lord Rivers said to Dunk. "You ought to beat that out of him."

"I've tried, m'lord. He's a prince, though."

"What he is," said Bloodraven, "is a *dragon*. Rise, ser."

Dunk rose.

"There have always been Targaryens who dreamed of things to come, since long before the Conquest," Bloodraven said, "so we should not be surprised if from time to time a Blackfyre displays the gift as well. Daemon dreamed that a dragon would be born at Whitewalls, and it was. The fool just got the color wrong."

Dunk looked at Egg. *The ring,* he saw. *His father's ring. It's on his finger, not stuffed up inside his boot.*

"I have half a mind to take you back to King's Landing with us," Lord Rivers said to Egg, "and keep you at court as my ... guest."

"My father would not take kindly to that."

"I suppose not. Prince Maekar has a ... prickly ... nature. Perhaps I should send you back to Summerhall."

"My place is with Ser Duncan. I'm his squire."

"Seven save you both. As you wish. You're free to go."

"We will," said Egg, "but first we need some gold. Ser Duncan needs to pay the Snail his ransom."

Bloodraven laughed. "What happened to the modest boy I once met at King's Landing? As you say, my prince. I will instruct my paymaster to give you as much gold as you wish. Within reason."

"Only as a loan," insisted Dunk. "I'll pay it back."

"When you learn to joust, no doubt." Lord Rivers flicked them away with his fingers, unrolled a parchment, and began to tick off names with a quill.

He is marking down the men to die, Dunk realized. "My lord," he said,

"we saw the heads outside. Is that ... will the Fiddler ... Daemon ... will you have his head as well?"

Lord Bloodraven looked up from his parchment. "That is for King Aerys to decide ... but Daemon has four younger brothers, and sisters as well. Should I be so foolish as to remove his pretty head, his mother will mourn, his friends will curse me for a kinslayer, and Bittersteel will crown his brother Haegon. Dead, young Daemon is a hero. Alive, he is an obstacle in my half brother's path. He can hardly make a third Blackfyre king whilst the second remains so inconveniently alive. Besides, such a noble captive will be an ornament to our court and a living testament to the mercy and benevolence of His Grace King Aerys."

"I have a question too," said Egg.

"I begin to understand why your father was so willing to be rid of you. What more would you have of me, cousin?"

"Who took the dragon's egg? There were guards at the door, and more guards on the steps, no way anyone could have gotten into Lord Butterwell's bedchamber unobserved."

Lord Rivers smiled. "Were I to guess, I'd say someone climbed up inside the privy shaft."

"The privy shaft was too small to climb."

"For a man. A child could do it."

"Or a dwarf," Dunk blurted. *A thousand eyes, and one. Why shouldn't some of them belong to a troupe of comic dwarfs?*

THE END . . .

. . . *of the beginning*

More travels and more travails await our hedge knight and his squire in the years to come. From Dorne to the Wall, their journeys will carry them across the length and breadth of the Seven Kingdoms, and even beyond the narrow sea to the Disputed Lands and the shining cities of Essos.

Along the way they will cross paths with lords and knights and sorcerers, and many a fair maid and noble lady, to write their names into the annals of Westeros, never to be forgotten.

But those are tales for another time.

Keep reading.

George R.R. Martin
Santa Fe
May, 2015

Acknowledgments

Over the eighteen months of illustrating The Seven Kingdoms, many people came to my aid. Thanks to my wife, Julie, daughters Niki and Gina, Raya and George, Anne Groell, Virginia Norey, Karl Gustafson, Pat Gustafson, Randy Broecker, Kay Kron, William and Christopher Neubauer and Forteza Martial Arts. Finally, I'm most grateful to Marcelo Anciano. His artistic guidance is the driving force throughout many of the books I've illustrated including *A Knight of the Seven Kingdoms.*

—*Gary Gianni*

About the Author

George R.R. Martin is the #1 *New York Times* bestselling author of many novels, including the acclaimed series A Song of Ice and Fire—*A Game of Thrones, A Clash of Kings, A Storm of Swords, A Feast for Crows,* and *A Dance with Dragons*. As a writer-producer, he has worked on *The Twilight Zone, Beauty and the Beast,* and various feature films and pilots that were never made. He lives with the lovely Parris in Santa Fe, New Mexico.

* * *

About the Illustrator

Gary Gianni is a book illustrator and a comic book artist. He has drawn Batman, Indiana Jones, The Shadow, Hellboy, and Monstermen in comics. He drew the Prince Valiant newspaper strip from 2003 to 2012. Gianni has also illustrated numerous books by authors ranging from Jules Verne and R. E. Howard to Ray Bradbury and Michael Chabon.